MW00760582

BREAKING the

DON'T PLAY IN THE SUN

EVIE T. McDUFF

ELLECHOR MEDIA

Copyright ©2015 by Evie T. McDuff

2015 Ellechor Media Edition
Don't Play In The Sun / McDuff, Evie T.

Paperback ISBN: 978-1-937844-56-1

No portion of this book may be reproduced, scanned, or distributed in any form without the written permission of the Publisher. Please purchase only authorized editions. For more information, address:

Ellechor Media, LLC
2373 NW 185th Ave, #510
Hillsboro, OR 97124
info@ellechormedia.com

If you purchased this book without a cover, you should be aware that this book is stolen property. It was reported as "unsold" or "destroyed" to the publisher, and neither the author nor the publisher has received any payment for this "stripped book."

Edited & Proofread by Veronika Walker
Cover Design by Damonza
Back Cover & Interior Design by D.E. West — ZAQ Designs

Printed in the United States of America
Sun graphic - Freepik.com

ELLECHOR MEDIA

www.ellechormedia.com

To my brother Clayton
Thank you so much for your
support! ♡ I love you

iii

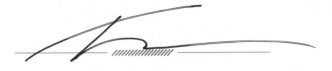

Inspired by true events.

DEDICATION

To my mom, Evangelist Blondell Williams:

I want to thank you for loving me, always supporting me, and raising me to be a woman not afraid to dream. My hat's off to you, Mom—I love you, more than words could ever say. You are the best!

The memory of that moment sends an unwilled shudder through her heart as it would through any mother's. But she knows she has to finish writing.

I thought I understood what horror was, but nothing can describe what that sound created inside of me. I knew then I had to put a stop to him and his filthy malevolence...

And tonight, my children, I've done it...

She recounts it steadily, unflinching. A few moments later, just as she finishes the last detail of her crime, the door behind her flies open and a frantic voice shouts out. Resolved, she stands but does not turn to acknowledge the ranting. Instead, she bends and signs her name with a determined flourish.

Resigned, she turns with a final nod to confront her fate.

CHAPTER 1

Life for me started out on the right road. I grew up in the lovely southern town of Beaufort, South Carolina, and my mother and father were loving and kind to me and to each other. Whenever I observed their strong, sweet relationship and how much joy they had with one another, I knew I wanted that same type of love for my marriage someday. I was sure I was destined for a beautiful life. How young and naïve I was then.

It was 1941 when I met Jack Miles. I was eleven years old. He entered my classroom on our first day of school, and since the only available seat was by me, we ended up sitting next to each other. He was raven-haired and green-eyed, and I thought even back then that he was handsome. Because he was the new boy and shy, neither he nor the other kids made any friendly overtures.

I had no friends either so I invited him to sit with me at lunch that first day and found a new friend. We discovered we were the same age, had no siblings, and shared a fascination with catching insects in glass jars. I invited him to church the following Sunday, and we introduced our families. Jack and I became the best of friends and were absolutely inseparable.

Over the next six years, our families grew closer. Jacks southern belle mother, Doris, and Mama would often go to market together and met up most mornings for coffee and conversation about all the latest gossip in Beaufort.

In fact, Mama loved and trusted Doris Miles so much that she decided to share the secret of our family history with her. Now, my eyes were gray and Mama's were sherry colored. We both had long sandy brown hair, which reached the center of our backs, and we both had a dusky skin tone, just dark enough to look kissed by the sun but the fact was, we were Negro inside.

Unfortunately, once that secret was revealed, Mrs. Miles stopped coming around. When Mama confronted her, Mrs. Miles claimed it had nothing to do with what she'd learned about us. But Mama knew better. Ever proud, she resigned herself to the fact that the friendship was over, and told me to be careful whom I confided in.

It wasn't a big deal to Jack, and soon we were "going steady." Despite Jack's frustration with his mother's prejudices, he thought I was the best thing that had ever happened to him, and often told me so. Surprisingly, his parents said nothing about our being in a relationship, at least not while we were in high school. In fact, things were so right with us, that on the night of our senior prom, as we danced the last dance of the evening, Jack stopped and got on one knee.

I was breathless as he held out a diamond engagement ring.

"I love you, Alice Whitmore," he said, eyes shining. "Will you marry me?"

I nodded and giggled. "Of course!" Jack had always been the one for me.

When I got home that night, overflowing with excitement, I told my parents right away. I could tell they weren't overjoyed, but they tried not to show their disappointment. Though we were both so young, Jack had always been respectful and polite to them. They knew from years of watching us together that he made me happy, and that was what mattered most to them.

I couldn't say the same for Jack's family, though. In deference to the strain between our families, Jack and I decided that we'd tell his parents together the following day. I hoped by seeing that we'd be a family soon, they'd accept our impending nuptials.

But Jack's father would have none of it and held nothing back when we told them of our engagement. "I know what you are, missy," he said, shoving a pointed finger in my face. "And you can't have my son."

Jack ignored his father's words, and in June of 1948, we married at the courthouse right after graduation.

A week after our wedding, Jack signed up for the Air Force. He'd always had a passion for mechanical things, and his sight was set on a career in mechanics, aviation-fighter planes, and engine schematics. Since we didn't have a house yet, Daddy and Mama offered to let us stay with them until Jack passed his military examinations and got us settled.

He did outstanding until the eye exam. They allowed him to try over and over, but even with glasses, he couldn't read the final required line on the eye chart. Jack was medically disqualified, and his dreams came to an abrupt end.

Since Daddy was the manager at the local paper mill, he offered Jack a job. My parents also helped us find a cottage nearby, and while Jack and Daddy worked, Mama taught me how to run a household. Though life for us newlyweds started off with disappointment, we were happy with our simple life.

That Christmas we found out I was pregnant. Jack was so excited that he broke down and called to tell his parents. After hearing his voice, however, his mother hung up on him. Though my parents were thrilled at the prospect of being grandparents,

Jack longed for his parents to be involved in our lives as well. In the months to follow, he called them several times, but received complete silence for his efforts.

Shortly after Denise's second birthday, we decided that an unexpected trip to Jack's parents' house was in order. With me at his side and Denise in his arms, Jack knocked on his parents' door and was met with the stoic visage of his father and the sour face of his mother.

"Hi, Papa... Mama." Jack smiled as best he could. I placed my hand on his back for support and could feel his muscles tense.

"I, uh...we want you to meet your granddaughter. Her name is Denise. Say hi, sweetie."

Raven-haired Denise, who never knew what shyness was, smiled, and offered a tiny, child wave. "Hi," she cooed.

Ignoring his son and his granddaughter completely, Mr. Miles glared at me and exploded. "Get out of here, coons! Don't you ever step foot on this property again, do you hear me, jiggas?" Then he slammed the door in our faces.

The look on my husband's face broke my heart. The anger that I felt on his behalf was indescribable. I myself had never been called such names, and to have him say that of my sweet little girl too?! But it was over; there was nothing else we could do. After that day, we never attempted communication with his parents again.

Life continued on, quiet and uneventful, as is often the case in the small towns of the South. But it was a good life, and I for one would have been happy to spend all my days in that sweet haven, surrounded by my loved ones while supporting my hard-working husband.

Jack, on the other hand, took a second job at a garage, both to give us extra for our savings account and to help satisfy his itch for mechanics. He longed for something more, something beyond what we had here. I prayed that he'd find the one thing—whatever it was—that would make him as happy as I was.

One evening shortly after Denise turned four, I was tidying our little living room when Jack came bursting through the front door, shouting my name.

"Alice, we've done it!" he said, beaming. In his exuberance, he picked me up and swung me around.

"Done what?" I replied, breathless and laughing.

"We've finally saved enough money to open our own car garage!"

"Oh, Jack, that's wonderful!" We had been discussing such a venture for a few months now. I could see a glimmer of joy behind those green eyes, the glimmer that had begun to fade over the past year. "Sweetheart, I'm so happy! I know Daddy can help you find a great place, and…"

My words trailed off as I watched the excitement fade from his face.

"Alice, honey, we can't open a shop here. We need to be in a big city if this is going to work. I want us to move to D.C. I've got great leads for work there."

Washington, D.C.? I sunk onto the couch, blindsided by this potential change in my perfect world. I simply stared at him.

"Jack, I…this is just too sudden," I finally sputtered. "I…I need time to think."

Jack was disappointed, of course, but after much talking and cajoling, he was resigned to wait on my decision.

"Honey, I know it's fast, but this could be good for us." With a hug and a peck on my cheek, he left the room.

I sat on the couch for a moment and thought about the wonderful life we were building in Beaufort. Were we really ready for such a big step at such a young age? But then I thought about how Jack had chosen me over his family, over his dreams. He had given up everything for me. I sighed, resigned; it was my turn to make the same sacrifice.

I went into the bedroom and told him I would move anywhere as long as we were together.

"Everything will come together, baby!" Jack said, excited. "This is our chance to start fresh, to make something of ourselves…you know, without your parents' help."

Jack appreciated Daddy helping him find a house and providing him with a job, but I knew what he meant. It was time for Jack to stop living in another man's shadow and go out on his own. I was sorry he often felt inferior to Daddy, but seeing Jack this happy and enthusiastic washed away all of my doubts about moving. I threw myself into our plans with no reservations. Well, no reservations except one—we had to tell my parents.

We waited until Jack returned from D.C. with the deed for our new home. We asked Mama and Daddy if we could come over for dinner, and Jack told them the news over coffee in the living room.

"So, you see, Mr. Whitmore," Jack said as he finished explaining our plans, "I've put down money on a house and signed the lease on the garage. I know Washington, D.C. is quite a distance away, sir…"

To say that my parents were astounded would be an understatement, but Jack forged on despite the looks on their faces.

"…if Alice and I are to have a real chance at fulfilling our dreams, we need to move to a big city with a growing population.

There will be more people with more cars that need fixing."

"Washington, D.C.," Daddy said gruffly.

"Well…yes, sir," said Jack as he clutched my hand. We exchanged nervous smiles and turned our hopeful faces back to my parents, who were seated across from us.

Mama wasn't accepting any of it. I swear I could feel her gaze burning through me. Trying to avoid that penetrating stare, I turned my attention to Denise, who sat contently on the floor, scribbling furiously in her coloring book.

"Sir, you know I love all kinds of engines," Jack continued. "Mechanics is my passion, my dream. I couldn't pass up this great opportunity. I'm grateful for everything you've done for us, but here in Beaufort, I'm always working. I miss my family. After the garage is up and on its feet, I'll have more time to spend with my girls."

"Your girls? Alice and Denise are my girls, too, you know." Daddy's voice was flat. "Alice was my girl and my responsibility a long time before you ever set eyes on her, son."

"Mr. Whitmore, I understand what you're saying, but with all due respect, sir, Alice is my wife now, and Denise, my daughter. They are *my* responsibility, and I have to do what I believe is best for them."

I squeezed Jack's hand, trying to give him quiet encouragement.

"I would like to have your blessing while I do it, sir."

"My blessing?" Daddy asked sternly. "What if I don't give it? Then what?"

The silent tension crackled as the wills of the two men in my life vied for dominance. I loved both of them but only one could have the final say.

"Speaking as your son-in-law, Mr. Whitmore, I would be disappointed and hurt to move them away without your blessing.

But as a man, I hope I won't have to make that choice."

Daddy eyed him, a glint of betrayal in his eyes.

"What about Alice?" Mama finally said, rather sharply. "Doesn't she get a say? Do you want to go, honey?"

I offered a smile, trying to lighten the tense atmosphere. "Yes, Mama, I do. We will see you often, I promise."

"And what will you be doing alone in a strange city while Jack is running his business, Alice? Huh? Jack's been very clear about his dream tonight, but what I'd like to know, is what about *your* dreams?"

I swallowed my sudden rise of tears. The truth was I really wanted to stay in Beaufort. It was my home. But I loved Jack, and he thought this was best. I gave her the answer I had been telling myself over the past weeks. Swallowing the lump in my throat, I said, "Well…I guess I'll be taking care of my family and being happy…just like I do here."

It would have been better if Mama had yelled at me or continued to try and convince me to stay, but instead she turned away from me, which hurt me deeply.

Not noticing my inner struggles, Jack continued, "Mr. and Mrs. Whitmore, we…Alice really needs your support." He looked to them both, soberly. "Please, will you give it to us?"

He stood up, walked over to Daddy, and extended his hand. Daddy's face was inscrutable, but I could tell that he was fighting with the decision. After an eternity, Daddy looked at Mama, her opinion plain on her face. Then he looked into my eyes and could clearly see me silently pleading for his approval.

When he finally stood, Daddy reluctantly proffered his hand to Jack and shook it firmly. With relief, I hopped up and gave my daddy a big hug.

Though he squeezed me back and forced a smile, he couldn't hide his unease. I glanced over at Mama, hoping she would offer an encouraging word. But her eyes were glistening with unshed tears, and she was struggling to keep herself together.

"Excuse me." She stood up and left the room.

"Charlotte…" Daddy made to go after her, but I stopped him and followed her out.

Mama never liked to lose her composure, so whenever she felt anxious or upset, she usually gravitated toward the kitchen to immerse herself in methodical tasks.

But she wasn't in the kitchen. *She must be in the bedroom,* I thought.

My heart became heavy as I climbed the stairs, passing a dozen pictures of our family hanging on the wall in a familiar array. Grandma Sheila, Aunt Blondell…they were all there staring at me with accusing eyes.

I paused outside of the bedroom door, hearing soft weeping. I had been loathing this moment all week but here it was. It was time to face the music.

"Mama?" I knocked softly and entered the bedroom.

She turned and wiped her eyes. "Hey, doll."

"Please don't cry, Mama."

"I'm sorry, honey." She dabbed her eyes. "I just don't want to see you move so far away. Denise is my only grandchild…and you… You're my only child, my little girl."

I sat on the bed beside her and put my head on her shoulder. It didn't matter that I was a grown woman; in that moment, I *was* her little girl. Mama drew her hand gently across my cheek and stroked my sandy hair.

"Mama, I'm sorry," I whispered. "I thought that—"

"Oh, Alice! You don't understand, do you?" There was an urgency in her voice that I was unaccustomed to. I sat up and looked at her.

"Baby, listen." Taking a deep calming breath, she continued. "I've told you many times about my mama and how she tried to be an example to me, right?"

"Yes, ma'am." Though I had never met Grandma Sheila, Mama told me she had influenced her greatly.

"She wanted independence for her children, Alice, and she had the will to do whatever it would take to see we got it. Honey, I know you love Jack. But why are you so ready to run off and help Jack fulfill *his* dreams? Don't you have your own dreams, your own desires?"

Mama took a deep ragged breath.

"Honey, stay. You can go to school, if you want, and I can help you with Denise. Jack can open a garage right here in Beaufort. After you graduate, you can start a career of your own. By leaving with Jack now, you're setting the stage for the rest of your life. Just think about it!"

I didn't know what to think. My only dream had been to marry Jack and start a family, and that was enough for now.

"Alice, honey, if it's really what you want, I'm happy for you. But it has to be what *you* want…whatever will make *you* happy." She tilted my chin, forcing me to look in her eyes. "This is *your* life, honey. Don't give it up for someone else's dream. Not even your husband's."

I wondered in that moment what Mama had given up for Daddy. I had never thought about it before, but now I knew that she was telling me she had given up a part of herself somewhere along the line, and was begging me not to do the same.

I looked deep into her eyes and smiled. "Mama, I love you so very much. You know that, right?"

"Of course, baby." She knew my decision and couldn't hold onto her tears any longer.

I grabbed both of her hands as I spoke. "My dream, Mama, is being a good wife and mother. That is what will make me truly, honestly happy. Really."

Her jaw set and she dropped her eyes. I knew she wasn't going to say anymore on the subject.

"Can I ask one thing of you?"

"Of course, honey."

"Will you try to be happy for us? When I leave Beaufort, I need to know you are going to be okay with my going. Please?"

She took a few moments before answering, studying me intently. I waited her out, feeling confident she would always be in my corner.

She raised a gentle hand and pushed a stray hair away from my face. "Where did my little girl go? When did she become this beautiful woman sitting in front of me? Yes, sweetheart. You have my blessing and my support."

Whenever I look back on that moment, it haunts me. She tried to tell me something very important that day, but I couldn't hear it then—either too young or too in love to understand. I know now that I should have listened.

On February 5, 1953, we left the only place I had ever called home. I was sad to leave Beaufort but excited to be on my own with my little family. I was twenty-three and all grown up with huge, innocent hopes for the future.

CHAPTER 2

The new house was a huge surprise. It was a soft yellow, two-story home with a two-car garage and large picture windows. I couldn't help but gasp when I saw it. It was so different from the little cottage we'd moved from.

The neighborhood was also a big surprise. In my mind's eye, living in the city meant dirty and grungy streets. But what met us was a middle-class neighborhood with well-manicured lawns and clean sidewalks. Jack took me to see his garage "in town," which was only a few blocks away from all the shops and restaurants.

We got settled in and by the following week, Jack's new garage, *Miles's Mechanics*, opened for business. Word-of-mouth got around about Jack's topnotch mechanical skills, and by October, Jack had to hire two more mechanics.

Michael Swartz and Jordan Gilyard both had uncanny mechanical skills, and the three men worked well together. Michael was married to Cadell and Jordan to Karen. The wives were both very kind to me, probably at first because I was the boss's wife, but soon we became fast friends. Every day saw us at one another's homes, shopping, or taking our kids to the park. We were all avid thrift store shoppers, and before long, I not only had a well decorated home that could rival any of my neighbors, but real friends too.

It was so glorious. In fact, I didn't miss Beaufort at all.

Jack, on the other hand, tried not to get too friendly with Michael and Jordan. He said it was because he was their employer and needed to keep things professional.

"It's the most important part of running a good business, Alice," he'd say.

Despite this, there were times he didn't have a choice; the girls and I would set up barbeques and birthday parties for the children, and he'd have to be sociable, which I knew he didn't mind…not too much, anyway.

By the middle of 1957, customers were coming to the garage from all over the city, and the guys had more work than time. It was also a highly charged political time. The Civil Rights protests were getting a great deal of publicity, and the more everyone buzzed about it, the more nervous Jack became. He was afraid that someone would guess my secret.

"This black and white thing is coming to a head, babe," Jack explained. "I think you need to keep your being a…'little black' to yourself." He shrugged in apology. "You never know what might happen, honey. Emotions are running high right now, and I wouldn't want anything to happen like it did with those kids at Little Rock. It could ruin our business, and all our hard work would go away just like that!" He snapped his fingers to emphasize his point.

Though I thought we were fine and nobody suspected a thing, I trusted his judgment and kept things simple with the neighbors. I'd wave and smile when going to the mailbox or when coming or leaving home. If I got cornered by someone raving about Jack's excellent business, I'd smile, nod, laugh, or hold a kind but shallow conversation, then make my escape. Having Cadell and Karen around made it easy for me to keep my distance from "the locals," as Jack called them.

My life was very satisfying back then. When I was not caring for Denise, Jack, or the house, I would sew. I'd always loved to sew and make clothes. I made dozens of dresses for Denise, and even pants, shirts, and jackets for Jack. He'd say with a proud glint in his eye, "Alice, you're spoiling me, baby! Your clothes fit me better than the ones in the store."

His compliments always made me happy, but in actuality, he was the one doing the spoiling. He purchased a TV for the living room, a new washer and dryer, and new carpet for the entire house. The ultimate surprise came when he left for work in our old jalopy one day and returned home behind the wheel of new sky blue Cadillac.

I was very proud of my husband, as were my parents. When they came to visit Daddy told Jack he approved of the direction we were going. Even though I knew she still had reservations, Mama nodded in agreement. It was obvious Jack and I were made for each other, and no matter what anyone thought, we were perfect together. I loved him in a way I couldn't explain or put into words. Jack was everything to me.

Then, things began to change.

--- //////////////// ---

I noticed it first on Denise's ninth birthday. We invited Michael and Jordan's families over for dinner and birthday cake. The children circled around singing "Happy Birthday," and the parents indulgently looked on. When I glanced at Jack, intending to share a smile, he had a peculiar look on his face.

In fact, he had no expression at all. The longer he stared at the candles, the farther inward he went. It was very bizarre, especially when we finished singing; I clicked on the kitchen light and Jack blinked, pasted an almost manic smile on his face, and let out a completely inappropriate laugh. It was all very unsettling.

That night when we lay in bed, I asked him about it. He sighed and admitted that he was coming to the realization that his business was the only way he had of providing for his family. If something happened, we'd be in trouble. When I asked him what could possibly happen, he didn't elaborate. I wasn't worried and told him so. When that didn't seem to make him feel better, I tried to coax him to making love, but to my surprise, he just kissed my cheek and said, "Not tonight."

After that night, his worries blossomed into increasing irritation and paranoia. He became short-tempered with Denise and me for the smallest things. When I asked him about it, he'd apologize and tell me everything was fine, but I knew there was something very wrong.

It happened bit by bit over the next year. Jack started spending less and less time with me and Denise. The wonderful presents and little gifts dried up. It became routine for a silent Jack to get up from the dinner table, kiss my cheek, and spend the rest of the evening in the living room by himself. Denise felt it as well. Normally a very vivacious nine-year-old, she became silent and withdrawn and would go straight to her room after dinner. Jack wouldn't come to bed until he was ready for sleep or wanted to be intimate; we had stopped laughing and having any pillow talk.

I asked him over and over again to share what was on his mind, but he'd say it was work-related and not to worry. But I was past worrying at that point. I knew I wasn't crazy; something was going on. I also tried talking to Denise, but she always said everything was fine with her friends and at school. We didn't discuss how things were going at home, and her tenth birthday was celebrated with little fanfare, at Jack's request.

If this change in my family wasn't frustrating enough, Karen and Cadell stopped calling and coming around as well. One day, feeling disheartened and lonely, I called Karen and asked if we could go to lunch, but she said she was too busy. When Cadell made the same excuse, I offered to pick up her children and take them to a movie with Denise, but she declined. When she started to hang up, I stopped her from disconnecting.

"Wait a minute, Cadell! Please, we were so close… Did I do something to upset you?"

After a long pause, she replied. "No, you haven't done anything, I promise. It's just that I need to keep some distance for now. I'll call when I can. I love you, okay?"

"Okay, I love you, too." I hung up, tears pricking the back of my eyes.

When Jack came home that evening, I asked him if he'd noticed any change in Michael or Jordan's attitude. He said no, nothing at all had changed. It was obvious that he didn't want to talk, so I left it alone.

One Saturday I tried to get Denise to go out to a movie and lunch with me, but she didn't want to. "It'll be fun," I said.

"No, Mom, please! I don't want to go!" she shouted.

Denise had never raised her voice at me. I was shocked. "What's going on, honey? I just—"

"Please, Mom, no…"

That became the pattern with Denise; she didn't talk anymore and never wanted to do the fun things that we used to do. I was miserable; my family was unhappy and I couldn't fix it. I couldn't figure out what I was doing wrong.

That December we went home to see my parents for Christmas, and they told us that Jack's mother and father had moved. Though Jack said it didn't bother him, it was obvious that it did.

During that visit, we pretended that everything was fine at home and did a great job of acting. We exchanged gifts, drank eggnog, and sang carols. After the three-day holiday, nerves stretched thin, I was ready to leave. No one spoke after we pulled out of my parents' driveway, and I cried silent tears on the ride home.

———————————— //////////////// ————————————

By spring of 1960, we were in a strange place. There was little communication with Jack and Denise, and I still hadn't seen or talked to Cadell or Karen. The silence began to wear on me something terrible. My very existence was gray.

Since we'd moved to D.C., I had always seen my parents twice a year, alternating visits between Christmas and the Fourth of July. As summer rolled around, I began looking forward to the infectious good cheer their visits always brought. I hadn't told them about our problems; I didn't want to give them anything to worry about or spoil the visit.

Three days before my parents were due to arrive, I got up as usual and made Denise breakfast. She was smiling today, which boded well; she was looking forward to seeing her grandparents, too. After she left for school, I gathered the laundry and started separating the clothing into manageable piles.

As I picked up one of Jack's work shirts, my heart stopped. There was a deep lipstick stain around the third button.

I was confused and felt betrayed. Then I got angry.

I called Jack's garage and sharply told him of my discovery. He said we would talk when he came home and hung up.

I was sick to my stomach all day. I couldn't do my chores, and my mind raced. Surely there was a reasonable explanation for this; my husband wouldn't do this. Not my Jack.

That night, I waited and waited, but Jack didn't come home. My emotions vacillated between fear and rage and back again until I reluctantly went to bed. I tossed and turned, unable to sleep. Finally, at three in the morning, I heard the Cadillac outside. I slipped into my bathrobe and headed downstairs.

Jack was still outside fumbling with the lock. My frustration and anger welled, and before I knew it, I'd wrenched the door open.

Jack was drunk! He had never been a heavy drinker, but there he stood, wavering on his feet, looking at me as if *I'd* done something wrong.

"Where have you been?" I demanded. Even I didn't recognize the shrew I became in that moment.

Jack's eyes—those beautiful green ones that could make me do anything—turned dark and cold. Without warning or explanation, he backhanded me so hard I ended up on the floor at his feet.

I stared up in utter shock and disbelief as he staggered inside and slammed the door. My head was spinning, and blood welled up from a cut on my bottom lip. When I saw my husband ball up his fist as if to strike me again, on instinct, I flipped over onto my stomach, covering my head.

This can't be happening… I thought.

Jack got a hold of my ponytail and pulled my head back so far it strained my neck.

"Listen, half-breed, and listen good," he growled through clenched teeth. His face so close, the smell of the alcohol turned my stomach.

Half-breed?

"I'm the man here," he said. "I don't answer to you, coon, you hear me?"

I was trembling, but more from despair and shock than physical hurt. My Jack had never called me names. I hadn't heard those words, not directed at me, since his father had said them. Jack had never looked down on me for who I was; in fact, I had almost forgotten it was an issue. Now I was filth in his eyes.

"You ever ask me where I've been ever again, you won't live long enough to get an answer! You understand me, jiggaboo?"

Paralyzed by fear, I kept my eyes closed and said nothing. He asked again, this time yanking my hair with each spoken syllable punctuating his words: "Do—you—hear—me?"

"Yes," I managed to reply, tears streaming with blood from my nose and mouth dripping to the floor. With a forceful thud, he shoved my head back down and turned away, staggering into the sitting room.

I lay there on the floor, shaking and terrified with a throbbing head. I was afraid I was going to scream—and then he'd come back and hit me again. I couldn't understand what I might have done to make him so angry.

Despite my pain and fear, I was thankful that Denise slept through the noise. I crawled to the edge of the stairway to listen, and after a few minutes, Jack began to snore. I managed to stand and make my way up the stairs inch by inch. With each noisy creak, I was expecting the monster to wake and grab me from behind.

Without cleaning myself up, I entered my bedroom and climbed into bed. I didn't understand. It had to be a horrible nightmare. Jack had never even raised his voice at me, let alone hit me. What happened to my gentle, loving husband? I knew somehow I was responsible. I stayed in bed, nervous and trembling, wondering what I'd done wrong.

The next morning I looked into the mirror and was horrified; my lip was split, and the left side of my face was red, purple, and swollen. My left eye had a huge bruise under it.

"Mom?" Denise tapped and began to open the door.

I quickly got back in bed and jumped under the covers. I threw the pillow over my head and started coughing and hacking.

"You're still in bed?" she asked, coming to my side of the bed.

I ducked my head farther under. "Yes, honey, I've got a summer cold. My sinuses are killing me, and I have a terrible headache. I think I'm going to rest for a while longer. Get yourself some cereal, and I'll see you when you get home, okay?"

My mind was racing after she left. I paced back and forth all morning, wondering what happened. *How could he do this to me? What did I do wrong?* I asked myself repeatedly.

Then I remembered: my parents were coming in two days! I had to figure out a way to stop them. *I'll never be able to explain this. No matter what I say, they'll know. Think, Alice!* I whispered to myself as tears fell from my chin onto my nightdress. *Okay, okay, calm down, you can do this.*

I wiped my face, rehearsed my lines, and called my parents.

I told Mama that Jack had surprised me with a trip to Vermont; a customer of his had a cabin out there and invited us to come spend a few days with their family.

"Mama, this is very important because this man is wealthy and has a large cab service here in D.C.," I fabricated. "He's considering signing a contract with Jack to keep up maintenance on his cars. So, it's kind of a business/pleasure sort of thing. And I could use a little relaxation time," I added, praying she didn't hear the lie. "You understand, don't you?"

She said she understood, but she and Daddy had scheduled time off with their jobs and couldn't reschedule. It would be Christmas before we could get together again. We agreed to discuss the details around November, and I managed to get off the phone without raising suspicion.

Breathing with relief, I went to the bathroom and put makeup over the bruises and my hair in it's usual ponytail. I changed my mind halfway through and parted my hair to include a bang to cover my bruised eye, pinning the rest in a bun.

Looking at myself in the mirror now was not so bad. I had done a good job covering everything up and found myself hoping that Jack and I could fix things.

Maybe it's not the death of our love, I thought to myself. *Maybe he didn't cheat on me… I will try harder to be a better wife, and by the time Mama and Daddy come, we'll have all this behind us.*

I went on with my day and tried to block out the memory of the vile names he called me. He'd never used those slurs against anyone of color…ever. Maybe it was just the liquor and his agitation. At least, that's what I hoped it was. I didn't know what I'd do if that was how he really thought of me. Then I chided myself. *Of course he doesn't feel that way; it was just a bad night.*

When Denise came home that afternoon, I got a breezy, "I'm home, Mom, going to do my homework."

"Okay, De—" and before I was finished speaking, she was gone. Normally that would have bothered me, her not stopping to talk after school. But today I didn't want to bring attention to myself and only felt relief.

The lasagna was ready by five-thirty, and the aroma of garlic bread danced through the house. Ready to put my best foot forward, I set the table especially nice, tossed a salad, and was ready to receive my husband.

Jack pulled up but sat in the car for a few minutes. *Odd,* I thought.

Determined to make tonight as normal as possible, I called for Denise and started making the plates. When Jack finally came to the kitchen door, I swung around, smiling.

"Hi, honey, your dinner is..."

He was drunk and reeked of alcohol. Denise, who was now standing by my side, just gaped at her father.

"Um, Jack," I said, trying to keep my composure, "dinner's ready. Uh...are you hungry?"

"Bring it in the sitting room," he drawled and walked in that direction. I warily took him his plate and came back to sit and eat with Denise.

"Mom, what's going on?" Her eyes were wide with confusion and fear.

"Nothing, honey," I said, stabbing methodically at my lasagna. "Your daddy...went to have a going-away drink with a friend of his. I guess he had too much, that's all."

"Alice!" Jack bellowed suddenly, stomping into the kitchen.

I jumped up, and as I did, he threw the plate at me. It missed me by an inch.

"This food isn't hot enough, woman!"

"Mommy?!"

It took me a minute to recover, but then I stepped to Denise's side, trying to comfort her. "Honey, it's all right. I just need you to go upstairs now, okay?"

"But, Mommy—"

"We'll talk later, but now you need to go."

Jack glared right past his frightened daughter at me, then turned around and staggered back to the sitting room.

I hurried my frightened ten-year-old to her bedroom and then heated Jack another plate of food. He ate it without comment and fell asleep on the couch.

I got the kitchen cleaned and went to talk to Denise. She was curled up in her bed with the sheet bunched around her as if for protection.

I did my best to keep my voice steady and explained that her father was under a lot of strain, but things were going to get better.

"What if they don't?" she whimpered.

"They will," I replied. "They will."

"What happened to your face, Mommy?"

I turned my head, chiding myself for not being more careful. "Nothing, honey, I'm fine. Go get your bath. And I'm sorry for your daddy's behavior… Please forgive him, sweetie. And forgive me too, okay?"

Denise nodded slowly, clearly still upset.

"I'll come and check on you before you turn in." I kissed her on the cheek and left.

I hoped Denise didn't hear the sobs that began before I made it to my room. I needed her to believe that we were still one happy little family. The truth was I needed to believe it myself. I clung to the possibility that this would all go away.

The next few months were hell.

--------------------------- ////////////// ---------------------------

By Denise's eleventh birthday, we were broke. Jack cleaned out our bank account, then Denise's college fund, and then sold most of our furniture and my beloved sewing machine. Instead of working, he spent many of his days gambling, drinking, and cursing me. The garage closed, and his once shining reputation as an excellent mechanic disappeared.

When he wasn't drinking, Jack would look for work, but no one would hire him. That led him to drink even more. He'd get upset about the simplest things and often resorted to calling me all sorts of names—stupid, good-for-nothing, dummy, and racist names, too. He even called me a whore. Then the beatings would start. I was the one who paid for his bad luck, often several times a week.

He'd sometimes apologize and bring me a rose or something from the store, but the nastiness and beating would just start over again within a few days. I didn't know what to believe. I knew by then he had cheated on me, at least the one time. It knocked the wind out of me to think on it. Meanwhile, Denise was growing more and more afraid. Every time Jack started, I'd tell her to go to her room.

One night, Denise and I were watching television in the sitting room when Jack barged in the front door. He stomped over to me, grabbed me by the throat, and slammed me against the wall. Denise grabbed for my waist, but he pushed her out of the way.

"Move, little girl, before you get it!"

Jack swept me up by my neck with my feet dangling in the air. "I've just seen Luciotti, that son of a…" he yelled in my face. "He called me a drunken wife-beater! Who you been talkin' to?"

"No one, Jack, please…" I rasped.

"He said I might as well stop looking for work 'round here 'cause nobody's gonna give a woman-beater a job! Nobody wants to hire me, woman. Nobody!" Jack raged, louder.

"Jack…can't…breathe…"

Denise, realizing my plight, found her voice. "Daddy, you let her go!" she shrieked, ineffectively pounding him with her fists, but Jack, enraged, didn't notice.

I gurgled, gasping for enough air to tell Denise to get away from him. I didn't know if he would hurt our daughter—and I didn't want to find out.

"G-Go...upstairs!" I gasped.

Denise ran upstairs, crying and screaming, and slammed her bedroom door.

Jack adjusted his grip on my throat, and I rasped again.

"You better stay out of my way, woman." He squeezed just a little harder, and everything starting going dim. "If I see your sorry face again tonight, I'm gonna bash it in, do you hear?"

"Y-y-yes," I managed, and with that he let go and I dropped to the floor, heaving and gasping for breath.

"Get your lazy, nagging ass up and fetch my dinner!" His voice grated. "And it better be hot!"

I soon learned that everyone in the neighborhood was talking about how Jack had thrown his life and business away for booze. Ex-customers called the house, demanding money back for work not completed correctly or not done at all. Even worse, one of the gambling sharks he borrowed from called and threatened me.

"Listen, lady!" he yelled. "You better tell your no-good husband that I know where you live. He's got two weeks, and that's a gift. If he doesn't pay his debt," his menacing voice softened, "I'll have to take it out on him, or that sweet little kid of his. Either way he's gonna pay."

I slammed the phone down and anxiously waited for Jack to return from his job hunt that day. I ran to meet him in the foyer and told him about the threat immediately. He listened intently to the entire story, and then his hands were around my neck. The next thing I remembered was Denise, with her book bag around her shoulder, screaming at me.

"Mom? Mommy! Get up! Please get up!"

Disoriented, I came to, still in the foyer but on the floor. "Oh my God…" I whispered and sat up as quickly as I could. Neck sore and hurting, I grabbed and held my daughter tight. "I'm okay, Denise, I'm okay, honey." But I was shaking and held her a few seconds longer.

When she helped me up, I checked the house for Jack, Denise trailing right behind me. When we were sure Jack was gone, Denise grabbed my sleeve.

"Mommy, we have to leave." She implored. "Please let's leave! Let's call Granddaddy. He'll help us. Please!"

"I have to do this at the right time, Denise," I said, calmer now.

"When will that be? After he kills you?"

I gaped at my daughter, stunned by her bluntness.

"He'd never go that far, honey."

"How do you know that, Mom?"

"I just do."

Though I lived in constant fear, I was determined to be a good wife and mother and forgive Jack for his betrayal and rampages.

If I did this right, my Jack would come back to me.

———————— ///////////// ————————

CHAPTER 3

Just before Christmas that year, Jack told me we wouldn't be going to Beaufort, offering no explanation. I called my parents and lied again, this time telling them Jack had so much work that he couldn't afford to take the holidays off. My plan backfired, and they decided to come to us instead.

When I told Jack of their decision, he said no. "It's my house, and I don't want them in it!"

I explained that I had tried to deter them, but it hadn't worked. It had been a year since they'd seen us; if we didn't let them come, they'd eventually come unannounced.

"Please, Jack," I begged. "I don't know what else to do."

He reluctantly agreed, and I prayed that the visit wouldn't have any incidents.

Mama and Daddy arrived at the door with lots of presents and boisterous good cheer. But when they went into the living room, they instantly became silent. The tree was a poor little pine, nothing like the ones we had in other years. Even worse, there were only two presents under it—a sweater for Daddy and silk gloves for Mama.

The longer they stood staring at the tree, the more uncomfortable it became. Anxiety was building in me, and I wanted to scream out, "Folks, everything's fine! It's Christmas Eve, and we haven't finished shopping yet."

But even if I had, it would still look the same tomorrow morning, and they'd realize I was lying anyway.

Daddy's instincts were up. His nose flared out, signifying that this was Jack's first strike. After a few moments of awkward Merry Christmas talk, the second strike hit.

Although I had makeup on, Daddy saw right through it. He kept staring and asking me if everything was all right, which made Mama get real close, focusing in on the right side of my face.

With false cheer, I averted my head and said, "Mama, please don't let Daddy make you paranoid. I'm fine, now come on, let's sit and catch up. I've missed you both so much."

We talked about the goings-on in Beaufort and here in D.C. Jack had warned me not to tell them about the shop's closing. I talked instead about my friends—ex-friends, now—classmates from Beaufort, the news…anything. I'd resorted to talking about the weather, when Denise came in from the movies. As she greeted them with much exuberance, I went to make dinner with relief.

Jack said he'd be home, and I was getting nervous. If this happy family facade would be convincing, he'd have to be here.

Jack never showed up.

Denise fell asleep while we were all pretending to watch a movie in the sitting room. I woke her and told her to go to bed. Though my parents said nothing about Jack being absent, the tension was mounting by the hour. No one wanted to mention the elephant in the room.

A little after midnight, I heard the key in the door and stood up with manic joy. "Oh, here comes Jack now!"

I hurried into the foyer with dread. It was as I thought: Jack smelled like he'd spilled an entire bottle of liquor on himself.

"Um, Jack…honey," I whispered, "Mama and Daddy are in the sitting room. Please don't—"

"Move, woman!" he yelled, shoving me roughly aside and tramping into the sitting room.

"Oh my God…" Mama choked in disbelief at the sight of him.

I looked at Jack and saw him through my parent's eyes. I was so used to seeing him this way that I'd grown numb to it. Growing up, Jack had always been meticulous in his hygiene and appearance. Now, with unshaven face, hair unkempt, and clothes appearing as if they'd been worn for a week, Jack looked like a thirty-year-old bum on the street.

"I knew it! I knew you were a good for nothing!" Daddy roared.

In an instant, Jack jumped in Daddy's face and started cursing him something terrible. He called Daddy a coon lover and said Mama and I were whores, nothing but niggers in hiding.

Daddy balled up his fist and swung at him, but Jack caught Daddy's arm and yanked it behind his back. He let out a yelp and Mama screamed. Jack wrapped his other arm around Daddy's neck and squeezed.

For the first time, I realized my daddy was no longer the strong middle-aged man I had always known. He had gotten old while I was away. My once powerful father was no match for Jack…even a drunk Jack.

"Please, please, Jack, don't hurt him!" I begged.

"Shut up, half-breed! This is your fault anyway. I told you I didn't want them here, so if break his neck, it'd be your fault. If you say another word, I just might."

He emphasized his point by squeezing Daddy's neck even tighter. I opened my mouth to beg him again, but his words stopped me. "I mean it, woman, don't test me!"

"You good-for-nothing bastard! Stop it!" Mama shouted, hysterical. "Let him go, or I'll call the police!"

"Lady, you better shut up you hear?" Jack turned on her. "You move one inch, I'll crack this old buzzard's neck!" he slurred. "So shut up and listen."

By now, Daddy was turning blue, and he looked as though he were about to pass out.

"You're killing him, Jack…" I whispered.

This seemed to reach him, and he eased up on Daddy's neck just a bit.

"Alice, go get their bags and put them and your mama outside the front door."

In fear for my parents, I did as he instructed. I gave Mama a hug on the porch, tearfully whispering I was sorry. With a final squeeze, I went back in to check on Daddy. Jack was muttering and cursing the entire time.

"Now," Jack said, "I'm gonna let the old fart go, and you're gonna take him outside, close the door, and bring your ass right back in this house."

I nodded, and Jack let Daddy go. I walked him outside as he cradled his arm.

"I'm sorry, Daddy," I said, "Jack's been…"

"Now, Alice!" Jack's voice barked.

I turned to hurry back into the house, but Mama put a hand out to stop me.

"Honey, come with us please."

"No, I can't. He won't let me take Denise; I can't leave. I'll call you, but please go."

"Alice, baby—" Mama said again, but Daddy interjected.

"No, Charlotte, let's go before I kill him. We love you, sweetheart. Tell my granddaughter Merry Christmas."

Mama touched my face one last time, and I wiped the tears from hers.

"We'll be okay, Mama. Really. We will be okay."

Christmas morning when Denise awoke, I told her they were gone. Hysterical, she kept asking me why. I couldn't tell her the truth, so I made up another lie. "Daddy left his medication at home, and he had to have it. Please Denise," I hushed her, "let it be. Just let it be!"

Things became worse after that horrid night. Denise completely disconnected from me, rarely talking or looking me in the eyes anymore. It wasn't disrespect; like me, she just had nothing to say.

------------------ ///////////// ------------------

In February, 1961, the car was repossessed. Jack had been out of work seven months with no job prospects in sight. He'd sold everything of value in the house to pay bills, drink, and gamble. The little money he brought in from his occasional gambling wins or odd car repairs went for food and electricity.

The few times Jack was sober enough to get a lead on a job, he would either not bother to interview or show up drunk pretending to be sober. Those nights at the house were particularly violent.

One night, I thought I would die at Jack's hands.

He left the house looking rather decent and sober for a change. He had an interview in Mt. Ranier, and I prayed long and hard that he'd get this one. But it was not to be.

"You!" he stabbed a finger in my face when he came back. "You and your stupid daughter!"

It was obvious he had been drinking, and I begged him to calm down.

"If it wasn't for you two, I wouldn't be in this blasted mess!" he raged, and lunged for me, hoisting me up onto his shoulders. I yelled and kicked, but he was too strong, even in his inebriated state.

When he got me into the bedroom, he threw me to the floor and ripped my blouse open. I grappled with him, trying to slip out from under him, but he was determined, holding me down with one knee while pinning my arms above my head.

Those moments were some of the longest of my life. I had never been molested. But the day I was, it was from the man I had sworn to give my life and love to…forever.

When he had worn himself out from his vicious and painful exertion, he shoved me to the side and rolled over, panting, his whiskey-induced rage now settled into stupefied drowsiness. I crawled away from him, and when I stood, I realized I felt wet between my legs. The blood was warm, though all the rest of me was icy cold.

The next morning, the look from Denise told me she had heard the entire thing. With a look of disgust, she left for school, not uttering a word.

Soon after, the bank foreclosure notices started coming. Jack was rough with me several more times, but with each new notice, the attacks decreased and he became more despondent. He started faithfully looking for work.

But it seemed to be a case of too little, too late.

In April, the bank sent the final notice. We had sixty days to move.

Jack was devastated. I think he realized that the foreclosure could only be laid at his feet; he sat in the sitting room for days.

He didn't go out, didn't drink, and didn't say a word. When I took him his dinner one evening, he was weeping. I hadn't spoken to him in the days of his despondency, too fearful that he would take his anger out on me, but tonight, his pain was obvious. I had to help him.

"Jack, are you okay?" I whispered.

"Come here, Alice, and sit down."

There was no inflection in his tone, so I didn't know what to expect. He reached toward me, and instinctively, I flinched.

"I'm not going to hit you, honey," he said. "I just want to hold your hand. Is that okay?"

I nodded, and he took both my hands in his big oil-stained ones. He took a moment to get himself under control. When he did, it was as if all the horrible years never occurred.

"Alice, honey…I don't know how we got here. In our relationship, in life… But from this moment on, there will be big changes."

Not knowing what to say, I stayed silent.

"I am so, so, *so* sorry, honey, for everything I've done to you. I'm a beast, and I can never make it up to you. It was the drinking, Alice. But I'm sober now, honey. And I will *stay* sober."

His green eyes looked into mine. "Can you ever forgive me?"

I nodded through tears, praying this was real. Of course I could forgive him. I loved him with my whole being. I always had. No matter what he did, I wanted to be the faithful one, the one that never gave up. He smoothed my hair back, and then pulled me into his arms, holding me like he used to, so gentle, so tender.

True to his word, Jack stayed sober, and I began to hope again. Within two weeks, Jack landed a job. Epson & Company, the local soda factory, hired him as a forklift driver. With only forty-five days left to move, another blessing came in. Mr. Gordon, a very nice ex-customer from Jack's better days, offered to rent us one of his houses. When Jack got off the phone, he explained the plan.

"I agreed to build an engine for his '32 Roadster, and he's gonna let me pay him rent in exchange for the work." Jack grinned. "Even better, he has an old car, and if I can fix it, we can have it!"

Jack was so excited that it made me really believe that this would be a turning point in our lives.

We packed our things and said good riddance to our first home.

We pulled into our new neighborhood in our "new" old car about nine in the morning. Children were already outside playing in the July sun, and adults were sitting on porches, drinking coffee and talking.

This isn't so bad, I thought. *The houses are small, but we can manage.*

When we reached the second to last house on our street, Jack pointed as he parked. "Here we are, girls."

Speechless, I got out of the car and stepped onto the sidewalk.

The two-story house had a tired, weather beaten gray exterior with an odd-looking red front door. Unlike the other houses in the neighborhood, it was small and had no porch. Wild bushes on either side of the door hid most of the front of the house and its windows. It was difficult to hold back tears as I followed my husband up the walkway, with Denise trailing behind us. This house definitely did not evoke the happy feelings our first home had.

Jack unlocked the door, and we entered a dark, box-shaped room. The interior walls were as tired and dull as the exterior. Right in the middle was a flight of tread-worn wooden steps that led to the second floor. To the left of the steps was a small sitting room with brown walls; to the right was the kitchen. It had only two small cabinets and very little counter space. There wasn't room for much else besides a small table and three chairs. A tiny side door opened to a scrap of backyard, filled almost entirely by a ramshackle shed.

Each step creaked under my feet as I went up the stairs to see the rest of the house. I went into the larger of the two bedrooms and tried to get an idea of how our furniture might be arranged—or if it even would fit.

As I surveyed the room, a premonition struck me. Something inside me screamed, *Alice, if you don't grab your daughter and run as far away from this house as you can, you will regret it!*

I turned to leave, but found myself face to face with Jack. At his touch, I flinched, but then relaxed as he softly kissed my neck and whispered in my ear.

"I'm happy, honey, and things will be good here. I promise." Another kiss from him chased away all of my apprehension.

Things settled down, and we were at peace. I added little touches to the house to make it feel more "homey." Though things were still at odds with Denise, I knew that it would just take time for her to trust the peace. In the meantime, she did make a couple of friends from the neighborhood. I figured with having other kids to pal around with, she'd eventually relax as well.

Jack still felt bad about how he had treated my parents and called to apologize. Mama didn't accept his apology, though, and Daddy wouldn't come to the phone. I told Jack that when we went home for Christmas, he could apologize then.

He said Denise and I should go alone. "I want to keep moving forward and forget about the past," he explained.

I appreciated that, but I'd never leave him alone for the holidays. Instead, I spent the next six months trying to convince my parents to give him another chance. But they wouldn't, and during a call in November, I'd finally had enough. Mama was on one extension telling me that Jack was no good, and Daddy was on the other, imploring me to leave and come back to Beaufort.

"Stop it! Both of you!" I yelled into the phone. "Mama, Daddy, this is my life and you can't tell me how to live it! I'm sorry I've let you down, but I am going to try to save my family. If you can't accept that, then I will stop talking to you! You're not helping…you're just pushing me farther away."

They both simmered down after that, but neither one said anything about forgiving Jack. I didn't go home that year, and they didn't visit us. After that, the calls were general and turned from weekly to biweekly, then to once a month. We spent most of that year purposefully avoiding talk about anything of importance, too busy trying not to say the wrong things.

Growing up, I had always been honest and talked to them about anything. Our relationship now was stilted at best, and I just couldn't let it remain that way. So that fall, even without a change in their attitude, I decided that Denise and I would go to Beaufort in the summer. I called and told Mama. She was ecstatic that we'd be visiting them, having felt the strain as I had.

I was so confident in the changes Jack had made, I was sure before summer, I'd be able to convince him to come with us. Once they saw the same loving man from the past, I was positive they would come around.

Jack's reversion started in the spring of 1963 innocently enough. He was invited by one of his coworkers to a friendly game of poker, and to another the following week. It didn't take long before he started losing himself to the gambling, and then the drinking started again. Denise had just started to interact with me again, but soon fell back into her reclusive and indifferent ways, and I began to despair.

Jack gambled away what little money we'd managed to save during our year of peace. When he got his paycheck from the soda company, he would only put a few groceries in the house and make partial payments on our bills. When the holidays rolled around, we couldn't even afford a decent Thanksgiving dinner or more than one present each under the tree for Christmas.

On New Year's Eve, Jack lost all control and attacked me again. Instead of ringing in 1964 with new hopes and dreams, I sat on my bed nursing my wounds. Remembering the ominous premonition I'd chosen to ignore on the day we moved to this house, I asked myself the age-old question, *Why?* Why didn't I listen? Why didn't I run? Why didn't I grab my daughter and get as far away from this house as I could?

Denise, now fourteen, had become more angry than scared now. Her principal was constantly on the phone with me, but no matter what I said, she still did whatever she wanted to do. One day, she got caught behind her school drinking beer with two older boys. When I told Jack and he confronted her about it, she paid him no attention whatsoever.

They argued all the time now. When he'd yell, she'd just fuss right back, as if daring him to hit her. He never did…though I often received her blows behind closed doors.

One afternoon, Denise stormed in an hour later than usual, slamming the front door and going straight up to her room. I started to follow her, but a knock on the door stopped me. It was sweet, elderly Mrs. Bailey, who lived down the street near where the children played. She responded to my greeting politely, then told me that Denise had gotten into a fight. Some of the kids had been teasing her.

"Teasing her? About what?" I asked.

Her face became flushed, but she offered me no answer.

"What happened, Mrs. Bailey?"

"All I have to say, Mrs. Miles, is that children can be cruel sometimes. Now, good day," she replied, turning to make her arthritic way down the walk.

"Please!" I called to her in desperation. "Please, Mrs. Bailey, if you don't tell me what happened, I'll... I'll never know. She doesn't talk to me." Although embarrassed by my lack of communication with my daughter, I stood there hoping this sweet old lady would offer me some solace.

She laboriously turned and walked back, rheumy eyes regarding me sympathetically.

"All right, dear," she said and took a deep breath. "Well...the children have been teasing Denise, saying that her father is a mean man who...beats her mother up all the time."

My face heated with embarrassment.

"Mrs. Miles, they...they were pretending to scream and thrash around, as if they were you—being hit, you understand?" When I gave the briefest nod, she continued. "Denise took all she could stand, but she finally had enough and jumped on the girls. That's when Mr. Sheffield from next door broke it up."

I was burning with shame and appalled that people—the children—suspected the truth. I forced myself to meet her eyes and spoke with as much dignity as I could muster. "Thank you so much for seeing her home."

"Of course. Please tell Denise I hope she feels better. And I...I'm so sorry."

I was so mortified that I just stood there. What I wanted to do was throw myself down in the middle of the floor and have a tantrum like a three-year-old, to scream and rage at the injustice of my situation. But I couldn't—there was no time. I needed to deal with this, to see my daughter and offer whatever comfort I could.

When I entered her room, Denise was lying across her bed, sobbing into her pillow. I sat beside her and put my hand on her back to console her, but at my touch, she scrambled up and scooted as far away from me as her bed allowed.

"Don't touch me!"

Her face was red and tear-streaked. New tears slid down her cheeks, and she wiped them away in irritation.

"I heard what happened, and I'm sorry," I said, trying to keep my voice calm against Denise's outburst.

"You always say that, and you're not sorry!" she cried out. "If you were, you'd get us out of here. But you just stay, and I'm stuck here with you. I'm stuck, and a freak, all because of you!"

"Oh, honey, don't say that. You're not a freak—"

"Yes I am! All the kids know that Dad beats you up all the time. Everybody knows!"

"Honey, please. Calm down…"

"Just leave me alone!" she shrieked, and before I could react, she jumped up and ran out of her room and out the front door. I couldn't catch her, so I prayed long and hard that she'd be back after she cooled off.

Evening came, but there was no sign of my girl, and Jack wasn't home either. I didn't know what to do. By midnight, I was sick with worry and called the police. They came immediately and stood in my tiny foyer with notepads and grim expressions. I was thankful that the latest bruises on my face had healed.

I was giving the officers a description of Denise when the front door opened. I rushed over and hugged my daughter hard, breathing in relief for what seemed like the first time since she'd left.

"Denise, I was so afraid! Where have you been?" I asked when I finally let go.

"Nowhere," she replied glumly, eyeing the officers with a scowl.

"Don't you ever scare me like that again," I said, now letting my anger in. She didn't answer me.

The lead officer closed his notepad. "Are you okay, Denise?"

She stared at him, expressionless. "I'll never be okay as long as I'm stuck here." She turned away, despondent, and went to her room.

I waited up for Jack to come home, but he was so drunk when he arrived, I didn't bother say anything. I believed in my heart it wouldn't have mattered if I had.

///////////////

CHAPTER 4

After that, Denise spent her time away from our neighborhood. I'd tell her not to leave the street and to be in by five-thirty, but she'd always come in long after curfew, usually smelling like alcohol. I tried punishing her by making her stay in her room, but as soon as I turned my back, she'd leave the house. Jack witnessed none of it because five nights out of seven, he didn't come home until after nine or ten o'clock himself.

Feeling helpless and not knowing what else to do, when he was less drunk than usual, I told Jack what had been going on.

"She needs someone to talk to."

"You mean like a quack doc? Hell, no!" he yelled. "I ain't paying for no doctor! There ain't nothing wrong with that girl. She's just trying to get attention. I told you she was too fast anyway, always outside around them older boys. If she gets raped, it will be her own fault."

I couldn't believe he would say that about his own child. He hadn't shocked me in a long time, but this was an all-time low, even for Jack.

"And, woman," he continued, "I find out that you spent one thin dime of my hard-earned money on some quack doctor, you're gonna be the one needing a doctor."

With no money of my own, there was nothing I could do to help my daughter.

When Denise went into a growth spurt that summer and started wearing heavier makeup, she looked almost grown. She was drop-dead gorgeous, curvy, and tall like her father. Her teeth were perfect, her bright green eyes almond-shaped like mine, and her jet-black hair grew long enough to sit on.

Jack didn't like how she was maturing or dressing and made a point of telling her she looked like a tramp every chance he got. His nasty words seemed to have no effect on her, though. Denise was immune to Jack's ferocious temper, and his disrespectful ranting meant nothing to her. He would tell her not to go outside after dinner, but as soon as he'd drunk his first six-pack, she'd be gone.

It was obvious she had no respect for either of us at all. The little girl I loved and who had loved me back was gone. She had shut me out, and I had no clue how to reach her and no one to teach me how.

I felt so worthless, so weak. I had nowhere to turn and no one to turn to. No friends, no family I could tell the truth to. No one. I missed Karen and Cadell—and Mama—fiercely.

Finally, I got to my lowest point yet. I even felt like killing myself. Without my husband's love, my daughter's smile, and the relationship I once shared with my parents, I had nothing.

What was the point?

———————— ///////////// ————————

I'll always remember it—July 10, 1964. It was as if God knew that I wouldn't make another day without his divine intervention. As I sat distraught, contemplating my possible demise, the phone rang.

"Alice? Hi, honey, how are you?"

It was Mama's sweet voice. I almost cried out in joy and desperation.

"Oh, Mama, I'm fine, just fine. It's so good to hear your voice…" I whispered a prayer of thanks to God.

"Did you get the box of clothing we sent Denise, baby?"

"Yes. You and Daddy spoil her rotten."

"Well, that's what grandparents do."

Her voice trailed off, and I could tell there was something she wanted to say. I wanted to scream, to tell her everything, but I didn't know where to start, how to form the words. So I kept pretending that all was well to stall.

"Where's that daddy of mine?" I asked. "Never mind, let me answer that. It's about four-thirty, so he's down at the lake fishing with the guys, right?"

Mama laughed. "Yes, he is. He should be home any minute. I kind of hope he didn't catch anything. You know how he likes for us to eat whatever he catches? Well, I'm running out of recipes for fish."

We both chuckled at that. Then, with a breath so deep I imagined it started from the depth of her soul, Mama continued.

"Sweetheart…I know you don't want to talk about it, but I have to say this, so please bear with me for a moment. I need you to know what happened that Christmas when we left."

I didn't want to go back to that memory. But I needed to hear her voice. "Yes, Mama, I'm listening."

Static rattled through the line as she exhaled. "Sweetheart, I've never seen your father like that, not even when his own mother died. We didn't get three blocks away before he pulled the car over and cried like a baby."

"Mama, I'm so sor—"

"Just, listen, honey. Your father felt helpless. He understood that leaving you and Denise with Jack would mean leaving you in danger. But he also feels that forcing the issue would create more of a problem in your house. Baby, it's killing your father." After a pause, she asked, "How long, Alice?"

"How long what, Mama?" I tried to make sure my voice was even, hoping to ease her worries.

"I saw the anxiety on your face that night and the terror in your eyes, child. How long has Jack been beating you and Denise?"

"He doesn't beat Denise, Mama, I swear."

"Alice…"

"No, no, he…"

"Please, Alice, the truth!"

It was over; she knew. I wanted to be forward with her. I wanted to tell her everything. To release the pain. But what kind of wife betrayed her husband?

"Well, Mama, sometimes he loses his temper with me…but it's not what you think."

"I believe it *is*." Mama's tone was steely, the mother bear protecting her cub. "I know I've said this before, but please listen, Alice. The first chance you can get, come home. You hear me? Don't ask him for anything, don't take any clothes—just come home. Do you know how many years it's been since we've set eyes on our girls? Alice, nothing good will ever come out of a man with enough rage to beat his wife."

I breathed deeply, trying to keep from crying, trying to quell the desire to grab Denise and do exactly what she said. And she was right. I had been denying it, all of it. I had to get us out of there…and soon.

As I contemplated in the silence that followed her last words, I heard a familiar sound in the background—the distinctive *shreeek* of the old screen door of my childhood home.

"Is that Daddy?"

Mama didn't respond. She wanted an answer. When I didn't give it, she relented with a sigh. "Yes, it is. Hold on… Honey?"

"Yeah?" Daddy replied in the distance.

"Your baby girl is on the phone."

"Well! If it isn't my angel!" Daddy's voice boomed. A minute later his warm voice came through the line. "How are you and that granddaughter of mine, sweetie? I bought her a fishing pole, Alice. I mean, I know most girls don't like baiting the hook and smelling like fish, but my grandbaby is spunky. I think she'll get a kick out of it." His laughter enveloped me like a warm blanket.

"I'm sure she would, just because you're doing it together."

I was crying silently now, my daddy's voice and characteristic warmth reminding me of everything I had been denying myself all these years. I wanted to go home.

"How are you, Daddy?"

"Oh, I'm fine, angel, just missing my girls, that's all. You need to come home and bring her real soon so we can give that pole a good try. And don't worry, I'll get her some overalls so she won't get dirty. When do you think you girls can come down?"

"Oh, I don't know, Daddy. I… Jack's been…"

He let out a heavy sigh. "Listen, you and Denise grab a train or a plane, either one. I'll pay for it. *Jack* doesn't have to worry about a thing. Just…"

He choked up, and tears poured from my eyes.

"Just come to where y'all can be safe, angel," he said. "Come home and let us take care of you."

"Oh, Daddy…"

I didn't know what else to say. Each of us held the phone in silence for a long while.

"Daddy?" I murmured. "You still there?"

"Yes, honey…" I heard the quaver in his voice. "I'll always be here, sweetie. Come home, angel. Please just come home, okay? Promise me you'll come."

"I promise I'll try." And I meant it. "I'll try to come before summer's end, or just as soon as I can."

He let out a breath, and whispered something to Mama, who was probably still standing next to him. "We'll be here, sweetheart. You take care of yourself, you hear? Denise needs you—we're far away and you're all she has. Remember that, okay?"

"Yes, Daddy. Give Mama a kiss for me. Goodbye."

"It's never goodbye, angel, because we're always with you. It's only good night."

"Good night, Daddy."

It was the last time I would ever speak with my parents. Two months later, they were gone.

One horrible car accident, and Mama and Daddy were dead. The foundation of my world, the only place I knew I could run and be safe and loved was gone… No more.

I went home alone to bury my beloved parents. On the train ride back to Washington, my mind gave way to the miles of track, thankfully numbed by the remembrance of the words of the Shepherd's Psalm and the clickety-clack of the wheels chugging beneath me. The motion of the train rhythmically drove the reassurance of two Bible scriptures used by Pastor Ronnie at the funeral:

> *Yea, though I walk through the valley of the shadow*
> *of death, I will fear no evil. Surely goodness and mercy*
> *shall follow me all the days of my life…*

"It's never goodbye, angel, because we're always with you. It's only good night." Those were the last words they spoke to me. So much hell existed in our home, I had not dared call them again. I couldn't pretend anymore, and because I couldn't…I didn't call.

When the train came to a stop, the porter's voice broke my chain of thought. "Union Station! Full stop at Union Station!"

I gathered up my things and stepped onto the busy platform. The crowd hurried past me in a whirlwind of motion, and all around me people were embracing as warm hellos or tearful goodbyes filled the platform. There was so much love in the dusky air.

I stood frozen and alone, gazing through the crowd hoping against hope to see my daughter and husband waiting to take me home. But their familiar faces were not there.

A man shouted my name above the crowd of people. I craned my neck…but it was not my husband. A woman standing close by shrieked, snatched up her bag, and ran in the man's direction with a huge smile on her face. I sniffed, then grabbed the long handle of my bulky suitcase, hauling it across the crowded train station. The shoebox-sized chest that Mama had left me I clutch-ed under my other arm, protecting it. I ducked my head and weaved my way through the crowd to avoid someone running into me with a hard shoulder or a heavy suitcase to my shins.

Alone, I began my twenty-minute walk home.

I passed St. Matthew's Cathedral and the Casa Italia Center where so many people in the community gathered. Realizing I may never get the opportunity again, I took a moment and said a prayer for my parents before the big doors of the church.

Two doors down, I passed *Mulden's Diner* and smelled the oregano and garlic from my once-favorite dish, salmon aioli. It had been ages since Jack took me there; I didn't remember the last time we had even gone out as a family, all those memories foggy and dim as if they were someone else's life.

Unable to help myself, I played the phone call over and over in my mind, the one from Aunt Blondell that told me of my parents' automobile accident. I shook my head to snap out of my sorrowful revelry and realized I was almost home.

I turned onto my street, which seemed to be teeming with a life I'd only been allowed to observe. The smooth sounds of Frank Sinatra coming from Miss Lucy's porch blared while neighborhood women exchanged gossip. Children whizzed about, hiding behind cars and trees, playing tag. The older kids wore ringer tees, bellbottoms, and hip huggers. They stood together in a haze of marijuana smoke, attempting intellectual conversation on the Vietnam War and the Civil Rights movement.

Inadvertently, I caught the attention of a freckle-faced girl who had long, beautiful red tresses draped under a patchwork cap. She gave me a peace sign and shined a smile. I didn't acknowledge her offering. It reminded me that so much was going on in the world, and I hadn't been allowed to be a part of any of it. I quickened my pace until I reached our house.

The hideous red door that Jack never got around to painting seemed to be a yawning mouth threatening to swallow me. I didn't know how, or if, I would survive this.

My parents' last phone call had given me hope. It was all so futile now. Maybe I should have gone home to visit then and just not come back. My eyes misted again as I thought about them. Mama and I wouldn't be talking about holiday recipes anymore; I wouldn't argue politics with Daddy again, or hear him grow quiet for fear of asking what he didn't want to ask. I was already missing how he would say my gray, almond-shaped eyes looked just like his mother's—wise and shimmery.

I clutched the chest from Mama closer, then swallowed the lump in my throat and braced myself. It took all my remaining strength to open the door.

I turned the key and quietly tiptoed inside. In the background, I heard President Lyndon B. Johnson talking on the television. Since President Kennedy was killed, it seemed nobody was happy—especially Jack. He wasn't fond of Johnson or the way he was handling the war and often railed against him to no one in particular.

I took one last breath and followed the thick cloud of cigarette smoke into the sitting room.

He was just as I'd left him five days ago, sprawled out on our old battered couch with a V&T bottle hanging from his hand. He had one foot planted in the bowels of the cushions and the other propped parallel to the six empty beer bottles on our cigarette-burned coffee table. His jet-black hair was uncombed, and the stubble on his face begged for a razor. News reports about Vietnam blared from the thirteen-inch black-and-white TV that displayed everything but clear images. Jack's eyes were glazed and unfocused. He was wearing a dingy undershirt accompanied by dingy underwear with holes and questionable stains.

Noticing me in the doorway, he sat up and cursed under his breath. Rigid, I watched as he slowly rose to his feet and turned toward me while pulling a cigarette out of his pack.

"H-hi, Jack," I stuttered as he lumbered closer. Though my knees were shaky and a sick feeling rose in my stomach, I did my best to stand up straight. "I'm home."

With his chin less than an inch from my eyes, he opened his mouth and exhaled the smoke into my face. I bowed my head trying to escape the disgusting billowing cloud.

"'Bout time you came back. You done running off to say goodbye to Mama and Papa?"

"I-I-I…"

"I-I-I-I…" He mocked my frightened stutter and staggered away in a fog of gray smoke and fell back on the couch. "Good riddance, folks." Jack waved his cigarette in the air then reached over, grabbed the liquor, and turned up the volume on the television.

The static aggravated my already frayed nerves, and with the conversation over, I grabbed my things and headed up the stairs. I had to get away from him.

I knocked on Denise's door as I passed, not expecting a better reception.

"Denise? It's Mom."

I knew she was awake, but didn't she bother to answer. It didn't surprise me; I knew she was still infuriated with me for not taking her to the funeral. I hadn't told her that her father wouldn't let me.

"Don't you even think about taking Denise," he'd said, "and if you try any funny stuff like trying to stay down there, I'll file legally for her, right here in Washington, and you'll never see her again."

He was nasty enough to do it. So I had to come back to my house of horrors.

As soon as I stepped into my bedroom, my nose was assaulted by the disgusting stench of man, booze, and cigarettes. Empty liquor and beer bottles were everywhere, ashtrays overflowed, dirty clothes and crusted plates were all about. It was an absolute pigsty. With one look around, the last bit of my mental hold vanished. My mind slipped back into the dark place, and I wanted it all to end.

"No!" I whispered fiercely. "No, you can't leave! Denise needs you, remember?"

I hugged the wooden box close to my heart and focused on the conversation I had with my Aunt Blondell, Mama's sister, just moments before stepping onto the train back to D.C.

"Grandma Sheila gave your mama this many years ago," Auntie said, pressing her hands tight around the little box as if reluctant to let it go.

I sniffed and wiped my nose again. "Do you know what's in it?"

"Oh yes," she replied. "Charlotte shared it with all of us when we were young, but it was always going to be yours. I vowed to your mama if she ever could not give it to you, I would."

I took the box from her as the train whistle blew in the distance, and rubbed my fingers gently over the bright pine-polished wood. There was a tiny lock on the front, and across the top and sides, a thick metal chain, of all things. It was impossible to open the box as it was now. I'd seen nothing like it before and was transfixed by the overwhelming pull it exerted over me.

"What is it?" I asked.

"Not so fast." Auntie waved a long, thin finger. "This box is one of the most important things you will ever possess in your life, child, so don't you go disrespecting it by rushing to see what's inside. You wait until it's time."

"When will that be?" I sniffed again, defeated.

"I don't know, but you will feel it in here." Auntie placed her hand over my heart. "Alice, close your eyes and be still for a moment," she said in a calm, soothing voice. "Concentrate and sit still. Listen for your Mama's voice."

The sounds from the station seemed to hush as Auntie's voice continued.

"Your mother loved you so much. Although she's gone, she's still with you in here." She pressed more firmly on my heart.

In the moments that passed, the love of my mother and the memories of her came flowing through into my soul. This time it didn't bring tears, but warmth.

"Now...can you hear her Alice?" Aunt Blondell asked.

"Yes," I said, almost in a trance-like state.

"Good," Auntie's voice was almost a whisper. "Do you think she wants you to open the box?"

I waited a moment more to be sure. "No."

"Okay then, there's your answer." Auntie patted my hands, and I opened my eyes, and all the swirling noises and bustle of the station rushed back into my consciousness.

"Whenever you're anxious and missing your mama," she said, "I want you to do what you are doing right now. Trust your heart and wait to hear her voice..."

Thinking of that memory now in my room brought a mist to my eyes. With a sudden inspiration, I dashed to my closet. There was a loose floorboard in the back. I knelt down, ripped it up, and tucked the box away inside where no one would find it—a piece of myself that Jack could never take away.

I removed my jacket and shoes and realized there was now silence downstairs. That meant Jack was most likely asleep, and I'd be able to have the room to myself. To be sure, I tiptoed to the door and pressed my ear against it.

"Kill the damn gooks!"

Jack's shout made me jump. My quiet serenity of the past few moments was shattered. Though it was early, I undressed and slipped into a nightgown. The bath I had looked forward to would have to wait till morning.

The sour stench of Jack's sweat and dirt caused me to pause as I pulled back the sheets; the smell was horrendous. But there was no help for it—I couldn't chance attracting his attention by making a fuss. I reluctantly slipped under the offensive covers and clicked off the bedside lamp. I could feel my heart racing.

I lay awake for almost an hour, sure that at any moment, Jack would make his way upstairs. When I heard nothing after a while, I closed my eyes and whispered a prayer.

"Oh God, please keep this house peaceful, at least for the rest of this night."

CHAPTER 5

A long sliver of early morning light sliced through the darkness of my dank bedroom. The bright light seemed more like a nosy neighbor disturbing my sleep than a welcomed guest coming in to wake me. I heard Jack stirring in the kitchen, getting ready for work at the soda factory. How he kept his job there, I never knew. His employers must have lacked the sense of sight and smell.

I usually made breakfast for him, but today I stayed in bed in the hopes that he didn't remember my coming back last night. I stayed put until the front door slammed, knowing then it would be safe for me to venture out of my room.

The silence restored a semblance of calm—but I wondered about Denise.

Tapping lightly, I eased her door open. She was still asleep. Though I should have been waking her for school, I stood over her bed and just watched her.

She looked angelic in sleep, dark hair cascading onto the pillow, framing her fair, heart-shaped face, with long eyelashes casting shadows against her cheeks. I took a look around her room, noting afresh that, despite it being as worn as the rest of the old house, she kept it tidy.

Denise stirred, and I jumped up, wanting to avoid a confrontation with her. I tiptoed out the door, easing it shut before she noticed me. I was halfway to the bathroom when I realized I'd become afraid of everyone in my life...even my little girl.

The long, hot shower helped replenish my grimy body and clouded mind. I told myself I was being silly—Denise was my daughter; I should be able to talk to her without hesitation. Slipping into my rose-patterned dress, I stood before the mirror and raked my fingers through my thick sandy curls. By reflex, I pull my hair into its usual ponytail. But then I remembered the freckled redheaded girl I saw on the walk home yesterday and left my hair loose to frame my face.

For once, I wasn't disappointed with the thirty-four-year-old woman facing me in the mirror. Perhaps seeing her mother groomed for a change might catch Denise's interest.

My good intentions proved useless. My attempted cheery greeting made no impact at all when she entered the kitchen. She tromped over to the refrigerator and pulled out the orange juice. I chattered away, unable to stop myself. I didn't care; I'd missed her.

"Hope you slept well, honey. Anything much happen while I was away?"

"Oh, sure. We won a million dollars." Denise rolled her eyes and got a glass from the cabinet.

I continued with false cheer. "I missed you, baby. The whole family sends their love and says to tell you hello."

She snorted.

"You would have liked how they put the funeral together, Denise." I didn't know what else to say. "I told them that maybe we can get together for a visit next summer. How's that sound?"

"Spiffy," she muttered. "Haven't seen any of them in five years, so I'm thrilled to spend a summer with total strangers."

She sloshed the orange juice into a glass and downed it in one gulp.

"Denise, I'm sorry I couldn't take you with me. Really, honey, I would have if I could but we didn't have the money and—"

"You mean you couldn't beg the money for another ticket so I could say goodbye to my grandparents?" she interrupted, slamming the glass on the counter. "And if they miss us so much, why hasn't anyone ever come to visit? Hmm?"

I was momentarily stumped by my fourteen-year-old's logical complaint. "Denise, just because they never visited doesn't mean—"

"I know why they never visited, Mom. So do you. Quit pretending." Her stare burned into me.

She wasn't a little girl anymore, not really. The same tricks would not work. I wanted to confess everything and opened my mouth to tell her the truth, but at the last minute, my words changed their course.

"It's a long trip from Beaufort to D.C., Denise, and our family—"

"Oh, just stop it, will you!" Denise's outburst halted my words. "Granddaddy loved us more than anything. He wanted to rescue us from this place, but he never did because *you* wouldn't let him!"

"Honey, I—"

"Stop lying, Mom. Man!"

"I'm not lying, Denise, I—"

"You *are*." Her eyes were aflame. I had never seen her that angry with me before. She had often raised her voice, but this wasn't just a put-on. She was enraged.

But it was over as fast as it started. "Whatever, Mother, it doesn't matter. Nobody cares anyway." She rinsed her glass in the sink, slung her school bag onto her shoulder, and headed for the front door.

"Wait, I made you some toast!" I rose and wrapped it up in a napkin.

"You eat it." The front door slammed behind her.

Oh God, I thought, *I've lost her. She called me "Mother"? Whatever happened to "Mom" or "Mommy"?*

Disheartened, I trudged upstairs.

I ended up back in my bedroom and stared at the chaos my week in Beaufort had caused. Stepping over the filthy clothes, I noticed the familiar pink smudges on the collars of several of Jack's shirts. Ignoring them, I crossed the room, pulled the old floral curtains aside, and flung open the window to air out the stench. Light washed over the dingy beige wallpaper, and a soft breeze entered the stuffy room.

"What happened? Where did I go wrong?" I asked to no one in particular. My question met silence; even the breeze seemed to consider my query.

Cleaning always helped me to distract myself, so I grabbed the dirty clothes from the bedroom and headed downstairs to wash them and start dinner. I numbly put a chicken in the oven and a pot of beans and rice on the stove, then ventured into the sitting room. I knew the filth would be there, waiting for me.

There were cigarette butts with lipstick smudges in the ashtray, which I again ignored. After dumping the ashtray and removing the glasses to the kitchen, I plumped up the worn pillows on the couch. Stuck in the cushion was a pair of Jack's underpants, crusted with dry spots with more of the now very familiar lipstick stains. Despite my best efforts, I gagged as the tears finally rushed in. I didn't stop moving, but scurried around to finish the room.

After putting the filthy garments in the washer, I went to rinse my hands in the bathroom sink. After what seemed a very long time, I became aware I'd been scrubbing my hands viciously. It was as though I needed to scrub off Jack's vileness. Taking a steadying breath, I dried my hands and went to lie down.

My mind raced as I thought about Denise that morning and how Jack treated me yesterday when I returned. And then the real pain flooded in. I'd lost Mama and Daddy. It was a physical ache that nothing could make better. I needed someone to hold me, to tell me it would be all right. Instead, I hugged myself, reaching out for the solace of ghosts. My words staggered between sobs.

"Mama, I need you…so much. Please…help me."

Wiping my damp cheeks, my eyes fell on the closet door, and I remembered what lay beneath its dusty floorboards.

"Mama?" I whispered. "Mama, is it time?"

I made myself calm down and did as Auntie had bade me—I listened for Mama's voice. A moment later, I stood by the closet door. I could almost hear the box coming to life, growing sentient… Calling my name.

I opened the closet and dropped to my hands and knees to pull up the floorboard. The box looked so innocent, yet heavy with importance. As I cradled it in my arms, the memories of Mama's love rose and settled around me like a warm blanket. I wanted to cry and laugh all at once.

It was time.

When I examined the box from all angles, the chain rattled and scraped against the hard wood. I turned the box upside down and saw a small key taped to the bottom. I inserted it and gave it a firm *click*.

Though grinning with triumph, I still couldn't get into it; the box was still securely encased with the chain. *How in the world am I going to get into the darn thing?* I pondered for a few moments. A minute later, wire cutter in hand, I went to work on a link at the center of it. At last, my fingers aching, the chain snapped and fell to each side.

"Whew, that wasn't easy," I said aloud as an afterthought. A breeze wafted through my open window just then, and I swore I could hear Mama's whisper.

"It wasn't supposed to be, Alice."

I smiled, because I knew it was real. Mama was watching me, still here with me. The chest was ready to divulge its secrets.

Heart pounding, I lifted the lid.

Inside there lay three small books tied together with what seemed to be shoestring. Safely tucked next to them was a yellowing envelope, which I opened gingerly.

Dear Kane daughters, it read,

    In this box, I have placed the accounts of Kane grandmothers, mothers, and daughters. I've wrapped a chain around it to represent the succession of slavery, both physical and emotional, that has held us in bondage for far too long.

    In these memoirs, you will find our hopes, dreams, truths, and fears. Through the years, we have fought the feelings of *worthlessness and entrapment that have been imposed by ourselves and others. Open the books and letters within, and as you read each one, experience the tears and treasures of your foremothers' lives.*

Then complete your mother's account and record your own—anything which you feel to be of value for the generations to come. Perhaps your life lessons will be read and embraced by your daughter someday...

Should you succeed, escaping the bondage of our past, hold this chain up toward the heavens so that all your foremothers may rejoice at your accomplishment. If you fail, return the memoirs, secure the box, and pass it on to the next Kane daughter.

Daughters of the Kane bloodline, I pray that after your own journey, no chain will ever encircle these accounts again.

Until that blessed day arrives, God be with you.

Your foremother,
Sheila (Kane-Wright-Jenson) Hanson

Sheila Hanson... I thought. Mama's mama, the grandmother I had never met. She must have collected these letters and diaries and given them to Mama. I looked at the signs of age on the book covers and was awed and humbled. My entire family legacy must be contained within this little wooden box. It was where I came from, the reality of who I was...the part of me I had promised Jack I wouldn't speak of.

63

ill feel Mama's presence as I picked up the first book
t. It was covered in soft black velvet and trimmed in
The center had an oval-shaped hole, framed in vintage
silver tw...e. I recognized my great-grandmother, Nicole Jenson,
from her wedding photo that hung in my parents' stairwell. She
was much older in this picture, no longer a young bride. Beneath
the noble portrait, I read the silvery, embroidered words: NICOLE
JENSON, BORN 1858.

I smiled and laid her book aside to pick up the second and
third books beneath it. They were made like the first, but one was
hunter green and the other red. The portraits on these two diaries
were instantly recognizable, even without the silver embroidered
names beneath them; it was my grandma, Sheila Hanson, born
in 1874, who collected the memories of this box, and my dear
mama, Charlotte Whitmore, born 1901. My heart constricted as
I gazed at these two wonderful women. Holding the books close
to my bosom, I breathed in, trying to absorb the enormity of their
aged and browned pages and every last memory I had of them.

Settling back, I took in the mementos spread before me. Not
sure which book to read first, I decided to start with the oldest
and reached for Great-Grandma Nicole's book. When I opened it,
three yellowed envelopes fell into my lap. Scanning the scrawled
writing, I felt goosebumps rise: I had words not from three, but
six generations of the women in my family right here in my hands.
Thanks to the labor of Grandma Sheila, I had their accounts and
their words of wisdom right here.

I picked up the first envelope and opened it with trembling
fingers. Grandma's elegant handwriting read: LILY FURRLY, BORN
1775 – LETTER WRITTEN CIRCA 1807

"Oh my God, that's almost two hundred years ago..." Heart

pounding in anticipation, I drew in a deep breath and pulled open the thick, coarse paper, reading its awkward, childish scrawl.

Mamie,

Jess herd Massa Dan say he takin me away so I need say sometings fust. I was born to Grace Furrly hare in Fayetteville, Nort Caroline. Soon I born, Massa sent Momma away an Nelly care fo me. When I lil gurl, dey wispers Massa Dan Furrly my papa.

Nelly dat troo? She say ya mite be a lil lite Mamie, but you still a nigga.

I growd up, fall in luv an jump da broom wit Isac. We happy. Den Massa Dan die an he step chile Massa Abe com boss. He tak me out my bed at nite from Isac. Soon Isac neva cood look at me.

My belly done swole wit child an I ask God to make ya Isacs baby.

Soon Isac see ya he cry an look so fill wit hurt an hate. I gone kill Massa he say.

I canna git up. I to week from pushin ya out. No Isac pleez done leev me. I screem for him but he run out an I neva see he agan. He ded fo what he gone try do.

Hurtin I look down at da lite skin on my new babe an drop teers on ya, den I screem out fo Isac, da pain in my belly an da pain in my hart.

Now yeers afta, my sweet chile, lak Massa Abe took my Isac from me, now he takin me

from ya. O what a dark dey dis be! Why God–
why do ya turn ya bak on me? Jess fo wite
man? Jess fo wite man...

Tears stung my eyes as I stared at the faded scrawl Mama
Lily used to relay these things to her only daughter. I had no idea
who this woman was, and yet I imagined her cries ringing in my
ears. I looked at my own pale skin and heard her haunting words
in my soul.

There was a light tread on the staircase, and I realized I must
have been sitting there all afternoon trying to get in the box—
Denise was home from school. She went straight to her room
without calling out to see if I was home. Her door closed, and I
sighed with a sense of relief. After the altercation in the morning,
I didn't know what I could say to her.

With the break in my concentration, I remembered dinner
and smelled the food simmering in the air. I headed downstairs,
contemplating the disturbing letter.

I'd often considered my Negro ancestors, but never
contemplated the reality of what that meant for them, how
horrible their existence must have been. I had had no knowledge
of Lily Furrly before, but her words were as real as if she'd told
me her story in person. My foremother, a slave, held down by
her master, robbed of her marriage bed and motherhood. What
tortures must she have endured?

While I pondered the enormity of this discovery and setting
the table, the rattling of the doorknob caused my bowels to clinch.

Jack was home.

I ran up the stairs and tossed the books and letters back into
the box. I wished I could place them gently and reverently as they
deserved, but I was shaking with terror—Jack couldn't know.
He'd destroy anything he thought I was hiding, no matter how
precious to me.

I'd just tossed the board over the box's hiding place when he came into the room and hoisted me up off of my knees by my neck.

"What in the hell are you doing in here, woman?"

"Please, Jack," I begged. "I was just...just reorganizing the things in the closet—"

"Don't lie to me, woman!" he barked. I could smell the alcohol on him. "You ain't gonna pretend to be a good little housewife now. I know the truth."

For a moment, my heart stopped.

"Your mama never taught you a damn thing. You don't know nothing about taking care of your man."

He turned me away from the closet door, hand still on my neck, applying even more pressure.

Though I was no longer afraid that he'd seen what I was doing, I was terrified in a new way. He dragged me toward the bed, loosening his belt with the other hand. I knew what was coming, and I begged for him to stop. But instead, he shoved me onto the bed.

"Take your clothes off," he said, slipping the belt from out of his pant loops. The sound sent me scattering backward.

"Please! No, Jack!" I begged again, but it was pointless. I undressed before him, my hands trembling. I didn't want Denise to hear us, and I prayed that someone, anyone, could intervene— could stop the monster.

But there wasn't answer from anyone. Not even Mama or the voices from the past hidden away beneath the floorboards. I was alone, in hell.

Jack knelt on the bed above me, face suffused with red. As he had done many times before, he began whipping me with his leather belt, subduing me more and more with each lash across my back and side. I struggled and cried and tried to get away from him, but it was no use. He'd started this new form of torture just after his second downward spiral. Giving in, I had realized, was easier than fighting the inevitable.

When I ceased to struggle, and he was satisfied with the beating, he had his way with me—hard, violent, and sickening. With every painful thrust, everything inside me screamed, *No more! Please, dear God!*

When he was finished, Jack pushed me out of the way. "Move. Go get my dinner."

Already on my stomach, I inched out of his way, trembling and sweaty, and slid out of the bed to go make his plate of chicken, rice, and beans. The smell of the food was now like rotten flesh to my senses.

Morning came far too soon. It was my second day back, but I felt like I'd been home for a month. My back and shoulders were swollen and stiff, and I wanted nothing more than to lie there. But I forced myself to get out of bed and quietly slip on a robe over my raw skin. Not wanting to wake a still sleeping Jack, I noiselessly drug my aching body downstairs to make a breakfast for which I had no appetite.

Half an hour later, Jack came downstairs and offered a cheery "Good morning," then gave me a light kiss on the cheek. It was if nothing happened. Knowing it was expected, I gave a weak smile of acknowledgement.

After I put his breakfast on the table, I started for the doorway. Before I could take a step, however, Jack stopped me.

"Alice, have breakfast with me."

Schooling my features to not show the fear that every muscle in my body was screaming, I tried to beg off.

"Oh, Jack, I…I'm not hungry. I'm just gonna get dressed and—"

"I said sit with me and eat," he said with more force, and tossed a piece of his toast onto the other side of the table.

And then he smiled.

"We haven't talked since you got back from Beaufort."

I glanced from the toast to him, unnerved and confused. *What in the world is going on?* my brain screamed.

"Eat it," Jack said again, not angry exactly, but I dared not refuse. I sat down across from him and nibbled at the dry bread, every mouthful like sawdust. My stomach was in knots, my entire body tensed, ready to flee.

He made small talk and told me, *chuckling*, about a joke someone told at the factory. If that alone wasn't enough to send me into a tailspin, when he finished eating, he stood up, reached into his pocket, and politely put some money on the table.

"Here's the grocery money. I want pork chops for dinner tonight."

When he leaned over to kiss me, it took everything in me not to scream at his touch. When I risked a glance up, he gave me a smile that said I was the love of his life.

"Have a good day, honey."

I sat for a moment with disjointed thoughts floating in my head about Lily, Isaac, and Jack's bizarre behavior.

When Denise trooped downstairs a moment later, I couldn't help but wonder if she'd heard us yesterday. She didn't bother to look at me; instead she snatched up her scrambled egg on toast and marched out the door without a word. My reaction in the quiet was utter devastation. My daughter knew what was going on—and I knew she knew. We had reached a point where we were not going to pretend.

Head still throbbing, I stood up from the table and went to get dressed. I had to go get Jack's requested pork chops. He would never accept my being sick as an excuse for not doing what he'd asked. I headed to the bathroom and eased my robe off my aching shoulders and stared in the mirror.

In the back of my mind, I knew I needed to have a conversation with myself. *You should leave, he may hurt you again, or worse. Why are you still here?* But the energy I needed to process the truth, to help myself, seemed but an elusive spirit; I simply had nothing left, no will to do anything more than survive.

Mindless and detached, I dabbed makeup over the bruises that showed past my collarbone and rummaged through my drawers and closet to find something that would cover the scars. I did all of this without a thought…without knowing even why I did.

But like a low, imperceptible rumbling that slowly breaks into one's awareness, my numbed mind felt the steady pull of the voices and the roar of time beneath the floor in my closet… The harsh memory of Jack almost discovering it and the beating that followed pushed me away, though. For now. I would return to it when I could.

On foot and drifting, I headed out to the grocery store. I started down our walkway and saw our neighbor, Mrs. Thornton, turning dirt in her front yard. She was a retired nurse in her late seventies and loved to talk. With nothing between our houses except for my slender driveway, most days, no matter how quickly I waved and tried to hurry away, she always stopped me to talk about her flowers. This morning was no different.

"Hello, dear!" she called out, waving her trowel to make sure she caught my attention. When she was close enough to speak, she offered her condolences.

"Denise told me about your parents' passing. I'm so sorry for your loss, dear."

"Yes, thank you, Mrs. Thornton," I said, edging further down the walkway.

"Alice, honey, can you wait one second?" She laid a gentle hand on my bruised arm, and I gave an involuntary flinch, which I instantly tried to disguise.

"Oh, I wish I could, Mrs. Thornton, but I need to run—"

"It will only take a second. Just stay put, I'll be right back." She crossed her lawn with uncharacteristic haste and entered her house. I didn't have the heart to make my escape, so I stood there feeling embarrassed. She returned a moment later with an envelope in hand.

"This is for you, dear. I want you to know I am here if you ever need to talk about anything, or need a shoulder to lean on." She looked at me deliberately. "I don't only mean about your parents, Alice. About *anything*, dear… Okay?"

I held her eyes a moment and then composed myself. "Yes, ma'am," I said as indifferently as if she were speaking about my dead chrysanthemums out back or the latest episode of *The Andy Griffith Show*. "Thank you."

I slipped the envelope into my purse and hurried away before she could pat my arm again. It was a sympathy card, I knew, and I couldn't open it. The thought alone made me want to wail.

CHAPTER 6

All the way home from the store, the pull of the wooden chest and the unanswered questions tugged at me. I prepared the pork chops and set them aside to marinate and put potatoes on to mash later. While waiting for the potatoes to boil, I switched on the television. When the image of people being beaten for their peaceful protests flashed on the screen, it was an all too real reminder of the box upstairs, and it drove me finally to investigate it again. I couldn't wait; I turned off the television and the potatoes and headed upstairs to steal another few moments with the women of my past.

I noted the time so I could anticipate Denise and Jack's return and then opened the box and the next letter. This one simply read, MAMIE, BORN CIRCA 1793.

Ma lil Claire,

I so happy that Massa Fred and Miss Ann let me be your mammy. It seem lak jus a day ago you were a lil baby I was rockin ta sleep. Now you gettin married tomarra and movin out of this hous. But befor that happen theer ar a few things ya need ta no.

I was born in Fayetvill, Nort Carolina on Abe and Betty Furrlys plantation. I wurk in the big house and when I was 'bout sixteen my massa rape me.

Late one nite Massa Abe came in me an mamas room. He smell lak corn shine.

"Oh Lord." mama whisper den she pull my backside as far into her belly as she could. Den massa pulled da cover off an started touchin me all over. Mama latched her arm so tite around my belly I cant breth.

"Massa please no," she beg but he tug and tug. I screem but he shush me. Mama kep holdin me beggin till massa got mad. He punch mama so hard she fell on da floor.

Massa put one hand over my mouth and took his pant down wit da ova.

He say ta Mama "Lily ya gettin in da bed or ya stayin on the floor? Eever way it gonna happen." I cry for her to get back in da bed wid me an wen she did, Massa forced his body in mine. Da mor I cry da more mama wisper for me to shut my eyes. Den da door open and Miss Betty screem. "Abe, dats your chile!"

Claire, I so shame. I ask mama if massa my papa why he do such a thing.

Mama say dat be the natur of a man. Dat don't make me feel no better and I cried til I fall sleep. The next thing I herd was the rooster crow. Massas men broke open da door *and da last thing I herd was mama screem my name all da way down the road.*

Den Massa's men took me to Massa Freds plantation. Wen I got heer Massa Fred Wilcox rape me too agin an agin til he fill me with chile.

I lade on dat dirt floor screemin an pushin. At firs I was sad God giv me a girl cause I didn't want my chile to go thru what me and mama did. Den, Bertha put her in my arms and afta I see her, all I want is to hold her and love her.

I say to her I gonna name you Lily. Then Massa Fred and one of his men came in an massa took Lily out my arms.

Him and da man stood theer lookin at her top ta bottom lak she was a horse. Da man say "Fred, this nigga witer dan you. The misses is gonn love her. She be hapy now."

Claire you dat baby, you my Lily. I never tell you cause Massa said he kill me or send me away. But that don't matta no mo. My lil girl is a free women.

Love your mama, Mamie.

Mamie's words seemed to leap from the page, entangling her sadness around my heart. Her emotions were tangible for me in that moment, and I felt as if I'd known her all my life. As I imagined the cold cruelty of Master Abe Furrly and Master Fred Wilcox, a chill ran through me. To be so close to your daughter and yet so far, all because of the cruelty of another…

I couldn't help but wonder why I felt the disparity between my own daughter and me. She lived in my house, yet I knew so little about her…as if we were strangers.

There was a knock on the front door that interrupted my thoughts. I put the letters away and went to answer it.

On my doorstep stood three of the neighborhood ladies, looking rather embarrassed and uncomfortable. I didn't know them personally, but I had seen them outside with their children before. After a polite greeting, the one in the middle—clearly the appointed spokeswoman—introduced herself and her cohorts.

"We're sorry to…ahem…bother you, Mrs. Miles, but we've come to talk to you about Denise…" Mrs. Mosely trailed off, earning short, approving nods from the other two ladies. "May we come in and speak with you a minute?"

Reluctantly, I stepped away from the door. "Okay." I definitely didn't want them in the house, but I was desperate to find out anything about Denise.

The ladies glanced at each other as they seated themselves, and as if by a predetermined script, one of the ladies, Mrs. Smith, started.

"Mrs. Miles, I don't want to upset or offend you in any way, but…" She stopped for a dramatic pause. "Denise has been running around with some boys that I'm sure you wouldn't approve of. Our children have been coming home with stories about her that are just awful."

"Yes," Mrs. Nelson, who completed the trio, said. "They say the boys at school are always harassing her, and the girls are so cruel with the names they call her. They…" she grimaced, "they also say she's been hanging around with several men. *Grown* men."

As she spoke, I couldn't help noticing that she had a very ugly mole on the side of her nose, and tried hard to look at her eyes instead.

"She's telling you the truth, Mrs. Miles," Mrs. Mosley chimed in, as if I had denied their censures.

It was all so surreal. I knew that Denise acted out sometimes, but it was another to have these…*women* come into my home and confirm what I tried to ignore.

"Just yesterday," Mrs. Mosley continued, "I saw her in front of the bar, smoking that stuff with some of those burnouts. At first, I wasn't sure it was her; she looked about twenty in those hip-huggers and all her cleavage showing. She's quite *endowed* for a girl her age…"

Mrs. Smith, who was sitting back with a superior air, emphatically continued. "Plus, she was wearing entirely too much makeup. Children that age shouldn't even be allowed to wear the stuff. I won't let my Betsy wear any of it. People are saying that she hangs around with all kinds of men—even *black* men—and will do anything for money, drugs and…"

As Mrs. Smith continued to talk, each word was more abrasive than the last. I knew she was telling the truth. There were so many times when Denise would come home with red eyes and smelling like alcohol and marijuana.

I refocused on Mrs. Smith's denunciations. "Dear, we came here today to talk to you because Denise is too beautiful a girl to waste her life like this." She closed her eyes and slowly nodded. Her artful performance was so comical that if the situation hadn't been so serious, I knew that I would have been hard pressed not to laugh. She finished her colloquy with "Well, it's so heart breaking."

"Yes, indeed," Mrs. Nelson parroted.

But Mrs. Mosley rounded it out with a more sincere closing statement. "Mrs. Miles, if this were my daughter, I pray that someone would have the courage to come and tell me."

As if on cue, the front door swung open and in marched the topic of our conversation in all her reckless glory. My heart sank at the sight of her. Denise arrogantly leaned against the door. She was dressed like one of the Indian women in a Saturday night Western, her long legs clad in soft brown leather-fringe boots. She had on a one-sleeved camel-colored dress with fringes to match. She certainly looked beyond her years, and she was flaunting every bit of it.

She stood in the doorway, taking us all in, and with a worldly smile no fifteen-year-old should have, said, "Hello there, ladies. How's the husbands?" Then she quirked an eyebrow and sauntered up the stairs without another word.

I had never felt more publically ashamed in my life. I escorted the ladies to the door, rushing them out as hurriedly as I could. They gave me looks of sympathy that nearly turned my stomach.

Denise appeared to be half asleep when I marched into her room, but I didn't care.

"Denise, get up. Now!"

She rolled over and covered her head with her pillow. I marched over and snatched it off her.

"What?" she barked.

"Don't you dare ignore me!" I said, surprised at how sharp my own words sounded. "Not this time, young lady. I want answers."

"No, you don't." She smirked and indolently sat up, regarding me with knowing eyes. It was like talking to an adult.

"Yes, I do. Where did you get those clothes? I sure didn't buy them."

"A friend," she replied nonchalantly.

"What friend? And who are these men that you've been hanging with?"

"Why? What do you care?"

"You're my *child*, Denise. I care because any grown person hanging around a child means them no good."

"They're just friends," she said again with a wave of her hand. "They wanted to give me a nice birthday gift. Nobody around *here* cares about it…"

It was terrible that my little girl had lost her grandparents so close to her birthday, but I didn't want to go there now. I was trembling with rage and fear for my little girl. "Denise, you know that's not true—but those people aren't your friends. From this day forward, I don't want you hanging out with them or in front of bars either. I don't even want you leaving this street without permission. Do you understand?"

Her scowl was one that I would recognize anywhere—her father had one just like it.

"You can't tell me what to do."

"Oh yes I can, miss! As long as you are under this roof, you will do as I say!"

"They're my friends. They love me." She jumped up off the bed, swaying a little.

It broke my heart to see her like this, but she wasn't going to get away with it. The disrespectful behavior she'd just displayed was all the help I needed to fuel my tirade.

"You're smarter than this, Denise. Those men don't love you, and they certainly don't respect you. If they did, they wouldn't get you wasted and keep you out all hours of the night! They don't have your best interest at heart, Denise."

"Dad doesn't have your best interest at heart—but I don't see *you* leaving." She glared at me, daring me to contradict her. "At least I get some nice clothes and money out of it. What do you get?"

Her words were like a slap in the face, and I could only lash out. "Thank God your grandparents don't have to see this!"

I could see it swell up in her eyes—the rage that had been building for a long, long time. I had pushed her too far.

"You are judging me, Mother? *You* are judging *me*? Why don't you fix your own life before you judge mine!"

"Listen to how you talk to me…" I stammered out. "Don't you have any respect for yourself? It's disgusting…"

She gave me an incredulous glare. "Seriously? Please tell me you're kidding."

"What do you mean?" I was dumbstruck.

"Do you really want me to say it? Can you handle the truth?" she retorted with a sneer.

"Go ahead, young lady," I snapped. "I can see you're itching to say what's on your mind. So say it."

"You're a human punching bag, Mother." She laid right into me. "Dad beats your brains out every day. He treats you like an animal…and just so you know, I've heard *everything* that happens in your room. It's disgusting, and creepy, but you have the nerve to stand here and judge my life? How could *I*, Mother? How could *you*? Tell me how you can stay with a man like that. He never gives you a dime for yourself, and even worse not even a kind word—which is free—but you stay. At least the guys I hang out with speak decently to me and give me all the clothes and dimes I want. So now you know how *I* could. But…how could *you*? You get nothing."

She was right, and there were no words that would make this better. I stammered out a half-hearted response.

"Denise, I know it seems bad now, but we will get out one day and—"

"Liar!" she yelled. "Liar! You stop it! Stop making promises you won't keep. No more excuses! No more for him or you. *No more!*"

She took a deep breath to get a hold of herself, then set her jaw. When I had no words to retaliate with, she spoke more calmly.

"How can I respect you, Mother, when you don't respect yourself?"

Right then, I saw the truth. My weak defense of Jack's treatment of me had made it impossible for me to establish any sort of rules or mandates for respect. I did nothing to deserve it… and my chance of ever having the type of relationship with her that I'd had with my own mama was impossible.

"Denise, I can't do this anymore," I said, defeated. I turned to walk away, unable to meet her accusing eyes. "What you are choosing to do with your life is breaking my heart. I wanted you to be better." I stopped at the door, still unable to look at her. "You deserve so much better, honey."

"Yeah…" Her voice was quiet. "So do you."

Over the next few days, I was more depressed than ever. I cooked and cleaned faithfully but did nothing else; I couldn't even read the letters. Jack continued to come in drunk and aloof as usual and slept in the sitting room. I hadn't seen hide nor hair of Denise and had no urge to. The guilt was killing me. I knew I should try to leave, but for once I was honest with myself: I was afraid—afraid to stay because Jack's behavior only seemed to be getting worse, afraid to leave because I didn't know what I would do or who I would be if I wasn't Jack's wife.

After several days of struggling within myself, I at last took solace in the words of my foremothers. I had nowhere else to turn, and my conscience was gnawing at me inside. I went to my room after everyone had left that morning, and pulled out the box. Just touching the old wood and memoirs settled my spirit, and I felt sure that something spiritual surrounded these aged words of my foremothers.

The third letter was from the daughter Mamie had lost to Master Fred and Ann Wilcox, Claire Kane. Her last name stirred my interest. Grandma Sheila had addressed all of us as "Kane" daughters…

Claire's letter began in a beautiful, well-educated hand.

November, 1857

My darling daughter Martha,

Of course you already know I was born and raised on Mama and Papa's plantation, Twin Oaks, in Greenville, South Carolina. I never wanted for anything since they indulged me in anything I asked for. They doted on me and showed me every kindness, and I loved them dearly in return. However, the demands of the land kept my papa away most every day. Between meetings, social calls, church, and her flowers, Mama hardly had a moment to sit down. Thus, I spent most of my time with my nurse, whose name was Mamie.

What can I say about my Mamie? She was a slave, and I was a daughter of the aristocracy; each of us knew our role. I was expected to mind my manners, cultivate my appearance, learn to create elaborate floral arrangements, and write thank you notes on monogrammed stationery. Mamie was expected to press my dresses, style my hair, clean my bed-chamber, cook, and serve my meals. No one told her she had to love me, but from my earliest years, I knew she did.

Though I was educated in reading, writing, how to curtsey and dance gracefully, I also learned the basics of being self-sufficient. Mama and Papa saw to it that I was educated to be a Southern Belle, but Mamie educated me about other, more useful things. Mama taught me embroidery; Mamie taught me to mend a shirt. Mama taught me how to trim roses without snagging my gloves; Mamie taught me how to shuck corn and snap beans. She was always saying, "Chile, you got to learn how to take care a yo'self. Your mama a good woman, but land sakes, she spoiled." I would smile and nod.

Mamie showed me her love in all she said and did. We talked about everything under the sun. We giggled, played games, and shared secrets just like real friends. My love for her was deep.

She was much paler than most of the other slaves. Though she never mentioned it, I knew she must have had a white papa.

To my parents, she was just another slave, and thus, our bond was a thing unspoken. But because of that, it seemed even more special.

The years passed, and I grew up and fell in love with your papa, Ernest Kane. He was a hard-working man who owned a farm in Charleston, a man of integrity and from a good family. He was a man whom my parents respected and approved of. Before long, we were betrothed, and I was caught up in the excitement of planning my wedding and embroidering my trousseau.

It was such an emotional time...and it grew even more so when, the night before my wedding, as Mamie brushed my hair, her demeanor changed. Finished with my hair, she abruptly set the brush on the dressing table and looked into my eyes.

"Oh, chile," she said, "look at how pretty you is. So pretty."

I turned to face her, and when I did, she gently wrapped my hands around a wad of folded papers.

"Claire, this is for you," she said. "But, sweet chile, this ain't for no eyes but yours. Read it when you alone. There ain't no hurry. I just wanted you to have it before you go. It be all I got to give my bride girl."

"Thank you, Mamie," I said. "But what is it?"

"The story of my life," she said.

My confusion must have shown, because she placed the palm of her hand gently on the right side of my face, something she'd done to comfort me since I was a child. Then, she bid me goodnight.

Martha, let me tell you, I had long known that my life was far more coddled and protected than Mamie's had been, but I never realized how violent and horrific a slave's existence could be.

The first page was a letter that appeared to be written by Mamie's mother, Lily. As I tried to decipher what she'd written, I couldn't help but wonder why Mamie thought I needed to have this, especially the night before my wedding. Its violence scared me. As I placed the first page aside, I was still confused.

The next page was addressed to me. That truly surprised me, as I hadn't known that Mamie could read and write. Reading her story, I was both alarmed and intrigued, and I couldn't stop reading till I came to the end. I read the last part of her letter three times before I understood what she was saying. My shock at this long-hidden truth was overwhelming: Mamie, the slave woman who had raised me, the woman who I thought of as my closest friend, was my birth mother!

Now, I loved Mamie deeply, but I'd always been taught that slaves were beneath me, that they served us because they weren't smart enough or capable of living on their own. Please don't judge me for this, Martha. I was still quite young, and the sheltered life of a plantation owner's daughter was all I'd ever known. Thus, learning that Mamie was my mother made me feel ashamed and somewhat tarnished. I was also afraid of what would happen if this truth were revealed… Me? Fred and Lois Wilcox's daughter. Me? A debutante, a society bride. Me…the daughter of a slave? I didn't want to believe that; yet, somehow, I knew it to be true. My mother was a slave woman, as was my grandmother. My doting papa, who I always thought of as being the most loving and kind man in the world, was in fact capable of unfeeling cruelty. He had forced himself on Mamie when she was a helpless, young slave girl. She gave birth to me, and he snatched me right out of her arms and gave me to his wife—like a bouquet of flowers.

Part of me wanted to confront my parents, show them Mamie's letter, and demand the truth. But I was afraid. Ernest fell in love with an aristocratic socialite. Would he still love a daughter of slaves? If my parents' friends found out, would my parents pick their status among the elite over me?

And poor Mamie, who had suffered so much, bravely gave me the power of truth. Didn't she deserve the protection of secrecy?

Somehow, I knew that betraying her trust would sentence her to death at Papa's hand. No, I knew that I couldn't confront them. But the thought of Papa being able to commit such an act made me sick.

In a blink of an eye, dawn came, and I had not slept a wink. The beautiful morning sun shone down on the plantation where I had been so happy. It warmed my heart and chased away the shadows of the letters. Despite my sleepless night, I was exhilarated; I was marrying the man of my dreams today and starting a new life in Charleston. I donned my exquisite white wedding gown, and Mamie did my hair while Mama—while Lois watched and cried. Neither Mamie nor I dared say a word about the letters with her sitting there.

And then it was time for me to get married. Oh, Martha, it was so beautiful; our wedding was like a real-life fairy tale. The ceremony was held on the lush green hill behind the house. We spoke our vows beneath the grand oak gazebo, adorned with long, colorful flower chains that Lois made. In front of all our friends and family, I kissed your Papa for the first time as his wife. I grasped his hand, unable to contain my happiness as the joyous love I felt for him filled me.

Afterwards, you're Papa and I mingled with everyone and accepted their congratulations and well-wishes. Yet, even with all the laughing and hugging, I was always aware of the small figure standing at the edge of the party.

After the ceremony, dinner was announced ready, and our guests drifted away. I excused myself for a moment and headed towards Mamie. I couldn't help noticing how she looked at me with so much love. She had always looked at me this way, but now it took on a whole new meaning. I wrapped my arms around her slender shoulders and breathed in her sweetness.

"I'm starting this family over," I declared. "As of this moment, there will be no more masters' last names. Today, I am Mrs. Claire Kane, raised a free woman. My daughters will be born and raised free. Thank you, Mamie, for your sacrifice so I never had to endure the pain and sadness you have."

My heart filled with affection, I added, "I love you, Mamie Kane. I love you… Mama."

Tears streaming down her cheeks, Mamie once again put her palm on the right side of my face. Knowing that this might be our last moments together, she pulled me in close.

Looking over Mamie's shoulder, I saw Ernest approaching. I wiped the tears from my eyes and pulled away.

"Claire?" said Ernest, concerned. "Honey, everyone's waiting for us."

I turned to look at Mamie one last time.
She squeezed my hand and whispered,
    "He a handsome boy. Now, go chile. This
be your wedding day." I nodded and went to
join my new husband.

I closed the book at that point and decided to take a relaxing bath—to dream about the picture that Claire painted of her wedding day. I couldn't stop thinking about the rice and white flowers and the sweet touch of Mamie's hand on her little girl's cheek. By living through Claire's happily ever after, I was happy. I'd forgotten what it felt like to have people all around me who loved me…and I wanted that in my life again.

///////////////

CHAPTER 7

As I dried dishes in the kitchen the next evening, contemplating the elusive wonders of new love and familial happiness, the front door slammed and Denise entered the kitchen. With plate and towel in hand, I turned to greet her, attempting to be cheerful despite our mutual disregard.

"Hi, honey, dinner's rea—"

I stopped midsentence, not believing my eyes. The dish shattered on the floor, breaking into a million pieces.

"Denise? What did you do?!"

"What?" She ran her long white fingernails through her chopped hair. Where silky black curls once fell to her waist, there was now barely enough hair to cover her scalp.

"Oh my God, Denise! Why did you do that?" I asked, my voice wavering somewhere between shock and fury.

"My buzz cut? Seriously?" Gold hoop earrings framed the smug grin on her bright pink lips as she pulled her thumb through the belt loop of her hip-hugger jeans. "I did this two days ago for my birthday. Where've you been? Oh, that's right, hiding in your room," she scoffed. "What've you been doing in there, anyway?"

"N-nothing…" Unable to control my tears, they ran in little salty streams down my face.

My grief didn't faze her in the slightest. She fixed her plate, plopped down, and ate noisily.

Jack, disturbed by all the commotion, staggered in from the sitting room, and I looked at him, speechless in my shock. "What's going on in here?" he asked. He took one glimpse at Denise and burst into a loud guffaw. "You'll do anything for attention, won't you, little girl?" He laughed his way over to the refrigerator, grabbed two beers, and laughed all the way back to the sitting room.

I was so upset, I became nauseous. The glimpse of happiness I'd shared with Claire was snatched away; the desire to think of or read about such happiness again now had little appeal.

Jack and Denise fought almost every day that week. As much as she ignored me, she found new ways to infuriate her father. He teased her and made fun of her "new" look. She yelled at him for his lack of hygiene and the disgusting company he kept. I wanted to interfere, to ask Denise not to agitate her father so much as I would often receive a beating following an intense argument between them.

I understood why he took his anger out on me. Directly or not, I contributed too much to his anxieties and failures. It was my responsibility to make up for it, even if that meant taking a hit sometimes. So far, Jack had left her out of it, probably because none of it was our daughter's fault. I prayed she wouldn't do something one day to make him forget that.

One afternoon shortly after Denise cut her hair, Jack lost all reason.

Still unable to bring myself to read further, I was trying to find something else to do in the kitchen when the front door slammed, harder than usual.

Without a word, he stalked past me through the kitchen door and went into the backyard shed, leaving the unpleasant odor of stale booze behind. He returned from his padlocked hideaway with a hammer and a small bag. My mind flooded with a dozen unasked questions as he stomped up the stairs, railing curses to no one in particular. I sank into a chair, knowing whatever he was up to wouldn't be good. I was terrified for myself and relieved that Denise wasn't home.

Then the hammering started, and I jumped with each resounding thud. Nerves twisting in my stomach, I couldn't begin to fathom what he was doing. When the banging stopped, I ran to the sink and began wiping down an already clean basin.

Jack walked up behind me and viciously grabbed my ponytail.

"Jack, no, please don't!" I begged, as he dragged me out of the kitchen and up the stairs, yanking my hair every time his foot hit the next step.

When we reached the top of the stairs, I struggled to get away, but Jack pushed me into the bedroom and slammed the door. I heard shuffling outside the door, but was too afraid to move. I lay there trembling, wondering how I'd provoked him this time; for the life of me I couldn't figure out what I'd done wrong.

When he didn't come back after a few minutes, I laid down on the bed. I must have drifted off into an uneasy sleep, because a little after midnight, I awoke to the sounds of him and Denise arguing.

"You can't keep me in this house!" Denise screamed.

"The hell I can't!" Jack shouted back. "Now get back upstairs!"

After that, there was more banging. Afraid for Denise, I got up to go and check on them, but I couldn't get out. I was locked in.

"I hate you, you drunk! I hate you!" Denise screamed as she ran up the stairs, slamming her bedroom door.

"Sure," Jack shouted, "I've got something for you to hate! Just keep playing with me, little girl, and you'll get it!"

The banging continued, this time from a different part of the house. When it stopped, fear of the unknown consumed me, and I lay back down, praying for answers to fix this mess.

Just before sunrise, I tiptoed to the door, hoping to use the bathroom, but it was still locked from the outside. After an interminable length of time, I heard shuffling again and despite my increasingly uncomfortable bladder, I jumped back in the bed and pretended to be asleep.

Jack came in the room, got something out of the dresser, and left without a word. I waited a few minutes until he left for work. Whether he forgot to lock the door again or not, it was now ajar, and I ran to it to see what on earth had happened last night. I gasped as I saw what all the pounding was about.

He had installed a padlock on the bedroom door. He could now lock me in whenever he wanted.

As terrible as Jack had treated me in the past, this new development left me more trapped than I ever thought possible. I ran downstairs to see if my fears would be verified.

To my horror, Jack had nailed boards over every downstairs window. He even put a padlock on the side door in the kitchen that led to the shed. It too was locked with no key. He had made certain there was only one way out of the house—the front door.

I was a prisoner in my own home.

///////////////

CHAPTER 8

*M*artha, our marriage started out perfect. Though we were not rich like my parents, there was more than enough money. Your papa worked hard running the farm in Charleston. I'm proud to say we paid everyone who worked our farm; not a single slave hand touched our land.

I now found comfort in the words of Claire and my other foremothers. In the agonizing hours that would follow Jack's often-violent hurling of me into the bedroom, I had little else to settle my agitated mind. I found an odd peace in rereading Lily and Mamie's letters and in continuing Claire's story. Perhaps it was because I realized that they would understand what my life had become.

The first few years with your papa, Claire's letter continued, I thought I was as happy as possible. But in 1833, my beautiful little boy Ernest Kane III was born, and I felt a joy so great that even at this very moment, I can barely find the words to explain it.

Our baby had his papa's big blue eyes, and when his hair sprouted out in tufts, it was just as blond and curly as my own. He was such a happy little boy, and he laughed all the time. Oh, Martha, how I wish you could have known your brother. He was a joy.

But it was to be fleeting. One chilly, wet spring, Ernie took sick with a vicious fever. Each day, I soaked his hot little body in a tub of cold water to bring down his temperature and did everything the doctors prescribed. But nothing relieved his misery for long, and his condition worsened.

The day before Ernie's fifth birthday, Ernest was away purchasing seed. Due to the seriousness of Ernie's illness, he'd held off going to town because the trip required him to be gone overnight. I snuggled in bed with my baby the entire day, reading him stories and trying to make him laugh by planning a make-believe birthday party.

That night, he complained that his head was hurting. Helpless, I watched his suffering, knowing that there was nothing I could do. It was now all up to my brave little fighter. I stayed with Ernie all night. When the clock in the hall chimed midnight, I softly sang happy birthday to him. He fell into a restless sleep while still tucked in the crook of my arm.

I woke the next morning to face the paralyzing devastation of Ernie's cold little body. Grief washed over me as I held him close in my arms and kissed his forehead, so recently burning with fever. Hours later, Ernest returned home to find me still in bed, holding our dead son.

We took Ernie back to Greenville to be buried alongside the beautiful, clear lake on the family plantation. It seemed fitting; he'd always loved it there. We placed him in the ground amongst fragrant bouquets of white roses.

Your grandmother Mamie was there standing far in the back. Even from the distance, I saw her pain-stricken face and the tears that flowed. At that moment, I wanted the comfort of my birth mother more than anything, but I wanted to keep our secret safe and so kept my distance.

That night, we stayed at the plantation, sleeping in my old room. Ernest and I cried in each other's arms until we fell asleep. I had no dreams that night; I think Ernie's death put an end to them all.

The next morning, laden with sorrow, I went to join my mother at the table in the shade of the porch. All those years ago, before my Papa snatched me from Mamie's arms, Lois had known the pain of being childless. She took my hand and offered words of comfort.

After a short while, Bertha, a mulatto house slave, came out of the house pushing a serving cart adorned with silver platters and polished silverware. As she removed the lids from dishes, I noted the distinct bulge of her belly. But when I looked into her eyes, I saw embarrassment, humility, guilt, and shame on her smooth creamy-brown face. At first, this confused me; she'd been serving us breakfast since she was a child. But then, I realized the reason for her embarrassment.

The ugliness of slavery's cruelties stood right in front of me, and a picture of my Mamie flashed through my mind. Had my Papa gotten this woman pregnant, too? Would my half brother or sister, if born too dark, be brought up in chains because they weren't white enough? Had these rapes been happening all around me the entire time? There were plenty of lighter skinned slaves here. None were as light as me, but that didn't mean my father didn't rape their mothers, too. Right then, I wanted to take this woman's hand and tell her what I was. I wondered if she knew the truth... if all our slaves knew.

"Thank you so much," I said, as she set a plate in front of me.

Lois looked at me in shock. It was poor etiquette to acknowledge a slave in those days. Bertha was just as shocked. She nodded and quickly disappeared through the large French doors.

Papa passed her on his way out, and I saw him glance at her lasciviously. I knew at *once who put that baby in her belly. All my sorrow instantly turned to rage in a flash.*

I stood up as hot, angry tears flooded my eyes. "It's not fair!" I railed. "You treat people like animals!" Papa stared at me, shocked by my sudden attack, but I didn't stop. "Papa, I may have been too blind to see it before, but I see it now. The way you treat the Negroes disgusts me! Some of them die from working in the hot sun, day in and day out. What gives you the right?"

For the first time in my life, my papa raised his hand as if to slap me. "Who do you think you're talking to, young lady?"

"Do not touch me!" I shouted, pointing my finger at him. I didn't have to take his abuse like Mamie and the other slaves did.

Mother stood and put a hand on Papa's arm, pushing it down. "Fred," she said, "please, Claire just buried her son! Your grandson!"

When Papa spoke again, his voice was low, calm—and cold. I'd never seen this side of him. "Our family," he growled, "has lived on this land for decades. We have slaves working the land so you can live in luxury and have everything you ever want. If that is troubling to you, you're more than welcome to go into the fields and join them."

I could not tolerate his words. It was impossible to look at him without imagining the cruel and sinister act of his forcing himself on Mamie all those years ago. How many others had he forced to submit? The relationship between us was damaged beyond repair. In my heart, he was no longer my papa. In fact, I wasn't sure I'd ever want to see him again.

"I never asked for this!" I spit forth. My hands shook as I clenched them at my sides. All the rage over my mother Mamie's mistreatment and all the grief for my baby boy came bursting out. I jumped up and ran to the stairwell. I found my husband, and with no goodbyes, we left to return to Charleston. I vowed that as long as slaves were being kept on the plantation, I'd never return. I also accepted that I might not see Mamie or my Ernie's grave again.

-------------------- ///////////////// --------------------

I would come to find that I had lost both my son and husband on that the evil day when Ernie died. Ernest became distant, uncommunicative, and even cruel with his words. Where we used to discuss the day's events over supper, most nights he didn't come home in time to eat. I cannot say that his time spent away from home was because he was out working the land; over the next few years, the crops yielded less and less, and we suffered because of it.

When I became pregnant with you, my darling Martha, I thought that your birth would bring back my laughing, caring husband. But my hope was in vain. Please don't misunderstand; your papa loved you, but it was as if he were afraid to get as close to you as he had with Ernie. Meanwhile, I was so excited and loved you so completely, I thought I could love you enough for the both of us.

When money became scarce, we had to release our household staff. I was so grateful for those early lessons that Mamie had given me on how to jar and preserve vegetables and fruits. I taught myself how to grow vegetables in our garden and even wash our clothes on a washboard. We had enough to make it, and I was very proud of my accomplishments. Although your papa and I had a somewhat distant relationship, I kept busy enough with housework, teaching you your letters, and tending the garden.

We are all but desolate, and it's taken me years to find the courage to write to you about my life; so much has happened, so much lost. I'm sorry that I did not give you the better things of this world. You remind me so much of myself as I used to be, as I was on the day you came into the world, bringing new life and hope. I loved and wanted you so much that I swore you would not know hardship. But when your papa died, we lost *the farm, and that became impossible.*

Now it's too late. I pray that your Edward will be good to you. But, even more, I pray that you will make something of this family. You are strong, and I have faith you will keep the Kane name moving forward.

All my love,
Your Mama Claire

When I finished Claire's letter, I was crying. Losing little Ernie was too real, too vivid for me. My hands went to my stomach, and I tucked my knees into my chest and thought back to when I carried life within me. I'd never buried a child, but I understood loss and death.

These women, all flesh of my flesh and blood of my blood, had suffered. Claire's defiance of slavery was courageous and impassioned. I wished I had her tenacity to stand up to injustice and cruelty. The rage of my husband, the death of so many American boys across the seas for who-knew-what, the feuds and slurs and chanting of rioters and haters I saw on the news... The world, I knew, and as Claire had found out, was a wicked, wicked place.

I searched for the next account, but there was no letter or journal, no record at all from Martha, and I felt my heart sink still further.

Would there ever be a Kane woman strong enough to confront the winds of injustice?

A few mornings after I finished Claire's letter, once Jack had unlocked the bedroom door and left for the day, I went to the bathroom to empty my Mason jars into the toilet bowl. I had stashed a few in the bedroom closet for whenever Jack locked me up for the night.

The *drip, drip* from the washbasin faucet tapped in my ears in rhythm, and I watched numbly as my own urine swirled around and around down the toilet drain.

I so wanted to leave my cruel home as Claire had done, with no turning back. But where would I go now that my parents were in the grave and my relatives were states away? I had no money for travel fare, and leaving Denise behind was not an option.

I thought of Claire laying her son's cold body in the ground and of Mamie, lonely and standing so far in the distance. My foremothers were strong women; they didn't let the cruelty of men, the cruelty of life, take away their spirit.

How had I let it take away mine?

I didn't have an answer. All I knew was that I had surrendered myself to merely existing. I knew what my foremothers wished of me, and what Mama hoped when she passed the box down to me. But I couldn't cast off shackles, lost dreams, and wicked masters; I couldn't even cast off the chains around my own soul and body. The weight, the pressure of the chains…they were all so, so heavy.

I gazed at the last of the yellow remnants swirling down the bowl and chuckled at the lunacy of it all. I was living like an animal.

No wonder my child hated me—my husband did.

I did, too.

Once I returned to the bedroom and the jars were back in the closet where I hid them, I gathered up the letters. I thought about how Aunt Blondell said the box would be mine. Why did they choose me? I would never have the strength or the courage to do what Grandma Sheila said needed to be done. How was I supposed to free the Kane women when I couldn't even free myself?

They had made a poor choice in me.

I folded each of the letters and carefully inserted them back into their envelopes. Then I grabbed Great-Grandma Nicole's book and opened it, feeling so unworthy. As soon as I flared the pages to read, though, an envelope fell out and onto the floor.

MARTHA WRIGHT, BORN 1841 –
LETTER WRITTEN MARCH, 1873.

There was Martha's letter; she had a story to tell after all. Perhaps she had not failed her mother's dying wishes. I glanced through the worn pages. I was thrilled to find this shred of hope, and yet after the humility of cleaning out my toilet jars yet again, I didn't want to read another word that would sink me further into despair and self-loathing.

I took the chance just before bedtime to read it, as Jack had yet to make an appearance. As soon as I read the first sentence, however, something—someone—told me I needed this, perhaps more than any of the others. That maybe something in here might save my life.

///////////////

CHAPTER 9

What have I done? Dear Lord, what have I done?
Martha's first words sent an instant chill through me.

I don't know where to start. Tonight started out like any other night. My husband was his normal, loving self. To my children, he was the best father, but I knew differently, having dealt with his persecution. But for their happiness, I have kept up the masquerade, and in the light of day confirmed his façade with my smiles and laughter. But in the dark of every night, I have endured his torture.

This life started when my father died. We were penniless and ordered by the bank to leave our farm But when Edward, the new sharecropper, arrived, he couldn't take his eyes off me. My mama, Claire Kane, noticed it right away and used it to her advantage. She explained our plight and told him if he'd let us stay, we would keep house, wash, cook, and clean for him. Edward continued to stare, and Mama's words fell on deaf ears until she added my hand in marriage as part of the package. Edward quickly accepted, and five days later I became Mrs. Edward Wright.

The first couple of months after our marriage, he was so gentle and loving. Though at first I had been angry for being used as chattel, I soon realized I couldn't have been happier being his wife. Over the next few months, for some inexplicable reason, my husband changed. Gone was the gentle love of my husband, and in its place, an aggression so rough it caused severe discomfort to my privates. I wanted to satisfy my husband, and so I said nothing.

By the fifth month of our marriage, I was pregnant. But even that didn't stop him. During my pregnancies, Edward took great pleasure in sodomizing me. Every time my breast filled with milk, he'd nibble and suck my nips raw. He once nibbled them to the point of mutilation, which made suckling hard for my babies and sheer torture for me. As the years passed, he came up with more and clever ways to arouse himself, scarring me in places no one else could see.

He'd even began finding pleasure in taking me with his hunter's blade at my throat. He would pierce me with the tips of his lit cigars and made vein like slithers of cuts anywhere he chose on my body including

*between my legs and on the soles of my feet.
If I so much as whimpered from the pain of
his sadism, he would cover my mouth, nearly
suffocating me to death.*

*I took it. I took it all because he
left me no choice. I always said nothing. I
said nothing because during the day, he was
the same kind and loving man he'd always
been. It was as if his nocturnal debauchery
belonged to someone else entirely.*

*Three days ago, I caught him watching our
oldest child in a way no father should ever
look at his daughter. I tried to overlook it
and convince myself that I was wrong. Last
night was the final straw; at the peak of
finishing his vile business with me, Edward
screamed out her name.*

*I thought I understood what horror
was, but nothing can describe what that
sound created inside of me. I knew then
I had to put a stop to him and his filthy
malevolence. This morning after he left, I
went to the barn and got the strychnine we
keep for rodents. This evening, I followed
my regular routine except when I fixed his
nightly port. I put a rather large amount of
the poison in his drink.*

*I made sure everyone was in bed, cleaned
the kitchen, and sorted out the children's
clothing. Before retiring, I checked one
last time to make sure that they were all
asleep. As I turned from their doorway,
Edward called out.*

Just as I reached our room, he started thrashing about. He told me to fetch Doc Gray, that he felt ill, and then he shuddered. I nodded, but just looked at him. I knew I should have felt something. Guilt? Triumph? But instead, I continued to stare at Edward, seeing the realization of what I'd done begin to dawn upon his stricken face. As I turned to go out the door, he began to convulse until I could see nothing but the whites of his eyes.

I dare not send my boys into the night, so instead I sit, having poured and drunk a port of my own. My nerves are now much calmer, though I don't know what will happen. But I don't care—my children are safe, and the devil will shortly be gone.

Nicole...all my sweet babes, while I beg your forgiveness for the sorrow you will feel upon discovering your father's lifeless body, I surmise that, given the same situation, I would do it yet again, for your sake's and my own.

Ever your loving mother,
Martha Wright

My heart felt like it was going to explode. Martha and I knew the same abusive demon, Jack with his torture and Edward with his. I succumbed to tears as I realized that someone else knew—they understood. Martha was just like me. She knew what it was like. I wasn't alone in this hell.

But how could I escape? I didn't have the courage to murder my husband. Did that make me a weak woman?

The front door slammed. I threw the box and the letter under the bed and pretended to sleep. Jack stumbled into the bedroom and called to me, but I didn't move, taking a chance he'd go away. I stayed put for about an hour, then tiptoed to the top of the stairs. He was snoring, so I silently slipped downstairs to steal a piece of fruit while the coast was clear.

For years I'd been peeking around corners, tiptoeing, and waiting to see what punishment he would inflict on me next. The absolute insanity of it all repulsed me when I thought deeply about it. When Martha had had enough, she ended her torture and any possibility of future torment of Nicole.

What of my Denise?

A new sense of purpose surged through me, far different than my usual dullness and lassitude. I was angry, livid at myself. Why was I living with this man's monstrosity? Why was I continuing to allow myself to be subjected to his torture? I needed the strength of my foremothers, of Martha Wright and Mamie, of my mother. I didn't know how to get it. But now I *wanted* it.

My ears perked up.

Jack had awoken and apparently encountered Denise in the hall. She was now arguing with him at the top of the landing—a familiar sound, but something in her tone was different.

I set the coveted apple back in the fruit bowl and strained to listen. I had to catch myself against the counter when I heard her scream those two words that would change everything.

"I'm pregnant!"

Oh, God... I prayed it wasn't true. But she was reckless, and had seen and learned a lot in her short life. *Please, Lord, please let her be lying!* I begged.

I dashed into the foyer and looked up the stairs to find them both on the landing above, Jack with a look of sheer disgust on his face, Denise with a semblance of—*Could it be?*— satisfaction on hers.

Standing there in her cotton nightdress, her short hair loose and disheveled, my once-innocent daughter looked right at me without any hint of shame or regret. She started down the stairs with a victorious visage, and I glanced worriedly at Jack, who stood as if frozen by Denise's announcement.

Then he lunged for her. But he overreached and slammed into her instead. They both tumbled down the stairs headfirst, crashing into a heap at the bottom.

I jumped toward them immediately, my heart racing. Jack wasn't moving, but I didn't care about him. All my concern was for my child.

"Denise, are you hurt, honey?" I asked, my hands trembling as I tried to help her to her feet.

She brushed my hand away. "No, I'm fine."

I saw she was, indeed, unhurt—thank God. So I asked. I had to know the truth. "Honey, I know you like to get your father riled up, but this isn't the time to—"

"I'm not lying!" she shrieked.

Desperate to help my baby, I grabbed her shoulder and lifted her face to mine, searching her eyes for the truth. I saw she meant every word; I also saw that, despite her bravado, she was scared. "Denise, no…"

"I'm pregnant, Mom."

The sarcastic satisfaction from a moment ago was gone; instead, tears rolled down my fifteen-year-old's face. For the first time in years, I saw the child inside of her.

"Honey, it's okay." My instincts took over, and I spoke to her the way my mother would. "It's okay, baby. We'll work through this together."

She fell sobbing into my arms. I held her, stroking the back of her head and squeezing her tight to my chest.

A noise from behind us sent a spike through my heart. Jack was trying to get up, his face crimson with fury. I didn't know if I could keep him calm, but something inside me was stirring. Whatever it was, it was going to make sure that Denise was safe from his rage.

He rose and I steeled myself, but before I could utter a word, Jack punched me so hard I was on the floor before it even registered that he'd hit me.

Rounding on Denise, he slapped her for the first time in her life. Blood gushed from her nose, and she ended up on the floor beside me.

Everything inside me screamed. I struggled to get up off the floor, still dazed, and Denise unsteadily scrambled to her feet as well. But Jack punched the side of her head, and she collapsed back to the floor again, whimpering.

Then something inside me raged. I lunged, throwing myself across Denise to shield her. I could feel her trembling beneath me.

"Jack, you will not do this!" I screamed. "You'll kill her! Stop, now!"

"Mom…" Denise shuddered.

Jack, deaf to my demands, kicked me in the ribs, cracking something, and I collapsed at Denise's side. He grabbed Denise by the hair and held her up, yelling at the top of his lungs as she flailed and struggled.

"You ain't nothing, little girl, you hear me?! You ain't nothing but mixed-up poor white trash, and I curse the day you were born!"

He tossed her backward, and she slammed onto her back but was up almost at once, scrambling away from him.

"Now get up and get the hell out of my house!"

She struggled to stand, and as she did, I caught sight of her from where I lay gasping on the floor. Her face was a gruesome sight, her pink and white nightdress darkened with blood.

My baby…what have we done to you?

She staggered toward the door, but swayed and crumbled to the floor.

Jack balled up his fists. I watched him stride toward my little girl with vicious intent. A voice—or perhaps many voices—inside me raged, roaring at me to *get up*. This was my fight. My chain. The chain I had to break.

Every maternal instinct rose within me, and I was off the floor and attacking my husband. I leaped onto his back and grappled to pin his arms back. I was screaming at Denise to run, to get away from him.

She was still balled up on the floor, her thin arms holding her knees tightly to her chest, dazed and unfocused.

"Get off me, half-breed!" Jack yelled as he tried to throw me off.

I clung tighter, maternal rage keeping me latched to his back. "Denise! Run, baby, please!"

Wrestling with me and cursing, Jack's temper surged to its fullest. "I ain't got nothing because of you! And now you and your sorry excuse of a daughter's trying to bring another beggar into my house for me to feed? Like hell you will!"

He shook me off finally and punched me, and I hit the wall. In shock, I saw one of my molars hit the ground.

I sat stunned for just a second, then lunged again, pounding my fists into his chest, his face, whatever I could reach. "Denise, run! Run, baby!"

She didn't budge. She was completely immobilized with terror.

Jack hoisted me up and threw me away from him, and I slid a few feet across the floor. He made it to Denise and kicked her thigh, jolting her slightly out of her daze.

"Get the hell out!" he bellowed, but she only mewled pitifully.

The throw to the floor had knocked the wind out of me. When I rose, I felt as though I were wading in molasses and stumbling back toward Denise in slow motion. But I was determined. *I will not let her suffer as I have…never, so help me God!*

Jack was standing over Denise, yelling for her to get out, and I kicked him hard between his legs. He crumpled, gasping and choking for air.

"Get away from her!"

"Denise, get *up!*" I made it to her and shook her hard, but it was as if her body were vacant, like she wasn't there. "Baby, you have to get up. Please, baby, come on!" I tried to pull Denise up onto her feet so we could flee out the door.

"Mom?" She blinked and focused on me. My heart jumped at her bloody face. Her left eye was swelling shut, and her nose and lip were painted with bruises.

Why didn't I do something sooner?

Jack's curses got louder, and she became hysterical. "Oh, God! Please help us!" she screamed, her eyes wide as she saw her father writhing on the floor a few feet away. "Somebody help us, please!"

I smacked her cheek just enough to get her to look at me. "Honey, now come on!"

As I helped her to her feet, I yanked the doorknob. Stark terror filled me when it didn't give. The door was padlocked! Jack must have done it just yesterday or just that evening. We *had* to find another way out.

I grabbed Denise's hand and pulled her past Jack, who was recovering and rolling to his knees. He attempted to grab Denise's ankle, but we were able to sidestep him. My instincts said to get to the side door in the kitchen, but then I realized my mistake. Of course he'd gotten to that one too, when he first boarded up the house.

Denise and I were completely trapped.

My mind was whirling. Only my daughter's trembling hand in mine kept me from giving up and letting my will melt into fear. There was nothing for it; we made a dash toward the stairs, and nearly slammed into Jack as he slumped against the foyer wall, still breathing deeply against the pain in his groin.

"I'm… gonna…kill you, Alice," he huffed, still doubled over. But his eyes didn't lie. "I'm gonna kill…you both."

I pushed Denise in front of me and onto the stairs, urging her forward as I kept my eyes on my husband.

"Yeah," Jack leered, stumbling forward, "you stay right there, jiggas… I'm gonna blow your brains out."

I was up the stairs before he took another step. I knew he had a gun—he'd bought it a while back from some hooligan, and I never knew where he kept it.

Denise and I made it to my bedroom, and I shoved her into the closet, throwing clothes on top of her, and slammed the door shut. She didn't utter a sound. My mind was racing. *What else can I do?* I turned off the lamp and slid under the bed, hoping Jack was drunk enough not to think about lifting the dust ruffle.

It was quiet for several moments, except for an occasional loud bang or clatter from outside the window; Jack was looking for his revolver. I contemplated whether we should stay put or risk trying to run out of the side door he'd just unlocked. Before I could make up my terrified mind, I heard loud, rhythmic thuds, and I knew Jack was back inside the house, coming up the stairs.

In the darkness I could hear my heart pounding, louder and louder as if battling for dominance with the sound of Jack's footsteps. The wooden chest was resting close to my face, still stashed under the bed where I had left it. I kept my wide eyes on it for strength, and sent a silent prayer to God for rescue.

Jack was in the bedroom.

"Alice!"

His voice jolted me, and I stifled a gasp.

"You can't hide from me, half-breeds," he growled as he came further into our tiny room. The venom in his voice sent shivers down my spine. "I know you're in here, sluts... I can smell you!"

I saw his feet from under the bed. When he went to the closet and yanked the door open, I held my breath. I could almost feel my daughter's trembling from beneath the clothes pile just inside the closet door.

After what seemed an eternity, Jack turned away, and his heavy boots walked out of my line of sight. I was still afraid to breathe.

Suddenly, the mattress and box spring above me were snatched up, and with surprising strength, Jack tossed them off the bed frame and threw them aside. "Hah!" he howled in triumph. "Got yah!"

I wiggled out from the other side and started scrambling toward the bedroom door. All I thought of was getting him away from Denise.

Jack anticipated my direction and snatched me back into the room by my waist. I struggled and was sent whirling out of his grasp, but then white, hot pain exploded in my side. He had picked up one of the thick bed slats, and whacked me in the ribs again.

I collapsed to the floor in agony.

He hit me again, the board making impact with my back. I couldn't inhale enough to gasp in pain. I couldn't…I had no more strength, nothing to fight back with.

A scream reverberated in my ears, and Denise leapt out of the closet in a fury. Above me, I saw her dash past her father as he raised the board above his head to hit me again. She snatched another bed slat and swung it with all her might.

The blow connected solidly with the side of his head with a sickening *thwack*, and Jack crumpled to the floor, hard.

Hysterical and still shrieking, Denise hit him in the head, once, twice, a third time, and was winding up again when I gasped aloud, struggling to get the words out. "Denise, don't… you're going to kill him…"

I couldn't get to my feet because of the intensity of the pain in my side and back. As I got to my hands and knees, crawling toward Jack's side, she hit him again.

I had to stop her. "Honey!" I gripped her ankle just as she raised the board one more time; my touch got through to her.

She lowered the slat and let it clatter to the floor. She kicked him for good measure.

"No more, Denise…" I whispered, stroking her ankle. "It's okay, honey… He can't hurt us now."

Jack was unconscious and his face a busted and bloody mess. *God, is he dead?* I thought.

When I looked up at Denise's bloody and swollen face, I saw she looked almost as bad. The pain of seeing her in that state was much greater than that which had been inflicted on me by Jack.

What have I let him to do you, baby?

In the stillness that followed those terrifying moments, Martha's words flashed in my mind, mingling with my own. *I don't know what's going to happen and I don't care. My child is safe, and the devil is gone…*

Body racked with pain from the blows to my side, I struggled to get to my feet and out of the house, Denise helping me as best she could. Halfway down the walk, we saw flashing lights and howling sirens racing down our dark street. Our nosy neighbors, God bless them, must have called.

I don't remember much after that besides the cops asking for Jack's whereabouts and if he was armed. The paramedics took Denise and me, and then everything was a blur.

///////////////////

CHAPTER 10

When I woke, the first thing I noticed was the afternoon sunlight slanting through a large window. I glanced around the sterile room, noticing a man in a white physician's coat standing near my bed, and I remembered it all in a flash.

"Hello, Mrs. Miles," the man said. "I'm Doctor Harvey. Do you know where you are?"

"Yes," I croaked. "In the hospital. Where's Denise? Where's my baby?"

"She's in another room down the hall, Mrs. Miles. Other than being bruised with some swelling, she's fine."

I sank back farther into my pillows relieved and then remembered... "And the baby? She's pregnant."

He smiled. "Yes, the baby's just fine." He snapped his folder closed and assumed a no-nonsense air. "You, on the other hand, have two bruised ribs and a slight concussion and need to get some rest."

I certainly felt foggy. "What about my husband?"

Dr. Harvey glanced down with obvious reluctance. "He did this to you, Mrs. Miles?" It was more of a statement than a question.

I swallowed. I couldn't admit it, not yet.

"Is he okay?"

"He's in a coma."

My head was pounding, and I lay back, squinting up at the doctor's kind but sober face. "What does that mean?"

"We can never be sure with this sort of injury, Mrs. Miles. He might wake up tonight, tomorrow, or never... There's no way of telling."

Maybe never? That would mean... I couldn't fathom a life without Jack's terror in it. I concentrated hard on what the doctor was saying, but only caught pieces of it.

"...as I said, you have two bruised ribs, but you should start feeling much better in a few days. Our staff will take excellent care of your daughter and husband. But you should sleep now."

My stay in the hospital was a true blessing. My battered body was confused with the rest forced upon it by the hospital staff. For the first time in years, I didn't have to worry about Jack beating me or locking me up, or the whereabouts of my daughter.

Every nurse who cared for me treated me with so much respect, I wasn't sure how to respond to it. When I was feeling better, a nurse was kind enough to take me to visit Denise's room. Despite the ravages of her father's brutal treatment, she looked beautiful—no longer afraid or petrified. In fact, she looked more like her old self, like the little girl I lost long ago.

Looking at her, I knew that though my hand had been forced, I had made the right decision in attacking Jack. I'd taken Jack's abuse, but like Martha with her Nicole, I was determined that my husband would not hurt my daughter.

The doctor released us later that week. Sitting in my wheelchair waiting to be discharged, I tried to keep my emotions in check as Dr. Harvey came in and offered me a warm smile.

"Hello, Mrs. Miles. You're looking much better. Are you ready to go home?"

Of course not! my mind was screaming. *How could I be? How could I ever be?*

"Yes, Doctor," I answered, swallowing.

"Good! You're going to be just fine." He offered to push me to the nurses' station where Denise would be waiting. When we arrived, he reached into his pocket and pulled out a card.

"Here you go," he said. "If you want to keep up with your husband's condition, just call this number and—"

Denise, who had come up from behind us, hurdled herself out of her wheelchair and slapped the card out of the doctor's hand.

"No thanks, Doc, we don't need it."

"Denise! Why'd you do that?" I said, shocked and embarrassed, as was Dr. Harvey.

"We don't want it," she said defiantly. "We don't need it, or him."

"Denise!" I was ashamed, not at her words, but at how rude she was being to the doctor who'd been nothing but kind to us. I felt guilty too: it didn't bother me in the least she wasn't concerned about her father. I wasn't sure I was concerned for him, either.

"What, Mom?" Denise glared at me. "He tried to kill us! We're lucky be alive."

"That's fine, Denise," Dr. Harvey graciously recovered, and reassured me with a glance. "It's standard procedure, that's all." He eased into the next topic. "I do, however, need you to take it easy as much as possible, young lady. You're a little over a month into your pregnancy, and you've been through a tremendous ordeal. The next few weeks are critical, and you can't let yourself get this upset; it's not good for you or the baby. All right?"

Denise hung her head with her jaw set, but nodded once. She was embarrassed now and seemed to understand what the doctor meant.

When we reached our neighborhood an hour later, my heart rate tripled when we stepped out of the taxi. I wasn't sure what Denise was thinking, but I shuddered at the sight of the yawning red door. My trepidation on taking the next step was physically making me ill, and the inner voice inside me shrieked for us to run.

"Come on, Mom." My daughter was right next to me. "It's all right. He's not here."

I swallowed when her hand clasped mine. It was the first time in a long time that she'd offered me a comforting gesture. I sucked in a deep a breath and looked at my daughter's face, at her bruises and cuts, her short, messy hair…her smile. I blinked back stinging tears.

"You are incredibly strong, sweetheart," I said. "Do you know that?"

She sighed and her own eyes filled. "No… I'm not."

I squeezed her hand reassuringly. "Okay, let's go." I lifted my chin up, resolved, and took the first step into our house of horrors.

Crimson and brown bloodstains on the walls and floor greeted us in the foyer. I took in the pictures hanging askew on the walls of the stairway and then went into the living room. The cruel boards on the windows allowed little light to come into the room. In the gloom, I saw lamps and other objects scattered over the floor—the remnants of our battle to survive.

"Denise, you head upstairs. I'll tidy up and get us lunch." I righted one of the lamps and turned it on.

But Denise insisted that we do it together. Her offer was touching and, with the ache of my ribs, much needed. We glanced around, taking in the chaos.

With silent agreement I got the hammer, and we marched to the windows to wrestle off the imprisoning boards. We pulled and strained at each one until they were all off.

As the early October sunlight flooded in, we stood side by side for a few long moments, drinking in the first bit of peace.

Giddy with this accomplishment, we then sprinted to get to the next chore. The tasks were difficult, and I had to stop often to catch my breath…but I knew who I was now, and it kept me going. I was Denise's mother—her protector. With each picture replaced or broken piece of glass discarded, I was flooded with a joy I had forgotten.

Once done, we rested over a lunch of turkey sandwiches and iced tea. It was pleasant, almost unfamiliar; we hadn't done something together like this since she was a little girl. The serenity was peaceful and unbroken, until Denise voiced the question I'd been asking myself since we left the hospital that morning.

"Mom, what do you plan to do when he gets out?"

I took a sip of my tea to give myself time to ponder. The truth was I was terrified and had no idea. But before I could say as much, a knock on the door interrupted my thoughts and gave me a blessed reprieve.

I eased my aching body up from the kitchen chair and went to answer it. Though the padlock was no longer hung, I could still see the clasp on the doorframe, taunting me. Trying to ignore it, I held my ear up to the door.

"Yes?"

"Police. I'm looking for Mrs. Alice Miles," a man's sober voice said.

Apprehensive, I looked through the side window and saw two broad-shouldered detectives, holding up their badges for me to see. I opened the door a crack and eyed them.

"Yes?"

"Good afternoon, Mrs. Miles, we're sorry to bother you," the older man said. "May we come in and speak with you for a few minutes?"

I opened the door farther and ushered them into the living room.

"I'm Detective Douglas, Mrs. Miles, and this is Detective Tate."

"Pleasure to meet you, ma'am," the shorter one said, giving me a nod.

"Likewise," I replied. "How can I help you?"

Detective Douglas's eyes shifted, and he smiled at a very angry Denise who was now in the living room doorway, arms crossed with a glint in her eyes.

"Uh, this is my daughter, Denise," I said awkwardly.

"Miss… Pleasure to meet you," Detective Douglas offered.

Denise only glared. Detective Tate asked her how she was feeling, but she just continued to scowl.

"Honey, uh…" I said clearing my throat. "Can you go upstairs and sort the clothes to be washed?"

She looked at me with a hint of the anger that was always boiling under the surface, but nodded and did as I asked. I waited until her footsteps faded up the stairs.

"I'm sorry, gentlemen," I said. "You must excuse my daughter. She's…we've both been through a lot…"

"Of course, ma'am, no explanation is necessary," said Detective Tate. "This won't take long."

I nodded in resignation. Since I entered the house, I had made a mental point of not reliving that night, but now I had to confront the memories. I urged the detectives to sit down on the embarrassingly battered couch in the sitting room as I sat on the equally battered side chair.

Detective Douglas pulled a pen and notepad from his jacket pocket. "Can you tell us what happened the night of the incident?"

I spent the next fifteen agonizing minutes recounting the story. By the time I'd finished, despite my determination, I was ragged from reliving the horrors.

"Just a few more questions, Mrs. Miles," Detective Douglas said gently, noticing my shakiness. "But I need the complete truth from you, okay?"

"Okay?" I echoed, not sure what else he might ask.

"Has Mr. Miles ever molested or tried to molest Denise?"

Wait, what? I was thrown completely off balance by his question. *Of course not...*

"Never."

"Are you sure, ma'am?" Detective Tate prodded further.

"Yes, I'm sure, Detective," I said, voice flat. "Jack may be a number of things, but a child molester he is not."

The two men glanced at each other, and Detective Tate scribbled in his own notepad.

They don't believe me.

To clarify, I added, "Detectives, if Jack had tried something like that, I promise you, Denise would not have kept quiet about it. I'm sure you noticed she is not timid."

That seemed to assure them, and the tension eased slightly. "Okay," Detective Douglas continued. "Mrs. Miles, had Denise been unable to stop him, do you think your husband would have been capable of killing you and her?"

This question was even harder than the last, but I didn't need to think long. I knew the truth.

"Sir, Jack was...extremely..." I paused to find the right word. "...upset. In our years together, I have seen his anger many, many times..."

Memories flashed through my mind. It was unsteadying, but I tried to keep calm. "Detectives, of the times I've seen him angry, this…this was the worst. He seemed…evil." I blinked back tears. "I've never seen him so crazy. It breaks my heart to say it, but yes. Yes, I believe he could have killed us. Now please, are we finished?"

"Just one last question. If Mr. Miles recovers and is released from the hospital, do you want him to come back here to live?"

I never thought I would say the words, not about the Jack I had been so in love with, but the resolve and fortitude of my foremothers gave me the strength to say them.

"For the safety of my daughter, I'd have to say no."

"Well," Detective Tate spoke again, "if you come to the station and sign a restraining order, he won't be allowed anywhere near you, Denise, or this house. If he violates the order, he'll go to jail."

The idea wasn't unappealing. *I need to think this through. I know I don't want Jack to come back…but I'm not sure I want to send him to jail, either.*

"Um… I'll have to give this some thought and get back to you."

"Mrs. Miles," Detective Tate's young face sobered, "you're still married, and Mr. Miles hasn't been formally charged with anything. This may be a difficult decision for you, but without an order of protection, Mr. Miles may come here whenever he wants." He shifted on the couch, leaning farther forward to emphasize his point. "He can hurt you both again or, God forbid…something even worse."

Detective Douglas nudged his partner, subtly quieting him. "Mrs. Miles," he said, "it'd be a mistake to assume he would not come back here. If your husband wakes and is released, this house will most likely be the *first* place he'll come. Do you understand?"

I bit my lip, but I still couldn't give them an answer. And I didn't know why. I wanted to protect my baby and myself but it was all so...extreme.

"Yes, I do." I stood abruptly, interrupting them before they could say anything else. "Honestly, with all due respect gentlemen, Jack has already lost his family, and his home. Isn't that enough?"

"No, Mom, it's not!" Denise's voice shrieked into my confused mind from the living room door. "How could you *not* file the order? He tried to *kill* us! He should be arrested and put in jail. You're thinking of taking him back, aren't you?"

She was hysterical in her terror, fragile even.

"If he comes back here, I swear I'll run away. You'll never see me again, you hear me?"

Sore as my body was, I stood and grabbed for her hands to calm her, but she snatched them away so fast, she lost her balance. Fortunately, Detective Tate, who had stood at her entrance, caught her before she could fall.

"It's okay, Denise," he said. "No one's going to hurt you."

I pulled my daughter gently from the detective's hands. "Gentlemen, please, we are not well—"

"Say no more Mrs. Miles," said Detective Douglas. "We'll see ourselves out."

He handed me a card and wished us a speedy recovery, followed more reluctantly by his younger partner. I stood holding my daughter's shaking frame until the detectives were gone.

"Honey, it will be okay. I promise."

She pulled away.

"No, Mom, it won't..." she said in a hoarse whisper, the fear and anger returning to her face.

"Honey, it will. You'll see."

"How, Mom? You don't want to sign the order to protect us from him."

"I didn't say that, Denise—"

"But you're thinking it. I know you, Mom! Why? Why do you want us to live in fear like this? You heard what the detective said. Dad will get out of the hospital and try to come back and kill us!"

I could see her desperation, and I knew I could never let him near her again.

"I won't ever let him hurt you again, I swear it. First thing tomorrow, I'll go to the police station and file the order. Then I'll…I'll pick up his paycheck and get our bills paid. And then…"

Then what? I still don't know.

"And then I'll look for a job. And I'll find one, honey. See, I have a plan." I attempted a confident smile that I didn't feel. "You have nothing to worry about, except getting better. We both need to heal and be strong, baby."

I pulled her close again, but I felt as scared and skittish as she did. *I have no idea what I'm doing*, I thought. *I've never held a job in my life, never been responsible for a household!*

Denise and I walked to her bedroom, and I got her to lie down and laid the coverlet over her still trembling body. As I stood at the door watching her slip into a light doze, my agitation increased. I painfully made my way back downstairs, intending to rest on the couch. I got aspirin and a bag of frozen peas from the freezer. I leaned back on the couch and covered my aching ribs with the bag of peas, but rest wouldn't come. My mind raced.

What are we going to do? After I pay our bills, there won't be enough left for food.

It was difficult enough with Jack working. Now, we had nothing.

Panic crept in slowly. The more I thought, the more alone and afraid I became. Jack had always been with me—since high school. Even if things with him weren't good…I had always had someone with me.

Now…I was on my own.

Although I'd promised Denise, I was truly dreading going to the station. The next morning, I picked up Jack's paycheck, ran my errands, and headed toward the police station, but when I passed *Mulden's Diner*, I decided to go in there first on impulse, stalling. Mr. Mulden always had a kind word for me. I believed he, like so many in the neighborhood, knew of my situation as well, and I needed to see a friendly face.

When I walked in, the stout, gray-haired Italian man surprised me with a big, careful hug and an encouraging grin. "Alice, glad to see you, my dear. We been so worried about you and Denise. How you feeling?"

"I'm getting better." I smiled and blinked back a stray tear, so thankful for the welcoming, gracious words. "Mr. Mulden, I…I need some help. Jack's in the hospital, and…well, I need work."

With a large Father-Christmas-grin, he led me by the arm over to the counter. "Say no more: I got a spot for a part-time waitress. It don't pay much, and you gotta get good tips, but if you want the job, it's yours."

"Oh, yes sir!" I smiled and thanked him profusely.

"You take the weekend to rest up and come see me Monday, at eleven. We work out your schedule then, yes?"

I was ecstatic, and for a moment I forgot all about Jack. I began to walk home as quickly as I could, eager to tell Denise.

Halfway there, it hit me; I hadn't gone to the station. My happiness dwindled, and I desperately began to seek an excuse. I kept a steady pace, but in my agitation, started to run. I regretted it as pain exploded in my side, and I clutched my ribs. Grimacing at my stupidity, I slogged painstakingly home as fast as I could. Now I definitely couldn't hobble down to the station…

When I opened the front door, the house was quiet. It was an odd sound, different than when I was alone cowering in terror of Jack's return. It disconcerted me in a way that makes one purposefully peek around corners to make sure no one else is around. I took off my sweater and hung it in the closet, then trooped carefully upstairs, still holding my sore ribs. The eeriness made me desperate to get to my room, to something familiar.

Denise was resting, so I settled onto my bed and opened the wooden chest, again smelling the ancient paper and wood. This was right, comfortable, steadying. I picked through them all again, remembering Lily, Mamie, Claire, and Martha, each one of them having taught me something about myself, about life and being a Kane woman. Each one giving me a sliver of encouragement that was more vibrant than the last.

I picked up Mama's book, tearing up over the beautiful portrait that graced the front of the hunter-green cover. All the other women before had helped me, comforted me…but I wanted my mama. I had the new job now, but I was still terrified. Life seemed so large and insurmountable, and I was left to conquer it alone.

Please, Mama? I prayed. *I know I'm supposed to read these in order, but…can't I read just a bit from you? I need you really bad, Mama… I'm scared.*

The moment I said the words, I felt in my heart that I would be cheating her out of the fullness of her gift. She wanted me to read them all, to learn them in order, as needed. I couldn't skip ahead.

Great-Grandmother Nicole Jenson's book was next, chronologically. I ran a hand over the intricately sewn lace and smiled at her neat little figure sitting there so perfectly. Excited now, I shivered. I knew Mama's grandmother had something to tell me, too.

///////////////

CHAPTER 11

inhaled a deep breath of the velvety scent and opened the book to page one.

Nicole Jenson, born 1858

I was only sixteen when my parents, Martha and Edward Wright, married me off to Milford Samuel Jenson, a long-time friend of the family. He was twenty-three years old and very handsome. Milford was tall and lean; his skin tanned from long hours working in the sun. He'd always given me a big, wide grin whenever we saw each other. But I was just a young girl; my only knowledge of men had come from playing and fighting with my brothers. I didn't understand what it meant if I couldn't take my eyes off him or why my cheeks felt flushed whenever he'd catch me staring. I didn't know what twenty-three-year-old men did with their wives… And, believe me, Milford was very much a man.

The feelings I had for him terrified me. After our parents gave us the news that we were to spend the rest of our lives together, we decided maybe we should get to know each other a bit better. Surprisingly, he was just as nervous as I.

Our families did everything together, church events, birthdays, and holidays. We both had large families, and we all got along well... It was a perfect combination. Milford often came over during the summers to help my papa and brothers, so it was as if we were already family. Maybe we weren't in love, but if marriage was something I was going to have to do, I was thankful that it would at least be with a good friend.

My only regret was I would have to leave our wonderful home my Grandpa Bert had left to my father. I was six when my Grandpa passed away. Not only did he leave us his house in Beaufort, South Carolina, but we also inherited thirty acres of farmland and Grandpa's good reputation with the local businesses.

Beaufort was already occupied by Union soldiers who'd set up a blockade on the river. Since our farm was considered small and had no slaves or political opinions, we were able to start fresh with little interference.

With our new life, my parents gained a beautiful home and a chance for financial security. We were all convinced we'd found heaven on earth, and since the fighting was *mostly on the coast and up North, it was easy to ignore the War.*

It was in those days that I came to love the lingering heat of a South Carolina summer. I can almost smell the heavy, Low Country air now. I'd step out onto the wide front porch in the morning and watch the rows of tall, resplendent sunflowers and golden stalks of corn illuminate as the sun rose higher in the sky.

In clean cotton dresses, me and my sisters, Shelby, Beverly, Carol, and Pat, tended the garden that Papa had set aside for us. Arrays of lush, crisp greens enveloped us as we cared for the crops, chatting, laughing, and bickering. The best part was after the day's work. In the cool dim of twilight, we'd dance about chasing fireflies while tall grass and dandelions tickled our ankles.

Oh, how I loved our farmhouse. It sat nestled between fragrant marshes to the east and towering mossy oak trees to the west. My sisters and I shared the largest room in the house, which was both airy and bright. But the best part was our porch. At sunrise, it felt like the world was sprawled out brand new just for us. If I found myself alone or frightened of anything in the big world, I knew that the second I set foot on that porch, nothing bad could ever touch me.

I always thought my Papa was a good man. He made sure to spend time with us and put effort into raising us right. He showed us the value of hard work, dedication, commitment, and most importantly, family. With cigar in hand, Papa loved sitting on the porch in his rocker, and we loved sitting out there with him. I felt that there was not a prettier, more peaceful place on God's green earth than our farm in Beaufort.

In 1873, I was told that I would be marrying the following year. That day when I awoke, I quickly scrambled out of bed, and rushed to join my siblings to start our morning chores. When I stepped out onto the porch, I noticed that the usual hum of summer was absent. I could sense something was coming, almost in the same way animals can tell when a storm is near. I tried to go about my day as normally as I could, but everything just seemed out of step.

Typically, summer was busy for us, but that particular day was slow, and we finished early. At dusk, my sisters and I decided to explore the cornfield. We ran blind like rabbits, feverishly giddy. The only sounds to be heard were our short catches of breath and the frantic tearing of cornstalks as we darted among them.

Our parents had a rule that none of us should ever venture out into the cornfields alone, as it was easy to get turned around under the tall arms of the stalks. I am still not sure if I wandered off on purpose or not, but for some reason when I heard the sound of my name being called, I didn't call back. I kept running. In the back of my mind, I felt that if my feet kept up their relentless assault over the earth beneath me, I'd be able to see past the pall that had been cast over the day. So I ran, arms pumping, feet pounding, lungs bursting, until my body's exhaustion ceased to exist. All that mattered was that I kept running.

I was so caught up with trying to clear my head of anxiety that I didn't notice Shelby's and my collision until I was falling. The ground rushed up at me, causing a sick crack as my head hit the sun-hardened soil. Though Shelby was younger than I, she was taller and much stronger, which meant it was never a good idea to ignite her fiery temper. She stood over me, eclipsing the fading sun, and before I managed to push myself up, she shoved her heavy hand into my chest and I fell back to the ground. Then she started scolding me about not answering when they called. I looked at her, sucked my teeth, and made to stand up again, but again she pushed me down.

Angry and wanting to get her back for knocking me down not once but twice, I pretended to be dizzy then waited for my opportunity to break free. I knew I wouldn't be able to outdistance her if I ran, but I could still tire her out. I slowly edged myself out from beneath her, and before Shelby could stop me, I took off running, disappearing into the corn again. It wasn't long before she caught up and pulled me down. Hearing our girlish battle cries, my older brothers Xavier, Felix, and Mack ran to find us, followed shortly by Aubrey and Jeff.

By the time they got to us, we were tussling about smacking and clawing at each other, until we found ourselves separated and carried back to the house.

Mama stood waiting on the porch with such a look on her face that I'm sure even Papa would have hesitated to speak. Shelby and I both squirmed to break free of our brothers' grasps. Mama commanded them to drop us, and soon as our feet touched the ground, it became a frantic race to see who could get to Mama first. We started yelling over each other, placing blame simultaneously, matching then exceeding the other's volume.

All the boys went to the porch laughing. Mama shot them a sharp, "That's enough, boys!" and gave everyone marching orders. Everyone that is…except me.

"Nicole," she said, wagging a crooked finger, "you, follow me." Mama turned and went into the house. For the first time in my life, the porch didn't feel like a safe *place to be. All I wanted to do was hide from whatever was coming. I knew Mama was upset, but I didn't think I had been that bad—nobody was bleeding. I stumbled over my own feet as I followed her through the house.*

After reaching her bedroom, Mama sat on the bed with a tired sigh and began rubbing her feet. Anxious, I stopped in the doorway and asked her if I were in trouble. She abandoned her foot massage in favor of throwing her head back and laughing. Patting the bed, she bade me to come sit.

Slowly, she grew serious. She told me how I'd grown into a beautiful young woman and how proud she was of me. It was nice what Mama said, but I was unaccustomed to her somber tone, and I didn't like this. She stared at me for quite a while with a look that I would never forget.

After several minutes, she told me that she and Papa had arranged for me to marry Milford Jenson. In that moment, all I could think was that my perfect world was about to end.

Two months after my parents' decision to marry me off, Papa unexpectedly passed away in his sleep.

"Passed away in his *sleep?*" I closed Nicole's book in thought, then swallowed in sudden realization. "Nicole...Edward didn't just pass away in his sleep. Your mother poisoned him!" My heart beat a little faster putting the pieces together. Nicole didn't know. Would she ever find out that her mother killed her father? Did she ever learn what kind of monster he really was? Surely she must have found out eventually; after all, Martha wrote her letter to Nicole.

I opened the book again to continue my read, but the phone rang just then. I would have ignored it, but the incessant ring would wake Denise, so I hurried to answer it, clutching my bruised ribs as I did so.

"Hello?"

"Hello, may I speak with Alice Miles?"

"This is she."

"Hi, Mrs. Miles, my name is Gemma Glen. I'm the liaison for Memorial Health's ACADA program."

"ACADA? What's that?" I asked, puzzled.

"ACADA stands for All Citizens Against Domestic Abuse."

"Oh, I see. How did you get my name?" I said tersely. *Just how many people know?!*

"I spoke to Detective Tate, Mrs. Miles, and he informed me that you might need someone to help you with your situation."

"My situation." I repeated flatly.

"Yes, ma'am."

"What kind of help do you mean?"

"Well, we offer many opportunities and are able to help you with lots of things," she explained eagerly. "Most importantly, we teach you how to protect yourself through our self-defense classes. We provide all these services with—"

"No, thank you, Ms. Glen," I interjected. "Services usually come at a cost, and we can't afford anything extra right now. Thanks anyway."

"There is no charge, Mrs. Miles. ACADA is a non-profit organization. Our goal is to help women who are victims of abuse, and I want to invite you to join us. Our meeting days are Monday and Thursday evenings and Saturday mornings."

An offer of help? Free of charge? Could someone truly, honestly care? It sounded almost too good to be true.

"Ms. Glen, it sounds helpful, but I can't take on anything right now and—"

"Mrs. Miles," she interrupted, a bit more firm, "before I let you pass an opportunity that can change your life, I'll just be honest."

"What?"

"As a liaison of ACADA, I am privy to information that others are not."

"Excuse me?"

Her tone was sober. "I saw the police report, Mrs. Miles. I know what happened. I understand the emotional toll it has taken on you. Believe me, I've been there... So with that being said, let me ask you a question. Your daughter Denise is very afraid, isn't she? Always on edge, somewhat withdrawn. Prone to anger, even?"

As she spoke, I traced the outline of one of the kitchen counter tiles with my fingertip. She knew. This woman I'd never met *knew*.

"Yes... I berate myself every day for failing to protect her," I whispered, surprised that I voiced my internal struggles so easily to this stranger. "I failed my daughter in so many ways, Ms. Glen. I've failed us, and I can't change that now."

"No, you can't change the past, but what if I told you that you could change her future?" she said, her voice sweet, almost maternal.

I exhaled deeply, my burden sitting right in my chest. "I don't think so. Denise has been through more than any child ever should. She's scarred for life..."

"Alice… May I call you Alice?"

"Yes."

"Alice, I'm scarred too. I am a living witness, a survivor, and you can be too. I can help you build a better life for you and your daughter, I promise. If you work with the program, you will win. Denise will become someone you can be proud of, and even better, she will become someone she can be proud of. So please, just come and give it a chance? You won't regret it."

My heart fluttered with hope. We were so broken. What Ms. Glen said made me hope.

I want nothing more than Denise's happiness.

"Okay, I'll come" I said, breathless.

"That's wonderful, Alice! We will be sharing stories and thoughts, then Mrs. Fluker from Stevenson Financial Corporation will be teaching interviewing techniques, so we ask that you come in business attire. All right? I'm looking so forward to seeing you, Alice."

I thanked her again and disconnected the line. I stood there for a long moment, processing the possibilities of the life I could have. The thoughts and memories of my foremothers drifted into my mind, and as unsure of my future as I was, I was certain of two things: I was proud to have come from such a strong bloodline, and I knew that Mama would have wanted me to do this. Perhaps all of my foremothers wanted me to do this… Martha had killed her own husband to protect her daughter, to give her a better life; Mamie had given up her daughter Claire so that she'd grow up a free woman.

Now it was my turn. I was ready to follow in their footsteps and free my daughter and myself from our emotional chains. It was my duty to become everything I could to see her through.

"Yes," I said aloud to myself. "Yes…I will do this for her. And for me."

--------------------------------- //////////////// ---------------------------------

Later that afternoon, Denise cornered me in the kitchen after she woke. "Hey, Mom, how did things go today? Please tell me you filed the claim against Dad?"

I flinched. I could see the fear in her eyes; she wasn't ready to hear the truth or my excuses… So for her sake and the baby's, I made a choice.

"Yes, everything's fine. Stop worrying, honey," I said. "Now let me tell you about ACADA." I wanted to move the conversation along.

"Whew, thank God that's done," she whispered with a long exhale. "What's ACADA?"

Excited, I told her all about my call from Ms. Glen. When I finished, Denise was beaming.

"That's great, Mom! I'm so happy for you! Maybe now we could actually start getting better."

I still had my doubts, but I felt happy as well. Without giving myself time to second-guess things, I jumped up from my chair and donned on my new conquer-the-world attitude.

"Let's go pick out something for me to wear tomorrow," I said, grabbing her hand and heading toward the stairs. We went to my closet and looked through my wardrobe.

Gingerly, I pulled out the suit that Jack bought me so many years ago. I hadn't worn it in a very long time. He had given it to me on my twenty-sixth birthday and told me he loved it because it matched my eyes. He used to give me compliments like that all the time, and I adored each one.

I remembered the anxious expression on his face as I opened the box. He'd always wanted me to be pleased with his presents, and every single time he brought me something, he would sit almost holding his breath until I opened it and gave my verdict.

I shut my eyes to the pain of the sweet memory as I held the suit close to my body.

"Try it on, Mom," Denise said, interrupting my thoughts.

I took the suit off its hanger and slipped into it slowly, savoring the feeling of dressing up. I turned this way and that, testing the material and seams. The suit still fit, and I was quite comfortable.

Next was my hair. With nimble fingers, I twisted it into an up-do knot and stood in front of the full-length mirror in the corner. The face staring back at me looked worn and tired; there was no mistaking my stress or my years.

"You look great, Mom."

I glanced at my daughter, astonished at how our relationship was already changing for the better. When we were trapped in our hell together, all I saw was her rage, her terror. I had forgotten her capacity for gentleness, her sweetness that used to make me smile so much when she was a little girl.

I squeezed her tight, and we embraced, savoring the moment of togetherness.

On Saturday, I took a hot bath, dressed in my beautiful suit, and headed to my first ACADA meeting. My heart was pounding as I stood in front of the building. I felt on the verge of something both terrifying and exhilarating.

I peeked through a dusty window to see the type of women who were in there, and was startled by a voice behind me.

"All of us did the same thing our first meeting."

I turn around to see a round-faced young woman, no more than twenty, smiling at me. "My name is Elizabeth," she said. "This is my fifth meeting."

I shook the hand she offered. "My name is Alice. Ms. Glen invited me."

"Gemma invites most of us." She still held my hand in hers and quirked a mischievous but sweet smile. "Since I'm still holding your hand," she said, "know that I'm going to be the strength you need to get you through the door."

I chuckled and squeezed back. "Was I that obvious?"

"No." She smiled warmly, reaching for the doorknob. "I just think that the first step is the hardest one. It's like there's a big wad of chewing gum stuck to the bottom of your shoe, and it holds you right there."

She certainly knew what she was talking about.

Elizabeth introduced me to the other women in the room, although Ms. Glen had not yet arrived. With each new introduction, I could feel my body relax more and more. I met Donna, who was still in a twenty-year marriage to a man who beat her. I met Mary, who fled her husband and home in Virginia in the middle of the night, only taking a few changes of clothing for her and her three small children; her oldest child was five. I met Tiffany, the only Negro woman in the group; she went into hiding after she poured boiling water on her husband while he was asleep. She was hiding from his family, not the police.

When Ms. Glen arrived at last, she took the time to make sure everyone was comfortable and acquainted, and beamed when she discovered who I was.

"Alice!" Her smile was big and warm. "I'm so glad you're here. You should be proud of yourself—taking the first step is always the hardest."

I exchanged a meaningful glance with Elizabeth and shared a smile.

Ms. Glen was beautiful and had an engaging demeanor. She was tiny at about five feet tall, with big brown eyes and a smile that could melt the stormiest of faces. Her hair was tied back in a neat bun that allowed full view of her thin oval face and high cheekbones. I felt an instant connection to her. We settled into our seats, and I tuned my ears to catch every word, not wanting to miss a thing.

Ms. Glen started out by asking each woman what it was that made her feel strong. As I listened to the others' answers—their faith, their will to live, and their children—I knew that each of those answers could be my own. When it was my turn to speak, the words just came.

"My daughter. My daughter makes me want to be strong," I said. "I look at her and see her will, her resilience, and I'm amazed. She makes me want to be a better woman, a stronger woman."

If it hadn't been such a private thing, I would have continued by saying that Mama and my foremothers added to that strength, that they gave me the will to try harder. But I knew the whole truth, and I hadn't told anyone about those letters yet; I didn't feel it would be right to share such a deep legacy with anyone...not until it was my turn to write a letter to put into the box.

Ms. Glen smiled, as did the other ladies. "Excellent, Alice. When things are at their worst, our closest connections are often what keep us going."

She moved on to the next subject, but I was lost in a few moments of deliverance. Having finally voiced something, even a small something, about what I was feeling, I felt awakened. Uplifted. Strengthened. I felt like I was someone, someone that mattered. I had a voice, an identity that was not defined by Jack.

We ladies talked, shared, and laughed, and I found myself becoming more determined to live and to move on without him. I didn't know how long he was going to be in the hospital, but I sure hoped that by the time he awoke, I'd be confident enough to tell him it was over between us.

Forever.

After Ms. Fluker outlined the interview techniques, she said her goodbyes and Ms. Leath, another counselor, took over. She broke us into small groups, and we each took turns acting out the role of boss and potential employee. Ms. Glen and Ms. Leath gave advice on how to conduct ourselves professionally and with confidence. By the end of the meeting, I felt more encouraged than I'd felt since high school.

On the walk home, I was actually humming a tune and stopped by my new place of employment for a large take-out plate of spaghetti and meatballs with Mr. Mulden's homemade garlic bread.

The aroma of the garlic and parsley teased me until I walked in the front door and called out for Denise. While she gathered herself to join me for dinner, I split the spaghetti onto two plates, went to the icebox, and grabbed the leftover salad from our dinner the night before.

"Wow, you're smiling wide tonight, Mom. I guess that means it was a good meeting!" Denise's excitement seemed to match my own.

"It was a *great* meeting." Maneuvering around the table, I asked, "Did you know that if you sit with your shoulders back and your head lifted slightly, you exude confidence in a job interview?" I sat to demonstrate.

"Nope, I didn't," she said. Unconsciously, Denise mimicked my posture, and I smiled to myself. "What else did you learn?" she asked.

"I learned that the best way to let someone know you're not intimidated is to maintain eye contact with them, and to let your eyes say whatever their eyes are saying."

"That I knew," she said. "It's one of the things you learn when you get into enough fights. If you look afraid, people will take advantage of you. But if you look as scary as they look, they might think twice about bothering you."

I was dumbstruck by her comment, remembering how often I had sat up at night hoping and praying she was all right and not getting into trouble.

"Unfortunately," I said, "I also learned that there are women like me who have lived in hell and some who *still* live in hell with men who are supposed to love them. Oh, but honey, the way some of these women talked about getting out, starting over, getting strong—it was amazing."

"I'm glad, Mom, I really am." Denise smiled, a real smile like she used to. We spent the rest of the evening getting to know each other again, long after dinner had disappeared from our plates.

///////////////////

CHAPTER 12

unday afternoon Denise was not feeling well, so after
lunch she went back to bed. I took the opportunity to rest
my body too, but my mind couldn't follow suit. I had to
keep reading Nicole's story, to find out if she knew the truth about
her parents. And what had happened to Martha? Did anyone ever
find her out?

I continue to read…

*After my parents' decision to marry me
off, Papa unexpectedly passed away in his
sleep.*

*I woke up in the middle of the night with
a terrible bellyache. I went down the hall
to Papa and Mama's room and knocked on the
door, but no one answered. Assuming they
were asleep, I gently nudged the door open.*

*"Mama? Papa?" I whispered. I tiptoed
closer and knew immediately that something
was wrong. Papa was alone in bed…and he was
pale as a ghost, with glassy, wide open
eyes.*

I screamed and ran out the room to find Mama. I burst into the kitchen and found her sitting at the table, writing.

"Mama!" I screamed again. "Something's wrong with Papa! Hurry!" Mama didn't react right away, and I found it rather strange. Of course I now know why, but at the time all I could think was, Why is she not moving?

The doctor came later and said that Papa had died of a heart attack.

—————————— //////////////// ——————————

With Papa gone, the only thing that kept me sane was planning my wedding. Mama worked tirelessly on my dress, stitching, pinning, poking and prodding. I thought her manner rather strange; she didn't seem the least bit sad about Papa's death. The other children and I were all reeling from the loss, but Mama just went on with planning the wedding as though nothing had happened.

A few days before the ceremony, Mama called me to the parlor. When I sat, she pulled out a stack of papers from an old tobacco tin.

"Nicole, come sit," she said. When I did, she held up the papers and gave them a pat. "I wanted you to see these. These letters were written by slaves a long time ago."

Quite puzzled, I asked her what the letters had to do with us. She didn't give me a direct answer. Instead, she smiled and began reading the letters while I listened attentively. When she finished, she told me they were letters from my foremothers.

Needless to say, I was shocked! How could that be? I wondered. I had Negro ancestors? After many long moments, I realized that because of all of those women's sacrifices, Mama, my brothers and sisters, and I were all able to escape such horrific lives.

I watched as Mama began nervously kneading the wrinkled skin on her forehead, clearly upset. Something was really bothering her.

"Nicole, I've failed your Grandma Claire...and I've failed you," she said. Now I was truly puzzled. She explained that Grandma Claire had married her to my papa in hopes that she would have a better life. "Now," Mama said, "here I am doing the exact same thing to you."

Mama took hold of both of my hands and looked at me deliberately. "Nicole," she said, "I want you to promise me that you will never be like me. That you won't start having babies the minute you say 'I do.' I want you to find something you like, something that you're good at, and figure out how to use it to try to support yourself. Most importantly, don't ever give your baby away in marriage like we did. You have to do

something different! You hear me? You have
to do something different now. Promise!"
Tears began to fall from her eyes as she
held my hands tight.

   "I promise, Mama. Please don't cry…"

The doorbell rang as I turned the page in Nicole's book. It was our first peaceful Sunday, and the fact that someone was interrupting it irritated me. I marked my place and tromped downstairs, but when I opened the door, I was completely at a loss.

There in my doorway was Cadell.

I hadn't seen her since before Jack lost the shop. Despite my hurt and feelings of abandonment, I hugged her fiercely. She was a reminder of when things were good in my life, and I wept with unashamed tears.

Cadell hugged me back just as fiercely, but soon she stiffened in my arms. "Hi, Alice," she said. "I need to talk to you. Can I come in?"

"Of course!" I said, wiping my eyes. I stepped back and allowed her to enter, joyous with nervous anticipation. It had been so long since we'd seen each other; it seemed a lifetime ago. "Would you like some ice tea?" I asked, escorting her to the living room.

"No thanks, I'm fine." She offered an uncomfortable half-smile. We sat…and stared at each other, at the floor, at the ceiling, in an awkward silence. I didn't know what to say, or if I should let her begin.

Cadell finally broke the silence, her Southern drawl sweet and apologetic. "Alice, I know what happened…with Jack." She reached for my hand. "Are you okay?"

"We will be," I replied, grateful for her kind touch.

"First," she began, "I want to apologize for staying away for so long. Our last phone call… I knew you were upset with Karen and me, and you had every right to be, but I didn't know how to tell you."

"Tell me what?"

Cadell looked at me with intent and with a firm resolve, confessed the sins of my husband and one of my best friends.

"Alice, Karen was having an affair with Jack," she blurted out. "I knew something was going on; Michael had started acting funny, and I was eventually able to drag it out of him. He told me that one evening he'd forgotten something at the shop, and when he went back, he saw Jack and Karen together in his office."

She paused, apologizing with her eyes. "Jack asked Michael and Jordan to have us stay away from you for a while, because he said you two were trying to work out issues with your marriage. Alice, I wanted to ask you what was going on, but Michael told me not to say anything or he'd lose his job. And I'm sorry. I shouldn't have let that come between our friendship, no matter what the cost."

I was numb. I'd known of Jack's cheating on me, but the details of the betrayal…

"Oh God," I gasped, the tears swelling. "She was my friend, Cadell! How could she do something like that? How long? Is it still going on?"

Cadell averted her eyes, and I had my answer.

"If it's any consolation, she and I aren't friends anymore." She went into her bag and pulled out tissue for me. "You will survive this, Alice. You'll see, honey. And this time, I will be here for you."

I smiled through my tears and hugged her again.

"Hey," she said, "if you don't mind, I'll take that tea now."

Cadell stayed about an hour, and when she left, we gave each other one last hug and promised to stay in touch.

"Who was that, Mom?" I heard Denise's footfalls on the stairs behind me as I locked the door.

"Cadell," I answered.

She eyed me, incredulous. "You mean Mrs. Swartz? Jessalyn's mom? What did she want?"

"Nothing in particular, we just talked. I told her about the baby, and she said to tell you hello." Not wanting her to see my upset, I changed subjects. "Are you feeling better? Are you hungry?"

"I'm much better, and these days, I'm always hungry." She grinned.

"Me too. Are you up to helping me make tuna salad?"

"Sure."

We prepared our dinner and chatted about potential names for the baby. We even laughed at some of the more outrageous ones; Oranjello because she liked orange Jello, and Chippy because she liked chocolate chip cookies. Though I laughed along with her, my heart wasn't totally in it. I was still trying to process Jack's adultery, and felt oddly *empty* inside. Then it occurred to me why I was feeling so alone in all this.

Mama and Daddy always took me to church back in Beaufort, and for a while, I continued to attend service here in Washington. I tried to remember when I had stopped going. *Probably when Jack started hitting me,* I thought.

On impulse, I cut Denise off in midsentence and blurted, "Denise, I'd want to go to church this evening. Will you come with me?"

Denise gave me such a strange look.

"Really?" she whispered. "It's been a long time, Mom."

"I know, honey," I said. "Will you come?"

We finished cleaning the kitchen without another word, then donned our best dresses and left the house with a feeling of celebration.

We decided to attend The Lighthouse Church of God, which was only a few blocks away. At first I was anxious, but the moment I saw the welcoming faces, I was at peace. When they called for special prayer at the altar, Denise and I went up with no shame or embarrassment. It was so good to be there…the missing piece. Though I didn't hear God's voice that night, I knew I was on the right path to the healing of my soul.

After service, Pastor Will and his wife, Lisa, introduced themselves to us. Sister Lisa complimented me on my dress, and when I thanked her and mentioned that I had made it myself, she raved that God had blessed me with such a talent. I was somewhat embarrassed, but had to admit that the compliment felt wonderful. I thanked her and the pastor for the prayer and welcome, and promised we'd be back.

While walking home, I thought of Jack, but I wasn't angry this time. My mind told me I should be enraged. But strangely, I was at peace, settled with what had happened to me and with where I was now. I had been hurt, of course, but I was now confident that I would get through it.

I smiled, realizing afresh that it was the help and wisdom of my foremothers and God's quiet but sustaining power that helped me get to this point. It had only been about two weeks, but I was stronger, more adept at processing my emotions and harnessing my pain.

Denise was on her way to healing, too. She'd started sketching again like she had as a child and was quite exceptional. When we returned home, she went upstairs to work on a piece she'd started the previous night. I gave her a kiss good night before heading to my room.

I snuggled deeper into my warm, fresh-smelling bed and opened Nicole's book, no longer feeling alone or afraid, but...*happy.*

"Okay, Great-Grandma..." I said. "I'm back."

———————————— ///////////////// ————————————

Milford and I married, and the promise I made to Mama didn't last two seconds. I got pregnant within the first six months. Though Mama didn't show it, I knew she was disappointed. As much as I hated to admit it, I was terrified...until I saw my baby's face. Sheila was a beautiful baby. I loved her so much it scared me.

After Sheila, the babies wouldn't stop coming. Next Frances was born, and then Valerie. Milford loved our daughters very much; but being a man, he wanted a boy.

"Nicole, I have these girls," he'd say, "but a boy is just what we need to make this a well-rounded family."

The good Lord must have listened to Milford's prayer, because two years later, we had Herbert. Imagine my surprise when the twins, Joseph and Reuben, came, and a year later our baby Tanny. Now Milford and I had seven children in all. I was often reminded of the old days at my parents' *house, except I now sat in a rocker on my porch, watching my babies tumble and play in the tall grass. There were moments when I felt myself running right along with them.*

Milford worked selling and trading livestock on the family farm, so as our boys grew, they helped him. The girls did their part around the house, but Sheila and I were like two peas in a pod. Whenever there were things that needed doing, including helping me take care of her siblings, she was right by my side following my instructions. It was like watching my childhood right before my eyes.

I cherished my family, but as the years progressed, a void in my heart became clearer, and despite my love for them, my children and husband couldn't fill it. Though Mama accepted that a mother and wife was all I would be, I still hoped to show her something different. Unfortunately, I never got the chance. One afternoon my sister Beverly went to visit and found Mama in her rocker, dead. I never got to say goodbye or ask if she was proud of me.

The years passed, and I found myself at loose ends, as each of my children needed me less and less. One day, missing Mama, I got out the old tobacco tin of letters that she'd given me years ago. When I opened it, there was a letter on top in Mama's hand, addressed to me.

She spoke about Papa...and it was terrible. I couldn't believe he was the man Mama described. The letter disturbed me greatly, but it answered many of my questions. Now I understood why there were times I saw Mama staring at Papa with such sadness. It was all clear, now that I knew. I thanked God that her secret had remained safe. With more determination than ever, I was determined to ensure that my children had a better beginning than I did, than my mother did, and I would show them by example.

With this thought in mind, after seeing a notice in town about a new school opening, I approached Milford about attending classes. I wasn't sure what I'd go for, but I thought maybe I could be a teacher. What better way to teach and show my children to reach for something outside of themselves...?

I woke to the morning sunlight, with Great-Grandma Nicole's book next to me. Still foggy with sleep, I snatched the book up, afraid that Jack was going to see it and take it away.

And then I remembered. Jack was no longer there.

I laughed at myself, amazed at the reality of my freedom from him.

When I peeked into her room, Denise was still asleep. Glancing at her hands, I noticed that she had chalk smudges on her thumb and index finger. I looked over at her drawing board and was immediately immobilized by her sketch.

My own eyes stared back at me from the paper, and beneath my outlined chin, her face gazed out as well; under her chin was the face of an infant, staring with big, wide eyes of wonder.

The consequences of not following through with the Commission from my foremothers were undeniably sketched in the beautiful lines of my daughter's hand. I was left speechless… and sobered.

We went to her school later that morning and cleared her for returning to classes. Afterward, we went to *Mulden's Diner* to pick up my new schedule as Mr. Mulden had said, and decided to stay for lunch.

As soon as we sat at one of the booths, two of the waitresses, Gabrielle and Sophia, came over to say hello. For the second time in as many days, I was complimented on my attire.

"Alice, where did you get your dress? It's lovely!" Gabrielle wanted to know.

I sheepishly told her I'd made it.

"Would you ever consider making clothes for someone else? I would love a new dress for my sister's bridal shower."

"And my daughter needs a dress for her recital," Sophia chimed in.

"Oh, I would love to help you," I said, "and we could use the extra money, but…I don't have a sewing machine anymore." I turned slightly pink, remembering when Jack had pawned it to pay off a gambling debt.

Just then Mr. Mulden deposited two glasses of water on our table. "You do now," he said.

"Excuse me?" I asked, confused.

"Now you gotta sewing machine. My wife…she pass three years ago, and I didn't wanna part with it. But she don't need it no more, bless her soul." He made the sign of the cross on his chest.

"It's a sign. I think this why I keep it so long. It was awaitin' for you," he concluded in his thick Italian accent.

"Mr. Mulden, I can't accept it. But thank you so—"

"Why not? You can use it, and I know you take good care of it."

"Um…" I hesitated.   Sophia and Gabrielle looked at me expectantly.

"Mom, it's a gift," Denise whispered, eyebrows raised.

Mr. Mulden put his hand on my shoulder gently. "Alice, you hurt my feelings if you don't accept." His eyes twinkled.

I hesitated a moment more and finally agreed. "Thank you so much, sir. I…I don't know what else to say."

He smiled and nodded. "*Fantastico!* I send Paulie to drop it off this afternoon."

"Yes sir," I said, blushing from his kindness.

"So it's a deal? You'll make the dresses, right?" asked Gabrielle when Mr. Mulden hurried back around the counter.

I held my head up and grinned. "It's a deal."

While walking home an hour later, it finally sunk in—I now had two ways to make money. It was a very good place to be. Sophia and Gabrielle's encouragement and Mr. Mulden's generosity made me realize that I was capable of doing something on my own.

It was a wonderful feeling.

Later that evening, I went to my second ACADA meeting and listened to all the women sharing their horrors and triumphs that night. I still didn't feel ready to share details yet, but I was confident I could do it next time. These ladies were wonderful.

After the meeting, I was surprised when Ms. Glen offered to give me a ride home. We chatted pleasantly until we pulled in front of my house. Then Ms. Glen turned off the car, took a deep breath and asked if she could share her story with me.

Not knowing where this was going, I said yes. Elizabeth had told me it was quite a tale, and that Ms. Glen always made sure to let each participant know.

But apparently it didn't get easier with the telling. Ms. Glen looked out the windshield, sober, as she relayed the details of her own haunted past.

"I married young, and my daughter, Carly, was born about two years later. My husband was a domineering man. He constantly bullied me into doing things that I didn't want to do, both in the bedroom and out. One day, he put a needle in my arm and I was too beaten down to object. He turned me into a heroin addict. A junkie. Just like he was.

"When my husband died of an overdose, he left me strung out, confused, and degraded. I did anything that I could for money, anything that you could imagine. Not to support my fifteen-year-old daughter, but to support my drug habit."

She was expressionless, but her knuckles showed white from the intensity of her grip on the steering wheel. I listened, hurting for her.

"When Carly turned eighteen, she disappeared. I didn't even bother to look for her. Alice, I didn't care. She could have been dead, and I never even told the police that she was missing. The only thing that concerned me was where my next high was coming from. Truth be told, I was actually relieved that she was gone. I hated myself for it, but with her gone, I didn't have to pretend to support her."

I was appalled that the kind of woman who was so dedicated to ACADA had ever been so heartless. I waited until she began again.

"A few years later," she continued, "I was in an alley trying to score some drugs, and I heard a familiar voice. I looked behind the garbage bin, and there was my Carly: filthy, barely clothed, begging a man for drugs. In my haze, I saw him capitulate and she started to unzip his pants. The sound of his zipper sobered me up quick. I yelled for her, but she didn't look up. That was it for me. I finally saw the reality of what my drug abuse had done to my daughter. I ran out of that alley, straight to Memorial Hospital for help. As soon as I was well, I searched the streets until I found her.

"Today, I'm eighteen years clean, and Carly seventeen. She is a registered nurse and an addiction counselor."

When Ms. Glen smiled at me, a weight seemed to lift off of her. *Anyone can get better—do better,* I thought.

"So you see, Alice," Ms. Glen released the steering wheel and wiped away a lone tear, "our stories may not be the same, but we all have one. And though it may be harsh and painful to tell, telling it helps us peel off one layer at a time—helps us to move on. Owning it, we grow because of it. We will never forget what happened, but we can learn not to let it define who we are. We can be happy even through the pain. Do you understand?"

I did. I had been sensing these things for a couple of days, both through Nicole's words and the comforting presence of the Lord. I knew what she was saying, and I knew that next time I went to ACADA, I would be ready.

"Thanks for sharing with me, Ms. Glen."

She smiled. "I hope to hear your story soon, Alice."

I nodded and opened the car door.

"Oh, one more thing, Alice."

"Yes?"

"Please stop calling me Ms. Glen." She chuckled. "That's my mother-in-law's name. Gemma will do just fine."

I giggled back and said my goodnight.

After checking on Denise, I took a bath and lay in bed for a while, pondering Gemma's story. I glanced at Nicole's open book on my nightstand.

Like her, I was at a crossroad. I was both nervous and feeling exhilarated at the possibilities of my future now. What did Nicole feel at her new prospects? I desperately hoped Milford would allow her to become a teacher, and flipped to my place in her journal to find out.

After I finished sharing my hopes of one day becoming a teacher with him, Milford stared at me, an incredulous look on his face. Then he let out a deep, hearty chuckle.

He told me that even if a school were to open, no wife of his would ever work. It was his job to support the family, and it was my job to tend house and take care of our children. Having dismissed the idea, he reminded me that nothing was more important than focusing on Sheila's upcoming sixteenth birthday party. I was crushed...

--- ///////////////// ---

Sheila turned sixteen on a beautiful fall day. All of our neighbors and family members gathered in the backyard to celebrate. Sheila herself was absolutely stunning...and I couldn't have loved my little girl any more than I did at that moment.

Milford lit the sixteen candles as our

guests gathered around and sang a rousing chorus of "Happy Birthday."

I attempted to join in, but my voice was rather fragile. A lingering summer cold left me with a nasty cough, and most days it felt as if my throat were coated with sandpaper. Another bout of the cough caused me to steal away into the house for a minute. My hacking quickly turned violent, and when I pulled my handkerchief away, I was startled to find sprays of blood on it. The pressure in my chest was so great. Breathless with the force of the cough, I was compelled to rest in my rocker.

As the cough quieted, I looked out the window at my children, and it was as if I was seeing them for the first time. I was amazed at how fast they were all growing up. My little girls were now young ladies, and my boys, young men.

The cough flared up yet again, accompanied by more blood. Hot tears clouded my vision. What if I'm not here when they are grown? I thought. What will I have left them? Will they make it in the world? Such big questions; such big possibilities.

Now, looking back on my life, I see that there is so much I wanted to accomplish that didn't get done. But, in acknowledging that, I realize that I have also had many successes, as a mother, as a wife...

A year has passed since that day, and as I write this, I realize that it may be my last chance to add to my family's legacy, so I will end it with a prayer for my children.

Lord, please watch over my babies. Keep them safe. Guide their footsteps, and help them get back up when they fall. Let them know that sometimes we have missteps—but we must always remember to be hopeful about the future and not dwell on the past. Though my path was chosen for me, help them to recognize that they are free to choose their own. Oh, and one more thing, Lord. Please help Sheila find a dream. She's so inquisitive.

In Jesus's name. Amen.

I closed the book on Nicole's story, suddenly feeling the enormity of everything Denise and I had endured over the years, what we had so recently escaped. I had done my best to bear up under it, to push away the feelings so that I could focus on getting us on our feet, but I hadn't really processed it all yet. Not really.

It all came crashing down upon me, and suddenly I was crying—heaving and gasping for air as the weight of reality and release and sorrow bore down on my soul. But I didn't fight it this time. I needed to cry—for myself, for Mama and Daddy, for Denise, for her baby... Even for the Jack I used to love.

And so I cried, long and hard, into the night.

CHAPTER 13

I read nothing for the next few days. Mr. Mulden worked me all week, and by Thursday I spun around in the diner like I'd been there for years. My feet, however, reminded me I was new in the waitress game.

Though my feet were hurting, I still had every intention on attending my Thursday night ACADA meeting and telling my story. I didn't know how much I would be able to tell, but I had to start somewhere. When I arrived, the women greeted me as though I were an old friend, and when it came time to speak, I was nervous, but less than I thought I'd be.

"Hello," I said, my voice quavering just a bit. "This is my first time speaking. I'm a little nervous, so please bear with me."

I glanced around the room at the friendly faces, and felt welcomed and safe. My voice got stronger as I went along.

"My name is Alice. My husband abused me...almost every day." I bit my lip, thinking. "One evening after I finished reading, I decided to take a bath. As I soaked, I thought about the sweet images of Claire, the bride in my book's wedding scene, and how happy she was. Considering I was afraid and depressed, for some reason the rice and white flowers, all of it, made me happy. It was a strange feeling, but good; I'd forgotten what it was like to have a moment of peace and happiness, but I welcomed it."

I paused and took a fortifying breath, then continued. This hadn't happened all that long ago…had it only been a few weeks or so?

"I finished my bath and stepped out of the tub. I was reaching for my towel when my husband plowed through the door, drunk as usual, with his belt wrapped around his hand. He shouted and asked where our teenaged daughter was. When I told him I didn't know, he screamed and raged that our daughter's whorish ways were my fault. Then, he lashed me with the belt… He had done it before, but he was so angry this time. And then he…he raped me."

I steeled myself against the horrible, fresh memory, and wiped the tears away. "I've never cheated on Jack. I never left the house except to get groceries or pay the bills, but he always accused me. I let my guard down that night for a few happy thoughts, just this one time…and it almost cost me my life. He could have killed me… I didn't even hear him coming."

I ended my tale almost whispering. It was shameful, but with the truth came comfort and release.

"Thanks for sharing, Alice," said Gemma softly. "That was very brave."

Tears streaming, I sat down and exhaled as another woman stood to tell her story. I realized that although I hadn't told my entire story, it felt good to share. Another brick off the load I carried.

Arriving home that evening, I removed my shoes, leaned against the doorframe, and slowly rubbed my sore feet. Denise saw me as she came out of the kitchen, and by the time I removed my coat, she had set up a foot-bath in the sitting room.

"Come on, Mom," she said. "You should sit for a few minutes."

I smiled. Such a warm gesture would never have come from her before. My daughter was shining now.

I let her soak my feet and told her all about my meeting and what I had learned about the different signs of abuse. She told me all about school and how much she hated math but loved art, English, and chorus. She went on and on as she massaged my feet, and all I could do was listen, her voice sweet music to my ears.

When my feet had received sufficient attention, we ate and dispersed to our rooms for the night.

I got settled and opened Grandma Sheila's book. This one I had been waiting for with eager anticipation. I had never met Grandma, but I knew of her veracity and can-do attitude, and was confident that of all my foremothers, she would teach me the most.

I read her name aloud. "Sheila Hanson—born 1874..."

Mama's last prayer was that I would find a dream. Well, Mama, I don't have to—I already know what I want to do. I want to be an editorial writer someday, just like Elia Peattie. If I could write all day, nothing would make me happier. So until I get my schooling, I will just contribute to my foremothers' stories. I will write in my spare moments until the entire tale is told.

Two years after my mother, Nicole Jenson, died of lung cancer, both my sisters, Frances, nineteen, and Valerie, eighteen, shocked me with their plans to marry. I was not pleased; I reminded them that Mama wanted more for us than to marry and have babies.

"Girls, what is the rush to get married? Can't you wait a bit and just enjoy being engaged for a while?" I asked, but neither one were interested. They both made it clear they wanted nothing else. Five months later, despite my disapproval, they married in a double ceremony, Frances to Willie Shedrick and Valerie to Lewis Stokes.

A year or so later, my father fell ill after working on the docks in Beaufort. He tried telling me all was well, that it was only muscle aches and back pain, but by day four, he was bed-bound with a high fever and headaches. The following week I had the boys go fetch the doctor, who told us that Daddy had contracted yellow fever. Daddy died shortly thereafter.

Though we struggled, with Daddy's insurance and the sale of the farm, my siblings and I purchased a smaller home with less property, and I was able to sustain us on what we made off of it.

Before too long, all of my brothers were out of the house. Herbert and Joseph had married and were living in Charleston, and Reuben and Tanny lived and worked on the same farm in Columbia. I was glad that they were on their own and taking care of themselves, but that left me home alone... and my aunts didn't let me forget it. They continually reminded me that I was twenty-five and becoming one of the "late bloomers."

"Sheila, you are so beautiful," Aunt Shelby would say. "When are you going to find yourself a handsome man to help you around the place?"

No matter how many times I told my aunts about my dream of one day becoming a writer, they dismissed my "fancies." I repeatedly explained, "There are no schools close enough for me to attend yet, but one day there will be. You know that marriage has never been at the top of my list."

One day Aunt Shelby said, "Sheila, Beaufort is a beautiful, quaint place. We like the simple things in life. A school may never open here. If it does fine, but don't waste your youth on a hope that may never come that's all, okay, honey? Now about this house... Your aunties and I have hired a yardman, Tom Hanson, to help keep the property. Expect him Monday morning around eight."

I didn't think any more on our conversation until Monday, when promptly at eight o'clock, I heard a knock on the door and found a very handsome man standing on the porch.

"Good morning, ma'am, I'm Tom Hanson," he said, removing his hat. "Ms. Shelby said you'd be expecting me."

With rays of morning sunlight glistening on him, all of Tom's features were defined. He had sea blue eyes, a straight prominent nose, and his dark brown hair was short and sort of messy. He was quite muscular and had to be at least six feet tall. This handsome man mesmerized me, and it must have shown on my face.

"Ma'am," he said, "are you okay?" When he smiled, the dimples in his cheeks seemed to dance.

I stuttered and felt the heat rising in my face. "Oh, I'm so sorry. Y-Yes, Mr. Hanson, I'm fine. Please...come in."

"Please, call me Tom," he said.

He told me he'd already taken a good look around outside and knew just where to start. While he told me his plans for the day, my stomach fluttered. I was awake in a way I'd never been before; my senses were all coming to life.

"Ma'am, you sure you're okay?"

Mentally I admonished myself for my flighty behavior. I was not like this. And after all, he was just a man. But my stuttering reply made a mockery of that. "Yes...yes, I'm okay. I know the place is a mess. P-please let me know if I can help with anything."

That morning changed my life. Every few days, Tom would come by to do odd chores, and many times I would assist him with little things. We talked all the time and grew very comfortable with each other. Within a few months, we realized that we had grown *to love one another, and Tom asked me to marry him.*

Before I accepted, I told Tom about my dreams of becoming a writer and asked him, if an opportunity arose, would he support and help me? He said he would.

We married in the winter of 1900. By the fall of 1901, I gave birth to my baby girl Charlotte. Over the next six years, we grew as a family. After two more girls, Blondell and Ginger, and one boy Earl, I thought I was done. A few years after Earl, our fifth child, Kitty, was born. She was a surprise, certainly, and I had to admit I felt more frustration than joy when I first learned of her coming. I loved my children, of course, and had found a great deal of happiness as a wife and mother. But like my mama before me...I was beginning to yearn for something new, and I had promised her I wasn't going to let life kill my inquisitiveness.

A few years went by before I saw my opportunity. One day while in town, I was visiting the apothecary and saw a notice in one of its windows:

Business Academy for Women

Opening September 7th

Enrollment Begins August 1st

I read the rest of the advertisement, and to my utter delight, one of the courses they would be offering was creative writing. Instantly, my dream to become a writer came roaring to the forefront of my mind. Here was my chance to make good on the promise I'd made to my mother—and to myself—so many years ago!

Several weeks passed as I deliberated. My little ones still needed a lot of my attention, but I persuaded myself that they were being trained right and we'd be able to manage it. I continued to hope for something bigger than diapers and meals and keeping house, until I was practically consumed with the thought of attending school.

During those few weeks, I'd also noticed that my breasts were a little sore. I'd put it down to my menses coming, but then I starting experiencing a few more familiar symptoms, and my heart sank like lead. I didn't have an official word, but the signs and sensations were there. I was thirty-eight and pregnant with my sixth child.

My dream was slipping away before it had even started. Saddened, I contemplated my situation for several days. Finally, I decided I simply would not have any more babies... I loved each one of my little ones; I truly did. But this time, I was going after something I wanted.

My decision made, I scooped up three-year-old Kitty and walked to my friend Kay's house. She once had mentioned she knew of a woman in a similar situation, and she'd found a way around it. After sitting with her and explaining my problem, I told her what I wanted to do. Kay seemed shocked to hear the suggestion come from me, but she got paper and pen and wrote down instructions.

Serious, she said, "Before I give this to you, you need to know all the possible consequences." She stared me down, emphasizing each point. "You could become sterile, go to jail, or even die. I want you to understand, Sheila; I have known people in all three situations, so be certain you want do this."

Kay extended the paper. Not hesitating in the slightest, I took it.

That evening when Tom came in from work, I called him upstairs into the bedroom so we could talk without the children hearing.

"Tom," I began, "I'm pregnant."

A joyous grin spread across his face, and he whisked me into his arms, swinging me around, laughing.

"Put me down, Tom," I urged. "Come on, honey. Stop it, please."

He continued to frolic as if he hadn't heard me. I knew I wouldn't be able to stop his child's play unless I got his attention.

"Stop it, Tom! Please listen. I don't want to have any more babies."

He paused mid-twirl and set me down on the bed, searching my face in confusion. "What do you mean, honey?"

"Do you remember the conversation we had before we got married, about my wanting to go to school to become a writer?"

"Yeah, a little, but that was so long ago. What kind of writing are you talking about?"

"I'm not sure yet. I'm only sure I need training if I am to consider working at something I love. I have to plan and—"

Interrupting me, he chuckled. "Planning for what?" he said jokingly. "Aw, shucks, woman, there's tons of work right here. And if love is what you're after, well, you've got plenty of that right here, too…with more on the way." He tickled my stomach, smirking.

This angered me. When I opened my mouth to tell him, I was interrupted by Kitty bounding into the room squealing, with Ginger right on her heels with a shriek, their usual sibling spat.

"It's my doll, Kitty, give it back!"

"No, mine!" Kitty screamed.

Tom gave me a humored look as if he'd just proven a point. Throwing his hands in the air, he chuckled once more and started for the door. But I would not let him dismiss my *dream or me the way my father had dismissed my mother.*

That night in bed, I brought the subject up again. Tom had his back toward me, but I didn't care.

"Tom," I said, "I will not argue with you about this, but I'm letting you know that I've already made plans to end this pregnancy. My mind is made up."

Tom flipped over, his eyes wide. "Are you crazy, woman? You are not going to kill our baby. That is not an option, you hear me? It will be a cold day in hell before I give you a dime toward it!"

"Don't worry, I don't need your money. I have my own," I said.

Furious, he sat up and grasped me firmly by both arms. "You will not be meeting with any law-breaking baby-killer!" he said forcibly. "I forbid it. Understood?"

I jerked away and glared at him. "I'm not keeping this baby. I'm going to school!" Tears tickled the back of my throat, but I refused to cry.

Seeing how resolute I was, Tom seemed to deflate. He flipped back over and lay unmoving.

I waited a few minutes, then hugged him around his waist. "Don't I deserve some happiness too, Tom?"

"Honey, what have I done wrong?" he said. "I've tried to be a good husband and

father and provide for us. I love you and the children. And when I'm home, I do all I can to help you with them."

"Yes, you do, and you have been wonderful about that, but–"

"Well then, what could be more important than us…than your family?" he asked. He was genuinely hurt. "Isn't knowing you are taking good care of us enough to make you happy?"

Hearing his words, I realized my husband wasn't being selfish–he was simply a typical man. Tom's narrow view of a woman's role was not his idea, but rather what men had been instilling in their sons for many generations before we were ever born.

The look on Tom's face said it all; he honestly didn't understand. At that moment, I could only empathize with the man I loved.

"Tom," I whispered, "I'm sorry for the pain I caused you tonight. Let's not speak of this again. Please forgive me, honey."

He turned and held out his arms to me. "Thank you, sweetheart, thank you. And once this baby is old enough, I promise I'll help you do whatever you want, okay?"

I nodded and went to sleep wrapped in my husband's warm embrace…

Frustrated that Sheila had given up so quickly, I slammed the journal closed. The darkness outside my window told me it was quite late, and I turned out the light with an angry *click*. Grandma

Sheila had disappointed me; I thought surely that the woman who had been Mama's everything, her role model, would have put up more of a fight. From what Mama told me about Grandma, if anybody could have told her husband no, it would have been her. I was angry, but I tried to keep it out of my mind for the night.

———————————————— /////////////// ————————————————

After I got Denise off to school the next morning, I invited Gabrielle over to get started on her dress since I didn't have to be at work until four. I was still angry with Sheila, and purposefully kept her out of my mind while waiting for my first "client."

Thirty minutes later, Gabrielle was there with material and pattern in hand. We chatted and laughed about girly things, the regulars at the diner, motherhood, and recipes. At one point, feeling bold, I told her I had Negro ancestors. It felt daring.

She surprised me when she had little reaction and instead said, "Everybody's got a little something in them; I've got Asian in my ancestry."

I couldn't help it—I laughed so hard that tears came to my eyes. Gabrielle, with her prominent Roman nose and stout body, was the most Italian-looking woman I'd ever seen!

As we chatted about our bloodlines and family histories, the thought struck me in a way it never had before: confidence stemmed from simply being unashamed of who you were. And that confidence was empowering.

After Gabrielle left, I continued to work and got the pattern pinned and cut. Before I knew it, I was humming and sewing up a storm. The fabric beneath my fingertips was comforting, like the caress of a long lost friend. I was pursuing *my* dream, even in a small way. And I was becoming more assured of myself and who I was. I knew I wasn't going to hide anymore. It was wonderful.

I lost track of time until the chime of the clock showed that I had two hours before I should be at work. I dashed around getting ready, grabbed a quick bite, and then sat down for a few moments of calm in my room before heading out to my shift.

Sheila's book toyed with my willpower from its place on the side table. Though I didn't think I would find her account satisfying at all, I was feeling ready for anything, and determined not to let her apathy disturb the surge of confidence and productiveness I was feeling. I picked it up for a few more glimpses of her story before I headed out.

That night, I told Tom what he needed to hear about the baby. The next morning, however, as soon as I'd gotten the children off to school and Tom off to work, I dropped Kitty at Kay's house. Afterward, I went straight to the beautiful brick building where my dreams lay: "Beaufort Academy for Women."

When I entered, I marveled at the sight of women registering for classes with smiles on their faces. Everything seemed so vibrant and just being there made me feel excited and important.

After I handed my completed application to the secretary, a woman called me into her office and introduced herself as Ms. Weaver. She explained the program and had me fill out several more forms.

She couldn't tell me exactly how much my financial obligation would be, but because of the size of my family, she was confident there would be several scholarships to pick up most of the cost. I was relieved because I didn't want Tom to find out…not yet. I told her about my story and how long I'd waited for this opportunity. I also told her I wasn't sure I could afford what the scholarships didn't cover.

To my delight, she handed me yet another form and told me about an office assistant job that had just become available. When I realized she was offering me the position, I almost jumped out of my chair! They even had a child care room for Kitty. It was looking like I'd be going to school…and working!

After my meeting with Ms. Weaver, I felt even more anxious about the pregnancy. I tried my luck and went to the address that Kay had given me. Although her instructions said to go after dusk, I thought that since I had time, I would go anyway. Soon enough, I was passing the shipping and boating docks on Bay Street and making a right onto a small side road.

As I walked, several questionable people approached me hawking their wares. I sidestepped them and continued down the road.

When I found the address, I was taken aback by the building's condition. I double

*checked the slip of paper and confirmed that
it was the right address. The house, if you
could call it that, appeared to be one,
maybe two rooms from the outside. It was a
faded, white-washed, sad little shack with
one tiny window and a patch-worked roof.
I gave a tentative knock.*

*An old woman opened the door a crack and
furtively looked out at me, then up and down
the road. Satisfied, she grabbed my arm and
snatched me inside.*

"What do you want, girl?"

*"If this is the right place," I said, "I
was told you may be able to help me with a
little…problem."*

*After my eyes adjusted to the dark, I
looked around the room with much trepidation.
It had a strange musty smell and desperately
needed soap and water.*

*"First, I don't like people coming here
during the day," the old lady snapped. "I
don't do no work during the day. If you
need my help, you have to come here afta
dusk. How far are–" She abruptly stopped
to knock four cats off the only table in
the dingy room. They appeared to have been
helping themselves to her lunch. "Mangy old
cats," she groused, turning back. "Well,
girl, how far along are you?"*

"About four weeks."

*"All right," she said, "you have about
seven more weeks before you'll be too far*

gone. I won't touch you afta that. It'll take about fifteen minutes, and it's gonna cost twenty dollars. I want my money up front. Now you come here alone, and you leave here alone. And afta I finish, I never want to see you at my door again. You got all that, girl?"

I agreed and got out of there as fast as possible.

I have to admit, walking down the road I couldn't help wondering if I was doing the right thing. But I believed that there was no way I could pursue my dreams and have another baby, too… It had to be the right thing, I thought.

As I made my way back to Bay Street, I passed one hawker, a thin man with hungry eyes that begged for money; he was holding up a beautiful pine box for my inspection.

"Twenty cents miss. Twenty cents, and it's yours," he urged. "This pretty box will bring you good luck, miss. Just twenty cents."

Good luck? Of course, I knew he was just trying to entice me to gain a sale, but maybe it was a sign—a sign from God that all would be well. The box was beautifully embellished, with a gold latch. The man gave me a toothless smile, and I thought, Heaven knows I could use the luck. I bought it.

After Tom left that evening for his night job, I went to my secret place in the bedroom. I pulled up the loose floorboard at the foot of my bed and got out the satchel of money I'd been saving. Between knitting hat and scarf sets for neighbors and extra house money that Tom gave me, I knew that I should have enough for the old woman, but I wanted to make sure. When I counted it, I was relieved to find I had more than enough.

I reached inside the floor space again and took out the tin box that Mama had given me. I picked up the little book written by my mama Nicole. I looked down at the picture she'd painstakingly framed on the book's cover, and had to smile.

On the heels of that happy memory came the disturbing thought that my foremothers and I were joined, like the rusty links of an old chain, each of us unwittingly following the same pattern as the one before. Like Tom and his chauvinistic ancestors, we too had been following the mindset and pattern of those before us. It was to our detriment, and I was resolved to change that.

I'd be the first to do something different.

Running downstairs, I threw out that old tobacco tin and grabbed my new box, then retrieved an old padlock and chain that had been collecting dust in the attic. Next, I placed the envelopes along with Mama's little book inside and wrapped the chain twice around the box and applied the lock.

Perfect, I thought. I'm going to a new school, I've got a new job, I'm writing my own book, and now I'm giving these letters a new home. At that moment, I made a vow to myself: I'd remove the chain as soon as I finished school and earned enough of a wage writing so that my husband would no longer have to work two jobs! I set right to it.

"I'm home, Mom!" I heard Denise yell. I looked at the clock; it was already three-thirty. I jumped up, much more excited and inspired now. I had grievously misjudged my grandma; she was the most determined woman in my family line yet!

I was energized by her ambition and swept into the foyer to give Denise a goodbye kiss on my way out to the diner. It was not the most glamorous job, I knew, but like Sheila, I was making my own way…and I would set right to it.

///////////////

CHAPTER 14

I took on my first early morning shift that week, and on Saturday when the clock struck 6:00 a.m. at *Mulden's*, I was *moving*. There were salt and peppershakers to fill, glasses to line up, and bagels and pastries to be tantalizingly placed within the glass cake plates on the counter. As soon as everything was in order, the race began.

That afternoon, still empowered from Sheila's words and the generous tips I had gotten that day, I raced out of the diner and headed to my ACADA meeting. I sat in my chair beaming—I couldn't help it. I had shared a small portion of my horrors, but today, Grandma Sheila's tenacity surged through me. When it was my turn to speak, I was ready to bear it all.

"Every Saturday night Jack went out with his friends," I began. "He never returned before two, sometimes three in the morning. That was fine with me because those were hours I didn't have to worry about him beating or raping me. I always thought nothing could ever be worse than that. But I was wrong."

I closed my eyes and took a deep breath. I felt a moment of weakness tempting me, but I refused to be cowed by the memories anymore. I forged ahead.

"I got up to use the bathroom one Sunday about two in the morning. When I entered the hall, I heard giggling. I checked my daughter's room, but she was asleep. I went downstairs and into the living room, and saw two figures in the dark. When I switched on the light, I saw Jack in his underpants and a woman straddling him in nothing but her panties.

"She was startled and reached for her bra, but Jack stopped her, and she said, 'I thought no one was here?' And...Jack said, 'No one is.' I couldn't speak; I was just too shocked. It was as if I were watching a movie. The woman told him she was leaving and keeping the money. And right in front of me, Jack tried to sweet talk her! I'll never forget it. He said, 'Come on, baby. Look, the old lady's not causing any trouble, is she? Let me talk to her. Give me five minutes, and if I'm not back, you can leave with the money, I promise.' The woman looked at me for a moment, and said, 'Okay, man, you got five and not one second more.'

"Jack kissed her cheek and scurried over to me. And then he grabbed me by my arm and pulled me into the foyer. I tried to break away, feeling frantic, but he had a strong grip on my arm. He was so angry. He gave me two choices: either go up the stairs on my own or unconscious. I knew he meant it so I didn't resist him.

"When we got to the room, he pushed me onto the bed. Then he punched me so hard in the stomach, I gagged. He put his hand across my face and pressed hard enough I could feel one of the springs pressed against the back of my head.

"He said he had paid good money to be with someone that was *all white*, and if he lost his money because of me, he'd kill me. And I believed him."

Standing there in front of the ACADA ladies, I felt my body trembling at the emotions surging through me with the remembrance of my husband's coldness and hatred. I looked up and saw Gemma's sweet face staring at me with sorrowful eyes.

But her genuine sympathy and understanding gave me the last bit of steadiness I needed to get through the last part.

"I believed him, but I felt I had to stop him; our daughter was home and might go downstairs at any moment, and I didn't want her to see this. He finally walked out, and I made my way to the door, still trying to catch my breath. But to my horror, Denise was standing in her doorway, listening intently.

"I whispered for her not to go downstairs. She gave me such a look of disgust... I'll never forget her face. She said, 'It's not like I've never seen it before.' She slammed her door, and I just stood there trying to figure out what she meant by that. I didn't know if she meant this wasn't the first time Jack had done this, or if she was telling me she was having sex, or something else?"

I sighed, looking down at my hands. "Ladies, please don't think wrong of me. I know I am her mother, but our relationship was so broken I couldn't ask her. Even if I had, she wouldn't have answered."

Several of the other ladies nodded sympathetically. "It's all right, Alice," Elizabeth murmured. "We don't blame you."

I smiled in thanks, but my voice stayed quiet. "About a week later, Jack informed me he was having 'company,' and I needed to stay in the bedroom. He grinned like the devil waiting for me to answer. I didn't know what else to do or say, so I just nodded slowly. And he kissed my check like he was proud of me! After that, hearing noises going bump in the night was just a regular occurrence."

My will finally faltered. "Oh, God...why did he do that? The humiliation..."

My entire body shook, sobs coming so hard I couldn't catch my breath to continue my story. It wasn't just the constant infidelity; I was letting go of it all. Accepting what had been done to me, or rather, what I had allowed to be done to me.

In that moment, I at long last came to terms with the fact that I'd been completely broken by the one who should have loved me most.

Gemma and the other ladies stood and surrounded me with hugs and tears and gentle hands of comfort. It felt so awkward and comforting all at the same time, and when it was over, I found I could smile again, and even share a small laugh with the ladies at how embarrassed but invigorated I now felt.

My heart was lighter than ever before. On the crisp walk home, feeling giddy with freedom, I said hello to complete strangers. I even held my head up and felt good about it.

Gemma was right; she'd told us again tonight the same thing she often said, that there's healing power in not keeping your pain silent. That thought encouraged yet challenged me, step by step. For me, telling this story was the ultimate test. The scars from Jack's beatings would eventually fade, but there was no pill or ointment that would ever take away the pain in my heart for his betrayals. I had to learn not let his disrespect define my worth. I was a good, honest wife, and I deserved a good healthy life.

When I got home, I was still happy, but I was mentally exhausted from processing the changes and emotional strengthening in my life. I called for Denise, but she didn't answer.

At first, I felt a jolt of fear but then I saw the note on the table in her handwriting: *Out to the movies with Jessalyn. Be back before midnight. Love you.*

I smiled. Cadell's daughter. That was good… It meant Denise was reaching out and reconnecting, too.

I shrugged off my coat, made some hot cocoa, and trooped into the living room. Since I had the night to myself, I could read more of Sheila's story undisturbed. I found great joy in connecting with her, seeing a culmination of sorts in the Kane women's legacy as Sheila went after what *she* wanted. I was doing the same. I hoped she made it to her desired end. Although…the question now swam in the back of my mind: If Sheila succeeded, as I hoped she did, why wasn't the chain already broken? The Commission would have been fulfilled—in fact it never would have come about if Sheila's dreams had been met; she was the one who gave it to us in the first place. Why did the box still have a chain around it?

I continued reading with trepidation.

> Over the next five weeks, I became accustomed to the school, my new job, and my schedule. I managed the home so well Tom never knew the difference. My grades were good, and as time went on, I became comfortable with my job.
>
> During those weeks, Ms. Weaver—Daisy—and I became good friends. I talked to her like a sister, a sister who understood my need to become a writer. We talked about everything, from my mother's hopes to my sisters' failings for not even trying, and even about Tom not knowing about the school. Through it all, Daisy never judged, and I grew to trust her and her opinion.
>
> One day while at lunch, I told her about the baby.
>
> "It's amazing that after you do all this here," she laughed, "you go home and manage a family. How do you do it all?"

I had to laugh back. "When you've waited for something your whole life, you do whatever it takes when the chance comes. I love my life and everything happening in it, but for the first time, I'm focused on something I want for myself, and will not let anything stop me."

Tears suddenly pricked my eyes as I thought about the child about to be aborted. "Daisy, I have a small problem. I call it small because I refuse to allow it to become big."

"What is it?" she asked, her brow furrowed.

After explaining everything to her, I pleaded with her not to think the worst of me…or to tell anyone. Tom didn't know about work or school yet, and he wouldn't know about this, either. I explained that I was scheduled to go in the following week, and I planned to tell everyone I had the flu while I healed. Mindful of Kay's warning, I told Daisy about my foremothers' letters and where the box was hidden and of my intentions of giving it to Charlotte, whether or not I succeeded. Of all my girls, Charlotte seemed the most interested in furthering her education, and would appreciate that piece of her past.

Daisy listened and only asked for further details, never questioning my decision or my plans. She only said, "All right then,

I guess we'll just have to work on getting you back to work and school as soon as possible."

For the next three days, I studied hard, and at the end of the week, I took my final exam. I couldn't wait to see the results.

Saturday evening I started my plan; I told Tom that I caught a terrible cold. Though I was anxious on Sunday, I was determined my jitters wouldn't stop me. Continuing with my ruse, I prepared meals that would take us through for the next few days.

Monday, when Tom came home from his day job, I was already in bed. I told him I had gone to Dr. Lewis, who said I had the flu and was to be on bed rest. To make sure no one else got sick, I told him that the doctor said I should stay away from the rest of the family. Tom understood and agreed to sleep in the sitting room.

That evening after he left for work, I told Charlotte that I had to go visit a sick friend, and left her in charge.

I went to Kay's house, where a prearranged horse-drawn cab was waiting. When we reached Bay Street, I told the cabby I'd be about twenty-five minutes and asked him to wait. I got out a few doors down from the old woman's house and walked the rest of the way.

Once again, I was snatched into the shack. "Give me the money, girl," her raspy

*voice commanded, her hand extended, fingers
moving in urgency for the cash. "Twenty
dollars."*

I quickly did as I was told.

*"Set your things there," she said,
pointing to a threadbare chair, "then take
off your drawers and lay on the bed."*

*Without waiting to see if I complied, she
went to a corner and began rummaging through
bottles. The room still smelled strange,
and though there was a lantern on the table,
it was still quite dark and disturbing. As I
removed my bottoms, her cats swarmed around
my feet.*

*Attempting to make conversation, I said,
nervously, "Ma'am, I never got your name."*

*"That's 'cause I never gave it, chile…and
I don't need yours, neither. It's best this
way. Now, prop your legs open and scooch
down to me."*

*I swallowed. "Okay, but can I at least
ask what you're going to do?"*

*She let out an exasperated breath.
"I'm gonna place these inside of you,"
she said, holding up a few thin brownish
sticks. "They're called slippery elm bark,
and they soak up the juices down there."
She indicated her private parts. "When they
swell big enough, they'll push the baby out.
Listen, you gonna have a high fever, and
you'll bleed with cramps like you have with
your menses. But in two or three days, it'll*

all be over. Now, just be quiet so I can get this done."

The whole thing took about fifteen minutes like she promised. When done, she tossed my bottoms onto the bed, then told me to hurry up and get out. I dressed hurriedly and without a backward glance, left the shack. When I arrived home, I was weary and sore, and surprised to feel so dirty and ashamed…

I flipped to the next page, and could see from the handwriting that Sheila had twice stopped recounting her tale for a time, and then started again later. The handwriting seemed to get shakier, more difficult to read than her usual fine hand.

Morning has come and I am still in bed, but I had to write down yesterday's events before I forget their vivid details. Again, I wonder if I have done the right thing: I lied to my husband; I left my children at home alone; and I've just endured one of the most humiliating things I could imagine.

What is the price of happiness, I wonder? Is it worth the pain and heartache now, or will it always haunt me, even when I achieve my joy?

―――――――――――――― ///////////////// ――――――――――――

Five days have passed, and my recovery hasn't been at all like the old woman

*described. The pain and bleeding has been
unbearable, and I had to go back to her
today. Soon as the children got out to
school, I grabbed Kitty and made my way to
Kay's. She took one look at me and took me
to Bay Street to see the old lady.*

*She dropped me off a few steps away, and
I laboriously made it to the door. Before I
could knock, the old woman opened the door
and snatched me in by my arm. The force of
her pull was so great and my weakness so
profound, I fell inside, sprawling on the
floor at her feet.*

*"Didn't I tell ya never to come here
again, girl? Didn't I? What ya doing here,
then? Huh?" She towered over me, eyes hard
as granite. "Ya got one minute to tell me
what you want."*

*It didn't seem to phase her one bit that
I was sprawled on her floor.*

*"Ma'am, I'm sorry. I didn't know where
else to go. Blood's pouring out of me, and
I can't stand the pain anymore. Please help
me." Tears streamed from my eyes, but I
didn't care. Something was very wrong.*

*She relented somewhat and helped me to
my feet. I was startled when she wrapped her
arms around me and whispered, "Girl, ain't
nobody ever tell ya that being a woman was
gonna be easy." She let me go and turned,
once again, to fan the cats off the same
rickety table.*

"Here," she said sharply over her shoulder. "This will fix ya right up." She gave me a vial of liquid. "When ya wake up tomorra, ya should be better."

I thanked her, but she shook her head, saying, "Don't thank me. Just get out." She peeked out the door, then pointed for me to leave. "Don't ya ever come back here again, no matter what, or ya gonna be sorry, ya hear?" I scurried out, and she slammed the door.

I am home now and resting. No matter the pain, I have to put this account in my book. I believe the medicine is already working, and I should have a better story to tell tomorrow.

But for now, good night.

Thank God! I thought. If Sheila hadn't acted when she did, the outcome could have been bad. I took a deep breath, resting Sheila's book on the sofa, and sipped the last of my now cold cocoa. It was unfortunate what Sheila had to endure and wrestle with in her conscience in order to gain a small amount of happiness. She stood her ground, though, and did what she thought was right for her. She didn't let Tom's dismissal change her mind. I prayed to God that I would never have to make such a choice and went upstairs to drift off to sleep.

––––––––––––––––– ////////////// –––––––––––––––––

That night, I dreamed that Jack was choking me. I woke in a cold sweat, heart pounding. As soon as Denise was off to school,

I called the hospital to make sure Jack was in no state to make my nightmare come true. I'd only checked with them twice since returning home.

I let out a pent-up breath when the nurse informed me he was still unconscious and showing no signs of change. I asked God's forgiveness a moment later; it was so wrong to be relieved by another's tragedy. On the other hand, though I now felt some measure of guilt for having to attack my husband...he'd left me no choice.

I was learning from ACADA that dwelling on past mistakes didn't help make the present any better. Determination, hard work, and owning your pain did. Going after your future made it all worth it, and that's what I would do...no regrets. I kept my mind focused on that resolution all through my shift at the diner.

That evening when I got home from work, physically exhausted, I stuck my head in to tell Denise good night and found her nibbling on toast. She was *always* eating these days. I smiled at her and glanced at her drawing board with her outline of the three of us on it.

"Honey...I love your sketch."

She glanced over at it.

"Me, you and baby," I said, "all together in that drawing. And soon to be all together in this life." Misty-eyed, I looked at her and smiled again. "I can't wait."

Denise smiled back. "Me either."

I took that opportunity to ask her a question that had been nagging me and came farther into the room. "Sweetie...can you tell me who the father is?" I hoped to God she hadn't been so promiscuous that she didn't know.

She looked to the ground and bit her lip. For once in her life, she didn't have any words. She just shook her head, once, twice, then her lip quivered and tears began to roll down her cheeks.

I put my arms around her and hushed her. "It's okay, honey. It doesn't matter. All that matters is that you, the baby and I are going to be here, together, and the rest we'll worry about later."

"I'm sorry, Mom," she said. "I'm so sorry."

"It's okay. Hey," I said on a brighter noted, "have you decided if you want a boy or a girl?"

She shrugged with a watery smile. "It doesn't matter. I just want her or him to be healthy…and not too loud and obnoxious."

"All babies are loud and obnoxious sometimes, sweetie," I chuckled.

She stuffed the last bit of toast in her mouth. "I know, but I can hope, right?"

We talked a short time more about her artwork, and I told her to think about what she could do with her talent; if I could loan out my sewing skills and make a few dollars, surely she could with her wonderful abilities. She nodded, pensive.

When I stood to leave, she stopped me. "Hey, Mom?"

"Yes, sweetie?"

She pursed her lips together, as though debating her words.

"Love you."

"I love you too, sweetie." With a swelling heart, I bid her goodnight.

A moment later, I was slipping into the new cotton nightgown I had made for myself. It was warm and soft, and seemed the perfect way to end a long, hard day. I settled into bed, whispering a prayer of thanks to God for the relationship rebuilding that Denise and I were working through.

Absent-mindedly, I picked up Sheila's book off the nightstand and removed the page marker from the last page I'd read, turning to the next one.

Nothing. The next page was blank.

What in the world? I thought. *It can't just end there!* I flipped back to make sure I was in the right place. I was—Sheila had just taken the vial of medicine to stop the bleeding and pain. There simply wasn't another entry.

My heart beat faster. *Where is the rest of Grandma Sheila's story?* I retrieved the box from under the bed, rummaging through all the papers and books again. There were no more loose pages, only my mother's unopened book.

"Charlotte Whitmore, born 1901," I said, reading the cover aloud and staring at it for a moment. Earlier I almost couldn't restrain myself from reading my beloved Mama's words, but now I didn't want to read a single word…not if Grandma didn't make it. She had gone through too much, experienced so much victory for her story to end in heartache.

"Mama, I don't like this. Something's wrong here. Please tell me everything turned out okay…"

I closed my eyes for a moment and held the book up to my nose, breathing in the scent of the velvet that Mama once held in her hands, and my heart calmed. For a moment, the unknown of Sheila's story faded, and I was just *there* with Mama. She had made sure that I would be here in this moment, with these women's lives and wisdom to guide me through. I would never have made it this far without them…without her. The thought settled into me like a sweet aroma, a breath of good, clean air into my lungs.

The truth suddenly overwhelmed me—this was the last mile of a long, hard journey. My journey. And I was going to end it with Mama's hand in mine.

Oh, how I've longed to read your words, Mama, I thought. *I know you have been here the entire time, even if I forgot sometimes. You've been the one whispering behind the voices of our ancestors as they spoke to me… Now it's time for you to speak to me yourself.*

"I'm ready, Mama..." I whispered aloud.

Lying back on my bed, unsure of what I'd find, I took a deep breath and opened Mama's book. Her first words hit me like a brick wall...

"Mama died when I was twelve, and I don't think I ever quite got over it..."

I heaved a loud sob and buried my head into one of the bed pillows. *Oh God, why? After all that, she died? Mama lost Grandma at twelve? Why have I never known this?!*

With that one sentence, I was a mess. I had lost Mama so recently and barely survived it. So how could anyone at such a young age process such a tragedy? I felt double the grief slam into me. My heart was breaking for Mama, Grandma, and myself... for all of us who'd endured so much.

///////////////////

CHAPTER 15

When I had finally cried myself out, I sat up straight, wiped my drenched cheeks, and did my best to prepare for whatever was to come next in my mother's writings. I knew these lessons were important, and I *had* to finish them. I wanted to move on, to know what Mama had desired for me.

Mama died when I was twelve, and I don't think I ever quite got over it. I was so angry, so hurt she did that to us, to Daddy. But I'm ready to relive it now. Alice, I'm sorry you never met your grandma. You would have loved her. I should have told you a lot of this before, but now that you're in D.C., I feel I need to put these memories down on paper. I don't know when you'll read them, but you should know...

I remember that we all thought that Mama had the flu. Imagine my shock when helping her to sit on the chamber pot and discovering that the bed linens were saturated with blood. I was scared to death, but all she said was she'd just seen Dr. Lewis about it *that morning, and not to worry—she would be fine. But she wasn't.*

I remember taking care of the kids for about four days after Mama got sick. On that last day, when Daddy came home, he greeted us and went straight to the bedroom. As usual, I followed behind telling him how her day had gone.

I almost walked into Daddy's back when he abruptly stopped in the doorway and yelled. "Oh my God, Sheila! What's going on?"

Stepping into the room behind him, I saw that in her restlessness, Mama had thrown off the covers, and the bedsheets and her nightgown were soaked in blood.

Daddy quickly turned and yelled for me to go get Dr. Lewis. I ran as fast as I could, praying the entire way. After I banged furiously on the doctor's door, I explained what had happened, and he snatched up his medical satchel and came with me back to the house.

When we returned, I swear Mama already looked dead. Her face had gotten so thin so fast. Her hair was stringy and lank with sweat, and her skin was paper white with deep bluish bruising around her eyes and mouth.

The doctor immediately started questioning Mama. "Sheila, listen. Did you get rid of a baby?" he whispered.

She nodded and looked at Daddy. "I'm sorry, Tom. I'm in school, you know."

Mama in school? A baby? How do you get rid of a baby? I thought, figuring that Mama was just delirious from the fever. Afraid someone would make me leave the room, I eased into the corner and said not a word, just listening.

Daddy fetched fresh water and sheets while Mama mumbled something else about school. Dr. Lewis finished his exam and beckoned Daddy into the hallway. I tiptoed to the door and listened.

He told Daddy that Mama tried to get rid of a baby and that whoever helped her had unsterile instruments. He said Mama's blood was poisoned and that he'd given her medicine to make her comfortable, but that was all he could do.

"Tom," he said, "I'm so sorry to have to say this, but Sheila's septic throughout her body... Her blood is poisoned, and she may not live through the night."

Daddy collapsed into Doctor Lewis's arms, sobbing. I didn't understand what septic meant—but I understood that my mama was dying. At first I couldn't think. What did that mean, exactly? Daddy continued to sob and Dr. Lewis tried to help him get himself together, but I didn't know what to do. I went back into Mama's room, numb and unsure. She smiled at me and held out her hand. I took it, and that's when my own sobs came. "Mama, please don't leave..." I stammered and tried to be strong, but I couldn't keep from shaking or sobbing aloud. She patted my head and held me to her, wordlessly.

A minute later, Daddy stepped back into the room and Mama turned to him and smiled. I sat back and wiped my tears away, trying to be strong for them both. Someone had to be.

"Looks like the medicine is working," Daddy said, in a valiant effort at keeping Mama smiling. But she wasn't going to let him deny it.

"I'm dying, aren't I?" she whispered.

Daddy kissed the back of her hand, not saying a word. I felt another sob coming, but I did my best to stifle it, for now.

She asked Daddy to go to the office at the business school in town and ask Daisy Weaver to come. Daddy refused to leave her, so I volunteered and ran to the school.

Panting and out of breath, I walked to the front desk where two women were talking. "Excuse me, my name is Charlotte Hanson," I interrupted. "Is Ms. Weaver here?"

"Why, that's me. I'm Ms. Weaver," she said with a smile.

"Ms. Weaver, I am Charlotte Hanson and…"

"Charlotte of course. You're Sheila's girl; you look just like her. Hello, honey. It's so nice meet you finally. I've heard so–" Ms. Weaver took a good look at my now tear-stained face, and her expression changed instantly.

"Charlotte, what's wrong? Is your mama okay?" she said, her eyes darting past me, hoping to see her.

"No, ma'am, she…she's dying!"

"She's what?!" Her calm voice escalated into a stunned shriek. "Where is she?"

"Home. She's asking for you…"

Ms. Weaver didn't wait for an explanation; she grabbed my hand, and we bolted out the door.   On the way, I explained as much as I could.

When we arrived, Ms. Weaver spoke with Daddy, then after gaining her composure, went in to see Mama.

"Hi, friend," she breathed, stroking Mama's hair.

"Daisy, I just wanted to go to school," Mama said. "I wanted to make Mama and my children proud."

"You already have, Sheila. Your husband, children, me, your coworkers, we all adore you, honey. You've done good, okay?"

Mama smiled. They talked for a few minutes, then Mama began to cry—soft weeping that seemed to be filled with so much regret. An unexpected pain hit her, and Mama inhaled deeply and shut her eyes tight as her body tensed. A moment later, she exhaled, eyes slowly opening.

"Daisy," Mama's whispered through short agonizing breaths. "Please get the box…and my family. Hurry…"

Ms. Weaver, with tears now streaming, quickly knelt down and grabbed a wooden box from a floorboard under Mama's bed. She kissed Mama on the cheek. "Got it," she said.

"Remember our conversation," Mama said. "Are you still willing to look after them?"

"Yes, I promise," Ms. Weaver replied. "I love you, friend."

"I love you too…and thank you."

Ms. Weaver looked into Mama's eyes, gave her hand a soft squeeze, and turned to walk away. "I will be back, Charlotte," she said to me. "You be strong, okay?"

My own tears silently flowing, I nodded.

With scared and confused looks on their faces, the other children all came into the room, standing just inside of the doorway against the bedroom wall.

Daddy propped Mama up on pillows as best he could. "Come on, babies. Don't be afraid," Mama said weakly.

We all slowly gathered around, darting scared glances at one another. I understood now what was happening, but I couldn't feel anything in that moment. I was just so lost… so empty.

Mama explained that she was very sick and that the doctor wouldn't be able to fix her. Daddy sat in the rocker across from the foot of the bed and watched us, eyes bright with unshed tears.

"Mama?" Blondell asked. "Are you going to die? Please don't die!"

Out of all of us, Blondell was the one we counted on to blurt out observations and questions that none of us had the nerve to ask. I told her to shush, but Mama quieted me. She took a ragged breath.

"You know how the preacher always talks about us going to heaven, where there is no more pain and sorrow?"

Everyone nodded sadly.

"Well, soon the Lord will take me there. Daddy will still be here, though, and I expect all of you to take good care of him, okay?"

"No, Mama," said Earl, "we want you here too. You said it takes all of us to be a family, so you can't leave!"

Everyone started crying, except me. I could tell that Mama was trying not to fall apart herself, and she needed me to be strong. She turned and looked at Daddy, who was no longer holding back his tears.

"Mama, can we lay with you?" Blondell asked.

"Kids, I don't think Mama can…" Daddy objected.

But my mother lifted her hand and, with a smile, stopped him midsentence. As if to gain strength, she closed her eyes for a moment, then nodded. "I'd like that," she said.

"Sheila, you sure, honey?"

Mama nodded and Daddy helped everyone carefully pile in. They were all lying on top of each other, trying not to jostle her. I sat at the foot of the bed, listening to everyone tell Mama how much they loved her. I just couldn't believe it was happening...

The room gradually grew darker, and I watched as Mama fell asleep. One by one, so did my siblings. But I was determined not to miss one minute with her. Daddy must have felt the same way, because he lit the bedside lamp and sat in the rocker, just watching his family. His expression said that these final moments with his wife wrapped in the love of her children would be a sight he would forever cherish.

I jumped when Mama's eyes suddenly opened wide. She looked up at the ceiling as if someone had called out to her. A minute later she blinked, then focused on me.

"Take care of them, Charlotte," she whispered. "I love you."

I wanted to hug her, but I couldn't move. It was like a dream. Was I really about to lose Mama forever?

Daddy got out of the rocker, went to the bed, and held her hand.

"I'm sorry, Tom. I love you..." she said as tears streamed down her face. "I just wanted—"

"Shh. No, Sheila," he said. "I'm sorry for not seeing what you needed. I should have been there for you… You…" His voice cracked with emotion. "Honey, I love you, and I'm so proud of you."

Mama smiled and opened her mouth to speak, but no words came out. With the look that passed between my parents, it was clear they no longer needed words to communicate their love. It was so bright and strong that when I closed my eyes, I felt it soar right through my very soul. I felt an odd calmness come over me, a warm feeling that let me know that somehow, it would be okay.

My eyes snapped open when Mama gasped, her peace gone. She took in her family surrounding her and softly exhaled. Her eyes closed, and it was over. Mama was gone.

"Sheila Hanson… Grandma," I whispered to myself. I had expected myself to bawl, to weep with my mama as I read her grief and pain. But strangely, the calm feeling she had felt settle over her seemed to have settled into my spirit as well. I ached for Grandma, for Mama…but I knew that the pain they had experienced was short-lived. They were both at peace. That thought permeated my mind as I smoothed out the page I had just read. My grandma was all right now. Mama was all right now. They were both in a place with no more pain.

I didn't expect to feel joy. But I did, mingling with the sorrow I also felt. The best word for it was bittersweet.

I found myself walking to Denise's room, just for a momentary respite. As I expected, she was nestled under her covers asleep.

Watching her, I thought about the times I had considered taking my life, and shuddered.

"I will never leave you like that, Denise," I whispered over her. "I wasn't lucky enough to have more children to help you through something that drastic, so I choose to stay, honey. I choose to fight."

Closing Denise's door, I returned to my room for the night, and dreamed of my mama and I back in Beaufort, eating chicken salad on the front porch and chatting about life.

————————————— /////////////// —————————————

I woke the next morning before dawn. The air had changed, and I guessed that our first overnight frost had come as I shivered a bit. I snuggled deeper into the covers and attempted to return to sleep, but now that I was awake, my mind seemed to churn with the voices of my ancestors. I sat up after a minute and flipped on my side table lamp. I was actually glad for the extra time alone with Mama; it was the perfect time of morning for us to finish this journey together.

I found my place in the journal, and propped myself back on the pillows. I took in a deep breath, and began the last leg of my journey.

A few days later, we buried Mama. It was the worst experience of my life. The following week, Ms. Weaver stopped by to invite us to the orientation program at the school. They had set aside time for a memorial in honor of Mama.

When we arrived, Ms. Weaver gave us a tour that included the office where Mama worked and the classrooms she studied in, and we even met her teachers. We were escorted to the assembly hall, and I was shocked to see over a hundred women filling the chairs.

When the orientation was over, a few of Mama's friends and coworkers stood up to tell stories of her time at the school. We were astonished by this secret part of her life…and even more surprised when they called Daddy up to the podium.

Puzzled but smiling, Daddy walked to the podium and stood next to Ms. Weaver, who handed him a lovely plaque with Mama's picture on it.

"Tom, we give you this plaque in honor of your wife, Sheila Hanson," she said. "There's a special place in our lobby where another plaque just like this one will be mounted. Sheila will never be forgotten here. She will continue to be an inspiration to every generation of women who will come through these doors. We hope that one day your girls will attend and share in Sheila's dream."

When Daddy took his seat, Ms. Weaver, who was struggling with her emotions by now, turned to address the audience. "Uh-um," she said, clearing her throat. "Sheila Hanson was one of the smartest women I've had the *pleasure of knowing. She wasn't afraid to excel or to dream. Sheila started here by studying to pass our school's exam. And as you know, we have one of the hardest exam qualification requirements in the State; scores decide not only admittance to the school but what scholarships are awarded.*

"Not only did Sheila pass, but she made history while doing it. The governor's office informed me that Sheila Hanson is the first woman—or man—in the State of South Carolina to score a perfect one hundred percent on the Business School's exam."

Everyone stood up and applauded, even shouting Mama's name. I will never forget the look on Daddy's face or anything about that day.

———————— ///////////// ————————

Fifteen years later Ms. Weaver, who'd now become Aunt Daisy, gave me Mama's box.

Aunt Daisy was a very important part of our lives—the voice and the spirit of my mother. It was she who dried our tears and taught us things that Mama hadn't gotten around to. Most of all, she tried to get us to attend a secondary school, though with little success.

Everybody had left to live their lives, except me and Kitty. Blondell was living in New York with her husband Clayton; Ginger married Thomas at eighteen and moved to Bluffton; and Earl married Theola, his high school sweetheart, and moved to Texas. Kitty, the baby, was now about to wed, and with no girls left to badger, Aunt Daisy turned her attention to me.

One evening, while Kitty and I were sitting at the kitchen table picking out flowers for her wedding bouquet arrangement, Aunt Daisy came in carrying a wooden box that looked vaguely familiar. She eyed me for a second, sat the box under the table, and began to talk to Kitty about attending school after her wedding, but Kitty stopped her before she could get too carried away.

"Auntie," she said flippantly, "I refuse to go to another school if I don't have to, and I don't have to. I love Leon. That's why I'm marrying him. And I hate school; that's why I'm not going back." Then with a big mischievous grin, Kitty kissed Aunt Daisy on the cheek and flitted over to the icebox. "Now, for a more pleasant conversation...anybody want a Coca-Cola?"

Aunt Daisy looked at me, and I shrugged, trying to hide my smile. We shared a few words about the upcoming nuptials and Kitty left the kitchen. Auntie set her gaze in my direction. I knew what was next, so I got up and went to wash the dishes.

"Honey, how's that beau of yours? Are you ready to marry him?"

"No, Auntie. Not yet."

"That's good, dear. After all, there's no rush, right?"

"Right," I replied. Here it comes, I thought to myself.

"Honey, you remind me so much of your mama. You've got a drive and a work ethic that your sisters just don't. I've watched you raise an entire family darn near single-handedly, and you weren't much more than a child yourself.

"With your being that focused and dedicated, just imagine what you could do as an educated woman! Your mother had dreams, baby—big dreams for herself and even bigger dreams for you. Yep, your success was so important to her; it's what she…"

I couldn't take another word. I'd heard this all my life, and today I'd had enough.

"Let me finish that sentence for you—it's what she died for, right?"

"What, Charlotte?" she said, astonished.

"I said it's what Mama died for. You always say Mama wanted me to dream big, but how could I when she left me no free time to do so?" Words running together, I continued. "I didn't have the luxury of sitting around dreaming when there was hair to comb, food to cook, clothes to wash, stories to read, homework to be done, a house to be cleaned, tears to be wiped, kids to be hugged and to dress for church, and so on and so on and so on!"

My voice rose in pitch with every word. "Aunt Daisy, you've seen what we've been through—what my life's been. There was no time for dreams. My God, I've barely had time to sleep!"

I realized I was hysterical to the point of disrespect and shut my mouth. I took a steadying breath and sat at the kitchen table with her. I wasn't sorry for what I said; every word was true—but I should have just skipped the yelling and the crying.

I explained to Auntie that had it not been for her, we wouldn't have had a constant woman figure in our lives. But then, with a deep breath, I told her the truth, how I really felt. It was the first time I'd ever voiced it to anyone.

"I'll always respect Mama, but I have a hard time accepting that she died for this elusive 'better life,' Aunt Daisy. If she hadn't left us, I would've accomplished the things she'd dreamed for me and much more. I'd have done it just to see her smile. Instead, she stuck me with the life she tried to escape. Ironic, isn't it?" I couldn't help the single tear that slid down my face. It was so unfair…

When I finished, Aunt Daisy stood up, tucked the box under her arm, and held out her hand. "Charlotte," she said, "I know you're not a little girl anymore, but you used to love walking in the garden with me. Would you walk with me now?"

*I held out my hand, and she grabbed it
just as she had when I was a little girl. We
walked through the garden in silence, the
fresh air a balm to my soul. Gradually, the
stillness brought me peace.*

*Aunt Daisy spoke softly, almost
reverently, in the silence of the garden.
She told me she knew I had had to grow up in
a hurry and had done an amazing job helping
to support the family. She told me it was
now time to think about myself—what I wanted
to do.*

*I reflected on that in the stillness.
Derek, my beau, had asked me to marry, but
I had turned him down because I didn't want
to leave Daddy alone.*

*"I love Derek so much, Auntie, and I
don't want to lose him."*

*"Listen, Charlotte," she said. "Don't you
dare miss out on your life because you're
too busy worrying about Tom's."*

*She looked at the box she was carrying
and slowly handed it to me. "Your mother
entrusted me with this chest and wanted you
to have it when it was the proper time. I
believe the time is now. Read it and you
will understand why your mother wanted you
to seek a life of self-reliance.*

*"Charlotte, your father has been alone
all these years, true, but maybe if you
move on, so will he. If he doesn't have
you to fix his meals and chat with every*

night, maybe it'll prompt him to change his life, too.

"Please know that I love you for who you are, not for who I wish you would be. Do whatever will make you complete and fulfilled—whether it's school or marriage or both. Do you understand?" She searched my eyes.

I sighed gratefully. "Yes, ma'am."

"Good. Let's head back," she said, giving my shoulder a light squeeze.

///////////////////

Your father and I married that winter and moved into a nice little house less than a fifteen-minute walk from Daddy. Our third year of marriage, you came along, and I loved you more than I ever thought I could love anyone. I cherished every milestone: your first smile, first word, first laugh, and first step—I was so blessed, so enchanted with my baby girl that sometimes I thought my heart would burst with love.

There came a time that my days seemed to lack the fulfillment they'd had when you were a baby. I had more time on my hands now, and I realized that I wanted to know the side of life Mama wanted to show me. So I went back to where it all started—the Beaufort Academy for Women.

A short stocky woman guided me on a tour of the school. It had changed a great deal from what I remembered from Mama's memorial. Near the end of the tour, I halted and stared at a plaque on the wall. Realizing I had stopped, my tour guide came and stood beside me.

"Isn't she beautiful? That's Mrs. Sheila Hanson. She was the first woman to ever qualify in this school for the Excel program. She was also the first person, of any gender, in South Carolina to get a perfect score on the business school exam. And—"

"—and she's my mama."

"Excuse me? Did you say she's your mother?"

"Yes, ma'am, she is," I replied softly.

"Oh, dear Lord! Well, isn't this a pleasant surprise! Your mother was a great woman, Mrs. Whitmore. Sheila Hanson set the bar very high."

"That's what she wanted," I replied as a tear slipped from one eye. More than you know, I thought. "If you don't mind, I'm ready to start as soon as possible."

I completed all of my courses in about a year, and though I didn't break any school records, I finished with excellent grades and references. With Aunt Daisy's help, I was hired for a great position as the front desk receptionist at a reputable real estate agency.

After seven years and a lot of training and hard work, I was promoted to office manager, and was making more money than Derek–not that he cared; he jokingly threatened to retire early from the mill and spend his days fishing.

I so wanted you to know that level of freedom, Alice. I had great plans for you, including a four-year degree from an accredited college. I had my eye on the College of Charleston, which was not too far from home. You may remember, I started planting the seeds when you were fifteen, promising we'd pay your tuition, and encouraging you to find a career before marrying. I tried to instill the importance of being independent...but it fell on deaf ears, I suppose. You never had any interest in school or a career. You married at seventeen, then had Denise. Alice, I was terrified for you... My mother's heart still trembles at the idea of what disillusions may come, but I pray to God that you will always be happy–always be at peace.

My heart broke as I read Mama's wishes and hopes for me. My eyes misted as I continued to read what would be her last words to me.

Dear God, my daughter and granddaughter are in trouble. Jack moved them away from us, away from Beaufort eleven years ago. We want her back. He is not a good man… He is a monster. Though she hasn't said it directly, I know he beats her…I saw the bruises, and he attacked Derek our last visit. Lord, I am so afraid that if she doesn't leave him soon, something bad will happen. We talked to our baby on the phone today, and she promised to come home, but my heart won't rest till she does, until she's here, safe…

Please God, open her eyes. I can't lose her like I lost Mama. I wouldn't be able to take it. I'd rather you take me home, dear God, before I see that happen…

Alice, honey… Come home, baby. Please… just come home.

Despite my resolve, my eyes filled with tears knowing what Mama went through because of me. It killed me to read those words. I closed the last book with a sense of purpose.

"It may be late in coming, Mama, but you've got your wish" I whispered. "Denise and I are fine and I am learning how to be independent. You would be proud of me now." I looked up to the heavens. "I hope you are all proud of me…"

///////////////

CHAPTER 16

The crisp chill of an early winter had, indeed, come. I crawled out from under the comforter, went to the window, and gazed out at the bright colors. The autumn leaves splashed spots of beauty over the neighborhood as the sun rose.

My soul was quiet. Mama's words melted into me, settling into my spirit like the warming harmonies of a sweet old hymn.

I knew now that I had let my fairytale of a forever take over, and I got burned…badly. I hadn't faced up to the reality that Jack was not the man I thought he was; I hadn't let myself believe it. By the time my dreams died, I was trapped, caged in the shadows. Through Mama's words, I understood that if your mind and feet weren't planted firmly in reality, dreaming could be dangerous.

During the bad years, I didn't take note of who that man had become. I had played in the sun like a little girl, twirling around and around without a care. But ignoring that needed reality check and my blind innocence had made me prey to the evil of the world, the kind that stalked and trapped those unaware.

I was at a crossroads again, this time in the very essence of who I was. I had my freedom from Jack, and a golden opportunity to walk into the sunlight eyes wide open, with feet planted firmly in my truth.

This time I wouldn't delude myself with a fairytale; I would work hard, setting my hands to the plow while soaking in the sunlight, both enjoying my independence and watching for the predator lurking with sweet promises that could snatch me back into the darkness. I would not get burned again... Never again.

Standing there contemplating the great, big, beautiful world, I realized that I had changed. I was neither the innocent dreamer nor the beaten down woman I once was. I was entirely disassociated from both versions of Alice Miles.

I would begin writing my story, as Sheila had mandated. I would also write a mandate to future generations—the chain would no longer surround the chest, but the priceless wisdom of the letters, the written words, would still remain under lock and key. For all future Kanes, it would now be their duty to read, reflect and write new letters of lessons they learned on their journeys. Though the chain would be broken and our daughters free—the legacy of leaving them with vital lesson would live on.

My name, my legacy, was Kane. And I was proud of it—black, white, all of it. I would own it. It was time to step out into the sunlight again—older, wiser. Brave.

———————————— ///////////// ————————————

Denise had been so patient and supportive with my working, and group meetings. It had left little time for us, so one day in November, I decided to make her a special dinner with the discount steak I'd gotten from the market. It was a rare treat.

I chopped peppers and onions to sauté and thanked God for the wonderful day; Thanksgiving was going to be wonderful this year, as Cadell had invited us over to her family's house.

I was feeling a renewed sense of purpose and contemplating where I should start in recounting my story to the next generation of Kanes as I bustled about the kitchen. There was certainly much to tell!

When the phone rang, I propped the receiver casually onto my shoulder and continued chopping. "Hello?"

"Alice? How are you, sweetheart?"

My heart stopped.

Jack?

"You there, sweetheart?"

"When did you wake up?" I was paralyzed. "Are you still in the hospital?"

"A little over a week ago," he said. His voice was calm. "I wanted to call, but…I didn't know what to say."

I didn't either. There was a long, uncomfortable pause. The only sound was that of blood rushing in my ears.

"How's Denise?"

My mind raced, and I leaned against the counter to help my body catch up. "She's fine." A canned answer, yes, but it would have to do.

"Listen, Alice, I'll be out of the hospital in another two weeks or so. I'd like to come by and—"

No way. I sobered up fast as that possibility struck me hard. Jack could not come back here—no matter what. "No, that won't be necessary."

"Alice, I really need to. You and Denise are all the family I've got." His voice sounded strained. "I…I love you both so very much."

I said nothing, but my breath caught in my chest. *Don't believe that!* my inner voice yelled.

"Alice, I am working hard on myself. I really am, honey. I've been going to therapy every day here at the hospital and talking to other people like me who want to change. It's called Alcoholics Anonymous. I'm learning how to talk through my problems, instead of blaming everyone else for my mistakes."

I steadied myself, pacing around the kitchen as Jack made his case. I hadn't been ready for this—not now. A war raged on in my mind and heart.

"I...it's helping me along," he continued. "You may not believe this, Alice, but...I've been going to the hospital chapel every day, too. I've asked God for forgiveness, to give me the strength to stop drinking, to be a better husband, a better father ...a better man."

God, how I wanted to believe him.

"Alice... Honey..." His voice was quiet, almost tender. "I know these problems can't be fixed in a day, but I am more than ready to work on them. I...I need you, baby. And I need to take care of both my girls and my grandchild and—"

"Jack, please..." My voice came out very small as I interrupted him.

"Honey, I lost control. What I did was terrible... And I... I know saying 'I'm sorry' doesn't make it better, but if you give me just one more chance, I will show you and Denise that I've changed and that we can move on."

"You tried to kill us!" I shrieked. The cold hard truth was that Jack had almost murdered me and Denise. Nothing he could say would change that. At least that's what I kept telling myself as I stood there listening.

There was a long, heartrending pause. Every little part of my soul was crying. I thought I had moved past it, past him, but hearing his voice again after all this time, I realized that I still loved him. Deep down, even with all that had happened, the reality was staring me in the face…

I still wanted a chance at redemption with him.

The static crackled as he sighed. "Alice, we had a good thing once."

A sob rose in my chest, and I covered the mouthpiece so he wouldn't hear.

"I'll admit that over the past few years, I've treated you badly, horrifically… But to outright kill my wife and daughter? No way. You're my girls. I know it sounds like a cheap excuse, but I had a mental breakdown, I'm sure of it. Even my doctor says it was a temporary mental break. Every time I remember how I hurt you both, it…it breaks my heart."

He took in a raspy breath.

Is he actually crying? I wondered.

"Sometimes I wish Denise had just killed me instead of putting me in that coma," he said. "But she didn't, and I think God spared me so I can make things up to you…to her."

Suddenly this didn't feel right. *Hang up!* my mind screamed. *Hang up* now!

"She doesn't want to see you," I managed to say. "Even the mention of your name frightens her."

Why am I still talking to him?

"But, Alice, I'm her father! I know I haven't acted like it," Jack implored, "but if you'll just give me this last chance, I'll prove to you that I can be the kind of father and husband you both deserve, honey."

I heard the pain in his voice. His heart was as truly scarred by what had happened as mine was. It seemed to be the real Jack who was talking to me, the one who disappeared for so many years behind all that anger. Tears burned my eyes, unbidden, mourning for the decent man he once was.

For a long time, I had hoped the man I had fallen in love with was still somewhere inside of him. Maybe he really was. But I couldn't risk it…even if it killed me to turn him away.

"I'm sorry, Jack," I said, finally getting a hold of my emotions. "You can't ever make this up to Denise. She's made it clear that she doesn't want anything to do with you."

"Yes, but—"

"She needs to focus on herself and her baby," I spoke right over him, "and we both are trying really hard to get our lives on track. That means not having you around."

"Alice—"

A rattling from the front door told me Denise was home. "I am finished talking to you!" I hissed into the phone, hoping she didn't hear.

"Honey, wait—!"

I slammed the receiver down, and as an afterthought, left it off the hook. I turned and nearly mowed over Denise as she came into the kitchen. Desperate, I tried to hide my guilt, but she knew me too well.

"Hi, honey, how was school?" I asked cheerily, turning back to the vegetables. I could feel my hands trembling, though I willed them to stay steady.

"Who was on the phone, Mom?" she asked me warily.

"Nobody important. How was school?"

"It was okay," she said, still eyeing me. "I felt a little nauseous on the way home."

"Let me get you the crackers," I said, perhaps a bit too hurriedly.

She didn't let me get away with it. "Mom, you're upset. Who was that on the phone? What's wrong?"

"Nothing, honey, everything's fine."

Denise's eyebrow rose. "If everything's fine, why is the phone off the hook? Why do you look like that?" Her eyes scrolled across the room looking for any abnormality. Then she paled. "Was that Dad on the phone? Oh my God, he's awake isn't he? Isn't he? Tell me!"

"Honey, calm down." She was panicking, and I grabbed her shoulders and forced her to look at me. "It was just the telephone company. I didn't pay the bill last month, and it's overdue. I'm going to take care of it."

She stared at me, and I stared right back.

"You sure that's all?" she asked, gradually calming.

"Yes, *Mother*," I teased with a quick rub to her stomach. "Now, can you please go and get comfy? Just relax, honey."

Denise smiled with relief, and I made myself smile back as normal as I could manage. But the smile drained from my face as she left and I hung up the receiver.

Jack was awake, and there wasn't anything that could stop him from coming home if he wanted. *Why didn't I file that claim against him? Or why don't I do it now?!*

I knew why—I didn't want to give up on him.

But it was impossible, I scolded myself, now that I knew he was awake, I had to start working on separating from him for good. It was time to seek legal help as soon as possible.

———————————— *///////////////* ————————————

Thanksgiving with Cadell's family was as sweet as I had hoped. Denise and I spent Christmas quietly at home, and it was so peaceful, exactly the way we wanted. Though we didn't have materialistic gifts, we had our new found freedom and rekindled friendships that were everything to us... something that no amount of money could buy.

With the help of the ACADA program, I had started an eight-week business/financial course at the local college at the beginning of the year. I finished the business course the last week of February with the highest grade in the class...just like Grandma Sheila. I was so proud of my accomplishment when I held my certificate in my hand; though it may not have meant much to the world, to me, it was everything. It was a symbol—I was not just surviving, but I was going after my independence one step at a time.

Since I'd met Gemma, she'd been so supportive and always gave me encouragement and continued to help after I received my certification. As it turned out, she was good friends with the hiring manager at American Way Bank and arranged an interview for me.

I was nervous that day, but as soon as my feet hit the cool tile of the bank's lobby, everything I had learned about interviewing from ACADA surfaced: stride in my step, head held high, big smile and a firm handshake. Why, I exuded confidence!

The following Wednesday when I got home from the diner, Mr. Riggans called and offered me the position. I was beyond thrilled. Mama's first job had been as a receptionist...and before too long, she was the manager. Could that happen to me? I was not discounting any possibilities.

There was a small hitch, however. He needed me to start Friday morning...so I had to tell Mr. Mulden I was leaving without any notice.

The next morning I went to the diner a half hour early to talk to him.

Mr. Mulden had been so good to me; I hated leaving him this way, but financially, this was the better choice. With a house to run and a grandbaby on the way, I was drowning on the meager waitress salary and odd sewing jobs. It wasn't an easy conversation, but Mr. Mulden was kind and told me he understood. The more difficult moment came a few minutes later after I fetched my apron for my last shift. As soon as I came out into the dining area, Mr. Mulden beckoned me over to a booth, asking me to bring the coffee pot for us both.

"Kinda quiet this morning, Alice. Should pick up soon," he said, sliding his cup closer so I could refill it.

I sat opposite of him and filled a mug for myself. He didn't look at me as he made general chitchat; instead, he looked out the window and focused on the people going into St. Matthew's Cathedral.

"They havin' special Mass at church this morning, for the ones that lost their boys in the war. Sad, you know. No matter what you think of war… Eh, truth is: men die. Some mothers, they never get to hug their son again."

I added sugar to my coffee and just listened, wondering where this was leading.

He took a heavy breath and placed an aging hand atop mine. "My daughter, she live in New York; her husband in the Army. I miss her so much, you know. I must go visit soon."

"I'm sure she would like that." I wondered if I should move my hand but left it under his gnarled fingers. It seemed he needed the contact—a comforting touch. "I'm sorry I have to leave the diner, really…"

He moved his hand and inhaled another deep breath. "It's fine, Alice, I tell you that," he said quietly. As if making a decision, he finally looked directly at me, and I saw real concern in his eyes.

"Alice…everyone in the neighborhood, they know about your husband, what happened to you. I would kill a *thousand* men for just raising their voice at my girl. I know you lost your mom and pop, too, but I'm sure your father, he feel the same way about you. Not a man's way to hit a lady. Not a real man…

"When you come in that door, looking for a job that day," he continued, "I was just so glad to see you *alive.* That's why I hire you. I remember your girl come in here sometimes… She sit in the back." He pointed. "That table over there. I fix her spaghetti all the time. Such a *bella ragazza.* She always give me that shy smile of hers, but never talk… Never talk."

I hadn't known that before. I felt a tear roll down my cheek, and Mr. Mulden handed me a napkin.

"No, no tears, *bella,*" he said sweetly. "What I try to say is your friend Mulden's here to help as long as you need. We…" he motioned to where his sons, Paulie and Anthony, stood talking behind the counter, "we not going to let anything bad happen to you again. You call us anytime, okay? *Seguire il tuo istinto.* Ah… what you say…?" He thought for a moment. "Instinct. Yes, you follow your instinct…You trust yourself, okay? You feel afraid, you no wait—you call right away, okay?"

I nodded slowly and smiled at him. He nodded once and scooted to the end of the booth, but I reached over and touched his arm, stopping him before he stood.

"Thank you."

"None of that now," he said, giving me his big Father-Christmas grin and a loving clamp on the shoulder. "Mulden always take care of *le sue ragazze.*"

The diner's front door opened just then, and an eager party of four came in. Mr. Mulden smiled down at me.

"Ready to go to work?"

After that, the stream of customers kept me busy enough to avoid dwelling on the fact that this was my last day. Still, I was glad that Mr. Mulden took the time to let me know there were men who would protect me if I needed them. Other than Daddy, I had forgotten chivalrous men existed.

Later that afternoon when things had settled down, I at last said my final goodbyes and left the diner, now feeling somewhat saddened. For the last few months, these people had sheltered me. I would still see them often, but I would miss the camaraderie and family-like atmosphere the place always offered. I was so excited to be moving forward with a better job at the bank, but walking away from this place was like closing an entire chapter of my life.

Though the air was frosty, I went across the street to the park to sit on a bench and think for a while. I mulled over the stories of my foremothers, which had helped me so much up to this point.

Mamie and Lily had never known the kindness and caring of a man like sweet Mr. Mulden, or the warm, tender embrace of a man like my Daddy. I thought about Claire, Nicole, and Sheila— all disappointed by their husbands. And Martha, my poor great-great-grandmother who had to resort to killing her husband to get a measure of freedom and safety for her children.

It just wasn't right.

"Why is life so hard for us?" I wondered aloud as I leaned back in the cool air and let the sunshine caress my face. "Is it just us Kane women, or are all women doomed to suffer like this?"

If on the rare occasion our husbands gave us leave, we held our own selves back and let the great, wide world scare us into a cowardly corner of fear and doubt. On the other hand, if we weren't raped or beaten by our men, we faced merely having baby after baby for them and being treated like possessions.

Why?

For some reason, an old memory that had been buried suddenly swept itself to the forefront of my mind.

Jack and I had gone to the movies that night. We even had a good time, something that had become so rare. As we were leaving the theater, I caught a glimpse of a strange man staring at me. Apparently Jack had noticed him, too.

We got in the car and I searched for something to say, trying to gauge Jack's mood. I started with the obvious.

"Did you like the movie?"

There was a long pause.

"It would've been better if you weren't acting like a slut."

My stomach twisted into a knot. After that pronouncement, Jack continued to mumble to himself. I knew in my gut I was in trouble; his violence had begun to escalate at this point in our lives, and I had to think of a way to diffuse his growing anger.

"Why, Alice?" he muttered, while parking the car in the front of our house. "Why do you keep testing me? Why do you keep doing things you know will upset me?" He started pounding the steering wheel to emphasize his words. "Why can't you be a *good—respectful—wife* instead of *such—a whore* all the time?" His voice rose. "*Why*, Alice? How could you *flirt—with—another— man? Right—in front of me?*"

"Jack, I...I didn't flirt with anyone. I swear I—"

Before I finished my sentence, he'd punched me on the side of my head and all went dark. The next thing I remembered was waking up alone in bed, wet and naked.

I snapped out of this miserable memory to find myself still sitting on the bench in the park across from *Mulden's*.

"Miss, are you okay?"

A distinct Spanish lilt interrupted my thoughts.

"Miss, do you need help?" The man speaking handed me a crisp white handkerchief.

I looked up at him, somewhat dazed; I hadn't realized I'd been crying. He had smooth, swarthy skin and dark chocolate eyes. Even in my distress, I couldn't help noticing his thick, beautiful eyelashes.

"Thank you," I said, wiping my eyes. "I'm fine, just thinking too hard, that's all." Now embarrassed, I attempted to hand back his now-soiled handkerchief.

"Oh, you keep it," he said.

"Are you sure?"

"Positive. My mother taught me to always keep a handkerchief handy; a beautiful woman may need one."

I smiled at his kind words and put the embroidered silk square in my purse. "Well, thank you, sir."

"Javier," he said. "And you are?"

"Alice."

"Nice to meet you, Alice."

"You too, Javier." I was blushing.

When I got up to leave, he asked, "Do you need a ride somewhere?"

"No thank you, I'm fine. Are you sure you don't want your hanky back? Its material is impressive, and I don't want your mother to think you didn't appreciate it."

Javier laughed. "I tell you what, you keep it in your purse, and if we ever meet again, you can give it back then. Okay?"

He smiled and so did I.

"Okay," I replied. "Enjoy the rest of your day."

"You too, Alice. You too."

CHAPTER 17

I started work at the bank that Friday morning, getting dressed in business attire and a full face of makeup. With Denise's help, I played with different hairstyles, including letting my sandy curls fall loose and free down my back. Denise said I looked like a different woman, and honestly, I felt different. I felt successful and steady.

I loved working at the bank. Not only did I work as the receptionist and have the opportunity to meet interesting people, I caught on quickly and began training as a teller. Within a week's time, I knew the procedures like I'd been doing them for years. I was so good at the job that Ms. Barton, my supervisor, made me a backup teller; I would cover the lead tellers during lunch hours, call-outs, or whenever needed.

Ms. Barton told me that I'd probably make it to full time teller someday if I kept up my hard work. As it turned out, her words were prophetic. When one of the tellers resigned, the bank promoted me to full time to take her place, just a month after I was hired! Mr. Riggins hated to move me so soon, but wished me well in my new position.

I couldn't wait to tell Denise about my promotion...and my raise. We laughed and giggled excitedly over dinner, but after a while, I noticed Denise had sobered.

"Denise? Honey, what's wrong? Did I say something to upset you?" I moved closer to her, ready to comfort, or apologize.

"No…" Tears formed in her eyes.

"Then what's wrong, sweetheart?"

"Nothing. I'm just happy to see you like this."

"Like what?" I asked. Her tears, I began to realize, were happy tears of joy, not the ever-present sorrow that had lingered about her in the past—she was smiling through her tears.

"I'm proud of how far you've come," she said. "I remember you always afraid and filled with worry, but now…"

Hugging her close, I whispered, "I'm glad you approve. Knowing that means so much; it makes the hard parts worth it."

She tilted her head up and lightly kissed my cheek. "Thanks, Mom, for everything."

"Thank you too, sweetie…for giving me another chance to be your mom."

My heart swelled as I held her. I finally had consequence; I no longer felt like a "waste of space," as Jack used to call me. He was wrong—and I had been wrong to believe him. Yet again, I clung to my resolution to stick to my guns and keep his ugliness and negativity out of my life.

That evening I couldn't wait to get to ACADA and tell everyone the good news. They were so excited for me, and Gemma so proud. I shared often now, becoming stronger and more assertive with each truth.

--- //////////////// ---

During the following weeks, Denise and I continued going to our little church. As our faith grew, we became more active and finally became official members. I worked in the women's ministry, and Denise helped in the youth group, teaching art. Our life grew into a comfortable pattern, with Denise in school and me at my new job during the day. On Sundays and Wednesdays, we had church, and of course I continued to attend ACADA, growing more confident and independent every day. Life was good; we were now just awaiting our little package, due to arrive in a few short months.

As Denise's stomach grew, so did her appetite, and I indulged her as often as I could. We were having dinner at *Mulden's* one night as a treat, ordering Denise's favorite dish of spaghetti and meatballs, when I glanced up and noticed Mr. Mulden signaling that he wished to talk to me. I excused myself from our chitchat with Sophia and Gabrielle, and approached him behind the counter. As I did, trepidation kicked in; his normal welcoming smile was nowhere in sight.

In a low, urgent voice, he told me that Jack had come in to eat earlier that week. "I no serve him," Mr. Mulden said vehemently, "and tell him he ever put his hands on you again, he get it back— from my own fist!" He nodded with emphasis.

"What did he say?" I asked, knots forming in my stomach.

Mr. Mulden pointed at his sons in the kitchen. "Don't worry, Alice; he understand completely. But I not like the look on his face. He not bother you, yes? You okay?"

"No, he hasn't bothered me," I replied, "and yes, I'm okay. Happy." I smiled to reassure him.

"Okay. But remember, he ever come to your door, you no open it. You call right away—I mean it, Alice. I no trust him!"

"Okay, I won't," I said. "Thank you for looking out for us. It means more than I can ever put into words." I kissed his cheek and prepared to return to our table.

"Eh, Paulie!" he bellowed across the diner. "You take Alice and Denise back when they done, see?" He looked back to me with obvious concern. "Stare attenti bello." At my puzzled expression, he repeated it in English. "Be careful, beautiful…"

At that moment, I could see my father's face in his.

I watched Denise closely the next morning as she headed down the walkway to school, Mr. Mulden's warnings echoing in my ears. When I heard the phone ring, my first thought was, *No one ever calls this early.*

"Hello?" I answered it.

"Hello, Alice."

His voice still made my breath catch.

"Alice, please don't hang up. Just give me five minutes, please."

"Jack, I can't talk now. I have to get ready for work."

"That's why I'm calling you, baby. I'm calling to tell you that you don't have to work at that bank anymore. I waited so long to call because I was trying to get myself together and…"

How does he know…? A chill surged through me.

"I've got a new job," he said. "It's paying me much better than the factory did."

"I'm happy for you, Jack," I said automatically, still reeling from the fact that he knew where I worked. "But that doesn't change anything."

"Um…honey," he hedged, "it's always been my job to take care of my family, and I want to do that now. I know you don't want me back at the house with you right away, and that's okay. I will do whatever it takes to…"

The rest of his words were lost in my growing anger. The chills from seconds earlier now felt like flames shooting through the top of my head.

"How do you know where I work?" I screeched. "Are you watching me?"

"No, Alice. I just happened to be going past the bank and saw you at your booth through the window…"

For a long moment, all I could do was stand there processing the fact that not only had he been watching me, but he also thought that he could move back into this house one day on good behavior. As Jack rambled on, his voice became more and more distant. In a surging moment of clarity, I heard my Grandma Sheila speak loud and clear above my confusion. *Remember my sacrifice, child! Your independence is important, Alice!*

Yes, Grandma, I thought, *I will never trade my newfound freedom for his imprisonment again.*

"Alice, sweetheart, are you still there?" Jack's voice brought me back to the present.

"*You* are a liar!" I exclaimed. "You can't see my booth from the window."

"Alice, please, honey. I'm worried about you. I—"
"It's not your job to worry about me anymore. You won't be living here again, you hear me? Never, Jack. Never again!"

I slammed the phone down. It rang again a few seconds later.

"Jack, no!"

"Alice—"

"Stop calling me! I swear if you call this house again, I'll call the police!"

Without another word, I slammed the phone down again, breathing heavily in my outrage.

When he didn't call back after a moment, I went to get dressed for work. Thinking further about Jack's call sent another eerie chill sweeping through me, and Gemma's words about safety came to mind. *"Follow your instincts,"* she always said. *"If that inner voice*

tells you to run—run. If it says to call for help—do that. Always,
always be aware of your surroundings."

"*You follow your instinct, bella…*" Mr. Mulden had said the
same thing.

Frantically, I looked out of my window, then went into
Denise's room to check outside hers. When I was about to leave,
I paused to put the double lock on the side door and check the
backyard. Lastly, I peeked out the window next to the front door.
Assured that all was well, I brimmed with pride having employed
things I'd learned from ACADA.

He didn't call back for few of months, and I hoped maybe I
had finally cauterized the last bits of my past. Maybe…

Either way, I spoke with Taneha, a girl from my group, later
that week, and she introduced me to her brother Jayden, an
attorney. He advised me to put together my finances and file for
a divorce soon as possible. I then began saving a little at a time,
determined that I'd be legally divorced from Jack one day.

—————————— *//////////////////* ——————————

Spring came and went, and in its place was a wonderfully
mild summer, full of bright skies and clear weather. I continued to
make and alter clothing for women around town, most of whom
wanted new sundresses for the warm days ahead.

I never told Denise about Jack's phone calls, and I didn't
regret it. We had been having so much fun while expecting the
baby's arrival, and I refused to ruin it for her. I enjoyed telling
her about the humorous things that happened at the bank and
learning of her school activities, and of course anticipating what
our baby would be like. We both got a kick out of my mimicking
Denise's walk, which had become a waddle, and the way she had
to rock four times before she rose from the sofa. It is always four

rocks—not three, not two, not five—always four. We determined that four must be her favorite number.

One sunny afternoon in June, while helping a customer, Mr. Riggans walked over and slipped me a note. *After you finish with this customer, grab your things, punch out, and come to my office.*

My first thought was that my good fortune had run out. I worried; maybe I made a mistake, or a customer had lodged a complaint against me. I offered the customer a final "Have a nice day," and put up my "Next Window Please" sign. This was it… *I was fired.* Nervously, I walked toward his office, rehearsing my apology the entire way.

"Sir, if I've done something wrong, if you could just find it in your heart to give me one more chance, I promise I—"

"Oh no," Mr. Riggans said, a smile on his usually stony face. "Calm down, Alice, nothing's wrong. Actually, everything's right: your daughter's having her baby! Bob is waiting outside to take you to the hospital."

"Oh my God!" I shrieked in excitement.

"Oh my God is right, and may He be with you through this blessed event."

"Thank you sir, thank you. I'm about to be a grandma!" With a gigantic smile, I left for the hospital as fast as I could.

I spent the next few hours pacing and praying. Finally, the doctor came out of the delivery room and informed me I had a healthy grandson. Before I could ask, he told me that I'd be able to visit mother and baby shortly.

A little boy… I wanted a girl. But it didn't matter; I was so excited wondering what my little grandson looked like. My hands itched to hold him as I waited, hoping that my baby girl didn't have too hard a time delivering him.

In my anticipation, I imagined what Mama and Daddy would've said. Knowing Mama, when Denise entered her last month, she would have made Daddy find a hotel room near us and been right by my side. This time, the thought of them made me laugh. It felt right remembering them as a new life entered our family.

I was so wrapped up in my own excitement, I almost didn't hear my name being called over the loudspeaker, followed by instructions to pick up the red courtesy phone in the waiting room. Assuming it was someone from the bank calling for an update, I ambled to the wall and spoke cheerfully into the mouthpiece.

"Hello? Doting grandma speaking."

"Hi, Alice," Jack said, and my happy mood evaporated.

"Jack? What are you *doing?*" I hissed. "How did you—"

"How is she?"

"How do you even know she's here?" I asked, glancing around the waiting room as if I might find him hiding behind a trashcan.

"A friend of mine saw Denise come in. I just want to know if she's okay."

A friend…? "She's fine," I answered.

"Good. Glad to hear it. After work, I was hoping to come up and visit the baby. I have something for Denise, too. I was wondering if you would ask her if it would be all right for me to stop by her room and—"

"Do you believe this is some sort of family healing moment, Jack?" I barked. "Denise isn't ready to see you. Don't ask. I realize that the hospital is a public place, so I can't stop you from coming here, but you'll just have to see *my* grandson through the nursery window like anyone else!"

He paused. "Will you take my number just in case?" He rattled it off.

"I have it," I said, pretending to scribble it on a sheet of paper. "If by some miracle she wants to see you, I'll let you know."

"Thanks." I could hear the disappointment in his voice. "How are you doing, Alice?"

"*I* am none of your concern. Goodbye."

I hung up and tried to rid my mind of him. *The nerve!* I couldn't believe he had tried *again*—and today of all days. I made myself replace his voice with images of kissing those little cheeks, changing diapers, and other ways in which I could spoil our new little one.

When the nurse gave me the okay, I headed to the nursery and peered through the glass at my precious grandson. He was so beautiful… I could already discern traces of my father's features on his tiny red face. I watched him through tears of joy until the nurse came to tell me I could visit Denise.

She looked so tired lying in the hospital bed: a navy blue blanket pulled up to her chest, eyes closed, her nape-length hair haphazardly pulled back. She stirred, her eyelids fluttering open. "Hey, Mom. Have you seen him yet?"

"Oh yes, sweetheart, and he is gorgeous."

"He is, isn't he?" Denise murmured, her eyelids drooped shut again. "Is it me, or does he look like Granddaddy?"

"You see it too? I thought the same thing when I saw him. Have you named him? We never settled on one…"

"No, I was waiting for you. But, now that you're here, how does Derek James Whitmore, Jr. sound?" she said, stretching each syllable as if to try them out. "We can call him D.J. for short. Isn't that the cutest? What do you think?"

"Oh, honey, that's a great name. Your grandfather would be honored. But what about Miles?"

"What about it?" she said with heated sarcasm.

"Honey, your name is Miles. Don't you want him to have your name?"

"No way! As a matter of fact, when I get old enough, I'm going to change mine too, and so should you. We don't want anything from *him*..."

"But, Denise—"

"No, Mom, he's my baby and I get to name him. I refuse to curse him with the name Miles."

She stared me down, and I said nothing else.

"Derek James Whitmore, Junior... D.J." Denise said the name again, and I smiled at her. "That's his name. And it's beautiful, just like him—just like Granddaddy was."

We chatted a bit more about the baby and how my parents would have loved him. I promised not to spoil him—too much—and she laughed at that. We talked until she drifted off into a tired slumber, and then I went back to the nursery.

The nurse invited me to hold my grandson for the first time. Derek peered up at me, squirming in his swaddled blue blanket. Then he cooed. I couldn't take my eyes away from his precious little face and wisps of dark hair. As I caressed his tiny nose and touched my finger to his cheek, he closed his eyes in the seamless way of newborns and fell asleep in my arms. After giving him back to the nurse, I went home to put down my thoughts about this wonderful day in my book.

———————— //////////////// ————————

After work the next day, I found Denise sitting up in bed, smiling as she gave Derek his bottle. "Look at your grandson, Mom. He's so greedy," she said.

"Yes, just like his mother when she was born," I teased, pulling up a green plastic chair. While Derek took his bottle, we talked about inconsequential things like baby clothing, the color of his eyes, and how perfect his tiny fingers were. Denise was fascinated with her son, as was I. I told her how watching her with Derek took me back to when she was born.

"No matter what was wrong in the world, honey," I said, "when I looked into your eyes, everything that had to do with you made sense."

"I know, Mom, that's how I feel too. Just perfect." She smiled again and leaned back into her pillows.

"Everything *is* perfect, baby. But, um…there's something I need to tell you." I had wrestled with myself all night on whether or not I should tell her. But I knew I couldn't avoid the subject forever. "Your father called here yesterday."

Her eyes snapped open, and she paled.

"I don't know how he found out you were here," I continued, doing my best to stay calm so as not to panic her. "I don't know why he thinks it is okay to even ask. But, he was hoping he could come—"

"No! No, Mom, I thought we agreed!" Denise shook her head frantically. "I don't want him anywhere near D.J. or me! I didn't even know he was awake. Why didn't you tell me?"

"Honey, because I didn't want you to worry and make yourself sick."

She ignored that. "How long has he been awake? Have you seen him? Where is he?"

"He's been awake a few months, honey, but no, I haven't seen him. Until now he's stayed away. He just wants to see Derek—"

"I said no, Mom. He can't see my baby!" She held him tight against her body, so much so he woke and started to fuss.

"All right, sweetie," I stood and came to her side, gently easing her tight arms and shoulders down again. "Listen, I don't want to see him any more than you do, but the hospital is a public place. I don't think they'll stop him from looking in the nursery."

She adjusted the little hat on her son's head, anxiously fidgeting. "Can't you call the police or something?"

"Honey, let's think: what could I tell them? That your father, who we haven't seen in seven months, wants to get a peek at his first grandchild through the nursery window? They can't stop him from doing that, sweetie."

"What about that order you signed? He's not supposed to be near us, or he can go to jail, right? Doesn't that cover Derek too?"

Denise can't handle this right now, I thought, stroking the baby's head to quiet him. *I can't tell her I never signed that* order. So I lied…again.

How did I keep putting myself into this position?

"Honey, that doesn't apply to the hospital, or at least I don't think it does. Now if we were home, that's different. Understand? But I don't believe he would do anything to hurt the baby, honey. He just wants to look at him."

"Why?" she said, lowering her head in defeat.

I felt terrible for bringing her low, but couldn't fathom what else to do. "I'll call Gemma and ask if there is something we can do while Derek is here," I said. "But in the meantime, honey, the baby is safe. There are lots of people and security officers walking around."

After mulling it over a minute, she said, "Okay, I guess… just keep him away from me. And, Mom, please tell the nurses if he comes, he can look, but he *cannot* touch. He is definitely not going to hold him—he stays on the other side of the glass."

"Now that I can do," I said. "I'll be right back."

I kissed her forehead and went to find the nurse to explain our circumstances. I felt better when the nurse said they often had situations similar to ours, and if Jack did show up, he would not be allowed into the nursery.

When I got back to the room, Denise was asleep, and the nurse was wrapping Derek up to wheel him back to the nursery. I kissed her and the baby goodbye and went across the street to the café for a bite to eat before heading to ACADA.

Staring down at my plate, I was frustrated when my thoughts turned from baby Derek to Jack. Pushing French fries around with my fork, I began to replay our life together. I remembered all the cruel things he used to do, like mashing his lit cigarettes out on my wrist because I politely mentioned that the smoke was bothering me. Or the day I walked into the house with groceries and Jack was sitting at the table in front of an empty plate with a fork in his hand. He had come home three hours early, but when I put the bags on the table, he leaped up and jabbed me in the arm with the fork, screaming, "Why isn't dinner ready, woman?"

I now rubbed the place where the fork had entered my skin. "Yep," I said under my breath, "he's done all kinds of mean things… But why? I still don't understand why."

I exhaled and took a bite of my tuna salad sandwich, enjoying the crunch of the onions and celery. It reminded me of the way Aunt Blondell made it. I did miss her. Before Mama and Papa died, I was too embarrassed to talk to her.

Since then, things had changed, and now we tried to catch up on the phone every few months. Since I started reading my family's history, it seemed everything reminded me of their importance. I decided that once I became eligible for a vacation at the bank, Denise and I would go to Beaufort for a visit; maybe we would even make our way to New York and visit Aunt Blondell and Uncle Clayton. We were never able to do those things before, and the idea excited me. After all, we had to show off Derek Junior.

I grabbed a napkin and began scribbling out our travel plans, but then a voice broke into my thoughts.

"Alice, do you mind if I sit?"

Time seemed to stop, and my heart stuttered. I looked up at him for the first time since he'd tried to kill my daughter and me.

He looked older—but at the same time, healthier, more pulled together. Perfectly sober and calm, the way he used to. He even had on glasses, which he hadn't worn in years. I tried to contain my emotions.

"You want to sit here with me? And if I say I do mind, would you listen?"

He stared remorsefully at the floor, guilt written all over his very familiar face.

Not wanting to cause a scene, I waved my hand at the chair across from me.

"Thanks," he said and slid into the booth. "How's Denise?"

"She's fine." Instead of meeting his eyes, I watched a little boy at the other end of the diner throwing a tantrum.

"That's good," Jack said, somewhat distracted. "I just got off work, and since I didn't hear back from you, I figured I would try to sneak a peek at the baby."

"Do what you want, Jack, but you're not getting anywhere near Denise, you understand me?"

I slid a few dollars under my plate and stood to go, but before I could take two steps, I was stopped by the heartbreak in Jack's voice.

"Alice…please wait. You're my *wife*…" He said it so low that I had to strain to hear.

I turned on him, shoving my face into his. "Since when did that matter, Jack? You never cared about that." My rage snapped, and the old hurt surfaced. "Why don't you try that sweet stuff with *Karen?*"

Jack looked surprised, but I marched away without as much as a backward glance. I did my best not to flinch when I heard a sob catch in his throat.

CHAPTER 18

The following day, my coworkers surprised me at lunch; instead of our usual Friday potluck, they showered me with gifts for Derek and Denise. Then one of the girls gave me the number for her beautician and said, "Alice, this is for you. After playing nurse and grandmother extraordinaire, you're going to need someone to make you all beautiful again!" I laughed at that, knowing how right she was.

I took one gift to the hospital with me that evening: a lovely navy blue outfit that would be adorable on Derek. Not paying attention, I almost collided with an attendant while coming out of the elevator. Amidst the apologies, I caught a glimpse of Jack down the hall, smiling and peering into the nursery window as if he hadn't tried to beat that little boy out of Denise's tummy.

Before he took notice of me, I turned around and started to ease away, though part of me wanted to beat *him* out of the hospital. I reminded myself that looking through the nursery window was not a crime, though. I did my best to put Jack's presence out of my mind and went to visit with Denise. Later when I was leaving to go home, a nurse pulled me aside.

"Derek's grandfather is here right now, Mrs. Miles," she whispered

My lips went tight. "I know, I saw him at the nursery when I came in. Thank you for telling me. I really appreciate your not saying anything in front of Denise."

That Saturday I slept in a little later than usual, having had a restless night. I wasn't really surprised to see Jack at the nursery window again when I arrived. I *was* surprised when I saw tears coursing down his cheeks…and it was my undoing.

Against my better judgment, I went to stand next to him to look at our grandson.

Jack quickly brushed his tears away. "He looks like your dad," he said, voice gruff.

"You see it too, huh? Yes, he does," I whispered, staring at little Derek intently. "Just like my father."

I had no intention of carrying on a conversation. But before I could stop myself, I said, "I wish Daddy was here to see him."

I felt Jack turn a bit more toward me. I still didn't move.

"I'm sorry, Alice."

I nodded absently. "Yes…so am I."

He shifted again and leaned one shoulder up against the window, continuing to stare down at me. "When will they be leaving the hospital?"

My guard was back up. "Why, Jack?" I snapped, finally turning to face him squarely. "Denise isn't going to let you touch him, so why does it matter to you?"

He appeared surprised by my outburst and quickly explained. "I didn't mean anything by it. I just didn't want to come to visit and him not be here—that's all."

Reluctantly, I groused. "Sunday. Tomorrow afternoon."

"Great, I'll be sure to come by early tomorrow, then." He looked back through the window, leaning his forehead casually against it. After a moment of silence, he straightened up and gestured to Derek's crib.

"You know, I've been standing here admiring our grandson every day, but this is the first time I noticed his last name isn't Miles." He started to clean his glasses on his shirt, trying to be casual.

"Sorry, Jack. It was Denise's decision."

I reminded myself that this entire mess was his doing, but he looked so dejected that I couldn't help feeling a little sorry for him.

"Would you like to get some coffee?" I blurted out.

Where did that come from?

He looked like I felt—stunned. "What?" he asked.

"Uh…the café across the street. Want to get coffee?" I swear I had no idea why I did it; I had nearly chased him out of there yesterday.

He looked at me for a long moment, then pocketed his glasses and offered a hint of a smile. "Thanks. I'd love some."

I walked in front of him down the corridor, steps quick and purposeful, all the while chiding myself and ranting. *This is stupid, Alice! What are you thinking? This man* cheated *on you! He almost* killed *you!*

But Jack honestly seemed broken up about Denise's rejection, I reasoned, and I determined that it was my responsibility to make sure he understood why it had to be this way…and keep my personal feelings out of it. Halfway there, I concluded that at least I had positioned myself to be in control of the situation.

In the café I instinctively knew how he would take his coffee: extra hot with two sugars, no cream. I ordered mine black. For several moments I sat wordlessly staring into my cup, unsure of what to say. Jack didn't deserve my sympathy or my kindness, but here we were. I wondered if he even recognized the woman sitting in front of him; I had changed so much… Even the way I dressed was entirely different from the frazzled housewife he had beaten for all those years, or the naïve young girl he had married so long ago.

I pushed the thoughts away and took a bracing breath. *Keep focused on Denise...* I told myself.

"Jack, it's going to take time for Denise to forgive you."

"Do you really think she will forgive me?" he said, as if he had been given a reprieve.

"You're her father, and nothing can change that," I admitted. "But the past haunts her. For months, she's had nothing but time to think about everything you put us through, and it's turned her sour. It's also made her extremely tough."

My voice grew more and more resolute the longer I spoke. I found I could look him full in the face and not feel intimidated.

"I mean, really, Jack—there's no way to sugar coat it. This child watched you beat her mother most of her life. Do you realize what that does to a *little girl?* And now she's a mother herself. She's angry, and she's protective of both her baby and of me. She *doesn't* want you around...*at all!*"

Though Jack kept his eyes on the table, I knew he was listening. In fact, he was hanging on my every word as if what I said actually mattered.

"I understand that," he said, his voice tight, "and I accept it. I'll never forgive myself for what I did. Not ever."

He clenched his jaw, fighting not to break down.

"If you don't mind my asking..." He paused, and then quickly interjected, "You don't have to answer, but I still would like to ask."

My stomach clenched, but I kept a neutral tone. "Yes?"

He looked directly up at me, and I could see—*What was it... trepidation?*—in those bright green eyes, a vulnerability that I had never seen in him before.

"You said it will take time for Denise to forgive me, but what about you? After all the mistakes I've made—after what I did that night, and…Karen—do you think you might ever somehow find it in your heart to forgive me, too?"

I hadn't realized it until he asked. The answer shocked me.

My voice was strong when I answered. "I've already forgiven you, Jack. I had to forgive you in order to heal and move on."

Jack straightened in his chair, a look of eagerness in his still handsome face. "Does that mean *maybe* we could still have a future?"

Not ever, I thought. My hands tightened around my coffee mug as I willed myself to speak calmly. I didn't want to break him anymore than I had to; it was obvious he was hurting so much.

"Jack…I realize that it hasn't been very long since we separated. But for me, it seems like a lifetime ago. I've changed a lot and view things much differently now. I'm no longer the person who needs your approval to feel good about herself. In fact, I've been doing well without you."

He took in a ragged breath and blinked quickly a few times. "Honey, I have to believe that one day we'll be a family again," he said. "I'll die if I lose that hope."

"Then you might as well stop breathing right now, Jack." My tone was more hostile than I intended, but I wasn't going to stay silent anymore. "I am *not* going to allow you to guilt me into telling you what you want to hear. I don't know what the future holds, but I *do* know that I will never live like that again. You were horrible, Jack, just horrible. You degraded and made me feel worthless every chance you got. You beat me, locked me up for days on end. There were times I didn't even eat. Even in jail they bring you food but you…brought women into *my* house—

you cheated on me with *my friend*—and had no remorse about any of it!"

"Alice, I am so sor—"

"Shut *up*, Jack! I've had enough. You are *not* the martyr here—not today, not ever, so you listen good. For years, I thought your pain, your frustration was my fault, but now I know that it's not and it never was. I was a good, faithful, *loving* wife to you. And to support your dream, I uprooted myself and moved away from my family just so you could drag me into this hell."

I was shaking in anger now. "You blamed me for every financial problem you had, but the money and materialistic things were never important to me. *You* were. I was so in love with you that I would have lived in a cardboard box if you'd asked me to, as long as we were together. But instead, you took my love for granted. You abused it. Well, sir, it's over now, and there's no turning back. So whatever you're concocting in that twisted mind of yours, forget it."

I could barely keep from screaming at him. Only my grip on the table's edge kept me from completely losing my composure.

"You made me hurt our daughter, too, just as much as you hurt me! Our daughter, Jack! You kept me in that room like a pet, and I kept her in that house when I should have done what my Daddy wanted and gone home!"

I stopped and took a large, painful breath. I was trembling in rage and release, and I had no doubt he had really heard me; tears were streaming down both of his weathered cheeks, and he shielded his face from the other customers in embarrassment.

In my anger, I had leaned in closer and closer to him and now checked myself, noticing one or two heads glancing over at our table. I sat back and took another swallow of air to help regain control of myself.

"I can forgive you, Jack, but I can't forget," I said, quieter but with no less emphasis. "There will never be a future between us. Never. I will live my life, away from every vile half-breed name and kick and rape you ever put me through. Understand?"

He was quiet, his sobs soft and low. No anger or retaliation. Just brokenness.

"Alice, I don't know *what* to say…"

"I do." I stood up, opened my purse, and slapped a couple of bills to the table. "Here you go, Jack…the coffee's on me."

For the second time in as many days, I turned my back on him and marched out the door, leaving him with only his misery for company.

———————————— //////////////// ————————————

When I entered the hospital a few minutes later, I headed straight to the ladies' room to splash water on my face. I took a few ragged breaths to calm my racing heart, but celebrated the fact I had not given Jack permission to control what I said, what I thought, or how I felt. Critiquing my part of our conversation, I believed that I'd become the woman Mama raised me to be—and the mother Denise had always needed.

Victorious, I freshened my makeup and went to Denise's room. She was lying in bed with her breakfast tray in front of her, looking healthier than ever. She didn't smile back at me when I entered, though.

Her brows knit. "Where were you, Mom? Your eyes are red. What happened?"

"Oh, nothing. I'm fine." I wiped at them, now self-conscious.

"No, you're not," she insisted, a bit terse. "What happened?'

"Denise, I'm all right."

She sat up straight and stared me down. "Mom…a nurse told me she saw you having coffee with Dad. I thought I'd give you the chance to tell me the truth yourself, but I guess you just can't do it." She glared at me, her jaw set.

"Honey, I didn't mean to—"

"Don't, Mom! I can't take it! I won't take it anymore!" she said. She pushed her tray aside and turned away from me, dangling her legs over the side of her bed. I could see her shaking, trying not to cry aloud.

I knew what she was thinking, and I felt terrible. I had meant to protect her, not hurt or scare her.

"Honey, honey, no…" I came around to the other side of the bed to face her. "It's nothing like that, I promise."

"You're seeing him again! If you aren't, why did you lie for him?"

"Baby, calm down and I'll tell you the truth, okay? Honest to God."

I put my hands on her shoulders, and she waited.

"I did talk to him. He tried to apologize for everything, but instead I told him exactly how you and I both felt. Now that I've gotten it all out, I don't intend to see him or speak to him again… and he will never set foot in our house." I put my hand under her chin to make sure she didn't look away. "Okay, sweetie? I promise you, he never will. That's what I told him, and that's the truth. Please, you have to trust me. We've been doing so well. Okay?"

Denise held my gaze, but her face softened.

"You mean that, don't you?"

"Yes, honey. I do." I kissed her forehead gently. "Nothing will come between us ever again, okay? I love you."

A tense moment later, she leaned in and gave me a tight squeeze, and I could feel the relief in her body. "I love you too, Mom."

"You get some rest now," I said. "I'm going to hold Derek for a while, then head home. See you in the morning."

"No, wait…" She didn't let go of my hand.

"Denise, if you keep getting agitated, you're going to make yourself sick, sweetie."

"I'm okay, there's…there's some stuff I need to ask you. After that, I'll rest."

"Okay…" I braced myself. I knew that this was a step Denise needed to take; she processed things so much differently than I did. I had been growing strong and into a different woman, but I needed to help her to do the same. "What is it, honey?"

She bit her lip. I gazed at her, knowing my little girl was purposefully stepping into a place of insecurity and fear in order to ask these questions, and my heart swelled in pride.

"Okay…one," she said, "why didn't you take me to Grandma and Granddaddy's funeral?"

I answered her with complete truth. "Your father wouldn't let me. Keeping you home was his way of making sure I'd come back."

Denise looked at me in full understanding and nodded.

"Okay, two," she continued, "why did Grandma and Granddaddy leave that Christmas morning like that?"

I shook my head at the memory. "Daddy got into a tussle with your father, and he put them both out."

"They had a *fight*?" The hurt in Denise's face was unbearable. I could sense from her tense body and balled fists she didn't want to be touched. She was processing in her own way, and I simply waited for her to speak when she was ready.

"Did Dad hurt him?"

I sighed. "Not badly, but enough that Daddy had no choice but to leave. I think Jack hurt Daddy's pride more than anything. It was a bad night, honey…"

A single, angry tear slid down Denise's face, but she continued. "Last one," she said, voice shaking. She looked me squarely in the eyes, and I hoped that for her sake I could answer this next question with as much straightforwardness and courage as I had the others.

"I remember a few years ago, before that Christmas..." she said. "You were, I don't know...happier than you had been in a long time. And Dad quit being so mean, at least for a little while. Well...I mean he didn't hit you as much. You didn't say anything to me, but you were humming lullabies a lot, and I saw you looking through my baby clothes a couple times."

My heart plummeted. I knew what she was going to ask.

Denise bit her lip. "And then lullabies stopped. You got sad again, and...you stopped humming. I liked seeing you like that... What happened, Mom? Why were you so happy, and why did it stop all of a sudden?"

I sighed and swallowed back the emotions that usually came with this memory. I had shared a lot with my ACADA group, but this was something that I could only share with one person—my little girl.

"I was pregnant, honey. Believe me, it wasn't intentional, but...it happened, and I was really hoping it was going to help things. You know, make your father wake up and see what he was doing to us. But...it only helped a little for a couple weeks. He got mad one night, like he always did, and beat me pretty badly. The next morning after you left for school, I began bleeding, and Mrs. Thornton took me to the hospital." I paused for a steadying breath. "Then I came home and rested. That was it."

Surprisingly, I wasn't sad or scared or even emotional as I told her what happened, my words almost mechanical. It wasn't from lack of sorrow over the loss of my other child, but I had buried the pain and recriminations. The new Alice could now reopen that wound and look at it without fear or devastation. This Alice was strong enough to talk about her pain and see the truth…not the lies that Jack had heaped upon her old self.

Another tear slid down Denise's cheek, and I hugged her like never before. I couldn't stand to see her so sorrowful.

"You have any more questions, honey?" I asked, but she shook her head no. "I love you, baby. No more lies, okay? Now, I'm going to go, but you have to promise to get some rest. I want nothing more than to have you both home with me." I smiled, trying to brighten her mood. "I'm getting lonely at home!"

"Thanks for your honesty, Mom," she replied.

"You're welcome, honey. It felt good to get it out."

As I headed for the door, I thought about the conversation I had had with Jack and turned back toward her. "Denise, I know you didn't want me to see your father, but I had to. I had so much to get off of my chest. You would've been so proud of your old mom." I grinned. "I gave him a piece of my mind. And guess what?"

"What?" She looked at me in eager expectation.

"On top of everything else, I looked him in the eye, and told him to shut up! I even threw the money on the table to pay for the coffee and walked out on him. Boy, was it liberating!"

"I'm sure," she replied. We both laughed. Even the nurse who came in on the tail end of the story snickered. With that, I headed to the nursery.

I held my little Derek for a while and told him a story about his great-granddad, King Derek the First, who hunted schools of fish and sea creatures in the lake behind his beautiful palace, in the great golden city known as Beaufort.

///////////////

When Denise and Derek were released from the hospital the next day, we arrived home to balloons festooning the kitchen. A banner with "Congratulations!" on it draped above the doorframe, and an iced cake with "Welcome Home, Derek" in large, baby blue sugar swirls waited on the table.

Denise squealed. "Mom! Thanks so much for the cake and the balloons! Even D.J. loves them. See he's smiling." She stroked the top of her baby boy's head.

"You're welcome," I replied, feigning a smile. I was in total shock. As Denise went forward, I coolly backed up into the hall and peeked into the living room to see if Jack was there. *Why didn't I think to change the locks?!* I was sure Jack was the one who had intruded and set this up. Although infuriated, I plastered a smile on my face. I would not allow him to ruin Denise's homecoming.

What really had me most livid was that I'd told Jack when Denise and the baby were coming home, and he had used that information to intrude in our lives—which told me he hadn't changed. Not in the way that mattered; he still didn't respect my boundaries.

Denise went upstairs to get the baby settled before we ate lunch. A few seconds after reaching her room, I heard another squeal of joy. Though I had no idea what she'd found, I assumed it was another gift from Jack. I went upstairs to find more balloons, a big teddy bear, a rocking chair, and a crib. The crib held a baby blanket, sheets, and at least five more stuffed animals!

"Oh, Mom…I love it all," Denise said, gliding her hand across the fabrics and polished wood.

That was it. I had to get the rest of the money even if that meant I had to borrow it from someone. Jack's interruptions in our lives were over.

"I am glad you like everything," I said, trying to keep my composure. I was infuriated, both with Jack and myself. I was displeased and steaming that Jack would be so invasive...yet at the same time, I no longer had the pressure to come up with the money for these things. All I'd been able to buy so far was a bassinette, diapers, and bottles—the other items beyond Jack's gifts had come from the ladies at ACADA, work, and church.

I never would have imagined Jack thought enough about Derek to do all this. How did he even know what she still needed?

I forced a smile and looked at my daughter. "Now, get yourself and Derek settled and comfortable, okay?"

Before going downstairs, I checked my bedroom to see if anything was out of place. Although nothing seemed amiss, I was uncomfortable knowing Jack had more than likely been through my things.

While fixing lunch, my thoughts turned to more practical matters, like how much more this dear baby would cost. Derek would grow fast, and his needs would grow right along with him. Absently, I wiped my hands on my apron and headed outside to check the mailbox. Sifting through two expected bills and an advertisement, I found an envelope addressed to me with no postmark. The handwriting was familiar.

> Dear Alice,
>   Here is one hundred dollars. I hope the money and the stuff for Denise & Derek will help some. All my love,
>   Jack

"Lord, you never cease to amaze me..." The prayer came unbidden from my lips." You know our needs and always supply.

I needed sixty dollars more to get the divorce paperwork started, and you have blessed me with that plus some, from a source that I wouldn't have thought possible."

Torn inside but knowing what must be done, I clenched the envelope to my chest and held my head down in total homage to God. "Thank you, Lord, for always, always taking care of me... of us."

/////////////////////

CHAPTER 19

About a week after Denise and Derek came home, I was at lunch with some of the girls from work when Jack came strolling in. "Good afternoon, ladies," he said, pouring on the charm.

His unexpected presence froze me in place.

"Jack, what are you doing here?" I asked, with a feigned smile. I didn't want to raise any suspicions with my new friends and coworkers.

"Hi, Alice. Can I please speak to you outside? It'll only take a minute." He smiled.

Every bone in me wanted to refuse, but I agreed and excused myself. As soon as we got outside, I rounded on him.

"Are you following me?"

His charm immediately dissipated, and he shoved his hands into his pants pockets, looking embarrassed. "No, Alice. I'm not, I—"

"How'd you know I was here, then?"

"I went into the bank, and one of the girls told me you all were here. I wasn't being sneaky. I needed to talk to you for a minute, that's all."

"It's invasive. And how dare you, Jack?" I got heated. "You had no right to come into our home like you did! I have every mind to call the police on you, do you understand that? You didn't bother to tell me you were buying Denise anything. And what the hell were you doing sneaking in to deliver it?"

I was so angry I had to remember where I was. I looked around quickly, noting a few people passing us on the other side of the street. *Calm, nice and steady, Alice*, I chided myself. *Controlled, like you were before.*

He scraped at the sidewalk with his shoe, eyes averted. "I'm sorry, Alice. I just wanted to help."

His plaintive words were so sincere that my indignation deflated. It seemed that Jack really was trying to make life easier for us as best he knew how, considering the current situation.

I exhaled. "Okay, Jack. I'll let it go this one time. But if you ever pull something like that again, I will report you, and I won't feel bad doing it."

He said nothing and seemed to shrink in front of me.

"Now, I have to get back. My lunch is almost up."

"Could I, uh…" He gestured for me to wait. "I was wondering if I could…you know, see Derek?"

"Denise is not going to let that happen."

"Alice, please. I—"

"No. She and the baby are just settling in, and she hasn't changed her mind about you. I'm not sure she will."

He winced, pained. "I was hoping you could try to talk to her, Alice. I love her so much, and the baby, too. I need to be in their lives."

"If you love them like you say, Jack, you'll give her time and space. You don't want to scare her, do you?"

"Of course not."

"Be patient, then."

"For how long?"

Probably forever, I thought.

"However long it takes. You almost *killed* her; so she may need a little more time to forget that," I said sarcastically. "You can't rush healing, Jack, and she needs to heal. So please, leave us alone for now."

"But, Alice—"

"But nothing!" I snapped. "If you love her, you'll leave us alone. Show her you love her by not being selfish and talking just about your wants and needs for a change. Respect what she needs…what *I* need. This is not about you. Can't you understand that?"

This was his test, his gauntlet. If he could do this, maybe— just maybe—I would believe that he had changed.

"Give me your number," I said, relenting somewhat when he didn't reply, "and if anything changes, you'll be the first to know."

He nodded, and handed me a business card with his number on it.

"Alice…" He bit his lip, as if afraid to tell me something. "I…I haven't seen Karen again. And I don't intend to, either. And I…I'm sorry. For everything." He shoved his hands back in his pockets and turned away without another word.

I watched him for a moment, then glanced down at the card—apparently he was working for a local garbage company. A far cry from the world of fighter jets and engines and adventures that he…*we* had once set our sights upon.

———— /////////////// ————

Since Derek arrived, we made many changes. Densie transferred to night school and either I or Mrs. Page, our neighbor, would keep him.

My divorce papers had arrived and only needed my signature and consent to serve Jack for his. I could finally take legal action against him.

Going through the paperwork, though, I mulled over if I should sign and send them back right away. Jack was causing no harm—not to mention his financial contribution, without which we would be in serious trouble.

I decided to wait. I put the papers back in the envelope and stashed them in my dresser drawer. If anything were to go wrong, they'd be waiting for me—my insurance policy against him.

Since Derek arrived, we made many changes. Densie transferred to night school and either I or Mrs. Page, our neighbor, would keep him.

Denise was a good mom; parenting D.J. had matured her. She was extremely attentive to him and had already learned all of his signals. When he was hungry, he cried and sucked his little fist; when he wanted to be held, he tried to roll himself from side to side and made a whimpering sound. He was full of personality, and people noticed it right away—though he didn't particularly care for people other than us.

Part of me had wanted a little girl for Denise, of course, but I wouldn't have traded my Derek for anything, and I knew Denise felt the same way. Her protective instincts were incredible, natural, and so fascinating to watch. When I shared my self-defense class from ACADA with her, Denise was intrigued by what she saw, and I became her instructor, teaching her the basic moves I'd mastered. It was heart-warming to see how her protective instincts had roared to the surface, just as mine had when I first had her. She gobbled up every instruction I gave, and we had more fun practicing with each other than was probably fitting for what we were doing.

Unfortunately, those carefree days were short-lived. One Friday afternoon in August, Mr. Riggans called me into his office at the bank and informed me I was being laid off.

He made it very clear that it was because of budget cuts and not my performance. The receptionist he had hired when I was promoted was also being let go. "Today is your last day," he said soberly. "I'm sorry it's such short notice, but I don't have a choice. It's protocol, Alice. Please understand."

I told him I did, even though I felt like the world had just collapsed around me. We had come so far…and had many more expenses and bills now with the baby. I was grateful that as a parting gift, Mr. Riggans gave me an extra sixty days' pay and an impeccable recommendation letter, yet all I could see was my forward momentum coming to a screeching halt.

I shook Mr. Riggans's hand and collected my things without much fanfare, but on my way home, I feverishly thought about how I would make it with a sixteen-year-old daughter and two-month-old grandson after the extra ran out. I still sewed on the side and could work on getting more business, but it would take time to drum up new clients. And, even with that and Jack's contributions, it still would not be enough to cover everything.

What was I going to do?

When I got home, I was drained. I didn't panic, but neither was I confident that everything would be fine. Sixty days… My emotions were in a state of flux; I loved working, but I was so tired of having to provide for us all on my own. I regretted feeling that way and tried to push it aside, but the lingering fatigue weighed on me. The tenacity that I had harnessed only a few short months ago was now nowhere to be found within me.

This is why so many of us failed, isn't it, Mama? I thought, thinking through the many Kane women who had tried to rid themselves of their burdens, only to sink farther under them. Breaking the chain around your life was hard…harder than anything I had ever done. Especially since I was on my own. I had Denise and Derek, of course; they were what kept me going every day. And the Lord had been faithful to provide friends and church members to encourage me… But at the end of the day, I was still alone with responsibilities that laid heavily on me. No one to emotionally help me shoulder the burden.

I was still much alone *inside*.

The phone's ringing broke into my oppressive thoughts, and I absently went to answer it. I had barely got out "Hello?" when Jack's excited voice rushed into my ears. For some reason, it didn't really surprise me this time.

He was overjoyed about his new job in the airport's mechanical department. I really didn't hear the words so much as the voice. The voice I once thought was music to my very soul. He kept going on about how hard it had been for him to stay away and that he really wanted me to know that he loved Denise—and me—enough to do as I had asked.

"I…I really do love you both, Alice," he said, almost child-like. "And I…I hope you're able to find it in your heart to show enough mercy to let me at least *see* my grandson…even for two minutes."

"Jack, what if Denise had answered? Huh?" I didn't have much strength to deal with him right now, and replied with only a watered-down anger. "Then what?"

"I would have hung up," he said. "But I know she's not there because she's in night school with my friend McGainey's daughter. That's the only reason I took the chance, Alice. But if Denise had answered, I promise I would have hung up. That's all. I didn't call to upset you or fight with you. I just want to see my grandson, Alice. Please?"

I didn't want to debate anymore. I was too exhausted. "Fine. Tomorrow at six."

"Thank you! Thank you so much," he said, jubilant. "You won't regret it, Alice, I promise!"

The phone's click in my ear was like a judge's gavel to my heart, condemnation shuddering through my body. It was all too surreal...

The next evening, Jack was rocking Derek in his arms for over an hour. He and I didn't speak much, and I stayed in the kitchen for most of his visit, scouring through the want ads. It was hard to watch Jack with Derek in his arms; it reminded me of happier days when it was Denise he had been holding and fondling over. To my chagrin, Derek didn't seem to mind him too much.

After a while I went to stand just at the living room door. "You have to go," I said quietly. "Denise will be here soon."

Jack whispered a tender word or two into Derek's ear. If it was anyone else, I would have thought it beyond cute, and I couldn't help wondering how important it would be for Derek to have a man who was a constant in his life. Would he miss something vital if there wasn't one? Would Jack ever be able to be that man?

"You've no idea how much I appreciate this," he said as we headed to the front door, Derek still in his arms. "Do you think I can visit him again? Maybe Thursday?"

"No," I replied. "Once a week. On Tuesdays only."

"Okay, whatever you say. What time?"

He took the restriction better than I thought he would; meanwhile, I couldn't believe I had just opened the door for a connection between them.

And you too, Alice, a small voice whispered. I grimaced to myself. *What is* wrong *with me?*

"Call me Tuesday at five-thirty," I said mechanically. "If Denise is going to class, she'll be gone by then."

"Thank you again, Alice."

He gave Derek another kiss and gently handed him to me. "See you then."

As he turned to leave, I said nothing, just stood there chastising myself and holding the baby close.

"Oh, I almost forgot." Jack pulled out his wallet and handed me another fifty dollars. "This is for Denise and Derek. I know you're doing real well for yourself, but a little extra never hurts."

I swallowed, thinking of the divorce papers collecting dust in the top drawer upstairs. "Jack, that's not necessary. You've done enough…"

"Well, it's necessary to me, Alice," he replied. "Take it—there's no strings attached. I'm only doing what I should have been doing all along." He looked away. "Okay?"

I nodded and looked at the money he'd just placed in my hand.

"Thank you," I said mechanically. When I looked up, he had melted into the dusk's shadows.

Maybe he means it, I thought to myself. *No strings attached…*

———— //////////////// ————

Jack faithfully visited Derek every Tuesday. He loved his new job at the airport and was giving me seventy-five to a hundred dollars every week. He brought diapers and groceries often, and I had to admit I sincerely appreciated the help.

Although he was contributing financially, each time Jack visited, my conscience and the voices of my foremothers chastised me for my weakness. Those old enemies—desperation and loneliness—were stalking my heart anew. I knew I had to keep my guard up, as I had promised Mama and myself...

But I was so very tired of fighting the daily battle.

During the day, I continued to look for work, but nothing panned out. I'd even gone back to Mr. Mulden's, but he had no openings. I was devastated and felt the grasp on my newfound life and freedom slipping away right in front of my eyes.

On one visit, Jack completely shocked me; not only did he come with money as usual, but he came with a receipt for our light bill.

"Paid in full? Why did you do this, Jack?" I asked, angered that he'd once again tried to take control and overstepped the boundaries again. But in all honesty, I was more frustrated with myself for not having the tenacity to tell him to get out of my life for good. "Are you checking up on me, Jack? You had no right to contact the energy company—why did you do that? I was gonna pay—"

"Alice, wait," he said, putting his hands up in surrender. "I know that you don't work at the bank anymore. The bill was two months behind..."

This will never *do,* I asserted.

"I know I let you come over a few times, but now you're in my personal business?" I said. "I won't have it, Jack!"

I opened the door and pointed.

"Get out. Now."

He waited a beat, eyeing me. Then he took a step toward me. Instantly, everything in me tensed. My heart started to race, and my breath came short.

He reached out slowly and put his hand on the door, pushing it shut, still holding my gaze.

Then his arms were around me.

Panicked, I screamed. "Let me go!" I worked hard to break free, struggling against him. "Get off of me!"

He held on. "Alice, honey, stop it, please! I'm not trying to hurt you."

"I'm not your honey, damn it! Let me go, do you hear me? I'm gonna call the police!"

"Okay, okay, please calm down, Alice," he said softly. With surrendered hands in the air, he took a step back.

I eyed him for a long, enraged moment, breathing hard, my hair askew.

Jack finally broke the silence. "I'm not trying to hurt you, Alice. I just... I thought maybe..."

I was trembling. "Well, you thought wrong."

He let his hands drop and sighed. A tense minute later, he nodded to himself and explained the bill.

"Please Alice, just listen. I ran into one of your friends from the bank, and she told me how sorry she was that the bank had to let you go last month. That's how I knew. I thought my paying your energy bill would be a welcome surprise. Please believe me. I wasn't trying to take control. If I made you feel that way, I am truly, truly sorry. I was just trying to help. Please don't be upset. We were getting along so well, and I don't want to ruin that."

He put his hands in his pockets and kept his eyes down, clearly uncomfortable and apologetic.

"If you want me to leave, I will. I just want you to know that I'm here to help you with whatever you need. I know we're not together anymore, but..." He risked a glance up at me. "You are not alone, okay?"

And there it was…my undoing. My mind reeled. I didn't want to let Jack into my life—at least, no farther than he already was. It wouldn't be right or fair to Denise.

But on the other hand, the extra money the bank had given me had dwindled to almost nothing, and until I found another job, we would be in trouble. Besides, I had to admit that I had come to not mind him being around. Just on Tuesday evenings.

This isn't right, Alice! He shouldn't be here! my inner thoughts screamed.

"Do you want me to go?" he asked. "I won't visit today if you're not up to it. I can come back whenever you say."

Derek decided to start crying at that very moment. I sighed.

"No, it's okay. You're here, and he's up now."

"Thank you, Alice."

I went to get the baby, all but cursing at myself. Jack had been so sincere and so humble…but this just didn't feel right. I wished Mama was there to give me advice. I had been brought up to be merciful and gracious to people, and not to harbor grudges against anyone. If Jack really was changed—and everything indicated that he had—then what was my responsibility to him now? I had told him I had forgiven him, as I knew God would have me to…

But how far should that forgiveness go?

///////////////

A couple of weeks later, the money was gone, and I was still unemployed. Denise and I still attended church regularly, and whenever they gave the altar call, I'd go to the front, get on my knees, and pray. God knew I needed help, and my faith was beginning to waver. Was this punishment for not getting us out from under Jack's abuse when I should have?

Thanksgiving came again, and once more we spent it at Cadell's. We had a great time, but it wasn't only us this year. Her brother John and his daughter Joye flew in from Oregon, and her sister Jennifer with her husband, Jimmy, came in from Florida. They were all so nice and made me feel as though they were my family, too. It was nice to get away from the reality of my truth— that I had no full time job; that Jack was still so very present in my life; and that I was still lying to Denise. I said a special prayer when I got home that night and went to bed longing for change.

Sure enough, the following week Denise received an exciting phone call. She had faithfully started to apply for a job of her own since her sixteenth birthday, and the nickel and dime store a few blocks away called to let her know she was hired. Denise was ecstatic.

"I'll be working during the day and some weekends," she explained, "so I can help with the bills while you look for work!"

I was grateful, as it came not a minute too soon.

Then a few weeks later, Gemma called to ask me to make a dress for her, and she gave me the numbers of two friends who wanted outfits made as well. I gladly accepted. After calling both ladies and securing the jobs that afternoon, I went out to pay a bill, and stopped into *Mulden's* on my way back.

Three of the regulars from my former waitressing days were there, and I chatted for a few minutes with them until Mr. Rowe, a rather stocky gentleman, mentioned that Sophia had praised my work. He wanted to know if I could let out a few of his suits. "The darn things keep shrinking, Alice," he said with a wink.

The other two regulars, Mr. Hinton and Mr. Alston, both claimed they needed tailoring work done as well, and made appointments with me. All of a sudden, I had multiple sources of income—six sewing jobs coming in one day!

On my short walk home through the crispy December air, riding the winds of excitement, I reflected on how good God was. When I got home, I went to my bedroom and dropped to my knees, crying, thanking him for always being so, so good to me… despite my weakness.

That Christmas, Jack brought the children presents but asked me to say they were from me. I knew arguing it would be futile, so I only said thank you instead and turned to focusing on the coming new year.

With 1966 came feelings of ambitious excitement. I had been on my own for a full year, and even though I was struggling, more jobs were coming in every few days now as more people from the neighborhood called seeking my services. I was so busy that I was only able to make my Saturday ACADA meetings. Gemma said she understood and that I should "stoke the fire while it was hot."

The more work I received, the more I appreciated Jack's visits with Derek. He was now coming over every evening Denise went to school. I knew it wasn't right, especially without her knowing, but what could I do? We needed the help, and if I'd told her now, she would be enraged; that wouldn't be good for any of us and would probably force Jack out permanently. Even though I had the extra work, we still couldn't afford not to have some of his help. It wouldn't be for much longer, I told myself.

February came and brought along with it a notice to appear in court as a witness in the state's case against Jack, I tore it up and threw it in the trash. Jack had been so helpful and unobtrusive; I couldn't take away his opportunity to redeem himself, not without a good reason. In fact, our troubles seemed to be making him a better person. Yet I knew Gemma would be so disappointed— and so would all the other ladies who taught me to watch out for myself and stay away from my abuser.

But how could I testify against him when he had obviously turned a corner? He had done nothing but be faithful in his monetary help and tenderness toward Derek over these months, never asking for anything in return. My abuser, it seemed, was gone forever.

I called the courthouse and informed the clerk that I would not testify against Jack. The police contacted me a week later to try to convince me to change my mind. They said that without Denise's or my statement, the charges against Jack would be minimized and possibly even dismissed.

"I don't want any part in testifying against my husband, or having my daughter testify against her father," I told the officer on the phone. "We just want to put the entire incident behind us, so please sir, respectfully I ask that you leave us alone."

The officer's response shocked and angered me. "Mrs. Miles, you may want to consider the possibility that if Mr. Miles is back in your life... Well, ma'am, it could be at the advice of his attorney."

"What do you mean?"

"Well, if he's being extra nice these days, it's probably because he's been advised to. If he can help convince you not to testify against him, he could only be looking at a few fines—a slap on the wrist, so to speak. Wouldn't that be convenient? At least for him..."

Is this man saying the only reason Jack's around is to help his case? That he's only using me?

I flinched at that. "I resent what your implying, officer. If he were in my life, I would have to be a fool not to think of something so obvious. I'm not stupid."

"I apologize, ma'am. But I'm asking you to please reconsider."

"Sir, it's been over a year since this incident happened, but you're just hearing the case now? No, absolutely not. I've gotten over it and so should you. *Goodbye.*"

I sat down at the kitchen table, closed my eyes, and began to rub my throbbing temples as the officer's words reverberated in my head. Had Jack come back bearing gifts hoping to keep me from going forward with the case? It would be just like him…

But then I thought about the man I'd been watching over the last months, loving and cuddling his grandson. No, that man was different. I was being kind to the one who had not been kind to me, not "repaying evil for evil." I couldn't just turn my back on him because someone still saw who and what he *once* was…

I stood up and wiped invisible dust off my skirt. Right or wrong, I'd made my decision.

A week later, I received another notice; unless I lodged a formal objection by the date listed, there would be no trial, and the state would accept Jack's plea. The deal called for him to be on probation for three years. For nine months of it, he would have to attend anger counseling, which sounded appropriate to me. Even though Jack had been in therapy at Alcoholics Anonymous for several months now, I still thought it would be good for him to be "officially" cleared with a government-sanctioned therapist. I tore up that notice as well.

Denise never knew anything of any of it. I decided there were just some things that she wouldn't be able to understand until she was an adult herself and this was one of them. She had matured a great deal and was handling her responsibilities with strength and exuberance. Every time she handed me her meager paycheck to help with what she called "her share of the bills," my heart swelled with pride because of who she was becoming. Still, in all, she was only sixteen, a new mama, and learning about how much joy life could hold for her. I didn't want to risk crushing any of that for a single instant.

So I continued to struggle behind the scenes to provide— and to quiet my conscience.

Now as I observed him, it was obvious that Jack loved Derek, and Derek loved him. And, though he'd been coming over for the past eight months or so, we hadn't spoken too often. When we did, we'd only exchange words about how big Derek was getting or how well Denise was coming along. Once or twice we talked about my sewing jobs or his work. But though our communication was limited, I had to finally admit...over this past year, I had become more comfortable around him. Even more so than when we were married.

One evening, as I was finishing a skirt for a lady Gemma had referred to me, a pin fell out of the waistline and I wasn't sure where to size it. Jack was just coming downstairs after putting Derek to bed, so I asked him if he would please put the skirt on, just for a minute.

"I will," he said, "on one condition: don't ever tell anyone I did this." He flashed a smile.

I grinned back. "I promise."

With that, he removed his pants and climbed into the skirt with just his boxers on. I pretended not to notice.

I went up underneath the skirt from the bottom with the stickpin. When I found the place, I shoved the pin through. I miscalculated the distance, though, and accidentally stuck him.

"Ouchie!" he yelped, his butt cheeks clenching together in pain.

"Oops! I'm so sorry!" I said.

We both burst into laughter as he rubbed the sore spot. "Dang, watch those pins, woman!" he laughed.

I slapped his arm playfully to punish his sarcasm, and the next moment, I found myself in his warm embrace. My breath caught, and those beautiful green eyes stared down at me, face drawn in silent emotion.

"Jack…" I said, breathless, "we can't do this. Everything's going so well…"

"Shh, honey," he murmured. "No promises, no regrets, okay?"

His lips pressed against my cheek.

"Let's just take this slow and see where it goes."

I was struggling for air as my heart pounded. I felt weak in his strong arms. "Are you sure, Jack? Because I don't want—"

"No commitments, Alice," he breathed. "Not unless you say so."

Another kiss.

"I promise…" he whispered.

I was still uncertain. Yes, I once loved this man. No, that love had not completely died within me. Yes, this same man abused me for years. No, the idea of being with him as he was now—the way he used to be—no longer filled me with terror.

You remember what I told you, Alice? I heard Mama's voice distantly in my head. *You remember, girl? He's no good for you.*

I pulled back a little to look into his green eyes, into the warmth I had not seen in years.

Yes, Mama, I know, but…

He kissed me on the neck, the soft place behind my ear… then the lips…

And to him, my answer was—

"Yes, Jack."

He carried me up to the bedroom and laid me down ever so gently on our bed, and that night, Jack and I we were lovers again.

CHAPTER 20

My conscience ate at me those first few nights, but the regret soon faded, and everything seemed new and right for a time. I was happy, even without an official job. The voices of my past sometimes broke into my dreams, but it felt so right to be back in Jack's arms, to have found that peace we'd lost so long ago.

Mama's voice especially bothered me. She was so angry and disappointed with my decisions. There were plenty of occasions when I wanted to tell him to leave, because with him, I was taking a giant step backward from the life I really wanted. But Jack seemed to be evolving into the man I used to know—maybe even better than him—and the hope remained kindled in my heart that he could truly be a part my new life. As much as he had been my captor, maybe he could now be a part of my freedom, my supporter.

We enjoyed each other and before I knew it, it was March. It seemed impossible that a year and a half had gone by since our hellish life had come to its climax; so much had happened since then, so many changes both physical and emotional for all of us. Little Derek, who'd just turned nine months old, decided one evening to crawl in front of Jack and me. It was a constant testament to the speed with which time flew by. We were so excited, and I couldn't wait for Denise to get home from school so she could see her son's newest development.

When Denise walked in that night, I excitedly told her to stand still and just watch.

"Come on, Derek," I said, placing his favorite toy on the ground in front of Denise's feet then picked him up and moved him a short distance away from her. Derek, smiling and dribbling, focused on his toy and slowly inched forward in a military crawl.

Finally, he reached his rubber duck and snatched it up in his fist triumphantly, a large grin on his face. Denise screeched in excitement and scooped him up while I clapped and gave him praises. Derek squirmed to get down, and she placed him on the floor with the ducky. We clapped a little more, and he cooed and looked at us as if to say, "What's all the fuss about?"

I was so proud of him and hoped for his sake that during his life he would have many more victories like this one. I went to bed happy but anxious, my conscience refusing to be silent.

Gemma showed up on my doorstep the next day with news that my anxious heart needed to hear. She had a friend who had just opened a tailoring shop and was looking for a head seamstress. I wondered, but told Gemma I doubted I'd get the position.

"Well, as it stands, Alice," she said firmly, "you don't have a full time job now. So, if you don't get hired, guess what? Nothing's better or worse, but at least you will have tried. Remember, honey, the only thing worse than failing is not trying at all."

"You're right, Gemma," I said, chiding myself. A surge of the old timid Alice had seeped back into me, and I needed to push her away before I undid all my progress, both mental and emotional.

Gemma got my interview set up for the following morning, and I was more than ready for it. After breakfast, I dressed in my gray suit and skirt and grabbed a few samples of my work before heading out.

As soon as I started down the walkway, Mrs. Thornton called me from her wooden rocker on her porch.

"Alice," she said, "I need a quick word with you, please."

"Oh good morning, Mrs. Thornton!" I called. "I really can't. I'm going be late for an interview."

"Child, that's not the only kind of late you gonna be if you don't stop what you're doing."

I paused, eyeing her across the hedge.

Her eyes bored into me. "I'd hate to see Denise and that beautiful little baby motherless. Now, come here please. This can't wait."

What in the world is she talking about? I thought. Mrs. Thornton had extended kindness to us in the years we had been neighbors—sometimes undesired—but despite her busybody personality, I never doubted that she had my best interest at heart. I walked up to her front porch and respectfully waited as if she were my own grandmother.

"Yes, ma'am?"

Her lips pursed together, her spectacles down low on her round little nose. "Alice, I see what you doing."

"What I'm doing?" I asked. "What do you mean?"

"Oh, you know just what I'm talking about, young lady."

She didn't flare up, and her voice stayed even. In fact, her steadiness and calm manner made the moment even more disturbing. She rocked back and forth, back and forth in her wooden rocker.

"Your little secret meetings and rendezvouses with that no-account husband of yours… Didn't you get enough when he nearly killed you, child?" Her eyes squinted. "Didn't that knock some sense into your pretty little head?"

I stiffened and pursed my own lips, but she wasn't done.

"Those kind of men never change, Alice. You're just going to get your brains knocked out again. And with that daughter of yours working so hard and going to school trying to better herself…this is what you do to applaud her efforts? You sneak around with the man that almost killed her and let him in your house with that innocent little baby?" She stopped rocking. "Shame on you, child. How could you do such a thing?"

This woman had seen me at my worst. She had known what was going on for years, but had never said anything to me about it.

But this was too much.

"Mrs. Thornton," I did my best to match her leveled tone, "I mean no disrespect, ma'am, but that's my business. I would appreciate if you stopped forming opinions about me and kept to your own affairs. I appreciate everything you have done to help us in the past, but that doesn't give you the right to butt into my private life. Denise is my daughter, and I will do what I believe is best for her and her son."

No, you won't, I heard the voices in my mind. *You know Jack isn't what's best for you. Why are you doing this, Alice?*

My voice and my temper rose to drown them out. "You shouldn't interfere in people's private lives, Mrs. Thornton—it's rude. Maybe I should tell that no-account husband of mine what you said about him… I wonder what his reaction might be."

I turned on my heel and stalked off her porch and down the sidewalk, trembling in anger and humiliation. *Oh my God, Alice,* I thought to myself, *did you just threaten an old lady?* I hadn't meant to say any of that, but I was a raging storm inside. My head wanted what was best for Denise—and my foremothers' redemption.

But my heart wanted Jack.

I barely made it to the tailoring shop on time, and was greeted by a dark-haired, smiling girl behind the counter, a welcome distraction to my turbulent mind. Dozens of manikins lined the large picture windows, many displaying luxurious and glittering fashions that I myself would never be able to afford. I could see rich, burgundy carpet gracing the entrances to the back fitting rooms. Still, the place didn't feel snobbish or stuck-up, something I appreciated; geraniums and other potted plants stood in various places around the lobby, and there was soft classical music coming from a radio behind the counter.

The smiling girl asked me to have a seat. "Mr. Menendez will be with you in just a minute, ma'am."

I nodded and sat down, feeling suddenly nervous despite the pleasant atmosphere. I bent my head down, holding my dress samples close to my chest with the recommendation letters from Mr. Mulden, Mr. Riggans, and Gemma in my sweaty hand.

Why is this so hard all of a sudden? I thought. *What is happening to that new me I loved so much?*

"Well, hello, Alice." A man's warm voice came into my ears. "So good to see you again."

I *knew* that distinctive Spanish accent. I looked up, startled at the recognition.

It was the nice gentleman from the park who had given me his handkerchief. I looked into his warm brown eyes and his ridiculously long eyelashes and couldn't help smiling, pleasantly surprised.

"Hello, Mr. Menendez."

Smiling as well, he said, "You look nervous. Don't be. I hope you're doing well?"

I stood. "Yes, sir, I'm just fine. But...I don't have your handkerchief with me," I said a bit sheepishly.

He chuckled. "No worries, Alice. You can give it to me some other time. Let's talk shop, shall we?"

He put out a hand to direct me behind the counter. After a rather brief interview and cursory inspection of my work, Mr. Menendez hired me on the spot. Suddenly, I was the new head seamstress and supervisor to three other employees at *Menendez Tailoring & Alterations*. I couldn't believe it.

When Jack came over that evening, I jumped into his arms and told him all about it.

"I will be in charge of a team of three, Jack, can you believe it? God is good!"

Although Jack wasn't jubilant, he seemed happy for me. "That's so great, honey. Congratulations." He gave me a big hug and twirled me around.

I was so grateful; now I really could go after my dreams again.

With my mind more relaxed than it had been in months, Jack and I laid down together and made the best love we ever had. When we were spent, we rested beside each other and talked, as easily as we used to when we were teenagers. He asked me to tell him more about Gemma and how I had gotten to where I was now. I explained the ACADA program to him and all that Gemma had done to encourage me along. He just nodded and listened. I had his full and complete attention, and it was wonderful.

As we faded off into a light doze, the thought gnawed at the back of my mind if maybe I wouldn't have to ease Jack back out of my life. Maybe the new Jack really could be happy with me as I was—a career woman, *and* a wife and mother…

My new job was pure heaven. Though he'd asked me to, I still couldn't bring myself to call Mr. Menendez by his given name—Javier. He proved to be a good employer: respectful, appreciative, and dedicated both to quality and his employees' wellbeing.

When Denise brought Derek to see me, I introduced them both to Mr. Menendez and the other staff. He greeted Denise with a sweet "Good morning, beautiful senorita," and then gave his attention to Derek.

"Hello, my little friend," he said, holding his finger to Derek's chubby hand for him to grasp. "So very nice to meet you."

Derek smiled in that gleeful way babies do and stretched out his arms to the handsome Spaniard. Denise and I couldn't believe it; Derek never willingly went to a stranger—*except maybe Jack*, I thought—but apparently there was something about Javier that made him comfortable.

The next few months went by in a rhythmic cadence, and Derek's first birthday was upon us. The year had flown by before I knew it. I still had not told Jack to leave. Instead, I found myself celebrating Derek's birthday with Denise one day and with Jack the next. My life had fallen into a regular pattern of daily work, chores, lovemaking with Jack, and avoiding the truth with Denise…

Deep inside I felt guilty, and the only thing that soothed me was that I loved my job. Though the bank had been a wonderful experience, and I excelled at it, the idea of creating and designing clothing was what my heart longed for. Spending my days creating wonderful designs and interacting with Mr. Menendez and the clients put a bounce in my step to and from work.

In fact, Mr. Menendez didn't seem like a stranger at all anymore. He made it his business to spend a few minutes with his "*pequeño amigo*," as he called Derek, when Denise brought him along to the shop to have lunch with me once a week.

I had to admit, Mr. Menendez was *very* handsome. I learned that he was Brazilian and Spanish by birth, as his dark, swarthy skin attested to. His wonderful accent made words seem to dance off his tongue, and his eyelashes still fascinated me. In fact, Denise and I both giggled behind his back about his "girlie" lashes.

Though he was a few years younger than I, he obviously understood the ways of the world. He told me his story one day while we were eating lunch. Born in Spain, he had lived there for twelve years and eventually moved to Brazil. His family had been in the tailoring business for over forty years, owning fourteen shops both in the United States and abroad, including the one here in D.C. which had just opened.

The *Menendez Tailoring and Alterations* shops in California and New York were well-known to the rich and famous. In fact, Javier had signed pictures of himself with Frank Sinatra, Sophia Loren, Dean Martin, and Jerry Lewis, just to name a few. I admitted to him I was jealous. He smiled and humbly declared that I shouldn't be; though he was a very well-known international businessman, it could be stressful to be in the world's public eye.

I was so lucky, and sincerely humbled, to be working under someone so talented and established. There was so much he could teach me, not just about the business but about life…and I was eager to learn. I was focused on doing well in my new career, and Jack knew it. Many times after making love, we'd talk about our day and the nuances of our jobs. At first, he seemed happy for me.

But as time went by, I began to notice that he would pointedly change the subject.

Soon I realized why. One day after my weekly lunch with Denise and after Mr. Menendez said his goodbye to Derek, Denise giggled unexpectedly.

"What's so funny?" I asked.

"D.J. absolutely loves Mr. Menendez, Mom. Wouldn't it be nice if he could see him more often? You should invite him to dinner or something." She gave me a wink and another little giggle.

I was shocked. "Denise, he's my boss, and a very rich man," I stammered, blood rushing to my cheeks. "I don't think he wants to or has the time to come and sit in our little kitchen and eat a home-cooked meal."

"You might be surprised, Mom," she said. "Being his employee doesn't mean a thing. You're still beautiful. And I can tell that he thinks you're beautiful, too."

"Okay, missy. That's enough." I grinned at the compliment in spite of myself.

"Come on, Mom. You can see he's extremely handsome, right?"

"This conversation is over, young lady," I said, patting her on the tush. "Now scoot. I have work to do."

"Okay, okay," she laughed, "but this conversation *isn't* over. See you at home."

Once Denise left, I thought about what she had said. If Denise, an innocent bystander, saw potential for me with Mr. Menendez, then Jack, being both my husband and a jealous man by nature, would too.

I never gave Jack a description of Javier or, as far as I knew, any reason to be jealous, but after that day, I watched him closely. Whenever I mentioned work or my boss, Jack's demeanor would change and our conversation became stilted. After that,

I was mindful of how much I talked about the shop with him, reserving my gushing for chats with Denise.

Early one evening, as Derek slept and we both lay in bed, Jack brought up the tailor shop on his own.

"How's work?"

"Oh, it's going great," I said casually, then tried to change the subject. "Anything interesting with yours? Are you still enjoying the airport?"

He didn't even acknowledge the shift in conversation, instead adjusted his arm over his head. "Good, I'm glad you're enjoying your job," he said.

There was a long, uncomfortable pause. My throat tightened, and I wracked my brain for a way to ease the sudden tension.

Before I could, he asked, "How's your *boss*?"

"Oh, he's...what do you mean?" I asked, now a little nervous. This was all entirely out of character for him.

Jack let out a breath, trying to act casual and failing miserably. "Oh, nothing much. It's just that I passed by the shop yesterday and saw Mr. Fancy Pants hovering over you." He eyed me as he flipped over onto his stomach and put his arms up under the pillow. "I was a little worried about whether you had enough air to breathe, that's all."

We both fell silent. Jack put his cheek down on the pillow, no longer looking at me. I continued to stare at the ceiling, hoping to God I would say the right thing. I couldn't let all our hard work unravel, not now. He needed to know that I still cared for him and him only.

That's the truth, right?

I took in a soundless breath and spoke quietly. "Jack, if you're worried, honey, there is nothing going on between me and Mr. Fancy Pa—Mr. Menendez."

"Oh, I'm sorry, honey. Did I say that there was?" His voice bit.

"No, but I assume that's what you were thinking." I didn't dare look at him. "But don't. He'd never be interested in anyone like me."

He seemed astonished by that and pulled up onto his elbows to look at me. "Like you? What do you mean 'like you'?"

I looked up at him. "I mean that Mr. Menendez is a wealthy and respected man who travels all over the world. He is busy looking for his next business venture, not romance. Besides he's only making sure his business is established here. Once he does, he'll be off looking for another area to do it all again. After he hires a shop director to oversee all operations here, he'll be gone." I smiled at him, hoping to ease his tensions on the subject. "As a matter of fact, I plan to apply for the position."

Jack's brows furrowed, but I continued blithely on. "In my spare time, I've been learning about every aspect of the shop, and I know I can do it. Just like Gemma says, the only thing far worse than not getting the job is not filling out the application."

"Alice, your hands are already full. Isn't the job you have enough? Besides, you've only been there what, five months?"

"Six. I started the end of March. Who knows, I just might get it. This is something I really want, honey. I love my work, and although I don't have all the fancy credentials the other candidates may have, I have hands on experience. I'm ready, I know it."

"It's amazing…" he said, a bit too sarcastically for my liking, and plopped back down onto the pillow.

"What is?" I asked, trying to keep the frustration out of my voice.

"How sure you are of yourself now. It's only been six months and look at you—ready to take on the world." He sounded almost accusatory. "You're obviously so far into his good graces you think he'll just let you take over for him. How interesting…"

Jack's tone was annoying me so much at this point I couldn't hide how I was feeling. The new Alice burst through to defend the old one—the one he apparently had forgotten would no longer cow to his insinuations.

"I am in his good graces—on a *professional* level," I said, not restraining the bite to my own voice. "Jack, there's nothing going on, and you need to accept that. Besides," I raised an eyebrow, "even if there were, we both agreed no promises, no regrets, remember?"

He raised himself up onto his elbows again, gazing in wonderment at me for a beat or two. Then he exhaled deeply.

"Yep, you got it, honey. Like my counselor would say, we're going to take it one day at a time. I know you love me, and you know that I love you. It'll all work out." His words seemed quite sincere, and he gave me a quick peck on the cheek before he turned over onto his side.

I was dumbfounded by his reaction. While it felt good to stand up to him now, I hadn't been expecting such an anticlimactic response from him. He had actually responded the way a husband should have. He was listening to what I said and needed…even when he didn't like it.

I reached over and rubbed his back gently. "Jack, I'm so proud of you."

"For what?" He looked over his shoulder at me.

"Well, for going to counseling, and for following the terms of your plea bargain, and…just for everything, Jack. You're being a man of your word, and I'm proud of you for that."

Jack smiled—a bit sadly, I thought—and rolled up off the bed, grabbing his shirt from the floor. "Yeah, well… I gotta start somewhere, right?" He pulled his shirt on and leaned over to kiss me again. "Guess I'd better go. Denise will be home soon."

I could see his despondency, and my heart twisted. He wanted to see his daughter so badly. Even though he was holding up his end of the deal, it was wearing on him.

"See you tomorrow," he said.

Before he left, I leaned up on my knees and kissed him firmly on the mouth, wanting to give him a little more assurance.

I laid there after his footsteps faded, replaying our conversation in my mind and wondering, once again, if I had done the right thing by allowing Jack back into my life, wondering if I was being real with him.

Somewhere along the way, I realized, my feelings for him had changed. Oh, there was still love, but it was different. We were lovers…but I no longer had that desperate kind of love that once consumed me. Even though Jack was finally treating me the way he should have all along, the reality was, with the empowerment my new position had given me, with all our needs met—and with the attentions of man as fascinating as Mr. Menendez stirring my emotions—I really didn't *need* Jack anymore. All I was doing was using him.

I was certainly in a different place than I had ever thought I would be with him. How had it all come to this point, anyway? I had almost forgotten.

I realized with a shock that I was being unfair to him. I didn't love him the way I thought did, and he was now waiting for something that could never be. Instead of love, all I had for him now was pity.

But perhaps my pity wasn't what Jack needed. What he needed, what Denise really needed, was my honesty instead.

————————————— ////////////// —————————————

CHAPTER 21

I was head over heels in love with my job. Denise and Gemma both noticed the change in me and asked where my glow was coming from. I told them my job and my grandson, which wasn't the whole truth… But it wasn't exactly a lie, either. What I didn't tell them was how much extra time Mr. Menendez had been spending with me…and how much I liked it. I hadn't thought much of it until Jack said something, but he was right—my boss did tend to "hover" around me.

The shop employed twenty people in all and was the size of a small factory. People came from miles around to have wedding gowns, suits, and dresses either made or altered. I soon found myself having to meet more and more deadlines, which meant I often had to work until nine or ten o'clock and even some Saturdays. It was exhausting, but I loved the thrill of the working world.

I had tried to see Jack as often as possible at the outset, but it was hard juggling everything. I wanted to have the much-needed discussion with him about our relationship, but oftentimes when we did manage to arrange a time together, I just wanted his comforting arms to rest my weary body in and go to sleep with little to no conversation.

Eventually, though, his disappointment and frustration with our limited evenings together began to show more and more. He complained about not seeing Derek, and I'd explain again that I didn't really see Derek that much either; most evenings when I got in, he was asleep and I could only give him a goodnight kiss. In the mornings, Denise and I were rushing around so much that I barely had enough to time to say goodbye.

But Jack seemed to miss the point.

"Alice, I've already told you," he said one night when he was leaving, "you don't have to work hard like this. Let me take care of you."

"Yes, I do have to work like this, Jack," I countered, frustrated that I had to explain it yet again. I thought he had heard me the last time, but maybe I had been wrong. "This is what I want, and I am working hard to get it. So, support me or don't, but I am going to continue doing everything that I am doing. I'm sorry, but that's the way it is."

Jack's mouth set, and even though he kissed me, his voice had an edge. "Call me when you find time, Alice."

Watching him walk away that time, I finally understood without a doubt how close I had me to relinquishing my new-found freedom, and it terrified me down to the core. Changed or not, Jack's involvement was a bump I could not keep trying to smooth out. I'd done what he had wanted for our entire marriage, but even if he was a better man now, I couldn't do that anymore.

I had attempted to ease Jack into the dreams I was going after...but he had become a distraction—a major distraction. I didn't like the loopholes I had to jump through, the secret life I had to keep, in order to have him in my life, even with no strings attached.

I hated to have to do it, but I had to find a good and proper time to tell him it was over between us. It would break my heart to do it.

And…it would most likely shatter his.

———————— ////////////// ————————

Since I was working late almost every night, I started bringing in dinner plates for Mr. Menendez and myself. Each night we would take a few minutes to eat in the break room while talking shop. One evening I went to get our plates out and realized I'd left them at home.

"Sorry, Mr. Menendez, we are out of luck tonight," I said glumly. "I don't know where my head is."

"Oh well," he chuckled. "Why don't I spring for dinner this time? Are you up for a change of scenery?"

He took me to a quaint Italian restaurant called *Guimarello's Bistro Italiano*. It looked expensive and exclusive, even from the outside. When we entered, the décor took my breath away. The walls were burgundy and gold, and a huge waterfall with hidden lights and lots of greenery created a serene atmosphere for the guests. The maître d' who greeted us looked like he'd just stepped out of an old movie, with his slicked back hair and his long, thin features.

"*Buona sera,* Giorgio." Mr. Menendez continued to converse with the maître d' in fluent Italian for a moment. Then he tucked my hand in the crook of his arm. "Shall we?"

"Why of course, sir," I said, feigning formality, then giggled.

As the maître d' led us to our table, I couldn't help but admire my worldly and handsome boss. "What did you say to him?" I whispered as we walked.

"I asked him if my favorite table was available."

"So you speak English, Spanish, *and* Italian?"

"And Portuguese."

"Oh of course," I waved my hand, "you're from Brazil. I'm still struggling to master English!"

He chuckled and pulled out a chair for me, making sure I was comfortable before seating himself across from me.

The place was beautiful yet had a cozy atmosphere, and I felt completely out of place. The last eatery that I had been in was *Mulden's Diner*. Despite this, I gradually relaxed in Mr. Menendez's company.

I enjoyed our relaxed and interesting conversation. We talked about current fashions, political fiascos, and our favorite films. At one point, when I was asking for more details about his family tree, I made a mention of my own heritage; he didn't even bat an eye. We shared plenty of laughs, more than I ever had with anyone else, except Denise. It didn't feel like a business dinner at all, not that I'd ever had one outside of the shop's break room before. But somehow it felt as if we were old friends who dined out all the time.

After a while, I noted the time and realized that we had been talking for over two hours.

"Oh! It's ten-thirty!" I said, surprised.

"It is! Where did the time go?" Mr. Menendez replied after glancing at his watch. "I'm sorry, Alice, I didn't realize. You must be exhausted."

"Actually, I am," I laughed. "If it's okay with you, I'd like to call it a night. My daughter will be wondering where I am."

As I stood up, he immediately followed and came around to place my sweater on my shoulders.

"Thank you, Mr. Menendez."

"Alice, do you think that we can stop being so formal now?" His eyes sparkled in the muted lights of the waterfall. They were a deep, rich brown, wise and patient—far different from Jack's haunting green ones. "After tonight," he said, "I feel like I know you much better…and, since you will be the new shop director, we should be on a first name basis, don't you think?"

"What? No…" I said, in utter shock.

"No?" He smiled. "I thought you might want the position. Was I wrong?"

"Oh no, no, Mr. Menendez, I want it. I definitely do!" I gushed.

"Javier, Alice. Get used to calling me Javier."

All I could think of in that instant is that I had a real title now, real power. Overwhelmed, I stammered, "Thank you so much…Javier."

"No thanks needed. You've earned it. I mean it, Alice. I am so impressed with the quickness of your mind, how quickly you have picked up on everything, and, more importantly, the dedication that you've shown. You're actually doing me a favor by taking this position, because I know that I will be leaving the D.C. shop in very capable hands. So strap in," he grinned, "you have less than six months to learn what you don't already know."

When we pulled up to my house, Javier jumped out of the car, opened my door, and extended his hand to help me out.

"Here we are," he said with a warm smile. "Shall I walk you to the door?"

I glanced up and noticed that Denise had left the porch light on for me. "Oh, I am fine," I replied, with my own smile. "Thank you for dinner. I really enjoyed it. And thank you so much for this opportunity. I promise I won't let you down."

"I know you won't," he replied. "Good night, Alice. See you in the morning."

After he pulled away from the curb, I made my way up the walkway. Still smiling at my good fortune, I waded through the odd paraphernalia in my purse that always seem to hide my keys. I looked up to unlock the door.

"Alice!"

"Oh my God, Jack!" I jumped backward, hand to my heart. He'd jumped out of the bush by the front door and was standing no more than two feet away, blocking it. "What are you doing here? You scared me!" I lowered my voice and glanced at the upstairs window. "You know Denise will have a fit if she sees you!"

"I thought I'd ride by the house and see if the coast was clear. Don't worry, I stayed in the bushes." His whisper was sharp in the dark. "I was going to stop and throw pebbles at your window like we used to when we were kids, but—"

"Jack, we've discussed boundaries," I interrupted, feeling my anger rising. "Now you're crossing them."

"What?"

"You're breaking the rules. We are not kids anymore. You can't just show up unexpectedly. You promised me you wouldn't do that."

"Yeah, yeah," he muttered. "Even if you had been expecting me, from the looks of it, you wouldn't have wanted me around anyway." He glared down the road in the direction of Javier's car.

I was immediately on the defensive. "Jack, I *told* you that when I first started working late that Javier would make sure I got home safely at night."

"Oh, excuse me—it's Javier now, is it? You've warmed up to a first-name basis. When did that start, Alice?"

"Tonight, after he told me I'd gotten the new position as shop director. Now please, we can talk about it later. You have to go."

Something was wrong. Jack was sounding more and more like his old self, and I tensed. I became downright petrified when I noticed, even through the fresh smell of breath mints, the distinct odor of alcohol on his breath.

All the old memories and taunting words and pain came rushing in. I swallowed but was determined I would fight them back.

Hoping that he could still be reasoned with, I calmed myself and kept my voice level. "Jack, I know what you're trying to imply, and I'm going to say this just one more time. There is nothing going on with my boss and me. Even if there were, it would not be a concern of yours. I owe you no explanations about my job or my boss. Need I remind you once again—no promises, no regrets?"

"Yeah, but...I thought we were past that now!" Jack's tone changed from suspicious to a child-like whining. "So, Alice, what are you saying? Are you saying that you will cheat on me if you feel like it?" The strangest expression crossed his face, and then he added sharply, "Do you want to cheat on me, Alice?"

That made my anger boil over, the memories of groans and sounds and lipstick stains flooding my mind. "You have a lot of nerve to ask *me* that, Jack Miles..."

Jack's eyes twitched, and I knew I had pushed him too far. I suddenly had the urge to flee. His anger was real, and my gut told me that he was about to snap, just like he always used to.

I did my best to stay in control of the situation, though, and get through to him. I made my voice get steady again. "Jack, you need to be careful... I'm sorry if I've made you mad, but you'd better keep a grip on yourself. You're acting like the old you, the one you promised I'd never see again." I held his gaze. "Please think about what you're doing and saying, okay?"

"Yeah... I am the man," he mumbled under his breath.

"What?" I asked, bewildered.

"Alice, I am still your husband, 'til death do us part,' and nothing in the world can change that. I have the right to know if my wife is getting it on hot and heavy with some Mr. Fancy Pants sewing man." The whiny child's voice had now turned venomous.

"Jack, that's enough." I hoped I was keeping the tremble out of my voice, but I knew the fear was plainly etched on my face.

How did I ever let it get this far?

He shoved in closer, and I couldn't help my flinch.

That made him stop. It seemed to freeze him for a moment, and suddenly his eyes changed. Everything about him softened a little; his face, his posture, his tone, everything just relaxed. And just like that, he was speaking in his normal tone of voice, not the child's whine or the venomous anger... Just Jack.

"Alice, why are you looking at me like that? Are you scared of me?"

All I could do was blink. His sudden transition had me even more frightened.

"You don't have to be, honey. I'm so sorry... I...I screwed up again. But it's just that I love you so much, and I'm hoping we will be a family again. I mean..." He seemed to choke on his words and backed a step or two away. "All the time we were spending together? You've had me believing that we were on the mend, sweetheart."

I was so thrown by Jack's chameleon-like behavior that I was at a loss for words. I knew he was right; I had been leading him on to satisfy my loneliness until it just became routine. I had been using him...

When I didn't reply, Jack seemed resigned. He just backed up slowly, turned around, and left without another word.

Shaken, I stood on the porch trying to pull myself together. The guilt began to settle over my spirit, mixed with anxiety and wariness. Something wasn't right with him... After a moment, I quietly opened the door, put all the locks on, and headed straight upstairs.

I let out a sigh of relief after peeping in and finding Denise and Derek both sound asleep. Still tense, I ran a warm bath to try to calm my nerves. I soaked my tense body for a few long moments, relishing the warmth covering me.

It felt so good, I took a deep breath and dropped my body down, submerging entirely beneath the water. The silence of it was utterly peaceful, and I gradually began to relax and just enjoy the stillness beneath the water with no worries, no anxieties... no Jack.

But he was in every part of my life...even my solitude. The peace began to ebb as the memory of the last time I had been submerged in this very tub came unbidden.

It was the day Jack had almost murdered me.

I had been languishing up to my neck, soaking the aching bones and bruises from the previous night. My clothes were strewn about the tile and sink, and though the warm water felt good on my aching body, it hurt to apply much pressure to my skin with the bar of soap. I did what I could, trying to wash away the dried blood around my neck where Jack had scratched me. My privates and legs still hurt.

Just when I rose out of the water to dry off, the bathroom door burst open and slammed into the wall. I dropped back into the tub, startled and feeling panicked. Jack was there against the doorframe—livid. I had seen Jack so angry many, many times, but never had I seen such hatred and hostility in his eyes.

I knew, even before he moved, this time he was really going to kill me.

"You black whore!"

He pounced, and I was under the water, both of his hands around my neck.

I struggled and gasped and took in air when he hoisted me up and screamed something in my face. I couldn't take in what he said in my struggle, and then I was under again.

The next time I came up, he held me to his face again, and I clung to his arms and soaking shirt to keep from slipping back in, coughing and shaking.

"You think you're gonna get prettied up for another man, you wench? You cleaning up for him? Huh? You so much as look at that man ever again and I'll kill you right where you sit, you understand me, jigga?"

"Jack! Wha—?" I pushed against the tub with all the strength I had and clung to him, gasping. "What are you…talking about?"

He shoved me under for so long the next time, I felt blackness pulling at me. I could see his face, distorted and white and ugly from the surging water above my head, and all I could think was, *Dear God, don't let me die like this.*

Now, all these years later, I opened my eyes under the water and the memory stopped. The light from the bulb in the ceiling trickled down through the clear sheen above me, and there was nothing but powerful silence. It so sharply contrasted the fright and panic I had endured in those eternal minutes of terror that suddenly, almost in a single flash of understanding, the clarity of mind and purpose I had been in need of since Jack reentered my life came crashing in.

I realized, in one devastating moment of reality, what I had done.

I jerked myself up out of the water, and tears flooded my eyes. Sobs lurched from my very soul, and I felt almost as desperately lost as that moment Jack had finally pulled me from the watery depths.

Alice, you idiot! How could you be so stupid? That man is not your lover. He hasn't changed. He's always blamed you for everything—his parents, his loss of work, his reputation going down the toilet...

I thought through our conversation outside. *He's drinking again, Alice. You* know *he'll never change. You* know *it! And you know you can't blame anyone but yourself.*

My crying softened, and I wiped my eyes, which didn't help because of my wet hands. I took several deep breaths to calm myself and stopped my self-recriminations to face the hard truth. The more I wailed inwardly to myself, the more my inner voice began to sound like Mama's.

You let him come back into your life, Alice. You did what felt "good" instead of being honest with him. You let your pity speak louder than your intelligence... And you gave him control again when you gave him your body.

"Oh, God! Forgive me!" I said aloud.

This man is a monster. Your Jack is dead, Alice. As much as you want him to still exist, he doesn't. A man like him will never change. Get that through your head!

I shut my eyes as tight as I could and voiced my last thoughts. "Get away from him, Alice. Get away while you still can. It's over. Done. Your husband doesn't exist anymore."

I felt the last of my weak spirit break, the last of the woman who clung to false hope and denied reality. She seemed to scream as she flowed down the drain along with my bath water...gone, no more. Forever.

I felt nothing now—no anger, no fear, nothing.

Emotionless and numb, I dried off and went to take the last look at myself in the mirror. It was an entirely different face that stared back at me.

"Goodbye, Alice Miles," I whispered. "Welcome, Alice Kane."

CHAPTER 22

Denise kissed me goodbye the next morning as she and Derek walked out the door, and I went to wash the breakfast dishes before I left for the shop. I was focused on my resolution from the night before, and though I had failed in many of my resolutions previously, I knew this one was different. This time, I meant it.

Something just wasn't right with Jack—his abrupt changes in tone and behavior last night weren't just moods. The more I thought about it, the more I realized that I didn't even know anything about how his coma or his medications had affected him. What if something was really *wrong*?

Just as the suds filled the basin and I turned the spigot off, I heard the front door open.

"Okay, Denise," I called out, grinning, "what did you forget? You're gonna be late."

"Hi, honey. How did you sleep?"

I spun around and there was Jack standing in the kitchen doorway. My stomach clenched.

"Fine," I said forcing my body to relax and my tone to be calm and natural. "What are you doing here?"

He looked at the floor. "I didn't get any sleep, Alice. I couldn't stop thinking about what I did last night." He glanced up at me.

"Honey, I was way out of line, and I had to come and tell you I'm sorry. You know I'm seeing my counselor, and I still have a ways to go…obviously. But I am trying, so…please bear with me."

I said nothing—just stared at him, watching for signs.

"Let me make it up to you," he said hopefully. "Can I take you and Derek to that quiet little restaurant? You like *Guimarello's Bistro Italiano*, don't you? Will you go with me? You have to… I won't take no for an answer." He tried to smile. "So…what do you say?"

Oh my God! He knew where Javier had taken me last night. Had he followed us there?

Though Jack looked calmer now, I noted that he had on the same clothes from yesterday and appeared…jittery. He kept fidgeting with his glasses and pockets, like he didn't know what to do with his hands, and his hair was a mess as if he jumped out of bed and only combed one side.

He was spiraling out of control. Whatever therapy and treatment he was receiving, apparently was no longer helping. At this point I was going to say whatever it took to make him leave, without agitating his unstable state.

"Okay, Jack. Yes, that sounds wonderful," I said, plastering on a convincing smile. "I'll be ready at six, but like always, call first so I can make sure Denise is gone."

His distraught face broke into a grin, and he dashed forward to hug me tight, so tight I couldn't exhale. But I waited him out; if he were convinced and happy, he'd leave.

"Thank you, baby," he said. "Thank you so much for understanding, and you'll see today that I can be just as charming as Mr. Fancy Pants. I know we can get through this, and then we can be a family again, right?"

He stepped back enough to look into my eyes for the answer, and I nodded.

"Right honey, of course."

Perhaps it was my new determination or the clarity of mind from last night, but my senses picked up everything now and the truth stood out like a beacon—Jack didn't love us; he was *obsessed* with us. All those gestures of kindness with the money and caring for Derek, it was his way of trying to hold onto something for himself. All those things he gave us—all our time alone as lovers—it was his way to keep us close…like prized possessions.

It frightened me that I had so naively allowed him to go this far. Until now, I didn't see that I was the one who had been too stupid and desperate for love and companionship.

I willed myself not to shudder under his touch as he squeezed my arm gently.

"Okay then. I'd better go and get everything set up," he said, eager. "I'll pick you up at seven. I love you, Alice."

The words were lead in my mouth. "I love you, too." I couldn't even fake the smile anymore and just prayed he didn't notice.

Jack grinned wider than he ever had and practically raced to the door. The resounding echo of the door slam pounded in my ears, and I fled to the sink, vomiting up my breakfast. I had let him get so close…so close to trapping me again.

And Denise and the baby…

"Oh dear God, please forgive me!" I vomited again, shaking and screaming inside at myself for having made such a horrible mistake that could have endangered my sweet babes.

"And for what?" I hissed at myself. "For a little sex? Some company?"

How could I have been so stupid and selfish?

"I'm so sorry, Mama!" I screamed.

My heart raced wildly, and I gripped the counter to gather myself. "Okay, Alice," I said aloud, "you have to fix this, *right now*."

I went to the chair and sat at the kitchen table. *Breathe...
Calm...* I told myself. When I gained my composure, I called
the shop. I told Javier I wasn't feeling well and couldn't come
in today. He seemed concerned over the slight strain in my
voice, but told me to take care of myself and to let him know if
I needed anything.

I thanked him rather hastily, hung up, and immediately dialed
Mulden's Diner.

Mr. Mulden answered the phone, and I nearly started wailing
again as I told him what happened, but he didn't let me get very
far. Thirty minutes later, his son Paulie was putting new locks and
deadbolts on both doors.

Paulie's hammering triggered something inside me. The
familiar pounding viciously reminded me of when Jack padlocked
the bedroom door and all the windows and doors. I jumped with
each bang, and finally fled to my bedroom to escape, throwing my
pillows over my head.

Paulie finished the locks and then gave me a ride to the
courthouse. I'd finally signed the divorce papers. They wouldn't
be enforced until Jack signed them too, but if that didn't show
him where I stood, nothing would.

When Denise came home from work and her key didn't fit
the lock, I blithely explained that I had lost my key and Paulie
had to pop the lock for me. She asked why the deadbolts had been
installed; I told her that Mr. Mulden had told Paulie to add them
so we'd be extra safe at night.

"Mom, what aren't you telling me?" she asked. "Please be
honest."

I sighed. "Okay..." I was truly done with lying to her. But I
had a bad headache by now and told her we would talk after she
came home from school that evening.

I went to lie down on the couch for a few minutes, and when she poked her head in to say goodbye before heading to school for the evening, I asked her to drop Derek off at Ms. Page's so I could get some rest.

Plus, I didn't want him around when Jack returned.

I stayed on the couch for the next hour, waiting in grim determination for Jack to call, mentally sifting through the stories and words of my ancestors. Some had had their children taken from them; others, their independence and fighting spirit.

Not me. Not this time.

Although I was expecting it, I still jumped when the phone rang promptly at six.

"Hi, honey. Are you ready?" he asked excitedly.

I inhaled and absorbed the passionate drive and determination of my foremothers that seemed to hover over me. My voice was not my own.

"I'm not going out with you tonight—or any other night, Jack. Whatever it was that we were doing, it's over now."

He didn't say anything. The silence continued long enough for me to wonder if he'd hung up.

"Wait, what? Sweetheart, what are you talking about? Things are going just fine. I know we just had a small bump in the road, but I apologized and you said you understood—"

"No, listen to me, Jack. I should never have let this happen. After last night, I realize that I won't ever be able to feel truly comfortable with you. I don't trust you and I never will."

I bit my lip and knew I had to say the full truth. "I don't love you anymore. The man I loved died years ago…and I can't make him come back! Nor am I the same person you married. I've changed, Jack, and you can't tell me how to live my life anymore. I can't—I *won't*—tolerate the jealousy, the anger, the infidelity, the fear—none of it! No more. It's over! We're done!"

The silence was nauseating, but I hung on, waiting for his response.

He was desperate. "Honey, please, wait a minute. Just talk to me. Tell me what it is you need, and I'll help you."

"No, that's just it—*you* are not going to have any control or say in my life anymore. This is my life, just like Gemma has been trying to tell me. It's time for me to help myself—without *you*!"

Another moment of silence.

"I don't think you mean that." He said it so condescendingly, it infuriated me even further.

"For once in my life, I know exactly what I mean and what I want, Jack! And I don't want to be with you anymore! You are the same drunk you've always been!"

The condemnation rang in the silence between us.

"That's right. Drunk! I know you're drinking again!" I couldn't help the slight shriek that came into my voice.

His voice sounded tight. "Alice, I know you love me in spite of that. I got laid off this week, honey, and I needed a little, you know...something to help me cope. I'm sorry—"

"It doesn't matter!" I screamed. "You can't keep making excuses for your behavior! I told you, I will not allow my former love for you to cloud my judgment about what's healthy or right for me and for my daughter. It's over..."

I took a breath.

"And to make sure, I've signed divorce papers."

"You what?!"

In the past, that bellowing tone would have sent me scurrying away, panicked. But now it only made me sure in my decision.

"Honey, I'm on my way over there. We need to talk face to face."

"Don't you dare!" I said. "You can't just walk in here anymore. I've changed all the locks, and if you don't stop bothering me, I'll file a police order against you like I should have in the first place. I really don't want to do that, Jack, but if you don't leave me alone, I won't have a choice. Now *goodbye*."

I slammed the phone down with finality. I meant every word this time, and I planned to hold my course, no matter how much it scared me or tugged at my heartstrings. This was it.

Fifteen minutes later, he was banging on the door.

"Alice, open up."

"*No,* get out of here now!"

"Alice…open the door!"

"No! You're doing everything Gemma said you would. You need help, Jack. Go get some help and leave me alone!" I stayed in the foyer a few feet away from the door, listening with my heart banging in my chest.

"Gemma this, Gemma that! Gemma, Gemma, Gemma!" Jack yelled. "Gemma needs to mind her own damn business! We are in this situation now because of her interfering ass. She's not your husband; I am. Open the door, Alice!"

I knew that tone, those words, that part of him so well. It wasn't surprising to hear him cursing at me again.

But then the pounding stopped. His insolent tone once again reverted to the sweet-voiced man I'd been keeping company with over the last months. My blood ran cold with the suddenness of the transition.

"Baby, please. I love you. And I'm not leaving." He wriggled his key in the lock.

When he realized that it wasn't going to budge, he banged on the door again, this time with greater intensity, calling me names in one breath and "honey" in the next.

The repeat of this bizarre behavior unnerved me so much I called Mr. Mulden.

"Paulie and Anthony be there in three minutes!" he said sharply. "Stay on the phone with me til then, okay?"

"Yes sir," I said.

I thought again about how I never followed through with the court restraint order, and I felt ashamed. The officer had told me this would happen...

Jack stopped banging. "Please, baby. I just want to talk. I'm sorry. Let's go to dinner. I need to see my grandson." Then he was angry in the next breath and hit the door again. "You can't keep him away from me!"

The sounds were terrifying.

A few seconds later, I heard a couple of car doors slam. I peeked out the window past Jack's figure, and took a breath of relief when I saw Paulie and Anthony quickly coming up the walkway.

"Hey, *stronzo!*" Paulie yelled at him. "You get the hell out of here!"

Anthony, the larger one of the two, shoved Jack away from the door. He staggered drunkenly, but snarled back at them.

"You better mind your business, gweedos! Get off of my damn property!"

When they positioned themselves between him and the door, Jack lunged at Anthony, and I watched out the window as the big Italians caught him and began pulling Jack backward down the walkway. He screamed my name all the way.

I hated every minute of it. No matter how many times he tried to run back up the walkway, they stopped and struggled with him, over and over, until finally they'd had enough.

On Jack's next attempt, Anthony suddenly grabbed and twisted both of Jack's arms behind his back, and Paulie hauled back and punched him with all his might in the stomach. Jack doubled over, but Paulie hit him again for good measure.

Jack dropped to the ground when Anthony let go of him, curled up in pain.

The brothers backed up a step and watched, waiting to see what he would do next.

A couple of minutes later, with saliva dripping from his mouth, Jack slowly pulled himself up to his knees, raising his hands in defeat. The brothers watched him warily as he got to his feet, but he slowly made his way to his car without another sound.

Every fiber of my body writhed at seeing my once-loving husband being manhandled and scuffed up. But this time, my resolve stood firm. He had caused this, not me. He had to understand that it was over. After he left, I opened the door, and I thanked the men for helping me.

"We gonna sit a little while." Paulie nodded toward their car. "Make sure he don't come back."

They waited in their car for a good half-hour. When Jack didn't show up again, they told me to call them right away if he returned.

When Denise got home with Derek, I was drained and didn't want to talk, but I had promised her the truth. After Derek was sound asleep, I ushered her to the kitchen table to sit with me as we had so many times before.

This time was different, though. This time the whole truth would be set before us.

Denise and I talked long into the night, with much crying and even a bit of yelling. She was especially furious that Jack had come anywhere near D.J., and at one point I thought she might flee upstairs to grab him and run away like she'd threatened before.

But when she understood that I was finally putting Jack physically and legally out of our lives, she quieted, eyeing me with a somberness I had never seen. Maturity that had been slowly

DON'T PLAY IN THE SUN

building in her came out in full bloom as she truly considered my position, and realized how things had gotten away from me so easily.

"I know how hard it is to let go of things, Mom," she said. "You were just hoping you…you could change him. I know how that feels."

I swallowed, speechless and broken.

She came to my side and put her arms around me, almost reversing our roles for a moment. "I'm still really mad at you… but I understand, Mom."

We hugged for a long time and I wept on her shoulder, then we went to sleep in my big bed together, little Derek in between us without a care in the world.

//////////////

After the night that my family and I had, I couldn't seem to pull myself together at work and remained on edge the rest of the week. The problem was I knew Jack wouldn't give up—and it didn't look like he could be reasoned with at all at this point. How was I ever going to be able to convince him to sign the divorce papers? I didn't know for sure if there was ever going to be a way out of this nightmare.

I spent most days keeping a close eye on my family, peeking out windows and making sure doors and window were always locked. Although I didn't hear from him, I couldn't shake the uneasiness that Jack was up to something. Where was he? What was he thinking? I knew after his erratic behavior that past week, he was, without a doubt, unstable. Even if he had meant a lot of what he said to me in our moments alone, his obsession with us was unhealthy, and apparently his temper was still triggered by negative responses. Therapy or no therapy, such a volatile man could not be allowed into any aspect of our lives anymore.

All that week I was distracted and moody, but Javier was nice enough not to say anything. At least, not until that Thursday when I showed up to work late and forgot key details on a client's wardrobe request.

We were sitting in the break room for our usual dinner that night, our time to go over the work and deadline schedules. He was quiet for a time, and I didn't offer any conversation either.

Finally he spoke, his voice casual but sincere. "This quiche is so good, Alice."

"Thank you," I replied absently.

He put his fork down. "Did you make it?"

"I taught Denise how to make it. This was her first try at it."

"Well, she's done a wonderful job. Tell her I give it a thumbs up."

I nodded once, not even bothering to make eye contact.

There was a slight pause, then he pushed aside his half empty plate and touched my arm.

"Okay, Alice I've been watching you since you came back from that sick day last week. You've been preoccupied ever since. What is going on?"

Still not meeting his eyes, I gave him a perfunctory answer. "Nothing, I'm fine. Thanks for asking."

"No," he said firmly, "I'm not asking to be cordial. I'm asking because I thought we were friends, and if something is wrong, you can talk to me. Sometimes talking about it helps to ease the problem. It takes the stress off, makes you not forget things at work." His dark eyes twinkled at that last part.

I finally looked up at him, embarrassed. "I know I've been scattered, and I'm sorry, Javier."

"It's okay. You're still one of the best at what you do. But seriously, Alice…what's going on? Please. Talk to me."

I saw the real concern in his eyes and knew without a doubt I could trust him.

Although I had been keeping company with Jack, technically we were separated when I applied for the seamstress position because we weren't living together. In my initial interview, I had mentioned Jack and being married, but as I looked into Javier's honest eyes now, I had to tell him the whole story. Maybe talking to someone on the outside of what had been going on might give me a different perspective.

So I told him everything.

During the recitation of all my stupidity and the failure of my marriage, not once did he look at me with anything other than concern. "That's why you were so upset in the park," he said. "The day we first met?"

I nodded, remembering. "Yes… But no matter how hard it is, I have to keep going," I replied, sitting up straighter. "My daughter and grandson are depending on me. Thank you for listening. It really helped to let this out."

"I'm glad." He smiled. "If I can do anything to make things easier for you and your family, or if you need to talk or take some time off, please don't hesitate to ask."

"Time off? Oh no, sir—I want you to know that I will continue to work hard for you. No more forgetting and letting my personal life interfere with my job. You can count on me, I promise."

"Don't worry about that, Alice. Your job is safe—and when you're around me, so are you." He held my gaze to make sure I was really listening. "Day or night, you call me if you need help, okay?" He wrote his home phone number down and gave it to me.

"Thank you, Javier. I appreciate that."

I moved to stand, but he softly grabbed my hand. I met his eyes and knew that he meant every word…and not because he cared about his employees. Something in those eyes said that he cared for *me*.

"I'd, uh…I'd better get back to work," I said, wavering.

As we both stood, I was overcome with emotion and fatigue, and tears welled in my eyes. Javier took out his handkerchief, dabbed my cheek, and placed it gently in my hand. Our eyes met again, and I could have sworn he leaned forward ever so slightly as though to kiss me.

I broke the contact and stepped back, nervously smoothing out nonexistent wrinkles on my dress.

"Gotta go. Time is money, right?" I said, stuffing his handkerchief in my pocket. Now I had two of them…

"That's right." He offered an enigmatic smile, and guided me back out of the break room, his hand pressing gently on my back. "As a matter of fact, get your things—this day's over. I'm taking you home to rest," he said.

I felt bad…but relieved. "Thank you, Javier. For everything."

///////////////

CHAPTER 23

It had been four months since I'd seen Jack. Not that I wanted to, but I just didn't know what to expect from him next. The holidays came and went, and Denise and I continued to move steadily forward. The business continued to grow as well, and my work hours increased, which gave me more time with Javier. Since he knew all about my secrets and me, I was more at ease and able to be myself. He took me to restaurants a few times a week instead of dining in the break room, and we became ever closer. He had a great sense of humor, and talking with him was as easy and comforting as soaking in a hot bubble bath.

One cold February evening, as we were closing up the shop, we both reached to turn off the lights, and I found myself standing uncomfortably close to him. Except…it didn't feel uncomfortable. It felt wonderful.

I didn't want to do anything to jeopardize my position in the company, though, so I stepped back, uncertain. Javier didn't share my hesitancy, however, and swiftly closed the distance between us.

"Alice…" He slowly wrapped his arms around my waist. "I should tell you I think you're amazing and…" He paused.

"And what?" I whispered, amazed at the comfort of his touch.

"I believe I'm in love with you."

He leaned in and kissed me, and my knees nearly buckled.

When he pulled back, I was smiling. "I believe I'm in love with you too," I said, breathless. We both chuckled. "So, what do we do about this?"

"I'd like to take you on an *official* date," he said. "Will you make me the happiest man on earth and let me take you out Saturday night?"

"Yes, I'd like that very much," I whispered, and we kissed again.

I told Denise about it as soon as she got home from night school.

"Yes! I knew it! I knew it! I knew it!" she screamed as she jumped up and down in excitement. "Told you, Mom! I knew it! I knew he liked you."

"Well," I replied, grinning ridiculously, "according to him, he's in love with me. And I'm almost positive that I'm in love with him too."

"Ah! Thank you, God!" she screamed some more.

"But…we are going to explore these feelings more just to make sure," I said, though I couldn't stop smiling. I knew it was kind of early to tell her about Javier, but I didn't care. Holding things back from Denise and lying to her was over. I wanted to build our personal relationship, to connect with her. So whether Javier and I became a long-term item or not, I wanted her to be the first to know.

After that, things moved forward at a much more varied pace than before. Javier saw life through different eyes and was happy to show me his world. He introduced me to some of the most amazing places and restaurants. We had dinners with some of our clients and vendors, as well as intimate dinners of our own—exotic cheeses, ornate venues, and aromatic wines. We shared Saturday afternoon picnics in the park and wonderful brunches he'd prepared. I loved his Belgian waffles, but I really loved the way we ended up feeding them to each other.

Javier was quite special. He taught me about fine art and classical music and made me feel just like a teenager being courted. He even accompanied us to Sunday services. My church family knew I was still technically married, but didn't judge me, for which I was relieved and thankful.

However, I still sought counsel from my Pastor Will and Lisa. I wanted them to know that Javier and I had decided to maintain a platonic relationship until I was legally divorced and we were ready to take our commitment to another level. They prayed for us and were very glad about the position we were taking.

In June, Derek's second birthday came, which we spent at Javier's house—just the four of us. We had so much fun, and Derek got plenty of presents. We danced, played with him, and when we weren't looking, he smashed both his hands all the way up to his elbows into his large double-layered vanilla birthday cake. He laughed and clapped as he ran around, giving each of us big hugs and kisses. There was cake all over us, on our faces and clothes, and in our hair, but it didn't matter; it was Derek's special day, and today he could get away with anything.

We were turning into a real family, I realized, and with each passing month, it became more real. One Saturday morning in August, Javier threw rocks up at what he thought was my window and ended up waking Denise instead. Imagine his surprise when a teenaged mom, exhausted from a hectic schedule, appeared at the window! He made it up to her when he took us all away on Labor Day weekend as an early eighteenth birthday present. We explored Washington, parts of Maryland, and even some of Virginia…just like tourists. Denise loved it, and I was ecstatic to see so many new things. We explored all the delightful little shops and historic sites I'd never known about.

"Alice," Javier said at one point as we walked, "the world calls out to each of us, and to experience it, we simply must respond. I once heard someone say, 'All you have to do is get up, step out, and live fully. And when you're given the choice to sit out or dance…'" He smiled at me. "Alice…I hope you choose to dance. Do you understand, honey?"

"Yes," I replied, "and every time that moment comes, like right now, I will always choose to dance, my dear."

Javier's strong arms then encircled me like his words as he gave me another warm kiss.

I thought about what he said as I watched him explain an object in one of the shop windows to Denise. I wanted to have more times like this with Javier, to see the world the way he saw it. To love life the way he did.

I adored him. I was in love and not afraid to savor and relish in it, either.

The first weekend in November, Javier flew us first class to New York for the weekend. We stayed at the Waldorf-Astoria and saw the Broadway show *Hair*, which Denise couldn't stop talking about for days. We were determined to keep our word and be a good example for my daughter, so Javier made sure that everywhere we went, we all had separate rooms, with Denise and mine normally adjoining.

Two weeks later Denise's Thanksgiving break from school came, and all of us flew to Los Angeles, California. Javier had a fitting scheduled with Ringo Starr, the drummer from the Beatles.

After the fitting, Ringo gave Javier front row tickets to their show, and that night, Javier hired a hotel sitter for Derek, and we all went out to the concert. I was so carefree, singing the Beatles' songs along with Denise at the top of my lungs. Javier just laughed at us. When the concert was over, as a surprise, Javier took us backstage to meet the group. Denise looked more and more awestruck as each Beatle shook her hand and offered a word of greeting. By the time she shook John Lennon's hand, she looked as if she were about to pass out. Not every teenager gets a memory like that, and we had Javier to thank for all of it.

A day later we were off to spend the rest of week and the Thanksgiving holiday in Martha's Vineyard. We stayed at Javier's family's summerhouse, a mansion with eight bedrooms, a tennis court, swimming pool, and large stable. It had a beach view only seen in the most prominent vacation magazines.

Javier told me that his parents used to vacation there every summer when he was just a boy, but as the business grew, the less time they were able to spend there as a family. The house was still pretty active, though; many of Javier's relatives used it for their vacations year round.

The staff consisted of one maid, a chef, and two property caretakers, all of whom were delighted to have us. The chef, in particular, gushed over little Derek and welcomed Denise into the kitchen to let her try her hand at a side dish or two, since Javier raved about her cooking skills. Denise was thrilled.

The more I learned about Javier and saw his normal lifestyle, the more I was impressed by his status and how important he was to people. But even more, I was overwhelmed that this wonderful, incredible man loved me. He was always doing something to show me his love. I never had to ask—Javier was just an old-fashioned romantic. His money didn't hurt, of course, but it was

Javier's genuine and calming way, his spirit that was peaceful—beautiful—that made me feel safe with him. I would have loved him no matter what.

On Thanksgiving Day the chef let Denise help him prepare dinner. The table was set so beautifully with china, crystal, flowers, and silver shining all around me. After dinner we all went to the living room to watch television together. As we sat laughing and talking, I basked in how much God had blessed my life, and how, despite his wealth, Javier had also given us the one thing money could never buy: a family full of love, right where it should always be found.

Our flight was scheduled to leave noon the next morning, but Javier came to my room and woke me at five a.m. to a bacon, omelet, and toast breakfast that he cooked himself.

"Good morning, beautiful, rise and shine," he whispered. "I have something very important to show you," he said with a grin, "so eat up and get dressed in something casual—a pair of jeans would be fitting, and put on these boots."

I blinked at the box as he laid it at the foot of the bed. "Yes sir," I said with a sleepily smile.

I ate and got dressed, still tired but intrigued by all the mystery. A little while later, I heard Javier's gentle tap on the door.

"Ready, *bonita*?" he said, smiling. He was dressed in a navy blue button-up sweater, khaki pants, and knee-high riding boots. I grinned at him and opened the door wider.

"Almost. You can come in...Javi."

He smiled at my pet name for him and took a step inside.

I went to stand in the bathroom mirror, brushing my hair back. A few seconds later, Javier came and stood behind me, and when I glanced up at him, I noticed him staring at me through the mirror.

I smiled wordlessly and drew my hands towards the nape of my head to twist my hair in a bun, but he softly touched my hands and stopped me.

"Can you leave it down this morning? For me?" He slowly lowered my arm, letting the curls fall back and cascade over my shoulders. His dark eyes twinkled.

"Of course I can," I whispered, still staring back at him in the mirror.

"Thank you," he whispered, and kissed the back of my neck.

"Anytime…"

We went to the stables hand in hand; the caretaker stood waiting for us with a beautiful gray stallion already saddled.

"Take a ride along the beach with me, *bonita*." Javier squeezed my hand. "There's one last thing you need to see before we leave today."

I nodded gleefully, and Javier hoisted me up into the saddle.

The faster the stallion galloped at the water's edge, the tighter I held my arms around Javier's chest. My hair blew back in the wind, and I could feel Javier's heart beating beneath my touch. I had never felt so free as we rode on and on, the waves breaking upon the beach in a glorious dance. It was like a dream, one that I didn't want to wake up from.

But all of a sudden, we stopped. I opened my eyes, not realizing I had shut them in sheer ecstasy.

"Look, sweetheart," Javier said. He pointed up at the sky to our left, above and beyond the water's boundaries. "Our first sunrise together."

It was breathtaking. To be in this moment with him and looking out at nothing but God's infinite creation for as far as the eye could see… There were no words to describe the joy and peace I felt.

This was my happily ever after, the one I had always longed for and never thought I'd find.

But I was not back in Washington a full day before life tried once again to unhinge my dream come true.

—————————— //////////////// ——————————

The hospital called me the day after I returned home, and told me that Gemma had given them my number. Her husband was out of town, and she wanted me to come as soon as possible. I tried to find out what had happened, but they insisted on not giving me any details until I got there. I walked to the bus station as quickly as I could, and arrived within the hour.

When I reached Gemma's hospital room, a police officer had just entered and was waiting to take her statement. I shuddered at the sight of my dear friend.

Her left eye was swollen shut, her right bloodshot. She was scared and shaking, and all I could do was hold her and stroke her hair as the nurse finished bandaging her up. All I knew was that someone had attacked her while she was closing up the ACADA facility.

She kept saying, "Thank you, Alice, thank you for coming, dear," and squeezing my hand hard. It was unnerving.

When the nurse had finished, Gemma was able to steady herself a bit and talk with the police officer who was patiently waiting. He told her to take her time, and she managed to relay what had happened, but held onto me the entire time.

"The center was closed for the holiday to everyone except the resident families who have apartments in the back," she said. "I was in my office, working. I always keep the door locked, but I ran to my car for some paperwork and must have forgotten to lock it back." She sniffed and dabbed at her bloodied lip. "I didn't hear the door open, but when I looked up, there was a man standing in my door. He was all red in the face and had his hands balled into fists."

"I asked could I help him with something. He rushed in, yelled at me, and started pushing me."

"What did he say?" the officer asked.

"'Who do you think you are?' He said that it was my fault he'd lost his family. I tried to ask him who was he talking about, but he just kept screaming 'I'm the man' at me."

Gemma shook as she talked, and I held her tighter, my hackles now up. It couldn't be…?

"I kept apologizing," she said, "but he punched me, and… and I fell down. And he…he ripped my blouse open…and…" She stuttered and started crying, a torrent of tears flowed from her eyes.

The officer stood by and waited for her to get control of herself. "Anything else, Ms. Glen? Did he say anything else?"

"He said that he almost had her back, until I introduced her to Mr. Fancy Pants."

I braced myself against the wall behind us with my free hand. *Dear God, this can't be happening!*

"Do you know who he might have been talking about?" the officer asked.

Gemma closed her eyes and shook her head. "No…"

I felt the blood in my veins turn to ice, and I could no longer feel my hand clutching Gemma's. I waited until the policeman got a description of her attacker, finished his questions, and left. I made sure Gemma was comfortable and all right for the night, and then told her I needed to leave and check on the kids. She nodded and mumbled something about not knowing what she did wrong, and all I could do was give her a brief, half-hearted hug and leave her to her exhausted slumber.

I made my way numbly home, then blurted to Denise what had happened the instant I came inside. Normally, I tried to shield her as much as possible, but I was nearly hysterical.

Denise gasped. "He did…what?"

I quickly related what happened, and she led me to the couch, looking at me with shock and hard determination.

"Mom, we've got to do something! He's crazy—you've got to tell the police. You've got to!"

I jumped up, making my way toward the kitchen. "I know, I know! I will, but I have to tell Javier first."

Confused and shaking, I dialed Javier, but after several attempts, I blew out my breath in frustration. In my state I'd forgotten that he had flown right back out because of business in New York. I wouldn't see him until tomorrow at the shop.

I paced the length of the living room, not knowing what else to do. After a while, Denise stopped my pacing and threw her arms around me.

"Mom, it's okay, it's not your fault! You couldn't have predicted anything like this. Neither of us saw this coming."

I hugged her back, but her words held no comfort. As forgiving as she was, Gemma would never be able to understand how I reasoned my way into letting Jack back into my life.

I thought about my romance with Javier. I thought about my friendship with Gemma. I didn't want to lose either one of them. Exhausted, I trudged to my room, and only after tossing and turning for quite some time did sleep finally overtake me.

The next morning when I got to work, Javier was already there. I told him what happened, and he immediately drove me to the police station; I told them everything I knew and gave them Jack's last known address. I also told them I *knew* he was the one who had assaulted Ms. Glen. It took a couple of hours for us to walk through the details, but Javier stayed with me throughout the entire interview.

Afterward, we picked Gemma up from the hospital. When we got her home and in bed, I told her of my suspicions, how Jack must have been spying on me, following me at work and at ACADA. But what I didn't tell her was the truth that Jack was still in my life. I couldn't stop apologizing for everything I surmised that Jack had done to her.

"Alice, sweetie," she mumbled through her still swollen mouth, "helping women is what I do. It could have been anybody's husband or boyfriend. It's not your fault." She patted my arm and told me to stop blaming myself.

Gemma had decided not to tell her husband anything until he returned from his business that day, so Javier and I stayed with her until he got home that evening. Mr. Glen asked us what was going on, but we sent him directly to Gemma's side, and left. It was her story to tell.

The days till Christmas went by without further incident, but I couldn't keep my mind off the fact that I had deceived my friend—that all of my problems had been because I couldn't face reality as it was or tell the absolute truth. Javier made a valiant effort to cheer both of us with hints of our Christmas gifts, but neither Denise nor I could rally ourselves enough to truly reciprocate. The gentleman that he was, Javier didn't take it personally.

In fact, he surprised us with a quick flight out to Vermont on Christmas Eve. "A change of scenery will do you good," he said, and sent us to pack. He took us to a cabin in the snow-covered mountains, and that evening, we drank mulled cider and sang carols in front of the crackling fireplace. Not until then did the

Christmas spirit enter my soul. Looking at my little family in the firelight, it felt as if nothing bad could touch this perfection.

I could only pray it would be so.

We opened our gifts Christmas morning. Javier bought me a beautiful diamond bracelet, and Denise and the baby got more presents than they'd ever received in their entire lives. I surprised Javier with a suit that I made in his favorite color, and Denise and Derek gave him a framed picture of all of us. The rest of our stay was like a storybook Christmas. We had a snowball fight, with Derek wearing his new snowsuit, and gathered chestnuts to roast on the fire while listening to Burl Ives and Bing Crosby. All the turmoil from D.C. went away, and for those few days, we had a wonderful time.

But on the flight home, I found myself instantly remembering the seriousness of our situation. Gemma had reassured me over and over that she didn't blame me, but I knew that if I hadn't told Jack about ACADA—if I hadn't been so naïve—he would never have known where to find her.

The police informed us on my return that Jack had disappeared. When they went to his apartment, they'd found that he'd moved and left no forwarding information. So now Jack was a crazy, angry rapist hiding out on the streets, and I couldn't help but feel guiltier.

If I had just signed that order in the beginning, he would be in jail. I wouldn't have got mixed up with him again. Gemma wouldn't have been hurt.

And he wouldn't be out there on the loose.

///////////////

CHAPTER 24

The beginning of 1968 was quiet. The sense of foreboding that hung over us lessened a bit as the days went by, but it never really went away. My relationship with Javier continued to deepen, and I was at least confident of where we were headed.

I hadn't expected to be in a serious relationship ever again, not after my experience with Jack. But there I was…choosing to dance, and loving it. Javier knew I was a bit skittish, and made a point to take his time, ensuring me that my heart and life were safe. Always constant and never pushy, Javier's love was real—a different sort to the one that Jack and I had shared even when we were young. Javier was not possessive; he respected me and did everything in his power to open up opportunities for me to grow. He was my biggest supporter, and I knew that my very soul was safe with him. I wrote in my journal about him nearly every night.

Denise finally graduated from night school that spring, and in June as a reward of sorts, Javier flew us to Brazil to meet his parents and to celebrate Derek's third birthday. He invited all of his relatives and their children to Derek's party, and I finally got to meet my love's family. I met his only sibling, his brother Marcelo, his wife, and a host of Javier's aunts, uncles, and cousins. I felt comfortable with all of them right away, and his parents were adorable.

Brazil was absolutely beautiful, and I wished I didn't have to leave. But reality beckoned. We said our goodbyes, and Javier's parents promised to come to the States in August, which I very much looked forward to.

When we returned to the States, Javier and I had a long talk. Jack hadn't been seen or heard from since attacking Gemma six months ago, and I still needed his signature on the divorce papers.

"What am I going to do, Javi?" I asked, resting my weary head on his shoulder.

"No worries, *bonita*." He kissed the top of my head. "Remember, I make clothes for everyone—including judges."

After I gave him permission, Javier went and spoke to a judge he knew, who pulled some strings and granted me a divorce. Within a few weeks, I was "Mrs. Jack Miles" no more—at long last, I was finally freed from all ties to my past.

Denise was soaring and asked Javi if he could help us get our last names changed as well. This time I didn't balk at the idea.

"That's a possibility, my dear," he said. "I'll see what I can do."

"You're the best, Mr. Menendez! Thank you for everything." Denise gave him a big hug.

"You're welcome, Denise. And while changing your name, would you mind changing mine?"

Denise looked at me, and I shrugged my shoulders in confusion.

"I don't understand," she said, turning back to Javier. "What do you mean?"

"Well, we've grown pretty close, wouldn't you say?"

"Yes," she replied.

"Then how about you start calling me Javier? Mr. Menendez sounds a little too formal for good friends such as us. What do you think?"

"I agree," she said with a smile.

"Good, now that that's settled, there something else I want to talk to you two about. I've been thinking…you girls need to be able to get around when you want, instead of having to hail cabs or wait for me to finish up with business. So, I tell you what…" His brown eyes sparkled. "If you study for your permits and pass the test, I'll teach you to drive."

Denise and I stared at him, speechless.

"Alice, I'll buy you a car immediately. Denise, you're obviously very smart, and dedicated, as you showed when you kept going to night school even while trying to raise D.J. here." He gestured to our little raven-haired youngster playing in his toy box across the room. "So, I have a proposal for you. If you're willing to go to college full time, I will pay for your education and begin giving you an allowance equivalent to your paycheck so you don't have to work. Instead, you can focus on school and D.J. And, if you can finish your first two semesters with a minimum GPA of 3.0, I'll buy you a car, too."

My eyes went wide, and Denise shrieked in delight.

"Deal?" Javier grinned.

"Oh my God! Yes, yes! It's a deal!" Denise hopped up and down in delight. "I can do it! Thank you, thank you so much, Mr. Menendez… Oops, I mean Javier!" She nearly tackled him with another hug.

I grinned at my eighteen-year-old's moment of childish excitement; it was so beautiful to see her this way.

"You're so welcome. I'm going to do everything in my power to see that you and your mom's dreams come true. *Entender?*"

"*Sim eu entendo!*" she squealed. "See, Javier, I'm learning."

"Yes, you are," he said, "you're a quick study, and I couldn't be prouder."

My heart surged with warmth and affection for him, not because of the offer of the cars, but because I knew that, unlike my first husband, Javi gave out of the kindness of his heart—not to buy our love. He truly wanted us to excel, to shoot for what we wanted. He had the means to help us achieve that, and he wouldn't think about holding anything back from us.

Over the next week, Denise and I studied for the driving test as much as possible. Meanwhile, I also moved up to another level at work. I'd always been able to sketch, but Javier now showed me how to sketch out professional designs, and with this new knowledge, I designed and made several outfits of my own, which turned out fabulously. Javi was very proud of my work and me and told me that I had a bright future in the business. I secretly hoped I would…while always at his side.

When Denise and I got our permits, Javi started teaching us how to drive, and within a few weeks, we were ready for the driving test. The day we took it, Denise and I were a bundle of nerves. I can't describe the racket we made when we found out we'd passed; everyone in the office stared as if we had lost our minds. Javi, who entertained Derek during the testing, shook his head in mock gruffness, but his broad grin broke through eventually. I knew he was so proud of us.

True to his word, he purchased a cream colored Pontiac for me, which Denise and I shared for now—just until she held up her end of Javier's "deal."

I could tell Denise had a whole new outlook on life, particularly when she went driving somewhere. Sometimes it made me tear up to see how beautiful and joyous my now-grown daughter had become—baby on her hip, a shine to her jet-black hair that flew in the breeze, a swing to her walk. She was so happy… More than happy—she was jubilant. My Javi had made us feel loved and respected by keeping us safe and supporting our dreams. I couldn't believe my life had come to a place so far beyond what I could ever imagine.

———————————— ///////////////// ————————————

The middle of August brought Javi's parents to town. They stayed for two weeks, and by the end of their visit, I had come to love them as my own, and they seemed to love me, Denise, and Derek as well.

On the last night, Javi took us all to dinner, and we shared plenty of laughter and good-natured teasing around the table. After dinner, the waiter brought out a platter with a silver-domed cover and placed it in front of Javier. He in turn pushed it in front of me.

"This is your dessert, sweetheart," he said.

That confused me; no one else had a dessert plate. He stared at me innocently.

"Take the top off, Alice," he urged.

Removing the cover revealed a small velvet box. Confused, I eyed Javi, but his face gave away nothing. I opened the box and caught my breath; it contained the largest diamond and emerald ring that I'd ever seen.

Before I processed what it all meant, he was on one knee in front of me.

"Alice, I never thought I'd find the perfect woman, but I have," he said softly. "You are the love of my life, and I don't know how I've lived so long without you. After today, I hope to never have to think about that again. Alice, will you marry me?"

I stared at him for a moment, completely shocked. But then the words were off my tongue before I even realized it. "Yes, yes, yes…!" I whispered.

He placed the ring on my finger and then kissed me, so passionately. Everyone in the restaurant oohed, awed, and clapped, and Denise hugged Derek close and squealed in excitement.

Then Javier stood up. "There's one more thing I need to do," he said with a nod to his father.

His dad reached into his jacket pocket and pulled out another velvet box.

"*Obrigado*, Papa."

"*Seja bem vindo*, Javi."

Javier opened the box, picked up a simple but elegant ring, and then surprised both of us when he turned toward Denise.

"Denise," he said, "now that your mother has agreed to be my wife, I'd like to ask you something."

Denise almost seemed nervous with the unexpected attention, and unconsciously squeezed Derek a little more. But she listened to him in fascination, as did I.

"You and D.J. have become equally important to me. I've grown to love you both so much, and I'm hoping we can continue to build our relationship, now as father and daughter, and as grandfather and grandson. With that being said, I have two questions for you. First, do I have your blessing to marry your mom? And second, since you want to legally change your last name anyway…would 'Menendez' be all right with you?"

Speechless, with tears streaming down her face. Denise nodded vigorously. Javi smiled, knelt, and put the ring on her finger, then gave her a peck on the cheek. It was like a fairytale— an absolute dream come true.

We set our wedding date for Sunday, December twenty-first, in Brazil. The next couple of months flew by as we made wedding and travel arrangements. By the end of September, we had sent out two hundred and fifty invitations, and by mid-November, over two hundred people had responded. I was very excited that thirty-two of the guests were my family; Javi had surprised us and said any of my family members who wanted to attend could fly in his family jet.

Javier still intended to follow up with his plan to leave D.C. and set up another shop along the coast. He would hear no argument from me or Denise or me, for that matter; we were more than ready to leave this wretched place behind us for good. The next shop would be the first one Javier would open as a married man, and he seemed even more excited about marking the occasion than I was.

I sketched and designed my own gown, and Javier sent it to Romel, one of his key designers in New York, who cleaned it up and made the actual dress. The four of us flew to New York in November, and while Javi took Derek to the zoo, Denise and I went to Romel's shop for my last fitting.

I had designed the dress to have a delicate floral pattern in a fine net overlay. Vertical seams extended from shoulders to hem, with the skirt curving outward at the waistline. But I was most excited about the train: it reminded me of the Antebellum-styled gowns of the 1800s.

I stepped into it, and Romel made some minor adjustments. Then he put on the finishing touch—the tiara-styled headpiece—and at last, I faced the mirror.

It was stunning… *I* was stunning.

I shook my head in disbelief. This was *really* happening…

Denise's eyes were shining. "Mom…you're gorgeous… I've never seen you look more beautiful."

I smiled to myself, quiet. Staring at the image in the mirror, the beautiful, strong woman who gazed back at me, I thought about Mama, and all of my foremothers before, knowing they at long last would be proud of me. I could feel their presence all around me in that little boutique, exuberant and joyful in my accomplishments.

All of us were about to be set free…

————————— ⁄⁄⁄⁄⁄⁄⁄⁄⁄⁄⁄⁄⁄⁄⁄ —————————

Two days before we were scheduled to leave for the wedding, I still had a hundred things to do. Javi and I were working late to tie things up before our trip to Brazil, and all the loose ends ran through my head as I worked in the main part of the shop. When the phone rang, I snatched it up, distractedly.

"Hello, is Mrs. Miles there?" the man on the other end asked.

"Who's calling?"

"This is Detective Tate."

Detective Tate? I thought to myself. Engrossed in my wedding plans, it took a minute to remember who he was. When I did, that old gnawing sensation edged to the surface.

"You were involved in Jack's case."

"That's right, Mrs. Miles. It's been a long time."

Detective Tate was the younger detective who had first questioned Denise and me about Jack's attack on us, alongside his partner. Though he had not been the one to tell us of Jack's disappearance, I vaguely remembered hearing his name referenced during that time, as well. He must have never dropped our case entirely.

"Yes, it has been a while," I replied.

"How are you, ma'am? How's your daughter…Denise, right?" he asked.

"Incredibly happy," I answered, "especially if you are calling to tell me you have Jack in custody."

"No, I'm sorry…not yet."

"Of course not," I said, sarcasm dripping from my voice. "How can I help you?"

"Mrs. Miles, I—"

"Stop calling me that, please. Just call me Alice, I am no longer Mrs. Miles. In fact, if you read the society page of the newspaper, you'd know I'm getting remarried."

I knew that I was being rude to him, but I couldn't help it. It was two days before I was leaving, and I didn't want anyone to remind me of the biggest mistake, the worst memories, of my life.

"No, I didn't read it," he said, still kindly. "Congratulations, ma'am."

"Thank you. Now how can I help you, Detective?"

"I was wondering if you would come by the station, Alice. I have some things we should discuss."

"I'm leaving for Brazil day after tomorrow, Detective, and I don't see my being able to fit a trip to the precinct in before I leave. Can you tell me what you need?"

He paused. "I, uh…I think it best if we talk in person."

"Why? Are we in danger?"

"No, not exactly but…we'd like to keep it that way, ma'am. If you would just give me a few minutes out of your busy schedule, I—"

"Okay!" I said, exasperated. "Tomorrow somewhere in between the fifty things I have left on my 'to do' list, I'll pop in."

He didn't seem glad for the news. "That would be great, Alice, thank you. I leave at six."

I hung up the phone just as Javi came out. "Who was that?" he asked, wrapping his arms around my waist.

I was fearless around him and took comfort in his strong arms as I told him about the call.

He was instantly on alert. "We need to go in the morning."

I tried to convince him otherwise; my faithful bridesmaids, Gemma and Cadell, had put together a dinner party for us the next day, and Javi had to finish his business affairs in order to make it on time.

"You're too busy, honey," I said. "I'll go, though I don't know what time. I have a ton of things to do—my hair, my manicure and pedicure appointments…and I'm sure I'm forgetting something," I smiled. "If I need you, I'll call you, okay?"

"Promise?" He gave me a kiss.

"I promise."

We finished closing up the shop, and since Denise had my car, he dropped me off at home.

"Do you want me to stay?" he asked, scanning the block as we stood at my front door.

"Honey, no. Quit being such a worry wart," I teased. "I'm fine. I will see you tomorrow when I've done all my errands."

He gave me one last kiss and left, obviously still uneasy. But I dropped into bed a few minutes later and quickly fell asleep, exhausted but anticipating our last day in D.C.

The next day, Javi and I were both as busy as I thought—me with my to-do list, and him with shop business. Before I knew it, it was evening, and I still hadn't made it to the police department. I rushed over to the precinct and found Detective Tate gone for the day. He left a note for me with his personal phone number, asking me to call him as soon as possible. I pocketed the information and stopped by the shop to see Javi before going home to get ready for the party at Cadell's house.

He gave me a quick kiss and a reproachful glance.

"What's wrong?" I asked.

"You didn't call me today, and I was worried. What happened at the precinct?"

I shrugged it off and explained that I had gotten there five minutes after the detective left. "I'm sorry, honey, but there was so much going on, it slipped my mind," I said. "Besides, I don't want to hear any unhappy news right now. We're getting married in four days, and I want to be happy. I'll call him as soon as we get back, okay? First thing, I promise."

I playfully gave him my irresistible puppy dog eyes and puckered up for a kiss.

He sighed, concerned. "Okay… But I'm letting you get away with this only because we're leaving the country and you will be out of danger. But the second—and I do mean the second—we get back, we are both going to the precinct. Understand, *bonita*?"

"Yes sir," I said with a nod and gave him a soft peck on the cheek.

"Alice…" His worried eyes told me he still wasn't convinced, and he took me in his arms. "Although we are moving out of Washington in a couple of months, we still need to make sure everyone's safe and away from that maniac until then. All right?"

I buried my head into his chest and sobered. "I'm sorry, honey. You're right."

He gave me a squeeze. "I love you, Alice."

"I love you too…"

He walked me to my car, and I went home to get dressed for the party, a little miffed that my joy had been momentarily deflated. But I was determined not to let it overshadow the rest of this wonderful week. Since I had time before Javi would be picking me up to go to Cadell's, I wandered into Denise's room and watched as she packed for the trip the next day.

"I'm sorry you can't come tonight, sweetheart." I picked up one of Derek's tee shirts, folded it, and placed it in the suitcase.

"That's okay, Mom. D.J. and I will wait up for you to tell us all the details. Besides, it's an adult-only thing; nobody my age is going to be there anyway." She shrugged.

I chuckled to myself. Sometimes I forgot that she wasn't technically an adult already, especially when she was in such a maternal mode as she was now.

She placed a stack of diapers in the bag and then paused. She turned to face me, suddenly quite serious.

"Mom, I want you to know I love you...so much. I can't wait till the wedding and you become Mrs. Alice Menendez. You deserve it."

"And soon after you will be Denise Menendez."

I smiled broadly, gazing at my beautiful daughter who had blossomed into such a lovely, determined young woman. Just a few years ago, we could barely have a civil conversation—and now look at how far we'd come.

I knew I had done a lot of work personally, and ACADA had been a remarkable asset, but Denise didn't know how tremendously my—and her—foremothers had helped me. Neither she nor I would be here if it wasn't for them, for their sacrifices. I wouldn't have had any of the courage I had now if Mama hadn't gifted me with the legacy of the letters and diaries of our beautiful ancestors—a true treasure.

Standing there watching my grown-up girl, I made an instant decision, and went to retrieve the box hidden away in my closet.

She was as fascinated as I had been as I showed it to her. She held it in her hands and listened intently as I told her a bit about its contents, and my contribution and rewritten Commission. She was truly excited to see the handwriting of our foremothers and wanted to dive right in. I couldn't help but chuckle…I knew exactly how she felt.

"You can start reading it when we get back from Brazil," I told her. "If I were no longer on this earth, you would have had to wait until your heart told you to open it, just like I did. But this is different—we are survivors." I put my hands on top of hers as she held the box close. "I think it only fitting that we break the chain together."

She nodded and smiled. "Okay, I'll wait till we get back. But how are we going to get that chain off?" She yanked at the links I had replaced with one hand, but of course they wouldn't budge. "This isn't going to be easy, Mom."

At that moment my soul filled with the memory of my own words to Mama as I had stood in my room clutching this box to my chest, longing for her words to answer me. Everything had come full circle at long last. And I was whole.

Complete.

I squeezed her hands, and it seemed as if my own mama spoke through me. "It's not supposed to be, sweetheart."

I kissed her cheek and left her to her packing, the box once again tucked safely away.

Javi picked me up a few minutes later, and off we went to our dinner party. Cadell greeted us at the door, with plenty of hugs and well wishes. Gemma gave us warm hugs and Javier chatted with her a bit, since they were old friends, and I glanced around the room. I was very surprised to see all my friends—Mr. Mulden and his sons, Sophia and Gabrielle, Elizabeth, and several of the other ladies from ACADA.

I was especially happy to see my neighbor, Mrs. Thornton. She, of all people, had been a witness to Jack's abuses and my subsequent bad judgment. Though I had apologized for it, I still felt bad about threatening to send Jack to her house, and I made a point to give her a hug and thank her for the advice and all she'd done over the years.

She gave me her grandmotherly smile and squinted up at me through her little spectacles. "Now you're right on time, dear."

That evening was lovely, and Javier and I were definitely riding the waves of ecstasy. Though it was after midnight when we got back to my house, we sat in the car for a few minutes longer, content to just bask in each other's presence, alone.

Spending time with Javi always felt new, like we both had just discovered our love.

"This is it, honey," he said at last, almost giddy. "Tomorrow, we're off to Brazil and our new forever."

"Well, we are off to Brazil tomorrow, but our new forever is not until Sunday," I said teasingly. "But it's close."

He chuckled and opened his door. "Come on, you'd better be off to bed. We have an early flight."

He came around and opened my door, and I stepped out into his embrace.

"We did it, Javi; we kept our word. Soon we will be joined as one, bringing our love full circle."

"Hmm," he grinned, "consummating our marriage is the part I'm looking forward to. I can't wait to feel all of you, my love."

We shared one last kiss.

When it finally broke, my eyes caught a figure rushing toward us. I knew that angry stride, with the tilt of the head just so.

It was Jack.

I flinched and Javier quickly turned. Before he or I could react, Jack struck him with a sharp blow from the pistol in his hands. Javier fell unconscious to the ground.

"You kissing my wife, Fancy Pants?! My damn wife?! You ready to marry her, huh? Fine, but you ready to die for her? Because I am!"

Pointing the gun down at Javier, he raged on. His eyes were wild and his face unyielding. Jack had become unhinged, a crazed maniac pushed beyond reason. I was frozen to the ground.

He turned on me. "Why do you make me do these things, Alice? Huh? Why?! You chose this idiot, this damn refugee over *me*?!" He waved the pistol in my face. "*I'm* the man!" he shouted. "I'm your husband!"

Javier let out a low groan at my feet. Without remorse Jack pulled the trigger, and two booming shots from his gun exploded in my ears.

He shot my Javi…

"What do you think of your Mr. Fancy Pants now, Alice?" Jack raged. "You still wanna marry him? How could you do this to me?"

He pointed the gun back at me, his hands shaking in ire. I held up my hands but couldn't find the coherence to utter any words. My mind reeled.

"You said you loved me! You…you ain't nothin but a lying tramp who tried to take my family!" Jack screamed. "Hell, no! We're all gonna die tonight!"

Hot fire exploded in my chest, and my back slammed into the car's side. Dimly, I was aware of a warm stickiness spreading across my body as I sank to the ground beside my lifeless fiancé.

I struggled to keep my eyes open, and noticed the neighbor's lights coming on just as Denise's screams scattered into the night.

I tried to get up to go to her, but I couldn't move—I couldn't catch my breath.

I wanted to tell Denise I was sorry—sorry for staying with her father for so long, for everything I had done that had contributed to this… I wanted to tell her to live, to complete the Commission, but my voice was stolen away.

"No, Daddy!" Denise screamed from somewhere above me.

I heard one final shot, and with my last exhalation, the darkness took me…and hope of a redeemed life died.

///////////////

ACKNOWLEDGEMENTS

To my dad, Aubrey Clayton Williams, who is no longer present on this earth, yet forever present in my heart, I want to say thank you. Thank you for being a dad who loved me unconditionally; a dad I could laugh and cry with; a dad who I could talk to and who always loved and supported me in my endeavors. I miss you, Dad.

To my mother-in-law, Hattie Pearl Clark:
Thank you for always loving me and being there for us. Your advice, your smile, and your laughter I will never forget, and I couldn't ask for a better second mom. I miss you so much, and the memory of you that I carry in my heart is priceless.

To my family, my friends and my supporters (you know who you are):
Thank you so much for your advice, your encouragement, your belief in me and my dream. Thank you so much for preordering and now purchasing my novel, and/or whatever you have done to go above and beyond to help me make this happen. My most humble thank you and "I love you."

///////////

SPECIAL ACKNOWLEDGEMENTS

To my husband of twenty-one years, E. Vedal McDuffie:

Thank you for all of your encouragement, the long days and nights of brainstorming, and all the laughs and love in between. We get each other, and no matter what we go through, we go through it as a team.

I thank you for all of your support and your non-wavering belief in my project and me. Thank you for listening to me whenever I felt unsure, loving me, and never hesitating to remind me of the person I am within.

Thank you for the commitment box you have made to accompany my novel. It is more beautiful than I could have ever imagined, and I hope many people will use it to break the chain and commit to a better future for themselves and their descendants to come.

Babe, you've worked tirelessly on this project while working your job, and there are no words that can fully tell you how grateful I am for everything you have done. I know you have dreams and talents as well, and I want you to know that I will be right by your side when you are ready. Thank you.

To E. Cadell Crawford:

There are no words to tell you how much I appreciate what you've done. Since the day I told you about my novel, you've never put it down. You've been beside me working out all the kinks, writing and rewriting. Thank you for all the long nights and early morning hours of reading when I was too exhausted to go on. Whatever I needed, even if you didn't have the answers, you didn't hesitate to take the initiative and step up and get the answers.

You have stepped into the role of writer, editor, marketer, proofreader, manager, administrator, financial advisor, even lawyer, and the list goes on. In my "woe is me" moments, you gave me no slack. Instead you'd say, "Oh get over yourself Evie, suck it up, stop the pity-party and get back to work."

The funniest part is, I did!

I celebrate not just myself, but you. I've finally given birth to my novel (my baby), and in doing so, I am officially making you my baby's godmother; I know beyond a shadow of a doubt that you are as concerned about how well she'll do in the world as I am. Thank you.

To Veronika Walker:

I want to thank you for all the time and effort that you put into this project as my story and copy editor. I know I wasn't the easiest author to work with, but I thank you for your professionalism and ideas, and wish you all the best.

To my Publisher, Rochelle Carter of Ellechor Media:

Thank you for all the time and effort that you put into this project as my publisher and strategic counsel. I thank you for your professionalism, your support, and for your belief in me as an author. We finally made it!

To Claudette E. Freeman and Samantha Phillips:

Thank you for all of your help with this novel. You both are great editors and I'm grateful.

To Shelby Williams, Beverly Hagood, Khalidah (Kay) Raheem, Sheila Williams and Phyllis Leath:

Thanks for your extra effort in helping me with this project. I so appreciate it, and I love you.

―――――――――― ////////// ――――――――――